BONES
DON'T
LIE

Center Point
Large Print

Also by Melinda Leigh and available from
Center Point Large Print:

Say You're Sorry
Her Last Goodbye

**This Large Print Book carries the
Seal of Approval of N.A.V.H.**

BONES DON'T LIE

MELINDA LEIGH

CENTER POINT LARGE PRINT
THORNDIKE, MAINE

This Center Point Large Print edition
is published in the year 2019 by arrangement with
Amazon Publishing, www.apub.com.

The text of this Large Print edition is unabridged.
In other aspects, this book may vary
from the original edition.
Printed in the United States of America
on permanent paper.
Set in 16-point Times New Roman type.

ISBN: 978-1-64358-315-0

The Library of Congress has cataloged this record
under Library of Congress Control Number: 2019943057

*To Rayna
for ten years of pep talks, pats on the back,
kicks in the butt, and plot hole fixes*

Chapter One

Bangs and muffled screams sounded from inside the trunk of the Buick. Standing in the weeds next to the vehicle, he stared at the closed lid.

Still alive.

Oh, well. A minor miscalculation. Didn't matter. This would all be over soon.

"Let me out. Help!"

He scanned his surroundings. No one in sight. Inky black in the darkness, the murky water of Grey Lake stretched out for miles. The crescent moon cast a pale light on its rippling surface. Thick forest fringed its banks. There were no buildings nearby. But there was always a chance of someone camping in the forest. His gaze swept the bank of the lake, but he saw no flicker of campfires, no brightly colored tents. No sign of human activity.

The public park, beaches, and boat ramp were two miles to the south. The wilder north end of the lake saw little activity.

A mosquito landed on his arm, and he swatted it away. Three more took its place.

The warm August day had cooled in the evening, but the summer stickiness remained.

Frogs croaked, and something small splashed. The tall grasses around the lake buzzed with insects. To the billion gnats and mosquitoes that lived here, his warm body was a free meal.

"You can't do this!"

The pleas for help triggered no guilt. No remorse for the series of events that had led him to this moment. His only regrets were the risk and inconvenience he'd brought upon himself.

But then, his lack of a conscience was one of the reasons he was here in the middle of the night.

He'd done things tonight he couldn't undo. Things that would ruin his life if anyone knew. His only option was to clean up the mess.

Besides, he'd be lying if he denied that killing a person wasn't exciting. He wasn't planning on doing it again. But there was a thrill, deep in his veins, over the control, the sense of power that came from extinguishing another human life.

More banging from the inside of the trunk. The vehicle creaked as weight shifted. Something metal struck the underside of the lid. Tire iron? Like that would do anything.

"Please. I'll do anything. Please let me out."

The plea was desperate.

Panicked.

And for good reason.

He ignored the cries, opening the driver's side

door and sliding behind the wheel. He started the engine, lowered the window, and stared at the lake ahead. The bank fell away on a steep grade. He knew the lake's bottom sloped to match the rapid descent. The water grew deep quickly. Farther out, a tiny sliver of moon reflected on the surface.

The Buick idled, its ten-year-old engine knocking and pinging. With the car door still open, he hesitated, his foot on the brake.

He eyed the brick on the floor. It would hold the gas pedal down when he was ready.

Was he really going to do this?

This was another indelible moment, one that would leave a permanent mark, one from which there could be no return. Unlike his impulsive action earlier this evening, this decision was born of careful thought and consideration. This was a conscious act.

This was cold.

Calculated.

Murder.

But what were his options? Admit his guilt? Go to prison? Ruin his entire life?

Hell, no.

He had plans.

Which meant he really had no options at all.

Bending forward, he positioned the brick on the gas pedal, then sat up and shifted into "Drive." When he eased his foot off the brake, the car rolled down the slope toward the lake. But the Buick wasn't going fast enough for momentum to carry it fully into the water. He pressed on the brick with the ball of his foot, and the car leaped forward.

A muffled scream sounded from the trunk.

He pushed himself from the moving vehicle. As soon as his shoulders hit the damp ground, he rolled. Thick grass cushioned his impact. He tumbled over a few times and slid over a rock, a quick jolt of pain zinging through his elbow. He came to a stop, sat up, and took stock by moving his arms and legs. *All good.* He'd get through this night with no more than a few bruises.

Ahead, the Buick struck the water with a broad splash. Momentum carried the car a few yards into the lake. Then it appeared to float for a minute, bobbing on the waves of its own making.

The weight of the engine pulled the front end down. The car began to sink, diving into deeper water nose first, its ass in the air.

Once the interior filled with water, the car sank faster. He wasn't sure if he actually heard more cries for help or if he imagined them. He was probably too far away. But they gave him a power-tripping hard-on all the same.

He climbed to his feet on the bank, watching. Water rose over the rear window, then the trunk.

Finally, the rear bumper disappeared beneath the surface. He checked his watch and then brushed some dirt from his arms while he waited.

Ten minutes passed.

All was quiet, except for the sounds of the lake and forest. Frogs, bugs, owls. No human sounds at all.

It was over.

The aftermath felt anticlimactic in its silence. The only sign that the event had happened was a path of crushed weeds leading into the lake. Those would spring back up in no time. One good thunderstorm would wipe away any trace of tonight's deed.

He turned away from the lake and hiked up the slope toward the road, a football field away. When he reached the top of the embankment, he paused to catch his breath. Despite the comfortable evening temperature, sweat gathered under his arms. It had been a night of errors, scrambling to cover mistakes, and discovery of his dark side.

Something he'd have to work to control. He couldn't repeat tonight's disaster. He'd been lucky in too many ways.

But now it was done. He took a deep breath, the first he'd managed in hours. The scents of summer night, pine, and lake water filled his lungs, cool, damp, and refreshing.

He turned back toward the lake.

The surface was smooth again, the ripples faded, with no sign of the earlier disturbance. No sign of what was hidden beneath the murky water.

Chapter Two

Twenty-three years later

Some secrets were better left hidden.

Lincoln Sharp stood on the shoulder of the road overlooking Grey Lake. He sucked in a hiss of air. The bitter cold pricked his lungs like a thousand icy pins. It was only the middle of November, but winter had hit New York State like a frozen sledgehammer.

Fifty feet from the shoreline, a sheriff's department dive team boat bobbed on the quiet water. Around the vessel, the lake's smooth surface reflected the leaden sky like a mirror, hiding everything within its murky depths.

The answer to a decades-old question lay just ahead of him, yet Sharp's boots remained rooted in the snow-dusted weeds.

What was wrong with him? He'd been waiting for a break in this case for more than twenty years. Now that it was here, he almost wished it would sink back beneath the water and stay there forever.

The ripples of this discovery would spread in ever-widening circles, stirring up waters that had long ago stilled.

Waking voices time had silenced.

Disturbing lives that had finally found peace. Unease stirred in his belly.

But there was nothing he could do to prevent the fallout. Maybe, just maybe, everything would work out, the case would be solved, and the family given closure. He exhaled, his breath pluming like smoke.

The high-pitched squeal of metal on metal carried across the open space, the harsh sound pricking his eardrums and lifting the hairs on the back of his neck. Sharp turned toward the activity on the shore. The winch on the back of a tow truck hauled the rusted carcass of a sedan farther up the bank, leaving a drag trail through the tall reeds. A group of law enforcement personnel swarmed the vehicle as soon as it stopped.

Sharp's breath froze in his chest.

A mid-1980s Buick Century sedan.

The same make and model car Victor Kruger had been driving twenty-three years ago when he went out for groceries and vanished, leaving a wife and ten-year-old son behind. Sharp, then a detective for the Scarlet Falls PD, had been the lead investigator. He'd worked and reworked the case right up until he'd retired from the police force five years ago and opened his own private investigation firm. There had been no sign of Victor.

Until today.

Sharp trudged past a pair of news vans. Just

outside the ribbon of crime scene tape strung around a handful of isolated pine trees, two reporters talked into microphones. The sheriff's department activity behind them provided a dramatic backdrop for their stories.

A young deputy stood as sentinel.

"Lincoln Sharp," Sharp said. "I need to talk to the sheriff."

The deputy shook his head. "The sheriff said not to let anyone through."

"He's going to want to talk to me." Sharp crossed his arms over his chest. He wasn't budging. This case was too important. "I'll wait here."

The deputy thought about it for a second, then walked back to talk to his boss.

Sheriff Paul King stood literally head and shoulders above the rest of the men, and his charcoal-gray cowboy hat added some height to his six-foot, three-inch stature. He bowed his head to listen to the shorter deputy, then the sheriff's gaze snapped around to focus on Sharp. The sheriff frowned, irritation dragging his face down like the jowls on a bad-tempered basset hound.

The deputy trudged back to his post. He cleared his throat. "The sheriff said you can go on through, but don't fuck up his scene."

No doubt the last few words were a direct quote.

"Thanks." Sharp ducked under the yellow tape and walked through the thick weeds.

Thin patches of ice and snow crunched under his boots. He approached the recovered vehicle. Rust coated the surfaces it hadn't eaten. Although heavily corroded, the Buick was in surprisingly good condition considering how long it had likely been sitting at the bottom of the lake.

The sheriff leveled an accusatory look at him. "Who called you, Sharp?"

"Word is out all over town." Sharp nodded toward the reporters, implying that's where he'd gotten the information rather than outright lying. He wasn't giving up his buddy in the sheriff's department who'd called him with the news. Twenty-five years on the force had given Sharp loyal contacts in every law enforcement agency within a twenty-mile radius.

"Did you call your partner?" The sheriff turned back to the Buick.

"Working on it." Sharp glanced at his phone, but his young partner, Lance Kruger, hadn't replied to his message.

"So he doesn't know we found his father's car?"

Where are you, Lance?

"No." Sharp scanned the clearing. He didn't want Lance to see this story on the news. "How did you verify it's Victor Kruger's car?"

"The diver brought up a license plate before

we even pulled the car out." The sheriff pointed to the license plate on the ground next to the rusted car, the letters and numbers still legible on the corroded metal. "I recognized the name and looked up the case. Wasn't surprised to see you listed as lead detective. It wasn't the sheriff department's investigation, but I vaguely remember when it happened." The sheriff had been chief deputy at the time.

"Not so much crime around here back then."

"No, there wasn't." The sheriff straightened. "How old was Lance when his father disappeared?"

"Ten."

Lance's mother, Jenny, had suffered from mental illnesses exacerbated by her husband's disappearance. When the missing person case had gone glacier cold, and it had become clear that Jenny Kruger couldn't cope, Sharp hadn't been able to walk away from the kid. He hadn't found Victor. The least he could do was look after his boy, who'd had no one else in his life capable of doing the job. No doubt affected by Sharp's mentoring, Lance had become a cop with the SFPD. After being shot in the line of duty the previous summer, he'd left the force and joined Sharp Investigations.

"Some cases stick with you," Sharp said.

A deputy to his right gave him a solemn nod. Every cop had at least one case that burrowed

17

deep into his soul. A crime—and its victims—that stayed with him forever. For Sharp, Victor's disappearance was that case.

Sharp turned back to the Buick. "Who found the car?"

"The state police SAR team was testing out their new sonar equipment. When they spotted the vehicle, they called us, and we brought the divers in." The sheriff pointed to the boat bobbing out on the water. "I'll request the official file from the Scarlet Falls PD, but since you're here, what do you remember about the case?"

Every. Damned. Thing.

Sharp shoved his hands into his jacket pockets. "At approximately nine p.m. on Wednesday, August 10, 1994, thirty-five-year-old Victor Kruger, known as Vic to his friends, left his house to go to the grocery store. He never came home."

"Signs of foul play?"

"None." Sharp had never even found a solid lead. The man had truly vanished into the thick summer air.

"Suicide?" The sheriff pulled a pair of gloves from his pocket and put them on.

"No evidence of depression or other mental illness," Sharp said.

Not with Victor, anyway. Lance's mother was a different story.

The sheriff walked around the front of the

vehicle and scanned the hood and bumper. "Any chance he was having an affair or was just fed up with his life and split?"

"I don't think so. According to everyone we interviewed, Victor was a family man who wouldn't have abandoned his wife and kid." Sharp moved closer to the vehicle. The sheriff didn't complain.

"If there's one thing this job teaches you, it's that everybody has secrets," the sheriff said.

As much as Sharp knew that was true, he hadn't uncovered any skeletons in Victor Kruger's closet.

Sharp leaned over to peer into the passenger seat. The interior was full of mud, weeds, and other lake debris. He spotted a plastic Coke bottle on the floor of the back seat.

But what Sharp didn't see were bones.

"Any sign of remains?" he asked.

Freshwater didn't waste any time reducing a body to bones, especially in the summer heat. Victor Kruger had disappeared in August. The water had been warm. Bacteria, aquatic insects, and other lake inhabitants would have gone to work on the flesh.

"Not yet." The sheriff rounded the vehicle, peering into all the windows.

"If he was in the vehicle, there should be bones," Sharp said.

"Who knows? The driver's window was down.

The door was open. The current could have pulled the body from the vehicle. We've had some wicked floods in the past two decades that could have shifted the car."

"Maybe."

"We don't even know that he was in the car when it went into the lake." The sheriff stuck his head in the open driver's door and then pulled it out again. "There's nothing in here but lake debris and some trash."

A deputy walked around to the rear bumper. "OK to pop the trunk?"

The sheriff swept a broad hand in the air. "Go ahead."

The deputy stepped up with a crowbar. The heavily rusted hinges gave way with a horror-film-worthy creak.

Staring inside the trunk, the sheriff grimaced. "Shit."

Sharp joined the sheriff behind the vehicle. His heart dropped. Inside the rusted trunk lay the disjointed bones of a human skeleton, the pieces scattered like Pick-Up Sticks. The skull rested against the spare tire well, next to what Sharp suspected was a humerus from its size and thickness. His trained eye also spotted some fabric too filthy to identify and a zipper. Vic had been wearing cargo shorts when he'd gone missing.

How would Lance take the news? Was it better

to know your father had probably been locked in his trunk and drowned in a lake or would it be better to assume that he'd been willing to walk out of your young life?

Sadly, the best outcome would be to discover that Vic Kruger had already been dead when he'd been locked in his trunk.

Not that there was an option in this case. It was what it was. At least Lance would have closure. He'd spent most of his life living under the weight of his father's disappearance. He'd taken on adult responsibilities at the age of ten. He'd stayed in Scarlet Falls to take care of his mother, passing up possible promotions elsewhere for the sake of family responsibility.

But last summer, Lance had met Morgan Dane, and everything had changed. Lance had just begun to develop an actual personal life.

And now this . . .

This was going to leave a fresh mark.

Victor Kruger hadn't left his family or committed suicide.

He'd been murdered.

Chapter Three

Morgan weaved through the crowded courthouse. At the other end of the hall, Private Investigator Lance Kruger stood with a woman in her early forties. Tall and jacked, Lance towered over her. The woman raised a crumpled tissue to her tear-streaked eyes.

Lance's blue eyes locked on Morgan's as she approached. He gestured between Morgan and the woman. "Nina, this is Morgan Dane, the attorney I told you about."

"Thank you for coming." Nina stifled a sob with her hand. "I didn't know what to do."

"Nina's son is Eric McCain, from my hockey team." Lance coached a group of at-risk kids. "Eric and six other boys were arrested last night. I don't have the specific charge, but it involved a video depicting classmates engaged in a sex act."

Most teens either didn't know that messaging explicit images of each other technically violated child pornography laws, or they just didn't think about it.

Nina sniffed and blotted her nose. "They held him in jail overnight."

Morgan pressed a hand to Nina's forearm. "I'll call the prosecutor's office, talk to Eric, and see what I can find out. Try not to worry. Today is just the arraignment. Eric will plead guilty or not guilty, and the judge will set bail. Our goal is to get him out of jail."

Last night, Eric would have been kept in a holding cell. Morgan did not want him in the jail's general population. Her last young client, who had been innocent, had been gravely injured there.

"Thank you," Nina said.

Morgan found a quiet corner. Her call to the prosecutor's office did nothing to allay her concern. In New York, in the absence of maliciousness, kids caught sexting were normally sent to educational programs. But Eric was facing a felony possession charge with a maximum four-year prison sentence. Was the prosecutor trying to scare him?

She did not condone boys-will-be-boys excuses. But sending teens to prison seemed like an overcorrection. She favored mandatory education and many hours of community service.

As her grandfather always said, *Tired teens have less time for shenanigans.*

Morgan made her way to the holding area near the courtroom where Eric would have been transferred this morning to await his arraignment. She requested to speak to her client and then settled on an empty bench in the corridor to wait until an interview booth became available. She removed a legal pad from her tote. Flipping to the second sheet, she made some general notes.

"Ms. Dane?"

Morgan looked up from her notes. A man in a well-cut gray suit stared down at her. He was thirtyish, with thick black hair, an olive complexion, and hard-to-read black eyes.

"I'm Anthony Esposito, the new ADA," he said. "I hear you're representing Eric McCain."

She knew from her phone call with the prosecutor's office that the new assistant district attorney had been assigned Eric's case. She flipped the top blank sheet of paper down over her notes and stood. "Yes. I'm Mr. McCain's attorney."

Her heels brought her to six feet tall and gave her a few inches on him.

He frowned up at her. "This case is straight-forward, but we're willing to offer a deal in the interests of saving time and money. If McCain pleads guilty, we'll agree to probation."

Ninety percent of cases ended in plea bargains, so Morgan wasn't surprised. "Would he still have to register as a sex offender?"

"Yes."

"Since I don't have the details yet, perhaps you could enlighten me," she said.

Esposito nodded. "Mr. McCain received an e-mail three days ago. Attached was a video of two minors engaged in a sex act. As I said, the case is very straightforward."

Maybe. Then again, Esposito wouldn't point out any holes in his case.

"I'll relay your offer to my client and get back to you." Morgan picked up the tote bag at her feet and moved to walk around him.

Esposito's mouth tightened, and he sidestepped to block her path. "This is a onetime offer. If your client enters a not guilty plea today, I'll withdraw the deal."

"I haven't even met with my client yet." Morgan wanted Eric's side of the story. Esposito could claim his case was as solid as Mount Rushmore. That didn't mean it was.

Esposito leaned into her personal space. "Your client will go to prison. Did I mention I have a signed confession?"

Shit.

How was she going to keep this kid out of prison *and* off the sex offender registry?

"I'll be in touch after I meet with my client." She took a deliberate step toward him, giving him no choice but to move out of her way. In her former career as a prosecutor, she'd interviewed rapists and murderers. She'd be damned if she'd let an ADA with a Manhattan-size ego intimidate her.

He backed up a step, his posture stiff.

Morgan blew past him, not yielding an inch of hallway. He was the sort you couldn't give a millimeter to. She made her way to the interview booth. Resembling a cubicle, it was open at the front and back for access with walls on both sides for privacy.

A guard delivered Eric, who plopped into the chair on the other side of the table. The overhead fluorescents highlighted a darkening bruise on his cheekbone. He'd likely have a black eye by tomorrow. "Ms. Dane? What are you doing here? They told me I'd have some random lawyer just for the arraignment."

"Lance called me," Morgan said. "How did you get that bruise on your face?"

Eric blew hair off his forehead. "My face hit the floor when the sheriff handcuffed me."

"Did you resist arrest?" Morgan asked.

Eric looked away. "Not really."

Which was not exactly a no.

Morgan moved on. "We don't have much time. The ADA has offered you a deal. If you plead guilty, you'll receive probation."

Eric jerked straight. "But I didn't do anything."

"Someone sent you an e-mail with a pornographic video involving a minor."

"Spencer's girl broke up with him. He sent the video of them doing it to everybody at school." He snorted, a disgusted sound. "How am I supposed to keep someone from sending me an e-mail?"

Good question. But if anyone found with e-mails containing child pornography could make that argument, conviction of pedophiles would be all but impossible. Morgan could argue lack of malicious intent on Eric's behalf, but the outcome would depend on the judge.

"If we go to trial, and you're convicted, the maximum sentence you could receive is four years."

Eric paled. "Four years? Because stupid Spencer sent me an e-mail?"

"Yes."

"But I didn't want it." His eyes creased in confusion.

Morgan's heart cracked. She used to be a tough-as-nails prosecutor, but her husband's death in Iraq two years before and the experience of being a single mom to three little girls had peeled away her tough veneer. "I'm sorry you're in this situation."

"I don't want to go to jail." He chewed on his thumbnail.

"If you plead guilty, you'll have to register as a sex offender, and you'll have a criminal record with a felony conviction that will never go away."

"This isn't fair." His eyes misted. He ducked his head and wiped his face with his hand. "What should I do?"

"Here's the thing. The ADA has said the deal is a onetime offer. If you plead not guilty, he'll pull his offer."

"What a pri—jerk."

"We don't know what other evidence he has at this time. If you enter a not guilty plea, he'll be forced to deliver that evidence. That's called discovery."

"I know. I watched *My Cousin Vinny* with my mom." His bleak gaze leveled with hers. "If I take the deal, my life is basically over. What happens if I say no?"

"You plead not guilty, then the judge will set bail. We'll try to get you out of here today."

"I won't have to spend another night in jail?" Eric brightened. " 'Cause that place is fu— messed up."

"That's the plan."

The smallest flicker of relief passed over his face.

Being defense counsel was new to her, but she was beginning to appreciate the importance of the role. When she'd worked in the prosecutor's office in Albany, she hadn't worried about sending innocent people to prison. Now she wondered if she ever had.

"The prosecutor says he has a confession," she said.

"I didn't confess to anything." Eric's voice rose.

"But you signed something . . ."

"Yeah." Eric swept a hand through his shaggy hair. "The sheriff made me sign a statement. He said if I didn't, the judge would go harder on me."

"Did he read you your Miranda rights before this?"

"Yeah." Eric nodded. "But he said calling a

28

lawyer would make me look guilty, and maybe I wouldn't get bail at all. Then I'd have to stay in jail."

Morgan had dealt with Randolph County Sheriff King before. Strong-arm tactics were his claim to fame.

"We'll argue that the sheriff coerced you into signing the confession. You said everyone at school had the video. Did you forward it to anyone?"

"No." Eric's lip curled. "I knew what it was. I deleted it as soon as I saw it in my in-box."

Morgan's pen froze. "You didn't open the e-mail?"

"No." Eric's voice rose. He glanced around and lowered his tone. "Why?"

The guard signaled to Morgan.

"Our time is up." She set down her pen. "Sit tight. I'll work on getting you out of here."

The guard led him away. Morgan headed for the DA's office, located in an adjacent wing of the courthouse, and asked to see Esposito. The receptionist directed her to a conference room. She went inside and set her tote on the table.

"Hello, Morgan." District Attorney Bryce Walters walked in, his smile white and predatory. Bryce had nearly been her boss, but two months ago she'd defended her neighbor in a high-profile murder case, upstaged Bryce, and forfeited any chance of working for him. She'd more than burned her bridges with the prosecutor's office. She'd sent them up in a mushroom cloud.

"Bryce, I didn't expect to see you. I thought Esposito was handling this case."

"I'm just checking in." He reached over the table and shook her hand, then pulled out a chair.

Normally, Bryce hid his emotions well, but he couldn't quite cover the small gleam of satisfaction in his eyes.

She breathed through a flash of anger. He saw Eric's case as a chance to get even with her.

"How is private practice treating you?" he asked.

"Very well, thank you." She sat down and rested her forearm on the table. "I appreciate being able to pick my own cases and set my own hours."

She had dinner with her three little girls almost every night, and she had an actual personal life. If she'd gone to work for Bryce, she'd have been lucky to get home by eight. But it was the smugness emanating from him that made her happy things had turned out the way they had.

This wasn't a game. A young man's life was at stake. No matter how aggressively she'd prosecuted criminals, she'd never treated them like pawns.

Esposito walked in, tossing a file on the table like he was dropping a mic. "Ready to deal?"

Morgan interlaced her fingers. "My client never opened the e-mail. He deleted it unread."

Crickets.

Esposito's mouth dropped open an inch before he snapped it shut. His eyes went cold and glittery with anger. Bryce's jaw tightened, and he frowned at Esposito.

"Coerced confessions are often false. Next time the sheriff hands you a slam dunk, you might want to verify the details." Morgan stood. She leaned forward, pressing her palms flat on the table. "I expect the charges to be dropped and my client released immediately." She pushed off the table and collected her tote bag and coat. "Goodbye, gentlemen."

Chapter Four

Lance followed Morgan into the duplex in the tiny business district of Scarlet Falls. His boss lived in the upstairs apartment, while the two-bedroom bottom unit had been converted into office space for Sharp Investigations. Two months ago, Morgan had rented the spare room for her new law practice.

They walked down the hall.

"Is Sharp in?" Morgan asked.

Lance ducked his head into his boss's office. "No."

Morgan stopped in her office to hang up her coat, then joined Lance in the kitchen. She went to the sink, wet a dishcloth, and dabbed at a spot on her skirt.

Lance pulled out his phone to check his messages. The battery was dead. He opened a kitchen drawer, took out a charger, and plugged in his phone. "Thank you again for helping Eric and his mom. They probably won't be able to pay you much."

"I know, but it was only a few hours of my time, and I wouldn't have let Eric sit in jail, no matter what."

"You can't do all pro bono work."

"I know that too." She scrubbed at the spot.

"But all I have on my plate is a DUI. I have the time."

Even if she didn't, Morgan never would have turned them down. Lance was a lucky, lucky man.

He crossed the room and took her face in his hands. "Maybe I can find some way to repay you for your kindness."

She tossed the paper towel in the trash. "What did you have in mind?"

He kissed her, pulling her close and wrapping his arms around her. "You were a total badass today." He leaned back. Enjoying the blush that stained her cheeks, he teased her a bit more. "I wanted to kiss you earlier, when we walked Eric out of that courthouse. But I know how prissy you are about PDAs when you're working."

"Prissy?" The corner of her lovely mouth turned up. "You call wanting to remain professional prissy?"

"Just a little. But I like it when you're strict. Makes me feel like a bad boy." Lance kissed her again and felt her laughter against his mouth.

"I hate to tell you, but you're more Boy Scout than bad boy. You always do the right thing."

"Oh, really?" He cupped the back of her head and angled for better access. Her bun got in the way, so he removed the hairpins and let her long black hair tumble to her shoulders.

"You're always doing that."

"I like it down." More accurately, he liked being the one to take it down. He cruised from her mouth to the side of her neck. He would never get enough of the taste of her.

She responded with a low moan, pressing against him. She was tall, and her body lined up with his perfectly.

"Well this Boy Scout is ready to blow off work." He checked the time on the wall clock. "*Fifteen* minutes early. Any chance you can stop at my place before you head home?"

"Fifteen whole minutes early?" She arched backward, her eyes shining. "I don't know if I can be with such a rule breaker."

"I'll make it worth your while." He slid a hand to the small of her back and pulled her hips tighter against his.

A spark of heat lit her eyes as she shook her head. "I don't have much time. I should be home for dinner. Stella is babysitting my grandfather today. Why don't you come with me instead?"

Morgan lived with her grandfather, who had broken his leg badly in a fall the previous month. Her sister, Stella, and Stella's boyfriend were pitching in to help care for him.

"I can work with a short time frame." He wrapped his arms around her waist, linking his hands behind her back. "I know where all the important buttons are."

She grinned. "You certainly do."

Between her recuperating grandfather, her three kids, and his mother's mental illness, their alone-time was limited. He'd take whatever moments he could get with her.

She pressed her hands flat against his chest. "Let me change my clothes. I don't know what I got on my skirt, but I need to drop it at the cleaners on my way home."

He watched her walk away, enjoying the view. Her fitted cobalt-blue suit played up her black hair, fair skin, and blue eyes, and the matching heels showed off a gorgeous pair of legs. "Need help taking it off?"

She glanced over her shoulder. One eyebrow arched in mock reprimand. "Behave. We're still in the office."

"Then be quick about it. We're on the clock." He crossed his arms over his chest and leaned against the counter.

The quickening of her step made him ridiculously happy.

She made him ridiculously happy.

On the counter, his phone buzzed. He reached for it. "Hey, Sharp."

"Where have you been?" Sharp asked. "I've been trying to get hold of you for an hour."

"No time for work now, Sharp. I'm on my way out." Lance picked up his keys.

"Lance—"

"Come on, Sharp. It's the end of the day. Can't it wait until tomorrow?"

"No." Sharp's tone was uncharacteristically grim and brought Lance to full attention.

"What happened?" he asked.

Morgan appeared in the doorway, wearing jeans and a thick wool sweater, her suit draped over one arm. Her brow furrowed. "Is something wrong?"

Over the phone, Sharp took a deep breath, his exhale audible over the sound of voices and wind. Where was he? "It's about your father."

The simple statement took the steam out of Lance. He eased into a chair.

"At lunch, one of my buddies told me that the sheriff's department pulled a 1984 Buick Century out of Grey Lake," Sharp said. "I'm sorry, Lance. It's your dad's car."

Morgan walked to his side. She bent down and wrapped an arm around his shoulders. She must have heard what Sharp had said.

Lance closed his eyes and leaned into her. The bright kitchen light colored the backs of his lids blood red. Even as he asked the question, he knew the answer. Sharp wouldn't have sounded so glum if the vehicle had been empty. "Was he in it?"

Sharp's next breath rattled. "Remains were found in the trunk."

Shock washed over Lance, leaving him numb.

The trunk?

His father had been murdered.

"I don't know why I'm surprised," he said. "I always knew he wouldn't have left us."

A flood of memories washed over him: his dad teaching him to catch a ball, mowing the lawn, driving him to hockey practice. He'd been a good man, a kind man. Who would have killed him? And why? Bitterness rose into Lance's throat.

After he'd processed Sharp's news, Lance had one overwhelming concern. "How am I going to tell my mother?"

Morgan's arms tightened around him. He squeezed her hand.

"I asked the sheriff to keep your dad's identity out of the news until we could notify her," Sharp said. "He agreed, but that's not going to buy us much time. The license plate on the car was still clear enough to read. It won't take the media long to find out who it was registered to."

"This is going to devastate her." Lance rubbed a hand down his face. "She's been doing so well lately."

His mother had a sort-of boyfriend. Except for their weekly group therapy sessions, she and her new man communicated entirely online. But it was the first relationship of any kind she'd welcomed in decades. She was also doing computer background checks and searches for Sharp Investigations. She seemed happy to be useful and enjoyed the investigation aspect. In short, she'd made huge strides forward in the past few months.

"This is going to bring everything back to her," Sharp agreed.

And it would likely cause a huge setback to her fragile mental health, and selfishly, upend Lance's life again, just when happiness felt like a real possibility.

"If you want to see the car, you need to get your butt out here," Sharp said.

"I'm on my way." Lance ended the call.

Morgan was on her cell phone.

He rummaged through another drawer for a portable phone charger and switched his phone to it. "I need to get out to the lake. I'll see you tomorrow."

She lowered her phone and slipped it into her pocket. "I'm coming with you."

"But you need to get home." The last thing he wanted was for his problems to negatively affect Morgan's three little girls.

"I'm coming with you," Morgan said again, enunciating the words just a little more clearly. "I called Stella and let her know I'll be late. She's going to stay until I get home."

Both her tone and the determination in her big blue eyes told him there was no point arguing with her. And if he were being honest with himself, he was grateful for her support.

"OK." Lance headed for the door.

Morgan was right behind him. She grabbed her coat from her office on the way out.

The ride out to Grey Lake took thirty minutes. The road became more and more rural as they drove. It was full dark when Lance parked on the side of the road behind two sheriff's department vehicles. He and Morgan got out of the Jeep. Crime scene tape fluttered between trees. On the bank of the lake, under stadium-bright portable lights, a rusted vehicle had just been loaded onto a flatbed truck.

The sight of the ruined vehicle filled Lance's throat. Next to him, Morgan took his hand and held it in a tight grip.

Sharp spotted the Jeep and broke away from the group of uniformed men. He met them halfway across the weedy ground.

"The medical examiner just left. The car is being taken to the county impound garage." Sharp narrowed critical eyes on him. "You all right?"

Afraid he'd choke on his voice, Lance nodded.

"The sheriff is handling the case?" Morgan asked.

"Yes," Sharp said. "The original missing person report was filed with the SFPD, but Police Chief Horner isn't going to fight the sheriff for a case this cold, and Grey Lake isn't in Horner's jurisdiction."

Lance didn't know if he should be relieved or disappointed that Horner wouldn't be handling the case. Horner was more politician than cop, but the sheriff wasn't any easier to deal with.

"Horner will send a copy of the case file over and wash his hands of the whole thing. The department is always shorthanded, and cold cases are notorious for racking up man-hours."

"But it isn't a simple missing adult case with no evidence of foul play anymore," Sharp said.

"No." Lance swallowed the truth. "It's murder. But will the sheriff be able to solve it? You tried to find my dad for years."

"I never had any physical evidence," Sharp said. "But now we do."

His dad had been in the trunk of his car on the bottom of the lake all these years.

Someone put him there. Had he been dead before the trunk filled up with water?

A sick feeling crawled over Lance.

Sheriff King gave Lance a solemn nod as they approached.

"What can you tell me?" Lance asked, his eyes fixed on the old Buick, memories of riding in it with his dad flashing in his mind. He pushed them away.

Not now.

"There isn't much to say at this point," the sheriff said. "The medical examiner took charge of the remains."

"Have you sent the divers back down to search the bottom of the lake?" Lance asked.

The sheriff shook his head. "Not yet. We'll evaluate the vehicle first. Whatever is down there has been sitting for twenty-three years. Another day or two isn't going to make any difference."

Underwater crime scenes presented unique challenges and costs. The crime had taken place too long ago to find any evidence on the lakeshore. Even the bottom of the lake was a long shot after all this time. The car and the bones were the keys to the puzzle. Lance understood, but he didn't like the sheriff's lack of urgency. But what could he do? He wasn't a cop anymore, and even if he were, Grey Lake was in Grey's Hollow, part of Sheriff King's fiefdom.

"I'll let you and your mother know when the ME officially identifies the remains," the sheriff said.

"I'd appreciate a heads-up when you want to talk to my mother." Lance debated how much information to give the sheriff and decided on, "She isn't well. The news could affect her health."

"Noted. Sharp mentioned the same thing," the sheriff said, which was not the affirmative response Lance would have liked.

"Does anyone in particular frequent this area?" Lance's gaze swept the lake, trees, and scrub grass.

"Only during hunting season. Most swimming and camping happens at the south end of the lake where the public boat ramp is. There are some good spots to catch bullhead down there." The sheriff pointed toward the water. "This end of the lake is muddy, which is probably why no one noticed the car all these years."

Lance backed away from the Buick. Staring at it wasn't serving any purpose, other than sledgehammering home the reality that his father was dead, and had been dead for a long time.

The flatbed started up with a roar and pulled away.

The sheriff nodded and headed for his vehicle.

After he was out of earshot, Sharp said, "I'll talk to the ME tomorrow and see how long he expects the official identification to take."

"No. I'll do it," Lance said. "It's my father."

Memories gathered in a ball beneath his breastbone. Pushing the past away was getting harder.

Lance slipped his hand out of Morgan's. "I have to go see my mother. The sheriff said he'd give me advance notice, but I don't trust him."

"Do you want one of us to go with you?" Sharp waved a hand between him and Morgan.

Lance shook his head. "I think it might be best if it's just me."

He didn't know how his mother was going to react. Morgan had never seen Jenny Kruger in the throes of her illness. Lance's mother had been stable over the past few months. Morgan had no idea how bad it could get.

And Lance wanted it to stay that way.

He didn't want to drag Morgan into the unpredictable reality of his mother's mental illness. He wished he didn't have to tell his mother about his father's car. But he had no choice. An agoraphobic, she literally lived online. If he didn't tell her, she'd find out on her own. The news would be far better coming from him.

"All right." Sharp turned toward the road, his movements slow and weary, as if the events of the day had sapped his strength. Usually, he had more energy than most twentysomethings.

Lance rubbed a hand across his scalp. After he visited his mother, he had only one thing on his plate: find out who had killed his father.

Chapter Five

Morgan watched Lance struggle, her heart breaking for him. On one hand, she wanted the closure for him and his mother. On the other, closure had a price. Old wounds would be reopened. The pain would be fresh. But hopefully, short-lived.

Lance turned to Sharp. "I'm kicking myself for not opening the case file when you gave it to me back in September."

"It was the right decision at the time," Sharp said. "You didn't want to dredge up the past when there was little chance you could solve the crime, but now there's physical evidence."

And the past was going to be stirred up no matter what Lance did.

He crossed his arms over his chest and stared out over the lake. Morgan followed his gaze for a few seconds. With no visible moon, the water undulated in shades of black in the darkness. She shifted her gaze back to his face, now shuttered.

A short while ago, they'd been embracing, happy and intimate.

Now everything had changed.

"Would you give Morgan a lift back to the office?" Lance asked. "Her minivan is there."

"Of course," Sharp said.

"Can you give us a minute, Sharp?" Morgan asked.

"I'll be in the car." Sharp walked toward his vehicle, allowing Morgan and Lance a moment of privacy.

She crossed the weeds to stand in front of him and put her hands on his forearms. His muscles were taut, rigid with tension. "How are *you* doing with this?"

"I don't know." He looked over her shoulder. Behind him, the flatbed retreated. Lance blinked, then looked at her. "It feels surreal."

"I'm sorry this is happening to you." She slid her hands down to grasp his. "Are you sure you don't want me or Sharp to go with you to your mom's house? I know you can handle things alone, but you don't have to."

"I'm sure." Lance's chest rose and fell with a sigh. "I don't know how she's going to react. If I need help, I can call Sharp. He's already seen her at her worst."

His words stung, even though she knew she was being overly sensitive. Sharp had been in the Krugers' lives for decades. Morgan's relationship with Mrs. Kruger was relatively new. Even though it felt as if *Lance* was part of *her* family, Morgan obviously hadn't reached inclusion status in his.

But she didn't push. She wouldn't have survived her husband's death without the support of her grandfather and sister. But Lance had had no one but Sharp for decades. Lance was more accustomed to being alone.

"I understand." Or at least, she was trying to. "You'll call me later?"

"I'll try. Depends on how she takes the news. I'll stay with her tonight."

"Of course you will." She nodded. "Is there anything I can do?"

He shook his head. "But thanks for asking."

That sounds so . . . detached.

She squeezed his hands, wanting more of a connection with him. "Call me. It doesn't matter how late."

With a nod, he turned back to his Jeep and left.

Morgan walked toward the road where Sharp's car was parked. Sheriff King stood next to the open door of his county vehicle.

As she passed him, his eyes narrowed.

"I hear you got one of those boys off this afternoon." His voice was low and deep and disgusted.

Morgan stopped and turned to face him. "Eric was innocent. Doesn't it bother you that he spent the night in jail for a crime he didn't commit?"

"Given the video his friends were passing around, I'm sure he's guilty of something." The careless lift of the sheriff's big shoulder said as much as his words. He swept his hat off his head and brushed back his gray-streaked hair.

"These entitled kids need to learn that there are consequences for their actions."

"Eric is hardly entitled, and even if he were, that's no excuse for putting an innocent kid behind bars." Morgan inhaled, hoping the damp night air would cool her anger. "Eric has a bruise on his face."

The sheriff shoved his hat back on his head. "Eric resisted arrest."

Exactly what Morgan had predicted the sheriff would say. "You could have gotten him killed. Your jail is hardly secure."

She and the sheriff locked gazes for a few seconds. His eyes narrowed at her reference to the attack on her previous client.

"Jail is a dangerous place," the sheriff said, his voice grating. "Now your client knows that. Maybe he'll stick to the straight and narrow."

"He was *already* on the straight and narrow," Morgan shot back. "The legal system assumes innocence until proven guilty. Eric didn't deserve the bruise on his face either."

"He shouldn't have resisted arrest." The sheriff's jaw shifted back and forth, as if he were grinding his molars. Morgan turned away. There really wasn't much else to say. Sheriff King was an old school hard-ass. He saw his job as putting as many people in jail as possible. He was not going to change.

"Tyler Green is out on bail," he said.

Morgan froze, her palms going cold as she slowly turned back. "Seriously?"

"Yep. He got a new bail hearing." The sheriff jammed his hat on his head. "I thought you should know, seeing as he threatened to get even with you."

Two months ago, Sharp Investigations had been hired to find the abusive deadbeat dad. Morgan had been instrumental in getting Tyler arrested. He'd attacked her, and unlike the wife who was too scared to testify against him, Morgan had pressed charges, and he'd gone to jail.

Supposedly.

"I thought he couldn't make bail." Morgan rubbed the base of her throat. Though her bruises had healed, she could still feel Tyler's hands around her neck.

"I don't know what happened." The sheriff lifted a shoulder. "I put him in jail. I can't help it if the system assumes he's innocent until proven guilty."

In light of the information he'd given her, she ignored the dig.

"Thank you for telling me about Tyler." Morgan wasn't surprised at the courtesy. Sheriff King could be harsh, but his manners were as old-fashioned as his dated approach toward law enforcement.

"You're welcome. Be careful out there, counselor." The sheriff got into his vehicle and drove away.

Morgan walked to Sharp's car. Her skin tingled with nerves, and a headache pulsed behind her ears. She slid into the passenger seat.

Sharp started the engine. "What did the sheriff want?"

Morgan summed up what had happened at the courthouse earlier. "He dressed me down for getting the charges against Eric dropped."

"He's a Neanderthal. I wrote *Mickey Mouse* on my ballot in the last election."

Morgan stifled a surprised snort. The sheriff had run unopposed.

"He also warned me that Tyler Green is out on bail," she said.

Sharp turned the car around and headed back toward Scarlet Falls. "Who would post bail for that useless jerk? He's a flight risk."

"Maybe the same family members who let him hide from subpoenas in their houses."

"Good point," Sharp said. "Are you all right?"

Morgan took a water bottle out of her tote and rolled the tension from her shoulders. "Yes. Lance upgraded our security system, and I'll tell the family to be extra careful. Hopefully, Tyler will appreciate being out of jail and stay clear of me."

"I wouldn't bet on Tyler Green making sensible choices."

"No. I suppose not." Morgan rubbed a ragged edge on her fingernail. "But I'm more worried about Lance."

Sharp nodded. "I know you are. I tried to help him as much as I could, but he learned to handle problems on his own at a very young age. That doesn't mean it's what's best for him or even what he wants. It's just what he knows."

And when people were hurting, they retreated to the familiar.

"Thanks, Sharp," Morgan said. "I'll keep that in mind."

She dug a bottle of ibuprofen out of her tote bag. She twisted the cap off the bottle and washed down two tablets.

Sharp frowned. "You shouldn't take those on an empty stomach."

Morgan found a candy bar in the bottom of her bag. "I'm not."

From the look of horror on his face, she could have been holding nuclear waste.

"Put that down." He opened the center console, pulled out a wrapped bar, and handed it to her. "Eat this instead."

"What is it?" In the dark, all she could read on the wrapper was the word *organic*.

"It's a protein bar. You'll eat candy, but you're suspicious of something healthy." Sharp shook his head. "You'd have more energy if you didn't eat all that sugar."

"Probably." She put the candy back in her bag, opened the protein bar, and took a bite. "It tastes like dust."

Sharp sighed. "You need the protein."

As usual, Sharp was right. By the time they reached the office, her headache had subsided. He parked and waited for her to get into her van and lock the doors before he disappeared inside the building.

Morgan drove away from the tiny business district of Scarlet Falls. A few minutes later, a pair of headlights in her rearview mirror caught her attention. The vehicle was too far away to make out the type of vehicle, especially in the dark. She made two turns. The car remained behind her, never getting close enough for her to see it clearly. She stopped at a red light and waited for the car to catch up. But it hung back instead. When the light turned green, she drove through the dark town, suspicion prickling between her shoulder blades.

It was after nine o'clock. Scarlet Falls rolled up the streets *and* sidewalks at eight.

The headlights were still there when she drove past the country road that led to her grandfather's house on the Scarlet River. Morgan dug her phone from her tote. She'd call her sister, Stella, a detective with the SFPD, and ask to meet her somewhere. The car behind her was probably a coincidence. Just someone headed in the same direction. But Morgan wasn't taking any chances.

Not with Tyler on the loose.

She was scrolling for her sister's number when

the headlights disappeared. Morgan blew out a breath.

You're paranoid.

She turned the car around and went home. But as she climbed out of her minivan, a cold breeze wrapped around her. She shivered, the hairs on the back of her neck rising, as if someone was watching.

She scanned the grass and trees but saw no one. The front yard was lit up like the Meadowlands. There were no big shrubs to hide behind. The dogs were at the window, barking.

She jogged up the front steps and didn't take a deep breath until she was inside the house. Other than the dogs snuffling around her legs, the house was quiet. The girls would have gone to bed hours ago. Morgan closed and locked the door.

"Hey." Her sister, Stella, walked out of the kitchen. Stella scanned Morgan's face. "What's wrong?"

Morgan told her about Tyler. "I probably imagined feeling someone watching me. The news about Tyler being out of jail has me on edge."

Snoozer, her French bulldog, begged for attention, but rescue dog Rocket brushed past Morgan's legs and went to the front window. Her white-and-tan markings and docked tail were bulldog like, but the mutt's lean body was some other breed altogether. A low growl rumbled from her chest, and the fur on the back of the dog's neck rose.

"What is it, girl?" Morgan knelt beside the dog and rested a hand on her back. The dog stiffened and barked. Morgan stroked her head.

Stella pulled her cell phone from her pocket. "The dog senses something. I'm going to have a patrol unit check the neighborhood."

Morgan rubbed the dog's shoulder. "Good girl."

Climbing to her feet, she dumped her coat on a chair and went into the kitchen. Both dogs followed at her heels. Her grandfather sat in his wheelchair at the table, a glass of milk and a piece of banana bread on a plate in front of him. His broken leg was encased in a plaster cast and elevated. He was trying to work an unbent wire coat hanger into the top of the cast.

"The doctor said you shouldn't do that." Morgan took the hanger. "You could scratch yourself and get an infection."

"It itches." Grandpa sulked.

She bent down and kissed his cheek. "I know. And I know you're bored out of your mind too. Two more weeks. Then the cast comes off, and you can put some weight on that leg."

Her heart clenched when she thought about how they'd almost lost him during surgery.

"I'll get through it." He reached up and patted her arm. "What was up with the dog?"

Morgan repeated her story about Tyler and the

car as she opened the fridge and poured a glass of milk. "I'm glad Rocket is here. The alarm system will tell us if someone is breaking into the house, but that dog will let us know if someone is outside thinking about breaking into the house."

Grandpa tossed the dog a piece of banana bread. She caught it in the air, her big jaws snapping like an alligator's.

Grandpa frowned. "Damn this leg. I'm not as useful as I could be."

Morgan smiled. A retired NYPD detective, Grandpa had broken his leg protecting her and her daughter. "You did just fine."

"Tell me about the rest of your day."

Morgan started with her afternoon at the courthouse with Eric and moved on to the scene at Grey Lake.

"So you trumped the new ADA, showed up Bryce Walters *again,* and ratted the sheriff out for coercing confessions from suspects?"

"Yes." Morgan sipped her milk, suddenly wishing it was wine. "It's been a full day."

"Nice way to make friends and influence people." Grandpa shook his head. "How is Lance?"

"I don't know." Morgan checked her phone. "He's with his mother now."

"That has to be rough."

"Yes."

And he hadn't called her.

Stella appeared in the doorway. "The patrol unit didn't find anything. They're going to do another drive-by later tonight."

"Thanks," Morgan said.

"I could stay," Stella offered.

"You were here all day. Go home to Mac. We have the alarm, the dog, and I'll break out my handgun tonight." But as sexist as it felt, Morgan wished Lance was there.

"OK." Stella took her keys from her pocket. "Mac doesn't teach any classes tomorrow. He'll be here at eight to help Grandpa get washed and dressed."

Morgan took the dogs out with her to walk Stella to her car. The dogs did their business while she watched her sister get into her car and drive away. A police car cruised past, and she went inside. She checked the windows and doors and set the alarm before walking back to her bedroom and opening her gun safe. She took her Glock out and set it high on her armoire.

Then she brushed her teeth, put on her pajamas, and prepared to not sleep. Once again, her family was in danger.

Chapter Six

Lance hesitated, his key an inch from the lock on his mother's door. Once he went inside, there was no going back. No taking back the words he would need to say. No resetting his mother's recovery train on its rails.

But he didn't have a choice.

He unlocked and opened the door.

"Lance? Is that you?" his mother called from the back of the house.

He made his way through the tidy house back to her office. His mom had succumbed to anxiety, depression, and hoarding after her husband's disappearance. At one point in Lance's youth, clutter had filled the house, leaving them narrow pathways to move from room to room.

She sat behind her L-shaped desk. A former computer science professor, she now taught online and performed freelance website design, security, and maintenance. Three monitors and a laptop stared back at her. A cat rubbed on Lance's calves. The other feline ignored him from the windowsill.

There was something different about his mom. Her eyes looked . . . She was wearing makeup.

Lance covered his shock with a cough into his fist. He hadn't seen his mother wear makeup in . . . never?

She waved him toward her. "Come here. I want you to meet someone."

Online?

Lance rounded the desk, set a hand on his mother's frail-thin shoulder, and kissed her on the cheek. The skin stretched over the bones on her hands was nearly translucent and streaked with blue veins. Years of chronic anxiety had aged her beyond chronological years. At sixty, she looked much older. But her smile had brightened over the past few months.

Today, he found her new happiness bittersweet.

"This is Kevin Munro." His mom gestured toward her main computer monitor.

On the screen, a gray-haired man of sixty or seventy waved. "It's nice to meet you, Lance."

"Um. It's nice to meet you too." Lance had seen him before, when he'd dropped his mother at her weekly group therapy sessions. Therapy and visits to the psychiatrist were the only times his mom left her house.

Kevin flushed and adjusted the collar of his plaid button-up shirt.

The quiet in the room turned awkward, and Lance realized this was probably the equivalent of a date for his mom and Kevin.

Lance stepped back. He did not want to ruin this for her. "I didn't mean to interrupt your conversation. I'll be in the kitchen. I need to talk to you when you're done."

"Kevin, I'll talk to you later," she said. Kevin responded with goodbye, and his mother closed the computer window. She swiveled her chair to face Lance. Anxiety creased the corners of her eyes. "Did something happen to Morgan or Sharp?"

"No. Nothing like that." Lance was bungling this. "It's about Dad."

She flinched. "What?"

Lance took a deep breath, crouched, and took both her hands in his. "The sheriff's department pulled Dad's car from Grey Lake."

His mother's face went white. But she didn't flail or faint or throw a fit. Her expression was blank. Too emotionless. Was she even processing what he'd said? "Are you sure?"

"I saw the car myself." He swallowed. "It's Dad's."

She stared at their joined hands for a few seconds. When she looked up at him, her eyes were tentative. "Was he inside?"

Lance hesitated. How much should he tell her? "They think so."

"So they're not one hundred percent sure it's Vic." Her voice dropped to a whisper when she said his father's name.

"No, but identifying him shouldn't take long. Dad's dental records are on file." Lance rubbed her fingers with his thumbs. "Tell me what you're feeling."

"I don't know exactly." Her forehead wrinkled. "On one hand, it's a surprise. After all these years, I never really expected to find out what happened. On the other, it's not. I knew something terrible had happened to him. He wouldn't have left us."

"That's what I always thought too."

"Was it an accident?" A tear rolled down her cheek. "Did he drive off a bridge or something?"

"No. There are no bridges near where he was found. The car would have been driven or sent into the water from the bank." Lance paused. Was she ready for this? Did he have a choice but to be honest with her? She was a very intelligent woman. If he didn't tell her, she'd find the details on her own. "I think someone killed him."

She pulled one hand free and covered her mouth. "You're sure?"

"Not yet. The sheriff will investigate." And so would Lance.

She wiped tears from her cheeks, her face frozen in a tragic smile. "I thought I was all cried out over your father. I guess not."

"I'll stay here tonight." Lance kept the essentials in his old bedroom in case of an emergency. "Will you be all right by yourself for a few hours tomorrow?"

"Lance, I don't want you to babysit me."

"Mom . . ." he protested. "That's not—"

"No." Her voice was firm. "I'm sorry. I know

you only want to help. But you've spent your whole life taking care of me."

"I don't mind."

"I know you don't." A sad smile turned the corner of her mouth. "How much did I tell you about the new counselor who's been running our group therapy session for the last two months?"

"You said she was pushy, and you didn't like her."

"At first I didn't. I was used to the old one. He'd been running the group the same way for twelve years. Change is hard for me, and some of the things Dr. Blake is encouraging me to do are uncomfortable." She blushed. "I've been meditating and doing yoga."

Meditation? Yoga?

Is this even my mother?

"I'm not fooling myself. I'm never going to be able to grocery shop or go to the movies or run errands like other people, but I *can* be more independent. I don't need to be mentally isolated even though I'm physically limited. It's a choice, not an inevitability. I can connect with people right here in my house."

"Like Kevin," Lance said.

She nodded. "You have a job to do. A life to live. Seeing you with Morgan has made me realize how selfish I've been."

"You're not selfish—"

She held up a hand. "Like any patient with a chronic illness, I have to learn to manage it myself." She straightened her frail shoulders. "*I* have to do it."

She looked determined and as grounded as he'd ever seen her. Maybe she could gain some independence. But in the back of his mind, a little voice whispered if she failed, she'd lose all the progress—all the happiness—she'd gained in the past few months.

She reached up and touched his face. "Lance, I don't want to be a burden on you. You've given up too much of your life for me already."

"If you feel comfortable managing things yourself, I'm behind you all the way," he said. "But I'm also here for you. What can I do to help?"

"Find out what really happened to your father." His mother dropped her hand and hugged her arms, rubbing her biceps as if she were freezing. "I'd like to put this behind me. I know it's asking a lot of you. He was your father. Maybe you don't want to delve into his personal life."

"I already intended to find Dad's killer."

"Then do it. I'll be fine here." His mother pressed a fist to her mouth and sniffed. Her shoulders curled forward, her posture projecting the distress her words denied. Lowering her hand, she swallowed. "We both loved him, but we need to move on. We need to put his death behind us."

"All right," Lance said. Tomorrow, he'd start by claiming his father's remains.

Chapter Seven

JOHN H ROGERS
CAPT
US ARMY
IRAQ
NOV 14 1982
JUL 10 2015
BELOVED HUSBAND AND FATHER

Morgan stared at the headstone. Half of her wanted to throw herself on John's grave. The other half wanted to run away as fast as possible in case the sadness she'd recently shed caught up with her again.

"Where's Daddy?" Three-year-old Sophie frowned up at Morgan. "You said he'd be here."

Sophie's misunderstanding added fifty pounds to Morgan's mood.

"I'm sorry, honey." Morgan searched for the right words. Did she tell her daughter that John was in a box six feet under the grass? Thinking of his body decaying in a box, alone, all that time, she shuddered. Her grief turned claustrophobic.

She looked to the open sky, the brilliant and glorious blue seemed like a betrayal, as if the world should not be so beautiful without John in it. There should always be some tiny, visible sign of misery to match the kernel permanently lodged in her heart.

While she was determined to move on with her life, she would never forget. Coming here was like ripping the scab off a wound before the underlying scar tissue had formed.

"Daddy isn't here," Morgan said. "This is his headstone. We put it here so we can remember him."

"Daddy's dead." Ava carried a white bakery box. At six, Morgan's oldest was the only one of her children who remembered their father. Usually, she used a know-it-all tone when she corrected her younger sisters. But today, her brown eyes, so like John's, turned up to Morgan for confirmation. Ava had the best understanding of the concept of death. At least she knew that her father was never coming home.

"Yes, honey," Morgan said. "That's right."

The frigid wind blew across the open landscape. Its harshness was somehow soothing.

Morgan spotted a pink hat on the grass. She picked it up and tugged it firmly over her three-year-old's light-brown braids.

"Mommy," Sophie said. "We need candles."

"It's too windy for candles," Ava said.

Frowning, Sophie plopped down on her knees in the cold grass. "We have to sing. You can't eat birfday cake unless you sing."

Five-year-old Mia tugged on Morgan's hand. Her serious brow crunched with deep thought.

Morgan crouched and tucked a stray lock of hair under Mia's purple hat.

Mia leaned close to her mother's ear and whispered, "Am I s'posed to be sad?"

Morgan blinked, trying to stem the sudden, hot flood of tears in her eyes. She squinted against a morning sun that shone too brightly. The grief she'd had firmly under control stirred to fresh life, threatening to drag her down like a weighted vest.

"You're sad," Mia said.

"I'm a little sad," Morgan admitted, her throat tight. "But you're supposed to feel however you feel."

Mia swiped a sleeve under her nose. The cold had turned her nose and cheeks bright pink. "I'm not sad."

"That's good." Morgan dug a tissue from her tote and handed it to Mia. "Daddy wouldn't want you to be sad."

"Mommy's not sad *all* the time like she used to be." Sophie plucked a blade of grass from the grave and spun it between her fingers.

"Where are your mittens?" Morgan asked Sophie.

Her youngest gave her a *what mittens?* look. "When can we eat the cupcakes?"

"Right now." Morgan took the blanket from

under her arm, spread it on the grass in front of John's headstone, and knelt on it. Tears blurred the rows upon rows of plain, pale markers. Sacrifice and heartbreak organized with military precision. It was all too neat, too perfect to represent the turmoil that each and every death had left in its wake. Lives destroyed. Hearts shredded. Worlds upended. She wanted a tornado to sweep them up, to smash and scatter them, to leave these identically shaped markers as broken as all the people left behind.

A few rows away, an older couple bowed their heads over a grave. A gust of wind whipped dead leaves around their feet. The leaves tumbled across the otherwise perfectly groomed landscape, a reminder that there would always be things that couldn't be controlled.

The girls gathered around her. Sophie took the lead singing "Happy Birthday." Despite her lisp, her voice was surprisingly strong and on key. The older couple turned and watched. The man reached for the woman's hand. Morgan could tell they were crying, even if she couldn't see them through her own tears.

The cold ground seeped through the blanket and the knees of her jeans. The rest of her was numb.

She took a deep breath and handed out cupcakes but couldn't eat hers. This had been a mistake. She'd been doing so well for the past two months. But how could she have said no after Ava spotted John's birthday marked on Morgan's calendar? Grief swept through her like a fever, reminding her of the dark place where she'd been trapped until just a couple of months ago. She'd almost forgotten how exhausting it had been. It was no wonder she'd done so little for the two years following her husband's death.

She forced herself to taste the icing. Sweetness burst on her tongue, bright and intense as the sunlight.

"Sophie has icing in her hair," Ava said in a disgusted voice.

Morgan pulled a box of wet wipes from her tote. She handed them out to Ava and Mia, then turned to her youngest. A gob of blue was stuck in Sophie's braid. More icing smeared her nose and lips and hands. How had she gotten it on her shoe? Morgan pulled out another wipe and started mopping up icing. In the back of her head, she could hear John's laughter. Instead of cleaning Sophie up, he would have smashed a cupcake on his own face to make his daughter smile.

John hadn't wanted Morgan to be sad either. The letter he'd left her had made that clear.

"Who's going to eat Daddy's cupcake?" Sophie asked.

"We'll take it home to Grandpa," Morgan said. "Is everyone ready?"

Three little heads nodded.

"I'm cold." Ava shuddered.

"Happy birthday, Daddy," Mia said. Ava and Sophie echoed their sister.

Morgan returned the wipe container to her tote and collected their trash. She stood and placed her hand on the top of the grave marker. The stone was cold under her palm.

Happy birthday, John.

She lifted her hand, then turned and led her daughters away from the grave.

Today, she would concentrate on all the things she was grateful for in her life: her children, her family, and her second chance at love.

She would be happy if it killed her.

They trooped back to the minivan. Morgan spotted one blue mitten by the front tire. She scanned the parking area and crouched to check under the vehicle for its mate. Instead of a blue mitten, she saw a flat tire.

The hairs on her neck waved in the wind. She turned in a slow circle but saw no one across the open landscape of the cemetery. Trees surrounded the fields. But still, she felt eyes on her.

Relax!

She'd been paranoid since the sheriff had told her Tyler Green had been released. Being out on bail, and with assault charges already pending, Tyler had every motivation to stay far away from her.

"We have a flat tire, girls. Let's get you all in

the van where it's warm. Then I'll deal with the tire."

She secured the children in their car seats, set the parking brake, and blocked the wheels. By the time she freed the spare tire from its location and dragged it out from underneath the vehicle, she was sweating, mentally cursing car manufacturers everywhere, and promising to start working out. Loosening the lug nuts proved to be another job requiring muscle she sadly lacked. Once she had the spare in hand and the lug nuts loosened, changing the tire was a dirty job, but no big deal.

After hefting the flat into the back of the van, she cleaned her hands with baby wipes and climbed into the driver's seat.

"I'm hungry," Sophie said.

They'd left the house early, and none of the girls had eaten much breakfast. She drove out of the cemetery. "Then let's find some food."

Fifteen minutes later, she found a diner, and the girls fueled up on pancakes. Still unsettled, Morgan stuck with coffee. Ava and Mia cleaned their plates. Even Sophie couldn't resist syrup-smothered pancakes. With the kids happy and full, Morgan led them back to the van and secured them in their safety seats.

She climbed into the driver's seat and shut the door. She inserted the key into the ignition and caught a heavy metallic odor. Cold wetness soaked into her jeans. *What the . . . ?*

Morgan put a hand under her butt. It came away covered in dark red.

Blood?

Her heart kick-started, and she leaped from the van. The van interior was black, but she could see the stain now that she was looking for it. The entire seat was soaked in it.

And now, so was Morgan.

Had she locked the car? She always did, but herding three small kids through a parking lot could make anyone forget.

"Mommy! What's wrong?" Ava called from inside the van.

"More car trouble, honey." Morgan scanned the parking lot but saw no one. The lot was only a quarter full. The other cars appeared to be empty. "Let's go back inside and call Mac."

Morgan hustled the kids back inside. She whispered an explanation to the waitress, who occupied the girls with crayons and paper while Morgan called the police and Mac.

"Mac is on his way," Morgan said to the kids. She kept one eye on the other patrons and another on the parking lot. She saw no sign of Tyler Green.

"Do you want to go clean up?" the waitress asked.

She would absolutely love nothing more than to peel her nasty jeans and sweater off and scrub her skin raw, but her own comfort took a back seat to her children's safety.

"I'll wait, thank you." Morgan wasn't leaving her girls alone for a second. She hadn't imagined anything. She should have listened to her instincts. She'd bet that flat tire hadn't been an accident either. Someone was doing much more than following her.

She was being stalked.

Chapter Eight

Lance parked his Jeep in front of the medical examiner's office in the county municipal complex.

He had been to the ME's suite in his days on the police force, but this time, his role was as a member of the victim's family. It was a new part for Lance and about as comfortable as a suit made of poison ivy.

Inside, the smell of burned coffee in the waiting area didn't help his nausea.

He gave his name to the receptionist. "Dr. Jenkins left a message on my phone asking me to stop by today."

The call had come while Lance had been in the shower.

Stop by if you can. I have a few questions for you.

Did that mean Frank needed more information to ID his dad's remains?

"Dr. Jenkins is in autopsy suite three," she said. "He said you could go on in."

Lance swallowed. He'd hoped the ME would be in his office.

He reminded himself that all he'd see would be bones. There would be no putrid smell. No rotting flesh. No bloated body. It couldn't be that bad or Frank wouldn't have invited him in. Right?

Right?

But Dr. Frank Jenkins was not known for his interpersonal skills.

Lance suited up in the antechamber. Gown, booties, gloves. He carried the plastic face shield. Damn things made his face sweat. He wouldn't put it on until he had to.

He opened the door and hesitated at the threshold, sweating even without the shield. The other tables were empty. For once, there were no bodies in sight, but the scents of formalin and decomp were permanent fixtures. The smells lay heavy in the air, coating the back of his throat and threatening to gag him.

"Lance, come on back." Frank waved him into the room. "I want to show you something."

Lance held his breath and waded in.

Let's get this done.

A sheet covered the stainless-steel autopsy table. On it, a skeleton had been loosely assembled.

Frank circled the table, his attention focused on the remains. "I had my assistant put the skeleton in order. Some of the small bones were missing, but we have a good number. Hopefully, enough to get a positive ID."

Hopefully?

Lance walked closer. "Then you haven't formally identified my father?"

"No." Frank looked up, his face confused. The

light glinted off his face shield. "Didn't Sheriff King call you?"

"He did not."

Frank muttered something that sounded like *asshole* under his breath. "I'm so sorry, Lance. I should have called you last night after I called Sheriff King. This isn't your father."

Wait. What?

The blood left Lance's head, leaving dizziness in its absence. "Excuse me?"

"It isn't your father."

Lance glanced at the skull. The jaw looked undamaged, most of the teeth present. He breathed through his mouth, but the taste of the autopsy suite only made him feel worse. "You have his dental records?"

"I don't need dental records." Frank gestured to the bones. "The skeleton is female."

Shock hit Lance like a cold slap. "Are you sure?"

Frank arched an annoyed eyebrow. With a sigh of great patience, he motioned to the skeleton and shifted into lecture mode. "Number one, the overall size and thickness of the bones, especially the femur, humerus, and radius, suggest this is a female." He moved down the table to the center of the skeleton. "Second, the female pelvis is wider than that of a male specimen. Lastly," he pointed to the skull, "the skull and jawbone of this victim also suggest it is female."

Lance stared at the bones, trying to take it all in. "Are you sure all of these bones belong to the same victim?"

Frank nodded. "We collected about eighty-five percent of the skeleton. Most of the missing ones are small: fingers, toes, vertebrae, etc. The bones are consistent in size, and there are no duplicates that would suggest a second individual was in the trunk of that car."

The medical examiner stepped away from the table and lifted his face shield. "Bones don't lie, Lance. This is not your father."

A few seconds ticked by as Lance absorbed Frank's words.

Not. My. Father.

Those were the last words he'd expected to hear from the medical examiner.

Now what?

Someone put a woman in the back of his father's car and sent it into the lake.

Who? Why?

Shit.

Where is my father?

His visit with Frank was supposed to answer questions, not generate a dozen new ones.

Pain thumped at Lance's temples. He'd wanted to visit the ME on an empty stomach.

Obvious reasons.

But now his hollow gut churned.

"You don't know who she is?" Lance asked.

This unidentified woman was now the key to his father's disappearance.

"No," Frank said. "Not yet. We'll start with any local girls who went missing in 1994 and work from there."

Lance's ears rang. His gaze swept over the skeleton, suddenly seeing its feminine slightness. "Can you tell me anything about her?"

Frank consulted a clipboard. "Measurement of the femur tells me she was approximately five feet, five inches tall, give or take an inch."

"Any idea how old she was?"

Frank gestured toward a row of X-rays on a lightboard. "Impacted wisdom teeth. She was likely at least eighteen."

"The fact that she didn't have the teeth removed could also mean that she didn't have access to dental care," Lance added. "Or she couldn't afford the procedure."

"Right." Frank waved a hand over the skeleton. "Some, but not all of her growth plates are closed. The clavicle, or collarbone, is the last bone to complete growth. The medial end is not fully fused, so she was under thirty." Frank picked up a magnifying glass and examined a rib bone. "The ends of the ribs change as people age. Based on the smoothness I see here, I'd estimate that she was in her early twenties."

"Any idea how she died?"

"Yes." Frank read from his clipboard, then set

it down and returned to the table. He pointed to a U-shaped bone below the skull on the sheet. "The hyoid bone is fractured."

The hyoid bone was located in the middle of the neck between the chin and the thyroid.

"She was strangled," Lance said.

"Most likely." Frank nodded. "We're lucky. That only happens in approximately one-third of strangulation deaths."

She wasn't lucky.

Lance stared at the tiny, meaningful bone. "So she was dead when she was put in the trunk?"

"It's possible to survive a fractured hyoid, but I hope she didn't." Frank frowned.

"Me too." Lance shuddered. Being strangled would have been bad enough, but he couldn't imagine the alternative.

"Do you remember anyone who meets her description in your father's life? Did your father have any female coworkers or friends that he was close with?" Frank was circling around the topic, but his line of thinking was obvious: infidelity.

"I don't know." Lance did not want to think about his father cheating, but he searched his memories. "No. My parents had some friends, but they were all about the same age as my parents, in their midthirties in 1994."

"If you think of anyone this could be"—Frank waved a gloved hand over the skeleton—"please call me."

"I will," Lance said.

Frank stripped off his gloves. "If she was a local and someone filled out a missing person report, I should be able to identify her. If nothing pans out, I'll bring in a forensic anthropologist."

"Good luck." Lance left the autopsy suite. He tossed his PPEs in the appropriate bins on the way out. As he walked across the parking lot toward his Jeep, his gut knotted.

Where was his father?

Chapter Nine

The wind whipped at Morgan's face as she crossed the parking lot from the diner to her minivan, where Mac was leaning into the open door of his SUV.

"Thanks, Mac." She rolled the top of the brown bag down. Inside were her blood-soaked, now-crusty jeans. Mac had brought her a clean pair.

"You're welcome." Mac had transferred the girls' safety seats to his SUV and was securing them in the back seat. "It's a little tight, but we'll manage. What are you going to do with the van?"

"I called a tow truck." There was no way she was sitting in a pool of blood to drive it to a garage. Besides, she wanted a mechanic to give the van a thorough once-over in case some other damage had been done.

"Whoever broke into your vehicle damaged the locks." Mac tugged on a child safety seat.

Morgan pressed a hand to her forehead. "I didn't notice when I opened the van."

Seemingly satisfied with the car seat's fit, Mac stepped away from the open SUV door. "That's because your fob still chirps when you press the button, but the locks don't work."

Sophie tugged on Morgan's hand. "Can we go soon?"

Morgan squatted to her level. "Yes. I just need to talk to the deputy for a couple of minutes. Stay right here with Mac."

"OK." Head low, Sophie turned back to Mac's car. She'd awoken early this morning and would fall asleep as soon as the vehicle was in motion.

Morgan approached the deputy typing up the incident report in the front seat of his patrol car. He pointed with his pen toward the Rapid Stain Identification Kit sitting on a clipboard in the passenger seat. Only one red line appeared in the test window. "It's not human blood."

"Some sort of animal blood, then." She glanced back at her van. Animal blood was less disturbing than human blood, but still creepy.

The deputy got out of the car.

"Were you able to get the feed from the security cameras?" she asked.

"No, ma'am." The deputy pointed toward the camera mounted on a street lamp. "The camera is covered in foam. From the smell of it, I suspect it's hornet spray."

Morgan walked to the pole and squinted up at the camera. She sniffed, catching the whiff of insecticide. "Clever. You can shoot that from twenty feet away."

"Yes, ma'am," the deputy said. "It sticks real well too, so it completely covered the lens. Maybe we'll get a hit on the fingerprints I took from your van."

Morgan expected the prints he'd found to be hers. Anyone smart enough to cover a surveillance camera with hornet foam wouldn't leave fingerprints.

"You'll check on Tyler Green's whereabouts?" she asked.

"I spoke to Sheriff King," the deputy answered. "He said he'll bring Tyler in for a talk. A copy of the incident report will be available in a few days." The deputy handed her a business card.

"Thank you." Morgan stowed the card in her tote and turned back to her family. The kids were hanging on Mac. Her sister had gotten lucky with him. He was a good man.

The tow truck pulled into the lot, and she stopped to issue the driver instructions. Then she checked the van for personal belongings before getting into Mac's SUV.

Exhausted from the morning, she nearly fell asleep on the drive home. Once the kids were settled in the kitchen with Mac, Morgan took a shower and dressed in a suit. She needed to visit the courthouse later. But not even a hot shower and fresh clothes could completely wipe away the skeevy feeling. She took her handgun from its safe and fastened it to her belt before heading toward the office in her grandfather's Lincoln Town Car.

What kind of person would pour animal blood in her van?

She reminded herself that Tyler Green had beaten his wife, hidden from process servers, and tried to strangle Morgan. Filling her car seat with blood was hardly a stretch for him.

A donut shop on Third Street caught her attention as she drove past. Thanks to her stalker, a simple visit to the cemetery had consumed her entire morning. It was almost lunchtime. Her crappy morning and a dull headache called for a sugar-and-caffeine fix. She went through the drive-through, then continued on to the office. Juggling her coffee, the bakery bag, and her tote, she unlocked the front door of Sharp Investigations. After the emotional storm of the morning, the quiet building was bliss. A general weariness nagged at her muscles.

She went into her office, dropping off her briefcase and coat, before checking out the kitchen. Empty. She settled behind her desk with her coffee at her elbow and opened the bakery bag. The scent of warm glazed donuts wafted to her nose. She sighed and ate the first one in three bites, washing it down with coffee. Fortified, she checked her e-mail and took her time with her second donut.

Footsteps in the hallway announced Sharp's arrival. He appeared in her doorway. Taking one look at him, she couldn't argue with the all-organic, mostly plant-based diet he attempted to foist on everyone around him. At fifty-three, the only signs of Sharp's age were his short salt-and-pepper hair and the crow's-feet gathered around his seen-it-all gray eyes. His lean runner's body wore jeans and an oxford shirt better than most men half his age.

He glanced at the white bag on her desk. "I'm not even going to ask what you ate today."

"That's probably best." Morgan licked the sugar from her fingertips.

"You eat enough sugar to give an elephant diabetes." His gaze lingered on her face, which was probably red and puffy. "Is everything all right?"

Where to even start?

"It's John's birthday." She fought a tear as she told him about the morning. Now that the incident was over, and her girls were safe at home with Mac, her self-control felt shaky.

Or perhaps Sharp was right, and she needed to cut back on the caffeine.

She thought about the third donut but decided Sharp would probably have a stroke if she ate it in front of him. Also, he was probably right about the sugar making her feel worse. Her sugar high was fading, leaving her queasy. "Whoever decided to suspend a spare tire underneath a vehicle should be flogged, and someone is harassing me. All in all, it was not the best of mornings."

And she still wanted the donut.

"I'm sorry," he said. "You OK?"

"Yes," she said. "As frightening as the morning's incidents were, now that I know there's a threat, I can take steps to protect my family."

And the grief that had crushed her at the cemetery had ebbed. She would miss John forever, and she would always be sad that he'd been taken from her and the girls. At every milestone, those feelings would resurface. But they wouldn't suck her under again. She wouldn't—couldn't—let them.

"Do you want to go looking for Tyler Green?" Sharp asked, his gray eyes narrowing, suggesting he'd love nothing more.

Morgan shook her head. "We have no evidence that it's him, and he's smart enough to file a harassment suit if we follow him around. The sheriff's department will handle it, and either Mac or Stella will stay at the house when I'm not there, so the family is covered."

Sharp nodded. "And I want me or Lance with you at all times until this stalker is caught."

"All right." Morgan was independent, not stupid.

"Have you heard from Lance?" Sharp asked.

"I called him early this morning." She updated Sharp on Jenny's condition. "He intended to visit the ME first thing."

"I'd like to set aside a chunk of time to review

Victor Kruger's case with you. I've been chasing leads for more than two decades. I'd like some fresh eyes on it."

"Yes. Of course," Morgan said.

"I'll make you a shake. It's lunchtime. You need some protein to balance out your stress— and whatever crap you just put in your body." Sharp left her office, still muttering as he walked down the hall. "I have no doubt you haven't eaten anything even remotely nutritious today."

"Thanks." Morgan didn't bother to argue. He'd just blend her a shake anyway. She needed real food in her body, but she ate the third donut while he was out of the room.

She drank more coffee and called out, "Where is the file?"

"Lance's desk," Sharp answered from the kitchen.

A blender whirred as she went into Lance's office. His desk was the only piece of furniture in the room. The file was in the bottom drawer. Dust floated to her nose as she pulled it out. She carried it back to her office and set it on her desk.

A few minutes later, Sharp set a gross-looking concoction by her elbow.

She sipped. Pineapple and blueberry. "Considering the color and what you put in them, I'm always surprised that these don't taste horrible."

"You can't even taste the leafy greens." Sharp's

current obsession was organic sweet potato greens. He eased into the chair opposite her. "This is going to be hard on Jenny—and Lance, no matter what he says."

"I know." She studied the man across from her. He rarely talked about his past, other than his police career. "Were you ever married, Sharp?"

"I was," he said.

Why did that surprise her?

His gaze drifted to the window, his eyes pensive. "The marriage was a disaster from the beginning. I wanted kids. She didn't. She didn't like being married to a cop. I didn't want to be anything else. We got a divorce. I haven't talked to her since I signed the papers. The last I heard, she'd remarried and moved to Boston."

"I'm sorry. I didn't mean to pry."

"It was a long time ago. I was a young man." Sharp shook it off, but sadness clouded his eyes, as if he had deeper feelings about the breakup of his marriage than he was willing to admit.

"When did you split up?"

"February of '94," Sharp said.

Three months before Vic Kruger had gone missing. Sharp must have been lonely. Morgan pictured him throwing himself into the investigation, taking an equally lonely child under his wing. Maybe his relationship with Lance hadn't been as one-sided as Morgan had thought.

"Anyway, I never came close to marrying again." Sharp patted the desk. "Enough about me. You can grill me about the rest of my life some other time."

Morgan stared at the file, thick and heavy with implications.

Before they could begin, the front door opened and closed. Lance appeared in the doorway. He took one look at Morgan's face and asked, "What's wrong? Where's your van?"

She told him about her morning.

Anger flared in his eyes. "I'd like to go after Tyler myself."

"The sheriff will handle him," she said. "Sheriff King is a pain, but this kind of situation is what he lives for."

"True. We can count on King to hassle Tyler." Lance rounded her desk, leaned over, and hugged her. "I'm sorry you had such a horrible morning. I wish I'd been with you."

If he'd been with her, she doubted her stalker would have been so brazen. But a mother focused on her three small children was an easy target.

"You had enough to deal with this morning," Morgan said.

Lance released her and straightened.

"Did you see the ME?" Sharp asked.

"I did." Lance's jaw sawed back and forth. "I just came from his office. You're not going to believe this, but the remains aren't my father."

"What?" Sharp snapped upright.

"The skeleton is female." Lance's eyebrows lowered.

Silence floated in the air like dust motes.

Female?

Was Lance glad the body wasn't his father? Or upset about the questions the news raised?

"Frank doesn't know who she is yet?" Sharp asked.

"No." Lance lifted troubled eyes. "I haven't told my mother. She took the idea of my father's remains being found better than I expected. But I don't know how she'll react when she finds out he's still missing. Plus, there's the obvious implication that Dad might have had some sort of relationship with this young woman." Lance went to the second chair that faced Morgan's desk, dropped into it, and recapped his visit with his mother.

It was typical of Lance to be more concerned about his mother when the news would affect him just as deeply.

Sharp got up and went into the kitchen. A minute later, the blender whirred, and he returned with another shake. He handed it to Lance.

Lance took it with a sigh. "I'm not really hungry."

"You have a headache, and you probably didn't sleep well," Sharp said. "The protein will help."

"You know he's always right about these

things." Morgan studied Lance's exhausted face. How did *he* feel about his father still being missing?

Sharp nodded. "I am."

Lance drank. Lowering the glass, he swallowed and seemed to brace himself. "Let's get started. I want to get more information before I tell my mother. I don't want to keep throwing conflicting reports at her. The ME isn't in a rush to release any information to the press. He wants to identify the remains and notify the family first. His assistant was pulling missing person reports when I left."

Sharp bowed his head and wrapped a hand around the back of his neck. "Now what?"

There was only one thing that would help Lance: an answer. Morgan opened the file on her desk. "Now we start at the beginning."

Chapter Ten

Lance turned to the whiteboard mounted on the wall. The board was empty, but what would they find when they dug in to the case?

Whatever it was, it was high time he faced the truth.

Morgan offered Sharp the file, but he clearly didn't need it. He leaned back in his chair and started talking. "We know that Vic left his house at approximately nine p.m. to go to the grocery store. When he hadn't returned at eleven o'clock, your mother called his closest friends, Stan Adams and Brian Leed, hoping one of them would help. Neither was at home. So she drove the route between the store and house in case Vic's car had broken down. When she didn't find him, she drove to PJ's Sports Bar, where he sometimes hung out with Brian and Stan. She didn't see Brian or Stan there. No one had seen Vic."

Restless, Sharp got up and paced in front of the whiteboard. "Jenny called the police a little before midnight. A uniform drove out to the house and took the initial report. Victor had no concerning health conditions or mental limitations. There was no evidence that he was especially at risk, though staying out this late was out of character. The uniform filled out a missing person report and issued a BOLO alert for Victor Kruger and his 1984 Buick Century."

Sharp stopped pacing and faced the board. Picking up a marker, he began a timeline. "The patrol officer had hoped, reasonably, that Victor had simply stopped somewhere or taken a different route. Maybe his car had broken down. Those were the days before everyone had a cell phone attached to his or her body. People still used cash for transactions. There was no E-ZPass. It wasn't so unusual for someone to slip off the radar for an evening."

Sharp used magnets to affix an old photo of Victor Kruger and two other men onto the whiteboard. The three men stood in front of a baseball field. They wore amateur baseball uniforms, with the logo for a local appliance store on their chests. Lance's heart squeezed as he stared at the wide grin on his father's face.

"That picture must have been taken at a game." Lance remembered sitting in the stands watching games. Memories of his dad teaching him to play flickered through his mind like a slideshow. "My dad loved baseball."

"Who are the other men?" Morgan asked.

Lance pointed to the men in turn. "Brian Leed and Stan Adams, my dad's best friends."

After a short pause, Sharp continued. "I took over the case in the morning. The first thing

I did was go to the grocery store and view the surveillance tapes. Vic never entered the store that night. His car never pulled into the lot. I made the rounds of gas stations and convenience stores, flashed a picture of Vic around, and checked security videos where available. No sign of him."

"Normally, an unexplained adult missing person case doesn't get a ton of manpower. But Mrs. Kruger was highly agitated. My caseload was relatively light, and I thought the disappearance warranted an investigation. Over the next few days, I visited locations Vic frequented. I called hospitals, morgues, police and sheriff stations, checked bus and train stations, the airport. I interviewed his boss, coworkers, and close friends. All the notes are in the file, but everyone agreed that Vic would never have just left his family. The more people I talked to, the more I became convinced that Vic Kruger hadn't left town on his own. I searched the house and his office. It didn't appear that he had taken anything with him except his wallet and car keys. I'd investigated people who walked, ran—and were taken—from their families, but in all my twenty-five years on the force, Victor was the only person to actually vanish without a trace. This isn't the city. People usually return from a trip to the grocery store."

Lance studied the board, trying to remain

objective. So far, none of the case details were shocking. Sharp's initial investigation had been by the book. But still . . . when the missing person was your dad, seeing his case laid out should have disturbed him.

But Lance felt as distant as he had been in 1994. It hadn't felt real then either. But then, his mother had used up all the emotions. Mentally, she'd crumbled quickly, leaving Lance to pick up the pieces. His life had felt like reassembling a shattered vase when you didn't have all the shards. No amount of glue could ever make it whole again. What else could he have done except bury his own reactions?

"So where do we start?" Morgan asked.

Sharp shrugged. "I updated the file and missing person database over the years, but not since I retired. Unfortunately, we don't have access to the NCIC, but I'll have to assume that the sheriff will utilize that system to look for like crimes."

The National Crime Information Center was an FBI database, only available to law enforcement agencies, not private investigators.

"It seems to me that you covered Vic's disappearance, Sharp." Morgan scanned the board. "So we should focus on the new piece of information."

"The dead woman." Lance got up and went into his office. He returned a minute later with his laptop. "We can start with NamUs. If she was a local and a missing person report was filed, her information should have been entered into the system."

The National Missing and Unidentified Persons System was a Department of Justice database accessible to law enforcement and the general public. It cross-referenced unidentified remains and outstanding missing persons across the country.

Lance tried not to think about the odds of actually finding his father. More than forty thousand sets of remains were unidentified in the United States, scattered in a patchwork of over two thousand coroner's and medical examiner's offices across the country. Even with his father's DNA on file, it was possible his body had been found years ago. NamUs didn't exist until 2009. Vic Kruger's remains could be sitting in a vault anywhere in the country, or they could have been buried or cremated long ago without being identified.

Focus on the task.

Lance typed. "In NamUs, there are 236 females missing in the state of New York."

Sharp leaned on the board and crossed his arms. "They'll be listed in order of date last seen. Start with July through September 1994. Then we'll whittle the list down by region."

"Four women were reported missing at that time." Lance scrolled. "Two were local girls.

Laura Dennis, from Albany, was twenty-two years old when she disappeared. She was last seen August 1, 1994. Mary Fox went missing from Grey's Hollow. Her description says she was sixty-four inches tall and weighed one hundred fifteen pounds."

"Local girl, close enough in height to Frank's estimate for the skeleton," Sharp said.

Lance continued. "She was reported missing August 25, but the file notes say she was last seen a week or two before. Though she lived with her mother and stepfather, her mother wasn't sure of the exact date she'd left. They'd had an argument, and it wasn't unusual for Mary to stay with a friend for a few days."

"No one reported her missing for two weeks." Morgan made notes on her legal pad. "That's horrible."

"Who's listed as the investigating agency?" Sharp asked.

"Randolph County Sheriff's Department," Lance said.

"King wasn't the sheriff in 1994." Morgan's chair squeaked as she shifted back and crossed her legs.

"No." Sharp shook his head. "Bob O'Reilly was the sheriff back then. He dropped dead of a massive heart attack on the job in 2001. King was the chief deputy. He ran for office, won, and has been sheriff ever since."

"Let me pull up the case report," Lance said. "I'll print Mary's photo."

The printer hummed and spit out a sheet of paper. Sharp retrieved it and fastened it to the board. Mary had brown eyes and shoulder-length brown hair.

Sharp pointed to the picture. "Does she look familiar, Lance?"

Lance shook his head. "No."

Sharp wrote Mary's name above the picture. "Lance, why don't you call Frank? If finding her was this easy for us, then he probably already has her name."

Sharp went back to pacing, as if physical movement jogged his brain.

The ME didn't answer. Lance left a message then set down his phone.

"While we wait, we should conduct a thorough review of the file and make a list of people to locate and interview." Sharp returned to the board. "Morgan, I want your eyes on this whole file. You're the one starting fresh with no preexisting opinions."

"If you don't mind, I'd like to copy the file for my grandfather as well," Morgan said. "He has decades of experience and nothing but time on his hands."

"I'd appreciate that." Sharp started a new column entitled *Interviews*. Underneath, he listed Stan Adams and Brian Leed. "Vic worked for

UpState Insurance. The company went bankrupt in 2012. His boss's name was Phil Dryer. Phil was a real company man and stayed with the firm for his whole career. His last known address is in the file. There was also a secretary, Dorothy Finch. She was sixty years old in 1994 and retired when the firm closed. The last time I checked, she was living in a nursing home."

Lance worked on his laptop. "Stan and Brian still live in town. Their addresses haven't changed in the last five years. I found an obituary for Dorothy Finch. Phil Dryer no longer lives at that address."

Under Find, Sharp wrote Phil Dryer.

As always, Morgan was making her own notes. "What else did Vic do? He must have had hobbies, other acquaintances. Were he and Jenny socially active back then?"

"Stan and Brian were the full extent of Vic's social life," Sharp said. "They played baseball and hung out at PJ's."

"Is that the same PJ's that's on Fletcher Avenue?" Morgan asked.

"That's the one." Sharp nodded. "It's still in business. Still owned by the same family."

Morgan turned to Lance. "What do you remember of your dad's friends?"

"Not much," Lance said. "Stan was single back then. Brian's wife's name was Natalie. Their kids were younger than me. Two were in diapers the last time I saw them." Lance shook his head, his mouth flattening as he remembered the sheer, stark loneliness after his dad went missing. "They didn't come around after my dad disappeared."

Sharp took a deep breath. "There were some things we've never talked about. At the time, you were just a boy. You had enough to cope with, and I didn't want to burden you. But now, if you really want to dig in to your dad's disappearance, you'll need to prepare yourself for the less pleasant details."

Lance straightened. His gaze met Sharp's briefly before he nodded. "I knew you kept things from me. Maybe I didn't want to hear the truth if there was no real chance of finding out what happened to him. But now there is, and it's time."

Over the years, he'd actively avoided learning more about the case. It was almost as if he knew the facts would change his memories of his childhood. No doubt he'd painted the period before his father vanished with a rose-colored brush. Understandable, since the years afterward had been hell.

"All right." Sharp took a deep breath. "Your father's friends, Stan and Brian, told me that Victor had been concerned about his wife's mental health. She had already begun exhibiting signs of anxiety and depression. She was still teaching at the community college but was struggling. They also said that your dad's company was having financial problems. He was worried about getting laid off. On top of all that, your mom's spending was getting out of control."

Lance digested the information. Bits of memory moved and clicked into place like a Rubik's Cube. "So his disappearance didn't cause her illness."

"It didn't," Sharp agreed. "But it sent her into a rapid downward spiral."

Given that information, the Krugers' marriage hadn't been the episode of *Leave It to Beaver* that Lance had always believed. Now that he thought about it, this version made more sense.

"Stan and Brian said Vic was unhappy," Sharp said. "He didn't know what to do about Jenny's problems. He was drinking too much."

Lance turned toward the board, away from Sharp. He'd always known he didn't have the full scoop. But none of this explained how a young woman had ended up in the trunk of his dad's car.

"Let's divvy up our tasks," Sharp said. "I'll search online records and the Social Security Death Master File for Vic's old boss, Phil Dryer. I can also make a few calls and see if there are any good rumors floating around about the case." Sharp knew everyone in local law enforcement who'd been on the job more than five years. "We need fresh background checks on everyone involved, and we obviously can't ask Jenny to do them for us."

"I'll take care of those. I'm not as fast as my mom, but I can get the job done," Lance said.

"Someone needs to go down to the county clerk's office and check vital records. We need to find out if Phil is still alive. If he is, I want to talk to him. Maybe now that he no longer works for UpState Insurance, he'll be more willing to share information than he was back then. I'd really like to know how precarious Vic's job really was. Phil would never give me a straight answer about the financial health of the company."

"Aren't vital records available online?" Morgan asked. "If he died, the county will have a death certificate on file."

"In Randolph County, you can request them online, but you might not receive them for a week or a month . . . or ever," Sharp said.

Morgan nodded. "I have to go to the courthouse to file a discovery motion for a DUI case I'm working on. It's Esposito's case, and the DA's office has been slow to send me information."

"What a jerk." Sharp shook his head. "Lance, go with Morgan to the courthouse. You can check vital records while she's filing her motion. I don't want her alone until her stalker is brought in."

Chapter Eleven

Morgan filed her discovery motion, then took the elevator to the ground floor and navigated the maze of hallways that led to the wing of the courthouse that housed the county clerk's office.

Walking briskly, she turned down a corridor. A man stepped out in front of her, and she bumped into him.

She stumbled and dropped her tote. Thankfully it was zipped, and its contents remained secure.

"I'm sorry." She drew back.

Esposito.

The last person she wanted to see.

She stooped to recover her bag. Standing, she said, "Excuse me."

He blocked her path, hogging the hallway. "You're always so focused. What are you doing here, Ms. Dane?"

She swallowed a smart retort. Antagonizing Esposito would not help matters. But his arrogant attitude slid under her skin like a big, fat splinter.

Morgan settled for, "I'm in a hurry. Is there something you need to discuss?"

"You should check that attitude."

"*I* should check *my* attitude?"

Esposito's black eyes went beady. He glanced

up and down the hall and lowered his voice. "You need my cooperation."

Morgan felt her eyebrow shoot up her forehead. *What is it with this guy?*

"I can make your life very difficult." He leaned closer, too close. He needed a breath mint. "We can do every single case the hardest way possible."

Enough was enough.

Morgan put a hand six inches in front of her to keep him from leaning any closer. She hated games. She just wanted to do her job. "First of all, back off."

He didn't. Instead, his eyes glittered with amusement as he shifted his weight farther forward, until his chest pushed against her hand. "You aren't a prosecutor now. You are a lowly defense attorney, a bottom-feeder. Your clients are the scum of the earth."

"Like the innocent kid you tried to railroad into a plea deal?"

His face reddened.

"What do you want?" she asked, her temper running short.

"Don't ever go out of your way to try and make me look bad again."

Morgan stiffened her arm to resist the press of his body weight. "I didn't have to do anything. You made yourself look bad. Next time you want to push hard on a case, verify your evidence first.

Bluffing is a gamble. Yours didn't pay off this time."

"I'm warning you, counselor."

"Warning me of what?" Morgan asked. She could *not* roll over for him. Her career would be over. "I take the law very seriously. My clients deserve the best defense I can give them. I will make you prove your case every single time."

His lip curled away from his teeth. "You're making a mistake."

He tried to take a step forward, to invade the last few inches of space between their bodies, but Morgan moved her hand into a horizontal position, until the tips of her fingers aligned with the hollow at the base of his throat. His forward momentum pressed her fingers into his jugular notch. Her fingertips sank into the soft flesh.

Gagging, he jerked backward. "You bitch."

A flash went off, followed by Lance's voice. "Hey, Esposito, why are you practically standing on top of the lady? I hope to hell you're not trying to intimidate the defense counsel, because that's what it looks like in this picture."

Lance held his cell phone in front of him. His light tone did not match his angry scowl or the fingers that curled into a fist at his side.

Still coughing, Esposito took a quick step away. "Ms. Dane and I were simply discussing a case."

Morgan didn't respond. Normally, she kept a decent hold on her temper, but men like Esposito set her off. His boorish and clumsy efforts to intimidate stunned her. Why would he think he could get away with this sort of behavior? Did other people allow him to walk all over them?

"You can discuss a case without breathing down her neck." Lance stepped to her side, using his own size to his advantage.

Esposito had tried to bully her, but he'd never try that sort of tactic with someone whose biceps were bigger than his head. Lance, in his tactical cargos and snug black T-shirt, did not look like someone to be messed with.

"We'll talk later." Esposito nodded and turned away. As he turned the corner, Morgan saw him rub the base of his throat.

"Thank you," she said, turning to Lance.

Underneath the grim anger, humor lurked in his blue eyes. "You're welcome, though it looked like you had him under control."

"He is such an . . ."

"Ass?" Lance finished.

"Yes." The encounter with Esposito had left a foul taste in her mouth.

Lance squinted down the hall where Esposito had disappeared. "We need to learn more about the new ADA."

"I'm sure he's been thoroughly vetted. Bryce is particular."

"Still . . ." Lance frowned. "I don't like him."

"Bryce is a politician. He barely won the

election. He can't afford to hire anyone with a questionable history."

Lance did not look convinced.

Morgan steered him toward the exit. "Did you find Phil Dryer?"

"I did." Lance opened the door for her. "He's dead. There was an error on the death certificate. They used his middle initial instead of his full middle name."

"That's why he didn't show up on the Master Death list. Then we can cross Phil off our list of potential witnesses. That leaves us with Stan, Brian, and Brian's wife, Natalie, to interview." If the skeleton's identity could be confirmed, the list would no doubt expand.

"Yes," Lance said.

He led her across the parking lot, and they got into his Jeep.

After the doors were closed, Lance leaned over the console and kissed her. "Are you sure you're all right? I wanted to punch Esposito in his smug face."

"I'm fine. I've visited violent criminals in prison. One ADA with the temperament of a seventh-grade bully isn't going to intimidate me."

"Did you file your motion?"

"I did." Morgan fastened her seat belt. "But the frustrating fact is that he *can* make things more difficult. He can drag out the process. He can delay delivery of important materials so defense attorneys have as little time as possible to review discovery evidence. I'll push back, but that's extra time billed to my clients. Public defenders have it even worse. They juggle a crazy number of cases. They don't have time for unnecessary motions and bullshit stonewalling."

"So his tactics will work." Lance unlocked the glove compartment and removed their weapons. Guns were not allowed in the courthouse.

She accepted her handgun and fastened the holster onto her belt. "Yes. He'll win cases simply because public defenders are overworked. The entire legal system is overburdened. Additional paperwork will not help matters. Either his ego is overinflated or he's trying to prove himself with an aggressive conviction record." Morgan took a deep breath. "There's nothing I can do about a difficult ADA. Where do we go from here?"

"We need to see the sheriff. The medical examiner hasn't returned my call, and we need to know the identity of the woman in my father's trunk."

"Oh, goody. Someone else who is not happy with me."

"Do you want me to drop you at the office?" Lance pulled out of the parking space.

"No. I want to go with you." Morgan settled into the seat. "The sheriff isn't as bad as Esposito."

"He's the exact opposite. Esposito wants to create extra legal steps. Sheriff King wants to skip as many as possible and send everyone to jail without passing Go or collecting their two hundred dollars."

Lance's phone buzzed. He looked at the screen. "Speak of the devil. It's King." He answered the call. "Kruger."

Morgan couldn't make out the sheriff's words, but whatever he said wiped all traces of humor from Lance's face.

"No. My mother doesn't leave her house. You'll have to go to her." A few seconds later, he ended the call. His fingers tightened around the phone, as if he wanted to crush it.

"What's wrong?" Morgan asked.

He shoved his phone in the console cup holder.

"Sheriff King is on his way to interview my mother. I want to get there before him." Lance pressed on the accelerator, and the Jeep surged forward. "I wonder if this means they've identified the body."

Chapter Twelve

Lance sat across the kitchen table from his mother, relieved that he and Morgan had arrived before the sheriff. Dark circles hung beneath his mom's eyes, and her skin was papery, as if she was dehydrated.

He glanced up at Morgan. "Would you get her a glass of water?"

"Of course." Morgan filled a glass at the tap and brought it to the table. She sat next to his mother. "Have you eaten lunch today, Jenny?"

His mother nodded. "Yes. I ate lunch at noon. Today is Tuesday. I had a tuna salad sandwich."

"Sheriff King is on his way here to ask you some questions about dad. Before he gets here, I have some news for you." Lance reached across the table and covered her hand. "The skeleton in dad's trunk wasn't him. It belongs to a young woman."

Shock filled her face for a few seconds. "Why would a young woman be in your father's trunk? And where is he?"

"That's what we're all trying to find out," Lance said. "Do you remember a woman by the name of—"

The doorbell rang.

Leaving Morgan with his mother, Lance went

to the door and opened it. Sheriff King stood on the front stoop. Lance went out onto the step and closed the door behind him.

"My mother suffers from acute anxiety and agoraphobia." Lance cut straight to the bone. "She hasn't had a stranger in her house in years."

King nodded. "Noted."

Lance led the way into the house and back to the kitchen.

"Mom, this is Sheriff King," he said.

In a gallant, old western gesture, the sheriff swept his hat from his head and held it in front of his chest. "Thank you for seeing me, ma'am."

The sheriff took the chair across from her.

She shifted backward, her shoulders curling in. She glanced at the sheriff from behind a curtain of her white hair. "You look familiar. Have I seen you on TV?"

The sheriff nodded. "I do press conferences now and then."

"You're here about Vic." His mother clasped her hands together in her lap, her arms tight to her sides, as if she could physically hold herself together.

"Yes, ma'am." The sheriff's tone softened. Maybe he wasn't a total hard-ass. "When was the last time you saw your husband, Victor Kruger?"

"August 10th, 1994," she said.

"And you've had no contact with him since? No phone calls, no e-mails, no letters?"

His mother shook her head. "Nothing."

"Does the name Mary Fox ring a bell?" the sheriff asked.

His mother frowned. "I don't think so."

"This would have been from twenty-three years ago," the sheriff clarified.

"I can't say for sure," his mom said. "I'm sorry."

The sheriff's upper body leaned an inch closer to the table. "Mary worked as a waitress at PJ's."

Lance stiffened. He'd been right. The remains were Mary Fox.

His mother's brows dropped. "We used to go to PJ's for burgers. Vic went more often than I did. He'd stop to have a beer with Stan and Brian a few times a week."

Lance's brain whirled.

His father had *known the dead girl.* Although the fact that she worked at his favorite restaurant meant that their connection could have been entirely innocent.

The sheriff pulled a photo from his pocket and slid it across the table.

His mother reached forward, her fingers touching just the edges as she slid it in front of her. "She looks familiar. Is this Mary?"

"Yes," the sheriff said. "We pulled your husband's car from Grey Lake yesterday. I'm sorry I didn't visit you then. Lance told me it would be better if he notified you. I also wanted to verify if the remains inside were his or not."

"Lance told me." Her fingers curled on the table.

Morgan took one of her hands and held it.

"But it was Mary's skeleton that was found in the trunk of your husband's car." Despite his polite tone, the sheriff studied her face, waiting for a reaction.

But Lance's mom just blinked. "I don't understand. How did she get there? And where is Vic?" Her voice rose as confusion segued into distress.

"That's what we want to find out, ma'am." The sheriff tapped the photo. "The night your husband went missing, did he say anything about going to PJ's?"

His mother shook her head. "No, he was going to the grocery store."

"Did he have a cell phone?" the sheriff asked.

"No." His mom's fingers tightened on Morgan's, the knuckles whitening. "They were expensive back then. The coverage out here was so poor, it wouldn't have been worth the expense. But Vic would have called me from PJ's if he was going to stop. He was good about not wanting me to worry." She looked down and opened her grip, releasing Morgan's hand. "I've always been a worrier."

"So he was considerate," the sheriff said.

"Vic was a good man." A tear rolled down Jenny's cheek.

"What did you do the night Vic went missing?" the sheriff asked.

"When Vic didn't come home, I drove around looking for him. I called everyone I could think of, but no one had seen him." She wiped the tear away. "Where is he?"

"I don't know yet, but I'm going to find out," the sheriff assured her. "You can help me by giving me as much information as possible. Did Vic go anywhere regularly except for PJ's?"

"I don't know." His mother's hands shook harder. She started picking at the skin around her fingernails.

"This is going to be a difficult question, and I'm very sorry for having to ask it," the sheriff said, his voice gentle, even apologetic. "To your knowledge, did your husband ever have an affair?"

Anger boiled in Lance's gut. At the same time, he understood the necessity of asking the question. So instead of punching the sheriff in the face, he gripped the table edge.

His mother's head shook hard. "No. He would never have . . ."

The sheriff rested his forearms on the edge of the table. "Did you receive any odd phone calls or hang-ups?"

"No," Jenny whispered.

"How much time did he spend at PJ's?" the sheriff asked.

Jenny ripped a piece of skin from her finger. Blood welled. "I don't know. I don't know. I don't know." She repeated the phrase in a monotone, almost under her breath.

The sheriff leaned back. His eyes flickered to Lance in question.

"That's enough, Sheriff. My mother has had a great shock." Lance stepped forward, but Morgan already had her arms wrapped around his mother's shoulders, and his mom was leaning into her.

The sheriff got up, and Lance led him toward the door. They stepped out onto the front stoop.

"Thank you for being considerate with her." Lance pulled the door closed behind them.

King nodded. "It wasn't something I wanted to do at all."

"Since you gave us Mary's name, I assume you've notified her family?"

"This morning." The sheriff nodded and blinked away. For a second—no longer—regret crossed King's face. Lance had done death notifications in his years on the police force, mostly after car accidents. Telling someone their loved one had died was one of the worst duties a police officer performed.

But the lapse in iron control only lasted a moment. The sheriff's jaw tightened, and all traces of vulnerability disappeared. "I'll need to talk with your mother again."

"If she's up to it." Lance's mother came first, the investigation second. "As much as I want to find out what happened to my dad, I won't sacrifice my mother for answers to something that was over more than twenty years ago."

Every secret exposed required sacrifice. The only question was who was doing the sacrificing. Unless his mother was under arrest, she had no legal requirement to speak to King, though she would cooperate. *She* wanted answers. But could she afford to pay the price?

"I understand your concern, but this is a murder investigation. Mary Fox and her family deserve just as much respect as yours."

Lance had nothing to say. The sheriff was right.

Sheriff King got into his vehicle and backed out of the driveway.

Lance closed the door and returned to the kitchen. Mom was still in Morgan's arms. He crouched in front of them. "Mom? Are you OK?"

She drew in a quivering breath, then straightened. "Don't blame the sheriff. He's doing his job, asking questions that need to be asked." His mother swiped a hand beneath her eye to catch a tear. "I can't believe Vic would have cheated on me." His mother's gaze shifted to the kitchen window, but her focus was inward. "He loved me."

But Lance had already discovered his memories were less than accurate. Were his mother's equally faulty?

If his mother had already begun her mental spiral in 1994, she might not have noticed if his father strayed. Her illness consumed her. It ate away at her interest in the outside world, taking giant bites and devouring them. Maybe his father had been lonely.

"I'm going to call Kevin." His mother stood. Her gaze landed on Morgan, then Lance. "Please find out what happened. Don't try and cover it up. I need to face the truth, no matter how difficult it might be."

She walked out of the kitchen, her gait slow, almost painful, as if she'd aged twenty years since the sheriff had arrived. Her office door closed with a soft click.

"So far, I'm impressed with the way she's handling all this." Lance stared at the empty doorway.

"She certainly seems determined," Morgan said. "What now?"

"Now we find out everything we can about Mary Fox."

"I'll call Sharp." Morgan pulled out her phone as they walked out of the house. She made the call while Lance locked the house. They climbed into the Jeep, and Lance started the engine.

Morgan ended the call. "Sharp wants us to talk

to Stan Adams and Brian Leed, but he wants to be in on the interview with Mary's mother. He says he'll meet us there later."

"OK." Lance drove away from his mother's house, but he couldn't escape the uneasy feeling in his chest as he left her behind.

Chapter Thirteen

"Should I call Stan and Brian?" Morgan asked, checking the time on the dashboard. "It's only three o'clock. They might be at work."

"No." Lance shook his head. "Let's surprise them. If they're not home, we'll come back. We can start with Stan. His house is the closest."

As he drove, Morgan read from her copy of Sharp's original interview notes and gave Lance the highlights. "Stanley Adams is fifty-eight years old. He's a founder of the accounting firm of Adams & Booker and a Scarlet Falls native. Ten years ago, he married Abigail Snyder. She is thirty-six years old. They don't have any children."

Lance turned into a new development and parked in front of a McMansion. "Looks like Stan has done well for himself."

A late-model black Mercedes occupied the driveway. They got out and walked up to the front door. Black iron railings flanked red paver steps. Ornamental plants and precisely trimmed shrubs screamed professional landscaper.

Morgan reached for the doorbell, but the high-pitched yapping of small dogs announced their arrival before she pressed the button.

The front door opened. A slim, fit man in his

late fifties scooped up a tiny mop of a dog. "Quiet, Ginger." He raised his eyes. "Can I help you?"

"I'm Lance Kruger," Lance said.

"Oh." Stan's eyes widened. He swept a hand into the house. "Please come in."

A second dog darted from behind his legs and snapped at Lance's pant leg. Stan blocked it with his foot, then picked it up with his other hand. He stepped back and gestured with his head for them to come in. "I'm sorry about that. Let me put them in the other room. Go on into the den and have a seat." He waved a dog toward an open archway and then disappeared down the hall. They heard a door shut.

Morgan went through the arch into a formal sitting room. On top of a thick white area rug, two white couches faced each other over a glass coffee table. Delicate glass sculptures filled wall niches. Everything in the room was lovely— and expensive. Stan definitely didn't have small children.

Morgan settled on one of the sofas and took her small notebook and a pen from her tote. Lance circled the room, impatient.

Stan returned in a minute. "My wife loves those dogs." His frown said that he did not. He offered his hand to Lance. "So you're a private investigator now."

"Yes." Lance shook his hand. "This is my associate, Morgan Dane."

"Can I get you anything? Coffee, water?" Stan asked.

"No, thank you." Lance joined Morgan on the sofa. "Thanks for seeing us. We didn't know if you'd even be home."

"I try to take time off when I can." Stan sat on the couch across from them. "Once tax season starts, I'll be too busy." He smiled at Lance. "What can I do for you?"

"I want to ask you some questions about my dad," Lance said.

Stan leaned back, crossing one ankle on top of the opposite knee. His posture was relaxed and open. "I wish I could help, but as I told Detective Sharp multiple times over the years, I don't know what happened to Vic. I wish I did."

"There's some new information that wasn't available back then," Lance said.

Stan tensed. "Really?"

"Did you see the news yesterday?" Morgan asked.

"No." Stan shook his head.

"They pulled my father's car out of Grey Lake," Lance said.

"What?" Stan straightened. His foot hit the floor with a thud and his mouth gaped for a few seconds, as if he didn't know what to say.

Lance shifted forward and rested his forearms on his knees. "Apparently, that's where the car has been all these years."

"Oh, my God." Stan brushed a hand over his receding hairline. Then his hand froze and his eyes snapped to Lance's, as if something just occurred to him. "Was Vic inside?"

Morgan had interviewed hundreds of witnesses in her career. Her internal lie detector was well honed, but she couldn't read Stan. She couldn't put her finger on it, but something about him didn't feel genuine.

"No." Lance shook his head. "But someone was. Do you remember Mary Fox?"

Stan frowned. His gaze dropped to the wood floor for a few seconds. Was he thinking or hiding his eyes? "I don't think so."

"She worked at PJ's," Morgan prompted.

"Oh." Stan's gaze snapped to Lance's. "There was a waitress at PJ's named Mary. Was that her?"

Lance dropped his joined hands between his knees. "Now do you remember her?"

"Yes," Stan said. He held eye contact for a couple of seconds, then looked away. "I didn't know her last name. Mary was memorable, all right. Vic and Brian and I used to meet for a beer at PJ's. Sometimes she waited on us."

"Why was she memorable?" Morgan asked. Until Mary's name had entered the conversation, Stan's responses had almost felt rehearsed. Now he seemed far less comfortable.

"Um." Stan glanced from Morgan to Lance.

His hands went in front of his chest, and he made a cupping gesture. "Frankly, she was stacked, and she wasn't shy about it."

"In what way?" Morgan pressed.

"She used to lean way over when she put a drink down on the table. It was impossible not to notice. They were in your face." A flush brightened Stan's face. "She had a reputation for being friendly, if you know what I mean."

Morgan had a vague idea. "Could you be more specific?"

The red of Stan's cheeks deepened. "She slept around. Once I saw her giving a guy a blow job in the parking lot. Rumor had it, if she was in the right mood and the electric bill was late, she'd do anything to anybody for fifty bucks."

Sadness filled Morgan, thinking of a twenty-one-year-old waitress trading sex to ward off the power company.

"She was a prostitute?" Lance asked.

"I don't know." Stan waved away the question, then his hand froze in midair. "I guess she kind of was. I didn't really think about it like that. You think hooker, you have a certain image in your head of a woman out walking the streets in spandex and high heels."

Lance shifted his weight. "Did you ever . . . ?"

"No." Stan shook his head. "I was never into sloppy seconds." He winced and shot Morgan an apologetic smile. "But some guys don't care."

Morgan asked the hard question. "Did Vic ever hook up with Mary?"

"No," Stan said, relaxing again. "I can't picture Vic ever doing anything like that."

"Did you see anyone taking particular interest in Mary in those days before Vic disappeared?" Lance's face remained impassive, and Morgan wondered how he was keeping it all in. She wouldn't want to have this type of conversation about her late father.

"Plenty of guys took her up on her offers." Stan shrugged. "I don't remember any specific names."

Don't know or won't say?

"Did you know anything about Mary's personal life?" Morgan asked.

Stan shook his head. "No. I'm ashamed to say, we thought of her as Slutty Mary. But looking back, I see her now as a sad case. She had no self-esteem." Stan examined his fingernails for a few seconds. "It's funny how age and life changes your perspective."

"It is," Morgan agreed. "What about Vic? Was anything going on with him in the weeks that preceded his disappearance?"

Stan's gaze flickered to Lance. "Your dad was worried about your mom. Her behavior was becoming more and more erratic. She was missing work and spending money like crazy. Vic spent a lot of time managing her. We used to play in a men's baseball league. Vic quit the team a few weeks before. He said he couldn't be away from home. He told me he felt like he was treading water twenty miles out to sea. If he stopped, he'd drown."

"In your opinion, is there any chance my father left?" Lance's mouth pressed flat. "Maybe he just couldn't take the stress anymore."

Stan considered the question. "No. I don't think he would have walked away from *you*."

For once, Stan's statement rang with truth.

"Was he suicidal?" Lance's voice dropped, as if he didn't want to ask the question.

"I have no doubt that Vic was depressed, but again, *you* kept him going. He once told me that if it hadn't been for you"—Stan nodded at Lance—"he would have let himself go under."

Lance's Adam's apple bobbed as he swallowed, and sadness clouded his blue eyes. He cleared his throat. "Do you remember where you were the night my dad disappeared?"

Stan nodded and looked away. "I can't count the number of times that Detective Sharp asked me this question over the years." Stan's voice shifted from conversational to mechanical. "Brian and I were at the baseball field. We hit a few balls, practiced some fielding, but mostly we were there to drink beer and blow off some steam. We called your dad, but he said he couldn't come."

"What time did you leave the field?" Lance asked.

Stan lifted his hands. "Around eleven. Your mother had left a message while I was out. She was looking for Vic. I called her back, but she wasn't home."

Jenny had been driving around looking for her husband at that time.

"Thank you for your time, Stan." Lance stood. "Can we call you if we have more questions?"

"Of course." Stan shook their hands. "I wish I could tell you what happened to your dad."

"Thanks." Lance led the way out of the house and back to the Jeep. "Is it my imagination or did Stan's statement about his whereabouts sound rehearsed?"

"It did, but remember he's answered those questions many times."

"You're right. Sharp kept poking at the case."

"Are you all right?" Morgan asked after they climbed into the vehicle and fastened their seat belts.

"Yes." Lance stared through the windshield. "I put my dad on a pedestal. I always thought of my life as two distinct time periods: before and after. Before was perfect, and my father's disappearance was an independent event that made it all go to hell. But that wasn't true. My parents had their share of problems before he went missing. Now I have to determine if those problems had anything to do with his disappearance." Lance paused. "Or Mary's murder. We can't forget that a young woman died that night, and her death is somehow connected to my dad."

Chapter Fourteen

"That's Brian Leed. He's a sales rep for a dental equipment manufacturer." Lance recognized the man raking leaves in front of a Cape Cod–style house in a middle-class suburb.

Morgan checked the photo in her file. "How old is he?"

"Too old to be wearing skinny jeans," Lance said. Brian had buttoned the tight pants below a small paunch.

"Maybe his kids bought them for him."

Lance parked at the curb, and they got out of the vehicle.

The man stopped raking and approached them. "Can I help you?"

"Brian Leed?" Lance asked.

"That's me." Brian leaned on his rake. His eyes narrowed. "Do I know you?"

"I'm Lance Kruger."

Brian straightened. "Geez. You got big."

Lance shook his hand. "This is my associate Morgan Dane. We'd like to ask you a few questions about my father."

"Of course." Brian turned, gesturing them to follow him. "Come inside."

The garage door was up. He hung his rake on the way past a long, low car covered in a tarp.

One corner had been folded up, revealing the shiny black fender of a sports car. Inside the house, a short hall opened into the kitchen.

Unlike her husband, Natalie Leed wasn't fighting the years. She'd gained weight. Her blonde hair was short and streaked with gray. A blue apron declared her the "World's Best Grandma."

Brian introduced Morgan to his wife and then said, "Nat, do you remember Lance Kruger?"

Natalie's mouth formed an O as she shook Lance's hand. "Oh. Wow. Didn't *you* grow up handsome?"

"He wants to talk about Vic," Brian said.

"Of course." She gestured to the table. "Please sit. I just made a fresh pot of coffee."

They slid around an oak table and Natalie served coffee in dainty little cups with gold rims. Morgan sipped hers, her eyes closing briefly with appreciation.

Natalie Leed set a thermal coffee carafe on the table, then went to the counter to open a cookie jar shaped like a rooster. She loaded a plate with cookies.

"I try to keep in shape, but Natalie is just too damned good of a baker." Brian's arms were muscled enough to suggest he spent some time in the gym.

In contrast to Stan Adams's pretentious and aloof McMansion, the Leeds' house felt homey and warm. Knickknacks—some of which looked like clumsy grade-school clay projects—and photographs of children crowded the surfaces of tables and bookcases. Not a speck of dust clung to any of the clutter.

Lance had been in the house before, a long time in the past. In his mind, he pictured a summer day, tables in the yard, balloons tied to the backs of chairs, kids running and laughing. *A birthday party?*

But as comfortable as the house felt, Brian's occasional side-eye triggered Lance's suspicion.

"Are those your grandchildren?" Morgan pointed to a pair of school pictures that hung on the wall.

"Yes." Crow's-feet crinkled around Natalie's eyes. Her smile beamed with pride. "Joshua is six, and Kayla is five."

"And Natalie spoils them rotten," Brian said with a hint of criticism.

"That's my job." Natalie shot him a look that said their marriage wasn't as perfect as Lance had imagined. "I'm their grandma."

Brian gave her a quick, irritated frown, then his face turned serious. "We saw that the police pulled your dad's car from the lake on the news. I assume that's why you're here?"

"Yes," Lance said.

"We haven't heard any updates." Brian lowered his voice. "They said a body was found in the car. Was it Vic?"

"No," Lance said. "Did either of you know a woman named Mary Fox?"

Brian stared at his plate, his brows lowered, his mouth set. "I don't think so."

Natalie shook her head. "That name doesn't sound familiar."

"She was a waitress at PJ's," Lance prompted.

Brian played with his fork. "There were several waitresses at PJ's. Can you describe her?"

"I can do better than that." Morgan reached for the tote next to her chair. Pulling it onto her lap, she removed a picture from the side pocket. "This was Mary."

Natalie took the picture. "I remember her." She frowned as she passed it to Brian.

Brian's jaw shifted as he took the photo. "Oh, *that* Mary. Her last name was Fox? Yeah, I remember her. Why?" He handed the picture back to Morgan, as if he couldn't wait to get it out of his hands.

Lance dropped the bomb. "Her skeleton was found in the trunk of my father's car."

Brian gaped. "That makes no sense."

"Did she seem to have a special relationship with Vic?" Morgan moved her notebook to her lap and wrote something down.

Brian looked away.

"I don't think so," Natalie said. "But I only went to PJ's once in a while. Brian, Stan, and Vic were the regulars." Natalie cleared her throat, her lips pursing in a prudish frown. "I don't like to speak ill of the dead, but she wasn't a very nice girl. She seemed to enjoy flirting with married men when their wives were sitting right there."

Brian stared at his plate. "She flirted with everyone. That's just the way she was."

"Did you hear anything about her soliciting from the bar?" Lance asked.

Natalie sniffed. "It wouldn't surprise me."

Brian winced. "There were rumors."

"Did either of you notice when Mary suddenly stopped working at PJ's?" Morgan asked.

"No." Natalie broke off a piece of cookie. "There were other waitresses. She wasn't there every time I went anyway."

"No. Maybe." Brian still wouldn't meet Lance's gaze. Was he hiding something or was Lance overly suspicious? "Like Natalie said, we wouldn't give much thought to a change in waitstaff."

Lance changed topic. "Did you notice anything unusual about my dad in the weeks before he disappeared?"

Brian toyed with a cookie. "He was worried about your mom. She seemed overwhelmed all the time."

Morgan turned to Natalie. "How well did you know Jenny Kruger?"

"Not that well. I invited her over for Tupperware parties, book club, that sort of thing.

She didn't seem very interested in being closer friends." Natalie gave Lance a pitying look. "I reached out to your mother several times after Vic went missing. She never responded, and I'm ashamed to say I didn't push the issue. I should have. I should have checked on you. I'm sorry. I assumed she had family or other close friends."

She hadn't.

Sorrow filled Lance when he thought of all the milestones his dad had missed. He couldn't think of any more questions. Emotions and memories were clogging his brain. "Thank you for your time."

He and Morgan left the house in a rush. Anger and frustration welled deep in Lance's chest.

Morgan took his arm as they walked to the Jeep. Her grip was solid and sure. "That must have been hard for you."

He didn't answer. He didn't know what to say.

She let go of him when they reached the Jeep parked at the curb. But she didn't drop the subject. "Talk to me. Tell me what you're feeling."

"I don't know."

"For all Natalie's perfection as a mother, she utterly failed to check on a child who needed help." Morgan shut her car door extra hard. "She keeps a perfect house. Probably cooks every meal from scratch. But she didn't do the one thing she should have."

"I'm sure she's not that bad." Lance had an epiphany. "My mother never had any close friends that I remember. She probably did push Natalie—and other people—away."

"Doesn't your mother have any family?"

"Not that I know of," Lance said.

Morgan tapped her armrest.

"What?" he asked.

"For a guy who loves his wife's baking, Brian didn't eat a bite of his cookie." She stilled her fingers. "Lying must have interfered with his appetite."

"You noticed it too?"

Morgan steepled her fingers. "He was definitely lying."

"But about what?"

"I guess we'll have to find out."

His phone buzzed with a message from Sharp. Lance read it out loud. "Mary's mother's name is Crystal Fox. Sharp wants us to meet him at her house in an hour."

"We should stop for dinner," Morgan said. "How about that deli on Oak Street?"

Lance was too preoccupied to think about food, but he didn't like it when Morgan skipped meals. He turned the Jeep around and headed in the right direction.

Maybe Crystal Fox would have the answers he needed.

Chapter Fifteen

Secrets.

So many of them.

Whispering in the woods. Sitting on the bottom of the lake. Threatening to rise from the past and grab him by the ankle.

He would not go down. He'd worked too hard to cover his misdeeds. But frankly, there were too many to bury in one place.

He'd thought he'd snipped off all his loose ends. But some threads had been pulled free. He must cut them off immediately or they would continue to unravel.

But which ends needed to be severed?

Who remembered what?

He couldn't risk it. They all had to die.

Starting with . . .

He drove past her house one more time. Not too slowly. He couldn't attract attention, not that he'd seen another car for at least a mile. He lowered his window. The sound of a dog barking floated on the morning breeze.

He fucking hated dogs.

A quarter of a mile down the road, he slowed the car, then turned it around. He needed a plan. No impulsive decisions. No acting without considering the consequences of his actions.

He would not let one mistake ruin his life. No one could know. Ever.

He could still see her mailbox, though trees screened the house from the street. He could park right in the driveway, and no one would know. She was even too far away from her nearest neighbor for the barking dog to be more than a nuisance. Turning at the mailbox, he stopped just past a thick stand of pines. An old Aerostar van was parked near the house.

He slipped out of his car and walked to the front door. A little dog barked on the other side of the door. Maybe he could talk his way inside, then surprise her. But she didn't answer his knock. The way the dog was yapping, if she was home, she was ignoring the door or in the shower.

The latter idea excited him.

He crept around the side of the house. Inside, the little dog followed his movement, yapping as it ran from room to room. A chain-link fence encircled the rear of the property. The gate squealed when he opened it, so he didn't bother to shut it. He waded through the high weeds to the back door. Donning a pair of gloves, he tried the sliding glass door. Locked. Cupping a hand over his eyes, he squinted through the glass, but the house was dark inside. He walked around the perimeter, testing windows, until he found one with a broken lock.

Someone needed a lecture on proper home maintenance.

He eased the window up and listened. The only sound he heard was someone snoring and the jingle of dog tags. He boosted himself over the sill, landing in a spare bedroom filled with boxes and random junk. He stood still for a few seconds, but the snoring continued in an even and steady pace.

With a tiny growl, the dog rushed his leg, grabbing his pant leg and hanging on. He kicked it with his other foot. The creature yelped but came back for another nip. The second kick sent it flying into the corner. As it tried to slink out, he grabbed it by the scruff of its neck and tossed it out the window.

Out of sight, out of mind.

His pulse kicked up as he slid out of the room. Adrenaline flooded his veins, giving him an instant erection. It had been years since he'd killed another person. How could he have forgotten the buzz?

A floorboard creaked under his weight as he crept toward the master bedroom. The snoring paused, and he froze just outside the open door.

How could his footstep wake her when the dog's barking had not?

Bedding rustled, and he held his breath. When the snoring resumed with a snort, his muscles relaxed.

He could feel every heartbeat in his chest, the blood pumping oxygen through his body. His limbs tingled, every inch of him more alive than he had been in years.

Twenty-three of them to be exact.

He peered around the doorframe into the bedroom. The moment of truth.

She lay on her back, one arm flung to the side, her mouth open. Once she'd been attractive, but hard living had taken its toll. Sallow skin and stained teeth showed a lack of personal care, echoed by the bottle of gin and a glass on the nightstand.

Maybe he was doing her a favor. She lived in a dump. She didn't take care of herself. She was squandering her life. But he bet that when faced with her imminent death, she'd fight to hold on to the very life she was wasting.

There was only one way to find out.

Crossing the room, he slid the rope from his pocket. The end was already tied in a simple noose. He shook out the loop. A tug on the ceiling fan convinced him that it would hold her weight just fine. Years of choosing alcohol over food had left her gaunt.

A chair sat in front of a vanity. He grabbed it and positioned it under the fan.

Easing up to the side of the bed, he leaned close.

"Crystal," he said.

She shifted in the bed. Her mouth closed, and she swallowed.

"Crystal." He touched her shoulder.

Her eyes opened. Confusion shifted quickly to alarm. She bolted upright. Her mouth gaped as if to scream, not that it would matter. There was no one close enough to hear. But he clamped a gloved hand over her face and dragged her from the bed. He put her back to his chest and looped his arm around her body. She struggled, her kicks and bucks surprisingly strong for a slender woman of her age. But she was no match for him.

He slipped the simple noose around her neck. No worries about screaming now. She stopped moving, paralyzed with fear. He yanked the noose tight.

"Please, no," she gurgled, the rope strangling her words, cutting off her air.

Using the rope around her neck and the arm around her body, he lifted her higher. Her feet frantically sought the chair to take the pressure from her throat.

Her head was just below the fan. He estimated the distance needed between her feet and the floor and wrapped the rope around the base of the fan. Before he tied off the end, he left a few inches of slack.

She wheezed as the extra length allowed her to take a single breath.

He smiled.

And kicked the chair out from under her.

Her eyes went wide, and her bladder released,

soaking her gray sweatpants. The sharp scent of urine hit his nostrils. He stepped back as her body dangled at the end of the rope. Her toes stretched toward the floor, but she couldn't reach. Her arms and legs flailed, her movements violent.

Panicked.

Desperate.

Her hands went to her neck. Her fingers clawed at the rope. Her nails raked her own skin, leaving bloody trails on her neck. But she couldn't free herself.

Death came in a minute or two as the tight rope cut off both her breathing and blood flow. He watched as her face slackened. Her arms and legs stopped moving. Life faded from her eyes until she stopped seeing him. Her body swayed for a few minutes, then stilled.

It was done.

This must be what an addict experiences when he finally gives in to his urges. Was the rush of heroin similar to this?

He *should* be ashamed. He *should* feel guilty, but all that surged through his body was satisfaction.

He'd silenced her so she wouldn't talk. But he'd enjoyed every second of the act. It didn't matter how long he'd maintained his self-control. Deep inside, he was a killer.

Crystal had been the first thread to be snipped. But there were more that needed severing.

He backed away from the swaying body, savoring the sight. The cell phone in his pocket begged to take a picture so that he could relive this moment forever. But he resisted. Stupid mistakes could get him caught. Instead, he simply stared, imprinting the sight in his mind. His memory would have to suffice.

A few seconds later, he backed out of the bedroom. He crept back to the open window. The overgrown yard was empty. He slipped out the window and back across the weeds to the driveway and his car.

He couldn't pretend he hadn't enjoyed the kill any more than he could pretend that he wasn't looking forward to the next death.

Chapter Sixteen

If Sharp closed his eyes, he could picture everything as it had been in 1994. Jenny becoming more hysterical as the hours passed. Ten-year-old Lance trying to calm her. He'd been just a boy, but he'd become his mother's caretaker that night. Sharp had helped as much as he could. His only other option had been to put Lance into foster care, and Sharp had seen too many kids destroyed by that system. In his opinion, unless a kid was in major danger, he was better off with his own family.

They'd survived, but neither Jenny nor Lance had lived a full life. Until now. Until Morgan had entered the picture. It had taken Lance bringing a woman around for Jenny to see that her illness had a death grip on her son as well as herself.

Morgan had made all the difference. And Sharp would be damned if he'd let Vic Kruger's disappearance put Lance's newfound joy in jeopardy.

This time, he was going to find the truth. This time, he would not fail them. But what if the truth was more painful than they'd ever imagined? Vic's car had been found in a lake with a woman's body in the trunk. If Sharp were investigating that discovery, with no previous connection to the case, he might conclude that Vic had killed the girl, covered up the murder by putting her in the lake, and left town because of his crime. But if he wanted to dispose of a body, Vic could have dumped her in the lake and gone home. No one would have known. There would have been no need to complicate the situation by using his own car.

Unless Vic also wanted out of his marriage and the stressful situation. In that case, it made perfect sense.

Shit.

Should he share the theory with Lance? Not yet. He'd keep it in the back of his mind and see where the evidence led.

Sharp cruised to a stop at the sign and turned right.

Crystal Fox lived in Grey's Hollow, a mostly rural community just north of Scarlet Falls. Weeds and woods lined both sides of the country road. At six o'clock in the evening, the sun had set, but the night wasn't yet full dark. In the gray twilight, Sharp passed a rundown farmhouse with a sagging porch and a barnyard full of knee-high weeds.

A quarter mile later, he turned at a broken mailbox onto a narrow, rutted driveway. Trees arched overhead and shadowed the lane.

Ahead, taillights glowed in the dim, and Sharp spotted Lance's Jeep. Morgan and Lance were already there. As soon as Sharp pulled in next to the Jeep, they climbed out and waited for him on the driveway.

The small one-story house was muddy brown and miserable looking. Paint peeled from the front door. Shutters and roof shingles were missing. A lamppost halfway between the driveway and the house stood dark. The porch light wasn't on either, and the lawn, more meadow than grass, hadn't seen a mower since the 1970s.

"The place feels empty," Sharp said on his way up what had once been a brick path.

A whimper caught his attention. "Did you hear that?"

Morgan was already on it, moving toward an overgrown shrub under a dirty bay window. Flashlight in hand, Lance hurried to get in front of her. Looking out for her took some effort on his part. That girl took care of her own business. Putting an arm in front of Morgan to stop her, Lance crouched, separated the foliage, and shone his flashlight into the shrubs.

Morgan stood back, arms crossed over her chest, one flat shoe tapping on the ground.

"I see something." Lance pushed his big shoulders into the bushes. Dried leaves crackled as something moved. "Ow. It's a dog, and it just bit me."

Morgan tugged him back. "Let me try."

"Be careful." Lance shook his hand. Blood welled from his finger.

Sharp leaned over to get a look at the wound. "Practically a paper cut. You'll live."

Morgan pulled a tiny packet of tissues from her bag and handed it over. Then she hiked up her skirt, got down on her knees, and crawled into the shrubs, talking in a soothing baby voice. "It's OK. I won't hurt you. That's a good baby."

A few seconds later, she backed out of the shrub with a small dog in her arms, a ridiculously tiny brown creature. A pink bow held the hair out of its eyes.

Sharp snickered. "It must weigh all of four pounds."

"Still has sharp teeth." Lance wrapped a tissue around his bleeding finger.

"It's a Yorkie," Morgan said.

Sharp let the little dog sniff his hand. It growled as he read her tag. "Her name is Sweet Pea Fox. She must be Crystal's dog."

Morgan set it on the ground. It took one step, dragging one leg, and she scooped it back up again. "She's hurt."

"Let's see why Crystal's dog is outside." Sharp headed up the walk. There was no doorbell, so he knocked on the door.

Something scraped from the back of the house. Lance put a finger to his lips and took off in a jog around the corner. Sharp motioned for Morgan to stay put. Then he headed around the opposite side. A rickety chain-link fence defined the backyard. Sharp went through the open gate.

He heard the scraping sound again. Shoving aside the branch of a monstrous rhododendron, he saw a hooded figure drop out of a window and haul ass through the weeds. Sharp sprinted after him. He could still clock a six-minute mile and closed the distance between them rapidly. Reaching the fence, the figure put one hand on top and leaped over. His feet hit the weeds on the other side, and he turned on the speed. Sharp followed him over the fence and continued to gain ground. He heard Lance's heavier steps and the rattle of the fence behind him. But Sharp focused on the hooded figure. He was tall and slim but clearly unconditioned. His strides were slowing.

As the man reached the end of the meadow at the edge of the woods, Sharp lunged forward, grabbing him by his hoodie and yanking him backward. Momentum worked with him. The man's feet continued forward, his shoulders pitched backward, and he landed on his back on the grass.

"Don't move." Sharp put a foot on his throat, intending to pin him to the ground.

The man grabbed his foot, knocked Sharp backward, and scrambled to his feet. Sharp got a boot under his body and launched himself forward. He landed on top. He was in good shape for his age, but the man under him was younger and stronger. A wild fist caught Sharp on the jaw. Stars exploded in front of him. In two seconds, he found himself on his back with a weight on his chest and hands around his throat.

The kid leaned on his hands, cutting off Sharp's air.

Sharp crossed his arms over his chest, using his elbows to bend his assailant's arms and ease some of the pressure, just enough to suck in one breath.

As suddenly as the weight had landed on his chest, it disappeared. Sharp gulped oxygen, his lungs burning, as a shadow fell over him. Lance had the kid by the neck of his hoodie, the kid's toes barely on the ground.

"What's going on?" Lance asked. He wasn't even out of breath.

Sharp looked up, wheezing and feeling old.

Lance shook the kid like a kitten. "Why were you running from Crystal's house?"

The guy was young, maybe eighteen or nineteen. His wide-open, panicked eyes made him look younger.

"I didn't do anything." His arms flailed.

Lance eased the kid's feet to the ground and released him. Sharp sat up and waited for the kid to spill his guts, but he clamped his mouth firmly shut. Sharp bet this was not the kid's first B and E.

"If you try to run"—Sharp jerked a thumb toward Lance, whose bowling-ball-size biceps served as useful threats—"I'll sic him on you again."

The kid's gaze darted back and forth between Sharp and Lance, then he nodded.

Sharp checked the kid's pockets for weapons and found a wallet. He read the driver's license. "Ricky Jackson. OK, Ricky, let's go see what you were so anxious to run away from." Sharp pushed him back toward Crystal's house. He pocketed the wallet, just in case the kid managed to beat feet.

There were no houses in sight. The dilapidated farmhouse a quarter mile away was the closest neighbor. Ricky dragged his feet, but he was smart—or experienced—enough not to give anything away.

"Are you cops?" he protested.

"No," Sharp said, keeping one hand on the kid's arm.

The kid tried to twist away. "Then get your hands off me."

"Walk." Lance pointed toward Crystal's place.

As they approached, Sharp studied the open window. Sharp caught a vibe—and a smell—that indicated bad shit had gone down. "I'm sure they'd love to know why you were climbing out Ms. Fox's window."

The kid went quiet.

They hauled him around front.

"What happened?" Morgan asked.

"Caught him climbing out a window." Sharp handed the kid off to Lance, then went to his car for a set of zip ties. Returning, he pulled Ricky's hands behind his back and fastened his wrists together.

"Hey, you can't do that." The kid wriggled.

"Shut up." Sharp dragged Ricky to a lamppost and used a second zip tie to hook him to the post. He patted him on the shoulder. "You stay here."

"You suck, man. I'm gonna sue your ass." The kid spat onto the ground.

"I caught you breaking into a woman's home. This is a citizen's arrest, my young friend." Sharp glanced at Morgan. Her face was set in a disapproving frown. He ignored her. His instincts told him they were not going to like what they found inside the house, and that the kid had been up to no good.

Besides, Grey's Hollow was Sheriff King's domain. The sheriff might not love PIs, but he would enthusiastically approve of heavy handedness when it came to punk-ass kids breaking into houses.

"Keep an eye on him," he said to Morgan, then motioned Lance forward. They approached the front door. Sharp pulled gloves from his pocket and tugged them on. Lance did the same. Sharp tried the knob, but the door was locked. He and

Lance walked the perimeter of the house, looking in windows. They tried the side entrance and a sliding glass door around back before stopping in front of the open window.

The sill was chest high. Sharp peered into a spare bedroom. He scanned past the boxes and piles of clothing to focus on the doorway. Across the hall and through another doorway, a pair of feet dangled just off the floor. "Shit, I see dangling feet."

Lance laced his fingers as a step. Sharp took the leg up and scrambled inside. He maneuvered his way through the piles of junk. Lance came through the window behind him.

"Let me go first." Lance shouldered ahead, his gun in his hand. "I'm armed."

But Sharp could already see there was no reason to hurry. The woman was beyond help. He stopped in the doorway, the breath whooshing out of him as he viewed the body. The smell of death brought back his years on the police force. The body had not yet begun to decompose, but the bowels and bladder had released.

She dangled from a rope attached to the ceiling fan, her toes not quite brushing the carpet. Her eyes bulged, and her swollen tongue protruded from her mouth. A chair rested on its back beside her.

"I'll clear the house," Lance said.

Sharp heard him moving through the rooms.

Crystal Fox had been the single best new clue in Vic's disappearance.

And she was dead.

"You really need to carry your gun." Lance stopped next to him.

"I generally don't need one, and I want people to feel comfortable talking to me," Sharp said. "Besides, you're the muscle, and I'm the brains in this operation."

Lance holstered his weapon and pulled out his phone. "I'll call the sheriff."

"No rush. She isn't going to be more dead five minutes from now." Sharp took a camera from his pocket and began snapping pictures. "Once King gets here, the scene will be off-limits. And the ME won't talk to us about an active investigation either. The sheriff will batten down all his hatches, as usual."

"But the kid knows we're here," Lance argued, sliding his phone out of his pocket.

"True."

"And I always get the feeling the sheriff would like nothing better than to toss us both in jail."

"Also true. King likes jailing people in general, but he has Ricky to lock up tonight. That should make the sheriff happy."

While Lance made the phone call, Sharp snapped more pictures, zooming in on the rope, the knot, the woman's face. "It's a simple slipknot. No special skill required."

"Do you think this isn't suicide?" Lance asked, lowering his phone. "The sheriff recently informed her that her daughter was murdered. Seems like a reasonable motivation."

"Maybe." Sharp photographed the body in sections. "But her daughter has been missing for twenty-three years. Don't you think the possibility that Mary had been killed would have occurred to her by now?"

"But the reality is very different from the possibility," Lance said quietly.

Damn. What a shitty thing to say to someone whose father had also been missing all that time.

Sharp lowered the camera. "I'm sorry. You would know better than I would."

"You could be right." Lance rolled a shoulder. "Even my mom, with all her problems, was almost relieved when she thought my father's body had been found. She's more upset now, knowing that it wasn't him."

"We'll get to the bottom of this." Sharp pointed to purplish red dots on the dead woman's swollen face. "Facial congestion and petechial hemorrhages are consistent with death by asphyxia caused by hanging, manual strangulation, or smothering." He used one gloved finger to lift the hem of her pant leg and expose her foot and calf. "No sign of lividity yet." The blood hadn't had time to settle in the lowest part of the body. "She hasn't been hanging here very long."

Sharp finished with the body and moved on to the room. His gaze landed on the dresser. The drawers were open and had been rifled through. A jewelry box lay on its side, its contents spilled onto the top of the dresser. "That little rat was robbing her."

"What's going on in there?" Morgan called from the open window.

"Don't let her in here." Lance frowned at the body. "She doesn't need to see this."

"She's tough," Sharp said. "She can handle it."

"But she doesn't have to," Lance said in a low voice, then he turned and called back to her. "Wait out front. Crystal is dead. I called the sheriff. He's going to be mad enough that we contaminated his scene."

Sharp gave him a look. "She is more durable than you think."

Yet, the fact that Lance was always trying to protect her was a good sign. For the last ten years, Sharp had been wondering if the young man would ever let himself have a personal life. But Morgan was the kind of special that had little to do with her pretty blue eyes and was all about her compassion, smarts, and pure grit.

"If we'd gotten here earlier . . ." Regret slammed into Sharp. A woman was dead, and his first big lead gone before he'd gotten a chance to talk to her.

Staring at the body, Lance's face tightened.

If Sharp was disappointed, he couldn't imagine how Lance felt.

"We'd better go outside and pretend we left the scene the second we saw the body." Sharp backed out of the bedroom. "But on the way out, look for signs of a break-in."

They left the way they came in, doing their best not to touch the windowsill.

Sharp examined the window lock and snapped a few pictures. "The lock is broken. The way it's rusted, it's probably been that way for a long time."

"If she didn't commit suicide, do you think Ricky killed her?" Lance asked.

"Hanging a person takes a lot of work," Sharp said. "Ricky doesn't seem like the industrious type."

They rounded the house and returned to the driveway.

"She was dead when I got there!" Ricky shouted the moment they were in sight.

Ignoring him, Sharp handed Morgan the camera. "Put this in your pocket."

"Why?" she asked.

"Because the sheriff won't search *you,*" Sharp said.

Nodding, Lance gestured between his own chest and Sharp's. "*We* don't intimidate him."

A few minutes later the sheriff's vehicle slid to the curb. Two deputies parked behind him.

King climbed out of his vehicle and stomped up the driveway. His face was locked in a stony expression. "What happened?"

"We came to talk to her and knocked on the door. No one answered, but we saw this guy"— Sharp jerked a thumb at Ricky, still zip-tied to the lamp post—"climbing out a window."

"I didn't kill her!" Ricky yelled.

Sharp gave the sheriff a very abbreviated version of events. "Lance and I cleared the house, verified that she was dead, and called you."

Sheriff King propped one hand on his hip and stabbed a finger at Sharp. "You should have called me and stayed the hell out of the house."

"What if she was still alive?" Sharp asked, though they all knew the chances of someone being alive when hanging by the neck were slim to none.

The sheriff glared. "Wait. Here."

He led his deputies to the front door. He checked the knob, then led the way around the house. Ten minutes later, he returned to the driveway. "Nobody leaves until I give them permission. And I want all three of you in my office at eight a.m."

Morgan shook her head. "I can't be there until nine thirty. I have to take my daughter to preschool and drop my nanny at dialysis."

The sheriff's jaw worked as if he were chewing nails. "Nine thirty, then."

He stomped to his vehicle, leaned in, and grabbed his radio mic.

"He's pissed," Lance said.

"Hey, we didn't kill her." Sharp shrugged. "But it's probably a good thing we have our lawyer with us."

"Who didn't see you break any laws." Still cradling the injured little dog in her arms, Morgan stroked its head.

"Exactly." Normally, Sharp was all about following the rules, but this case was different.

This one was personal.

He would do whatever it took to learn what had happened to Vic Kruger, and he thought Crystal Fox's suicide was just too convenient.

Chapter Seventeen

Two hours later, Morgan was relieved that neither Sharp nor Lance were in jail, though she wasn't ruling out that possibility for the near future. In her office, she made a cup of coffee. While the machine gurgled, she dug through her desk for a candy bar.

Sharp walked into her office, a grayish-green shake in his hands. His hair was damp. He'd gone upstairs to his apartment over the office for a five-minute shower and change of clothes.

"Are you sure I can't make you one?" Sharp took a huge gulp. "When was the last time you ate?"

"Lance and I had sandwiches on the way to Crystal Fox's house." Her coffee machine beeped. She swiveled her chair to retrieve her steaming mug of energy. "One liquid meal a day is my limit."

"That stuff will kill you." Sharp shook his head. "You need to eat better, sleep more, and stop relying on caffeine to get you through the day."

But the hot coffee smelled and tasted like heaven.

"Spoken like a person who doesn't have three kids under the age of seven." Morgan drank, grateful to the first human who'd decided to crush and boil coffee beans.

Sharp checked his phone.

"Any word from the vet?" Morgan asked.

"Not yet." Sharp had dropped the little dog at a twenty-four-hour veterinary clinic. "You can go home to your kids."

"I called and let them know I'd be late." Again. She hated missing dinner and bedtime with her girls, but her family would take care of the kids and Grandpa. "Lance needs me, even if he doesn't want to admit it."

"You're right," Sharp said. "And don't listen to him when he tells you differently."

"I won't."

The front door opened and closed. Footsteps sounded in the hall. Lance walked through her office doorway. Like Sharp, he'd felt the need to shower after being in close quarters with the body. Lance had stopped at his house six blocks away from the office to shower and change his clothes.

In Morgan's office, he made himself a cup of coffee.

"I can't believe you're going to drink that." Sharp's face wrinkled with disgust.

"Not now, Sharp." Lance drank deeply. "It's been a crappy day. I need some sustenance."

"Go ahead. Poison yourself." Sharp flipped a hand in the air. "Let's get down to business." Sharp tapped the open lid of his laptop on Morgan's desk. "I'm downloading the photos I took of Crystal Fox's body. We can view them when I'm done."

"I'm adding Crystal and Mary Fox to the list for background checks. I'll work on those tonight from my mother's house," Lance said.

"We all know the sheriff won't share beans with us," Sharp said. "What do we know about Crystal Fox?"

Morgan began, "Crystal Fox was sixty-two years old. She lived at her current address for the last thirty years. She married Warren Fox in 1983. There's no divorce on record."

Sharp made notes on the board. "What do we know about Mary?"

"She was twenty-one years old when she died in 1994. She dropped out of high school at the age of seventeen. She'd been arrested once at eighteen for shoplifting, and again at twenty for solicitation of prostitution. She plead guilty to both charges, paid a fine for the shoplifting offense, and received probation for soliciting." Morgan scrolled. "She worked as a waitress at PJ's and supplemented her income with prostitution."

"We need to talk to someone who knew Crystal." Sharp studied what was now their murder board.

"There was one house down the road, but it would be best to wait until tomorrow to knock on the door," Morgan said. "The sheriff has had quite enough of us tonight. We'll be seeing him again early tomorrow morning. At that time, I'd rather be able to honestly say that we haven't tampered with his case."

Sharp glanced at the clock. "After we're done with the sheriff, then."

Lance set down his cup. His face was drawn, and dark circles lay like bruises under his eyes. He needed a good meal and a full night's sleep. But he wouldn't allow himself either. "We need to know how Mary was connected to my father."

"They knew each other from PJ's," Sharp said. "But you're right. That isn't enough. Your father wasn't at PJ's that night. Both your mother and the responding patrol officer verified that."

"We need to know if Mary worked that night." Morgan tapped her pen on her blotter. In the back of her mind, a much darker possibility had formed. If Vic had had a sexual relationship with Mary, could *he* have killed her?

"Putting a visit to PJ's on the list, though I can't imagine anyone on the current staff was working there all those years ago." Sharp made a note on the board. He checked his laptop. "The pictures are downloaded."

He and Lance shifted their chairs, and he angled the computer so they could all see the screen. Morgan flinched at the images.

"At first glance, this appears to be a suicide." Sharp clicked through to the pictures of the knot.

"The chair had been knocked over. She struggled a little, maybe her feet kicked."

Sharp squinted at the screen. "In the few suicide hangings I've seen, the knot was on the side of the neck, typically rising behind the ear due to the weight of the body in suspension. This one is at the back of the neck. It's atypical, but doesn't necessarily imply anything sinister."

"The rope looks like a common nylon type," Morgan said. "I have some in my shed."

The woman wore sweatpants and a worn sweater. Her feet were bare.

"What's smeared around her eyes?" Lance straightened. He leaned closer to the computer. "Sharp, do we have a close-up?"

"We do." Sharp tapped the touch pad mouse.

"It's mascara. She'd been crying," Morgan said in a soft voice. "That morning the sheriff had told her her daughter was dead. Let's see the whole room."

Sharp switched pictures.

"She went back to bed after the sheriff left. She drank, and she cried." Morgan pointed at a box of tissues on the nightstand, next to a glass and a bottle of gin.

There wasn't enough alcohol to numb that level of grief. Morgan had lost both of her parents and her husband, but she couldn't fathom the depth of pain that came from losing a child.

"The bedding is half on the bed, half off."

159

Sharp leaned closer to the screen. "But the whole house was a mess, so it's hard to say if there's any sign of a struggle."

Lance said, "If she was drunk, she wouldn't have struggled much anyway."

They reviewed the rest of the photos, but nothing else stood out.

"My eyes are crossing." Sharp stood and stretched his back. "I think we should all go home and get some sleep. Nothing is happening tonight. Tomorrow, we'll split up to interview Crystal's neighbors and the staff at PJ's."

Morgan took her coffee mug to the kitchen and put it in the dishwasher. Then she returned to her office to collect her tote.

Lance took his keys from his pocket. "I have to go to my mother's house. Sharp, could you follow Morgan home?"

"Of course. Give me five minutes." Sharp walked into the hallway.

Morgan followed Lance into his office. He was stashing his laptop into a computer case.

"What about *you?*" She reached up and cupped his jaw. Buried under all that strength was a soul-deep vein of vulnerability.

He covered her hand with his. "I can't even think about me right now."

And she worried about that very fact. "Don't shut me out. I'm here for you."

"I know. Thank you." He pulled free of her grasp.

"I'll be at your house by nine. We can drop Sophie and Gianna on the way to the sheriff's office."

"Goodnight." She rose onto her toes and kissed him on the lips. "Call me anytime, even if you just need to talk."

"I will." He walked out of his office without looking back.

But would he?

Morgan collected the copy of the file she'd made earlier that day. On the way out of the building, she turned to Sharp. "Something occurred to me tonight. Do you think there's any possibility that Vic killed Mary?"

Sharp sighed. "The same thing had occurred to me. Unfortunately, I don't know. No one even remotely indicated that Vic had a temper or a violent side. In fact, everyone said just the opposite. Vic was a nice guy."

"We haven't established any close link between Vic and Mary, other than he frequented PJ's and she worked there."

Sharp stopped beside his car. "Let's see what we can find out about Mary's movements on the night of her death and go from there."

But it *was* a possibility. One that would devastate Lance and his mother if it were true.

Sharp followed her back to the house. He waited at the end of the driveway until she'd unlocked the front door, opened it, and waved. Then he drove off.

She went into the house and was bombarded with small creatures, some furry, some not. Before she could take off her coat or put down her tote, they set on her. Her evening greeting could be more accurately described as an attack.

The dogs tangled around her legs. Ava took Morgan's tote bag and dragged it to a nearby chair. As soon as Morgan's hands were free, Sophie leaped into her arms. Expecting the jump, Morgan caught her. Not wanting her middle daughter to feel slighted, Morgan leaned over and kissed Mia on the head.

"Why are you all still up?" Morgan allowed herself to be pulled into the kitchen.

"We missed you." Sophie smacked a kiss on Morgan's cheek.

All three girls wore their pajamas, and the scent of No More Tangles wafted from their still-damp heads.

Gianna stood in the hallway, a towel tossed over her shoulder. "I hope it's OK that they're still awake. They wanted to see you."

The young woman was all smiles, and Morgan was happy to see the tired look on her face was the healthy kind brought on by an active day nannying three little girls, not the sort that came from poor nutrition. She still needed dialysis three times a week, but Gianna had come a long way since she'd moved in with them last summer.

"It's fine." Morgan set Sophie down and turned to the girls. "Have you brushed your teeth?"

Three little heads nodded.

"Then you can each pick out a picture book." Morgan crouched to their level. "I'll be in to read to you in five minutes."

They scurried down the hall to the room they shared. At the doorway, Sophie elbowed Ava out of the way.

Morgan went into the den. Her grandfather was in his wheelchair, his casted leg elevated on a pillow. He wore clean pajamas. His thin, white hair combed. Mac sat on the couch, the TV remote in his hand.

"You need help getting into bed, Art?" Mac set down the remote control and stood.

"Hell, no," Grandpa grumbled. "I feel like one of the children. Can't even wash and dress myself."

"You'll be rid of that cast soon," Morgan said, then turned to hug her sister's man. "Thank you, Mac."

Her sister had found a man the polar opposite of Lance. With his shaggy surfer hair and lean body, Mac always looked a little like the wild creatures he studied as a wildlife biologist.

"Anytime. Are you sure you're all right here alone?" he asked.

Morgan perched on the arm of the couch, the two dogs at her feet. "We'll be fine. Snoozer isn't much of a watchdog, but Rocket doesn't miss a thing."

And she would be keeping her gun close.

As if she heard Morgan's praise, Rocket cocked her head toward the front door.

"All right, but call if you have any concerns." Mac and Stella lived just a few minutes away. "I canceled classes for the rest of the week. I'll be back in the morning." Mac taught biology at the local university and used his wilderness experience to aid the local search and rescue team.

"You didn't have to do that."

"No worries. I just assigned a boatload of reading and a research paper instead." He grinned.

Morgan followed him out of the den to the front door.

"I don't know what I would have done these last four weeks without you, Mac."

"In two weeks, a simple shower won't be such a production." Mac went outside. "I just took the dogs out ten minutes ago. They should be good for the night. Lock up. Set the alarm. Call us if you need anything."

Morgan turned the dead bolt, set the alarm, and returned to the den. "I'm going to read to the girls."

"I can't wait to be useful again," Grandpa said.

"Speaking of useful." Morgan opened her tote.

She pulled out the file. "Sharp asked if you'd go through his case file on Victor Kruger."

"Really?" Grandpa sat up straighter.

"Yes. Really." She handed him the file. "And if you get through this whole file, Sharp might have some illegal crime scene photos for you to look at."

When she emerged from the girls' bedroom fifteen minutes later, Grandpa had the file open in his lap, his reading glasses on his nose, and his entire demeanor had changed.

Only a Dane perked up when confronted with murder.

Chapter Eighteen

Lance parked in front of Morgan's house just as the school bus pulled away from the curb. Ava and Mia waved from the bus windows. Joining Morgan on the sidewalk, he waved back.

The bus rumbled away, and he and Morgan turned toward the house. Her breath puffed in the frosty morning air, and she rubbed her arms.

"You need a coat," he said.

"We're always in a rush. The bus comes at the same time every day. You'd think we'd be ready."

"At least you're wearing shoes today."

In her black heels, she was only a couple of inches shorter than him. She wore a red suit and her black hair was twisted in one of the no-nonsense updos she favored for legal business.

"The girls have missed you the last few days," Morgan said.

"I meant to get here earlier." Lance glanced back at the retreating bus. He'd waited until his mother was settled in her office, with a website design to occupy her, before he'd left.

Morgan opened the front door. Sophie leaped at Lance. As he caught her, she wrapped her skinny arms around his neck and pouted. "I haven't seen you all week. You pwomised to take me skating."

"I know. I'm sorry." Guilt speared him like a fork. "My mom has been . . . sick."

"Like Grandpa?" she asked.

"Yes. Something like that." Lance hugged her. When he'd first started dating Morgan, the fact that she had three small children had terrified him. Now, catching one in midair felt natural. He'd never thought he'd look forward to dealing with the sticky chaos, but their smiles and hugs—their acceptance—filled him with gratitude.

But how could he possibly be there for Morgan and her three kids *and* take care of his mother? No matter how hard Mom tried to be independent, one of life's curveballs could wipe out her efforts as fast as a rag across a whiteboard.

"Are you driving me to school?" Sophie squirmed away from his chest.

He set her on the floor. "Yep."

"Yay!" She raced for her bedroom, stopping and giving him a stern look over her shoulder. "But we hafta leave now or I'll be late. I don't wike to be late."

Lance lifted both hands. "Hey, *I'm* ready. Where's your backpack?"

She shot into her room.

Gianna came out of the kitchen and took her coat from a peg on the wall. A bag over her arm held her dialysis supplies: a warm blanket, a thermos, and the iPad Morgan had given her for her birthday. The young woman was still sick, still dependent on her treatments, and still waiting for a kidney, but there was energy in her step and hope in her eyes. "Thanks for driving me today, Lance."

"It's my pleasure," Lance said. They went outside. While Morgan locked the door, he loaded Sophie into his Jeep, double-checking the fit of her safety seat and harness.

Gianna slid into the back next to Sophie, and Morgan fastened her seat belt in the passenger seat. He drove Sophie to preschool. She made Lance walk her in and introduced him to her teacher before allowing him to leave. Next, he dropped Gianna at dialysis, and then they headed for the sheriff's station.

"Sharp is meeting us there?" Morgan asked.

"Yes," Lance said. "He wanted to check on the dog."

"He's such a softie."

"Don't let him hear you say that." Lance drove out to the sheriff's station, located near the county jail and municipal complex.

Sharp was already parked in front of the ugly-ass brown brick building that housed the sheriff's station. He climbed out of his car.

"Safety in numbers?" Lance joked as they walked toward the door.

Sharp snorted. "I wasn't waiting for you. I was waiting for my lawyer."

"How's the dog?" Morgan fell into step beside Sharp.

"She has a broken leg that needs surgery, but she should be fine for you to take home in a day or so."

"Me?" Morgan laughed. "Why do I get the dog?"

"You're the one who collects strays." Sharp opened the glass door and stepped aside to let Morgan enter first.

They went inside the lobby. At the counter, they were met by the sheriff's watchdog, a sixty-something-year-old woman with sensible shoes, a navy-blue cardigan, and a laserlike gaze that could cut a man in two.

"Hey, Margie." Sharp leaned on the counter.

Margie rested both hands on her hips. "Lincoln Sharp. I haven't seen you in ages."

Sharp inclined his head beyond the counter. "There's a reason for that."

Margie's head shake said it all. "It isn't personal. He doesn't believe in the whole concept of private investigation. I'd tread extra carefully today if I were you." Margie dropped her voice. "He just canceled his annual hunting trip because of this case. This will be the first deer season he'll miss in fifteen years. He is *not* in a good mood."

Was he ever?

"Thanks, Margie," Sharp said.

169

Margie continued to shake her head as she gestured over her shoulder with a thumb. "Go on back. He's expecting you."

The sheriff greeted them with a nod and a grunt in the corridor. King had showered, shaved, and donned a fresh uniform, but his eyes were weary. He hadn't slept much, if at all. He issued commands to a deputy at his side. "Put Sharp in room one, Kruger in room two, and Ms. Dane in my office."

Only Morgan warranted a title.

"You realize neither Mr. Sharp nor Mr. Kruger will answer any questions outside of my presence," Morgan said without moving.

The sheriff muttered something that sounded like *oh, hell* under his breath. "I give up with you three. Just go in there."

With a frustrated wave, he motioned toward an open doorway on their left. Lance led the way into a cramped conference room full of stale air and the smell of burned coffee.

The sheriff came in behind them. The office chair squealed as he dropped his bulk into it. "No doubt you've had plenty of time to get your stories straight anyway."

"Mr. Sharp and Mr. Kruger gave full statements last night," Morgan pointed out. "Were there any discrepancies?"

"No," the sheriff admitted.

"Before we get started, I have news for you."

King nodded at Morgan. "I had a talk with Tyler Green about your stalker problem. He claimed not to know anything about it. But the most interesting takeaway from our conversation was that he has struck a deal with the prosecutor's office."

"What deal?" Morgan stiffened.

"His case was given to Esposito, who offered him reduced charges for time served." The sheriff's frown deepened. "I impressed upon him the importance of staying far away from you if he wanted to avoid further incarcerations. But Tyler isn't known for his self-control or intelligence. Please be careful."

"Thank you," Morgan said. "I appreciate the notice."

King nodded, then turned to Lance. "Now back to the case. Do you remember going to PJ's when you were a boy?"

"Yes," Lance said.

Sheriff King cocked his head. "Your dad went there a few times a week. Mary Fox worked there. Do you remember her?"

"No." Lance shook his head. "I was ten."

All he remembered was that the burgers were huge and he could watch TV while he ate.

"Your father's friends remembered Mary. You talked to them yesterday, right? Brian and Natalie Leed and Stan Adams?" the sheriff asked. "How well do you remember *them* from your childhood?"

"I have some memories." Lance shifted his weight. The hard plastic chair dug in to his back. "But once my dad went missing, I didn't see any of them."

The sheriff leaned forward. "Do you remember your mother acting strangely back then?"

"No," Lance said. His father had hidden that well.

"Do you remember your father being depressed?" the sheriff asked.

"No," Lance answered.

"Kids don't always know what's really going on with their parents." The sheriff leaned back and crossed his arms.

Discomfort swam around in Lance's chest. Where was the sheriff going with his questions?

King turned to Sharp. "Your original reports mentioned that Vic was upset, depressed about his wife's deteriorating mental health."

Sharp nodded.

"Mary Fox had a prior arrest for soliciting." The sheriff scrutinized their faces, one at a time. "But I suspect you already knew that."

Discomfort curled Lance's fingers into fists. Next to him, Morgan must have felt his tension building. She pressed her leg against his, a silent plea for him to cool it.

"Where are you going with these questions, Sheriff?" she asked.

Sheriff King straightened. "Once we cleared

172

the mud from the vehicle, we found a brick on the floor on the driver's side, as if someone had used it to jam the gas pedal down so the car would drive into the lake all by itself."

Lance's gut twisted. He wanted the sheriff to get to the point, but his mouth would not form words. He felt like King was toying with him, leading him along, like a cow being coaxed into the slaughterhouse. They all knew Mary hadn't driven the car into the lake.

"Yesterday, the dive team scanned the lake bottom where we found the car. They found no other remains." The sheriff leaned forward, his elbows hitting the table. "You're sure you haven't heard from your father over the years?"

"What?" Shock freed Lance's voice. "No."

"How about your mother?" King interlaced his fingers. "Are you sure she hasn't heard from him?"

"Yes." Lance's spine snapped straight.

"I'm giving this to you." The sheriff pulled a folded paper from his pocket and dropped it on the table. "These are the things I'd like from your mother. Either you get them for me, or I'll be forced to go to her." His big hand settled on top of the page. "I'm doing my best to be considerate of her fragility, but I can't let it undermine the investigation."

Morgan beat Lance to the paper. He kept his eyes on the sheriff while she unfolded and read it. "He wants the last twelve months of your mother's e-mail and phone records."

"My mother is a victim here." Anger replaced Lance's unease.

The sheriff held up a hand to cut him off. "Here's what I think might have happened. Your dad was depressed and lonely. He turned to Mary for comfort, maybe even paid for it. But she was known for being less than kind. Maybe Mary threatened to tell your mother. Maybe Vic strangled her, put her in his trunk, and sent his car into Grey Lake. Maybe that's why your father left town, never to be seen again. And if Vic *is* alive, I also have to wonder if he's contacted your mother over the years."

Lance surged to his feet. Morgan had him by the arm on one side, Sharp on the other.

Morgan was whispering in his ear. Her tone was calming, but Lance couldn't hear the words over the roar of fury in his head.

She shoved her way in front of Lance, blocking him with her body. "This interview is over, Sheriff."

"My father was a victim." But Lance's voice was strained. Could the sheriff be right? How much did Lance really remember about his dad? Some of his memories had already been proven false.

"Will you call your mother about these records or should I?" the sheriff asked.

"I'll do it." Lance forced the words out of his locked jaws.

The sheriff's posture eased and his tired eyes gleamed with satisfaction. He didn't retreat from his position or his statement. "I think your father skipped town because he'd committed murder. Now I need to know if your mother was an accomplice."

Lance wasn't sure how he left the sheriff's station. Suddenly, he was outside. The sun broke through the clouds, blinding him.

Morgan took his arm and led him across the parking lot. "Your mother doesn't have to comply with the sheriff's request. He doesn't have a search warrant, nor does he have the grounds to get one."

"She'll give him whatever he wants, and he knows it." Lance put both his hands on his head. "He'll tell her not providing the information will slow his investigation. But giving him access to her personal records will upset her."

His mother wanted nothing more than to find the truth. She'd been waiting more than two decades to move on with her life.

"You can go for a power of attorney and block him from seeing her," Morgan said.

Lance shook his head. "I'd have to convince her psychiatrist that Mom is incompetent at the same time that she's been making improvement with her new therapist. It won't fly. And she would feel that I'd betrayed her."

And that would hurt her more in the long run than anything the sheriff could do.

"Then let her comply." Morgan stopped next to his vehicle. "He won't find anything. He's just spinning his wheels."

Lance swallowed a lump of anger the size of a volleyball in his throat. If Morgan hadn't dragged him out of King's office, he might have taken a swing at the sheriff and ended up spending the night in jail. Losing control would help no one.

But was he losing his shit because the sheriff's theory was way off base?

Or because it was all too logical?

Sharp came out of the building and crossed the parking lot. "The sheriff is a dick. You want to get even with the SOB? Let's find out what happened to your dad before he does. King will never get over it."

Lance breathed. Angry air hissed out of his chest. "As much as I don't want to, I can follow the evidence to the sheriff's theory that my father killed Mary. In fact, if I wasn't too close to the case, I would have already considered it. But to suggest my mother conspired with him is too much."

"Your mother did nothing wrong, and she will be fine," Sharp said. "She'll send him copies of her e-mail and phone records. Hell, she's better than any forensic computer tech I've ever worked with. Even if she had been in contact with your dad, the sheriff would never find the evidence in her permanent records. All communication would have been routed through some village in Turkey."

Lance paced a tight circle in front of his Jeep. His mother was in no danger from Sheriff King. Right?

"I might not have been right about my parents' relationship when I was ten," Lance said. "But I know that my mother hasn't been in contact with my dad since that night."

"Of course she hasn't." Sharp waved off his comment. "The whole line of inquiry is ridiculous. Unfortunately, it makes me think the sheriff is desperate, and that he doesn't have squat in evidence or leads to follow."

"Did the background checks reveal anything useful?" Sharp asked Lance.

Lance looped a hand around the back of his neck. The hours he'd spent online the previous night had given him a stiff neck. "Brian and Stan both have multiple mortgages on their homes. Stan is the more leveraged of the two by far."

"Brian had a sports car in his garage," Morgan said. "Maybe he has other expensive toys. Stan has a big house, a Mercedes, and expensive furnishings. But as a partner in an established accounting firm, I'd think he'd be able to afford those things."

"Maybe the firm has problems," Lance said.

"It's worth a deeper dive," Sharp agreed.

"Then let's get to work," Morgan said. "Lance and I will talk to Crystal Fox's neighbor."

Sharp nodded. "I'll go to PJ's when it opens this afternoon and see if I can track down anyone who knew Mary. I'll see what I can dig up on Stan Adams's accounting firm as well." He headed for his car.

Morgan held her hand out for Lance's keys. "I'll drive. You are too angry to get behind the wheel."

Lance dropped his keys in her palm. They climbed into the Jeep. Lance called his mother and explained what the sheriff wanted. He didn't elaborate on the whys of the request. "I'll stop by later and pick up the documents," he told her.

She sounded confused but steady as she agreed. He lowered the phone.

"Was she upset?" Morgan glanced at him.

"I don't even know anymore." He leaned his head against the seat. He could tell Morgan wanted to talk. She was desperate to help, to share his burden and lend him some of her tremendous strength. But Lance was unable to process any more emotion. So he took the cowardly way out. He closed his eyes and didn't say another word until they arrived at the farmhouse down the road from Crystal Fox's house.

Morgan parked on the shoulder of the road.

Lance lifted his head. The farmhouse sagged

under the weight of its history. The structure seemed wobbly and precarious, as if the removal of one cinder block from its foundation would bring the whole building crashing down like a giant Jenga tower.

"Looks like the kind of place where the residents cook meth in a shed." He scanned the tall weeds that surrounded the property. The carcass of a barn, its timbers exposed like the ribcage of a skeleton, lay behind the house. "Maybe this is a mistake."

A low throb started in Lance's leg. The memory of approaching another rural house with an abandoned air hovered in the periphery of his mind, the way a predator hides in the shadows. He surveyed the windows, looking for movement but saw nothing.

No shifting of a curtain. No silhouette of a man. No rifle barrel.

No criminal waiting to shoot him in the leg and nearly kill him.

"We're just going to ask a few questions," Morgan said.

He rubbed his leg. He'd been shot approaching a front door to ask some simple questions. He shook off the memory of lying on the grass, bleeding out, but his bullet scar continued to ache. "Maybe you should wait in the car."

"No one answers the door when you knock." Morgan got out of the vehicle.

Lance followed her to stand in front of the Jeep. "Sure they do."

She shook her head. "You don't look casual. You still look like a cop. You intimidate people."

He glanced down at his clothing. Black cargos, T-shirt, leather jacket. "This is casual."

"Sure. For a SWAT team. It wouldn't matter what you wore. You just have that look in your eyes, and your muscles bulge out all over." Shielding her eyes with one hand, she surveyed the house. "Looks abandoned to me, but tax records say the house belongs to Elijah Jackson. He must be related to Ricky Jackson."

Which made the meth lab even more likely.

"There's only one way to find out." She walked toward the porch.

Lance tamped down his emotional turmoil as he refocused on the house. Ripped screens covered the windows. A gust of wind blew through a set of rusty wind chimes. The high-pitched metallic pings lifted goose bumps on Lance's arms.

He checked his weapon and tucked Morgan behind him as they walked up the driveway and approached the sagging porch.

"Watch yourself." He steered her around a hole in the porch step.

Moving away from him, Morgan raised a hand to knock on the door. Lance tugged her to stand behind the doorframe.

He whispered in her ear, "Never stand dead center."

In case someone shoots through the door.

Despite the cold air, sweat dripped down the center of his back. His senses went on high alert, and his bullet scar itched with the intensity of an electrical current.

Or an instinct.

An early warning system designed for survival.

Standing to one side, Morgan knocked on the door. Something moved inside. A thump and a scrape sounded behind the door. Then another.

Thump. Scrape.

Lance's hand inched toward the weapon on his hip as the door creaked open.

Chapter Nineteen

Morgan edged in front of Lance, who looked ready to shoot the homeowner. The door opened two inches and hit the end of the chain lock on the other side. The eye that looked through the gap was blue and rheumy. Next to her, Lance removed his hand from the butt of his gun. His body didn't exactly relax, but he was no longer poised to rush the door.

"Mr. Jackson?" She smiled.

"Who are you?" the old man asked.

Morgan introduced herself and Lance and offered her business card through the gap above the door handle.

The old man took it. A few seconds later, he squinted at Lance. "You look like a policeman."

"No, sir. I'm a private investigator," Lance said.

"What do you want?" Mr. Jackson asked.

"We just want to ask you a few questions," Morgan explained.

The old man grunted. The door closed. Metal scraped, and the door opened fully.

"I'm Elijah Jackson." He was at least seventy-five, likely closer to eighty, and leaned with both hands on a four-pronged cane. A body that had once been tall and strong now bowed under a lifetime of hard work and disappointment. "If you're defending Ricky and you want money, you've come to the wrong place."

"Do you know Ricky Jackson?" Morgan asked.

"He's my grandson." Mr. Jackson nodded. "The sheriff was here last night."

"I'm sorry," Morgan said.

"Me too." Mr. Jackson shuffled backward a few steps and motioned them to enter the house. "I need to sit down. This damp cold is hard on my arthritis."

Morgan and Lance wiped their feet on a rag rug and stepped into a wood-floored foyer. The old farmhouse was falling down, but the inside was tidy. There were none of the dust-and-fur bunnies that bred in the corners of Morgan's house.

Mr. Jackson led the way down a narrow hall to a huge, old kitchen. A fire crackled in the adjoining living room. A picture window overlooked a weedy barnyard. Rickety wire fencing encircled a chicken coop. Inside the enclosure, a dozen hens scratched at the dirt. A second fenced-and-cleared rectangle held neat rows of plants.

He gestured toward a scarred oak table. Morgan and Lance sat at ladder-backed chairs while Mr. Jackson filled a teakettle and set it on the stove.

"I'm out of coffee, but I still have some tea," Mr. Jackson said.

"We already had our breakfast, but thank you

anyway." Morgan couldn't take one of this poor old man's last tea bags.

She rested her forearms on the tabletop. The gray-brown surface was worn smooth from decades of plates and elbows and scrub rags. In the center of the room, a butcher-block island held a basket of brown eggs. Chipped ceramic bowls held carrots, beets, kale, and brussels sprouts. A large stainless-steel pressure canner on the stove and a line of mason jars suggested Mr. Jackson was getting ready to preserve his harvest.

"If you're looking for bail money for my grandson, I don't have anything left. He's bled me dry." Perched on a stool, Mr. Jackson leaned his cane on the island, picked up a vegetable peeler, and began scraping the skin from a fat carrot. "I took him in when my son got hooked on drugs and disappeared. I fed the boy. I clothed him. I tried to teach him some sense. But he's just like his daddy. All he can think about is drugs." He shook his head. "That heroin will be the end of this country. I bailed him out twice. He's taken every dollar I have. If it weren't for my chickens and my garden, I'd starve. Before he left last night, he emptied my wallet. I guess it wasn't enough. Miss Fox wasn't much of a neighbor, but there isn't much lower a human can sink than stealing from a dead woman."

Unless it was stealing from his own elderly grandfather.

"I'm not representing Ricky," Morgan said.

Mr. Jackson tossed the naked carrot into an empty bowl and started peeling another. "Then why are you here?"

"How well did you know Crystal?" Morgan asked.

"She lived up the road as long as I can remember." Mr. Jackson shrugged. "We were neighbors, but I wouldn't say we were close. Crystal had her problems."

"Do you remember when her daughter disappeared?" Morgan asked.

"I do. Mary wasn't any better than her mother." Mr. Jackson attacked the next carrot. "My Gracie, God rest her soul, was a hell of a woman. A lot of people go to church, but my Gracie, she walked the good walk." Sadness wrinkled his tanned face. "Anyway, I remember this one time that Gracie heard Crystal had lost her job at the five-and-dime. Knowing Crystal had a teenager to feed, Gracie took her some eggs and a casserole. Crystal told her to mind her own you-know-what business and shut the door in her face." His wrinkles hardened. "After that, I had no time for Crystal. No one should've treated my Gracie that way. She was only trying to help."

"So you haven't seen Crystal lately?" Morgan asked.

"I've seen her long enough to wave as she drove by. We didn't talk. Grace would be disappointed in me, but polite distance was all I could muster for Crystal." He paused. "If you want to know what Crystal was doing lately, you should talk to Abigail Wright. She plays the organ for the church. She also owns the Roadside Motel out on Route 99. Crystal worked there."

"Do you have Ms. Wright's phone number or address?" Lance asked.

Something outside the window caught Mr. Jackson's attention. He dropped his peeler and carrot, grabbed his cane, and moved toward the back door as fast as he could shuffle.

"What is it?" Lance was on his feet, his body shifting back into ready.

"Damned fox is after my chickens." Mr. Jackson flung open the back door and rushed out. Tripping on a loose floorboard, he nearly fell on his face.

Lance caught him and set him on his feet. "Let me."

Morgan followed the men onto the back porch. A flash of orange disappeared into the tall weeds around the property.

"I'm down to twelve hens. A hawk took one last week. She was one of my best layers." Mr. Jackson leaned on his cane. "I trade with some of my other neighbors. Eggs and vegetables for bread and bacon."

Morgan couldn't imagine how he managed to

tend his garden and care for his chickens when he could barely walk.

"Your fence is broken. Do you have more chicken wire?" Lance called from the yard.

Mr. Jackson waved toward a shed. Lance crossed the yard and disappeared inside the outbuilding. A few minutes later, he emerged with a roll of chicken wire under one arm and a toolbox in the other. In ten minutes, he'd repaired the break in the fence and checked the rest of the enclosure.

"I used to be strong like that." Mr. Jackson sighed. "It's an insult the way your body turns on you as you get old."

When Lance had finished securing the chickens, he returned to the porch.

"Thank you." Mr. Jackson went back into the kitchen. He filled a carton with eggs.

"I don't need payment," Lance said.

"Give them to Abigail." Mr. Jackson put the carton in Morgan's hands. Then he took a piece of paper from a drawer and wrote on it. "This is her address. Tell her I sent you. She'll be able to tell you more about Crystal."

"Do you have a phone number?" Lance accepted the paper. "We could call first."

Mr. Jackson shook his head. "Won't matter. At this time of day, she'll be outside working in her garden." He walked them back to the front door.

Lance and Morgan returned to the Jeep, and

Lance headed for the driver's side. "I'm perfectly calm now. I can drive."

"All right, but why do you need to drive?" She dropped the keys into his hand.

"I like to be in control," he admitted.

Which no doubt sprang from having so little of it over his life.

He drove to the address Mr. Jackson had given them. Abigail Wright's cottage was as perfect as Elijah Jackson's was dilapidated. A white picket fence enclosed a neat garden rioting with fall blooms. Blue clapboards and white gingerbread trim shone with fresh paint. Purple cabbages lined a brick walkway. Morgan led the way up three wooden steps to the front porch. The wind rocked a white wicker swing on the opposite end of the porch. Two cats ignored them from a sun patch next to the swing.

Holding the carton of eggs, Morgan pressed the doorbell. Standing back, she admired the deep purple of some daisy-type flowers that crowded a flower bed in front of the porch. "These are gorgeous."

Lance barely glanced at the flowers, but he'd relaxed somewhat since they'd left Mr. Jackson's house.

No one answered the door, but a red sedan was parked in front of the cottage.

"Let's try out back. Mr. Jackson said she'd be working outside." Morgan followed a brick path around the side of the cottage, calling out, "Ms. Wright?"

Lance fell into step beside her.

The late-morning sun took the bite out of the raw wind, warming Morgan's head and shoulders.

They walked under a trellis. Blue jays splashed in a birdbath next to a stone bench. After the dark and depressing news of the past couple of days, Morgan suppressed the desire to stop, sit, and enjoy the sun on her face for two minutes. They rounded the side of the house and scanned the rear yard for a little old lady.

"Hold it right there!" a voice yelled from a shed fifteen feet away.

Morgan lifted her hands, raising the egg carton in the air. The shed door stood ajar. From the three-inch opening, the double barrel of a shotgun stared them down.

Lance caught Morgan around the waist in a tackle. She hit the ground hard, Lance on top of her, covering her with his larger body. He rolled them behind the stone bench and slid his handgun from its holster.

Chapter Twenty

"Put down the gun!" Lance shouted. He lifted his head, scanning the yard over the bench. He couldn't see who was inside the shed. The bench was solid and would provide good cover.

Unless the shooter moved . . .

Underneath him, Morgan wheezed. He slid off her body, and she took a deep breath.

The shooting that had ended his police career and almost killed him rushed into his head. Sweat poured from his back and chest, and his heart jumped as if he'd been defibrillated.

Gun in hand, he peered over the stone bench again, his free hand on Morgan's shoulder, pinning her to the ground. "Keep your head down."

The sun glinted on the dark metal of the barrel poking out from the slightly open door of the shed.

"Ms. Wright!" Lance shouted. "We just want to talk."

The shed door opened a few more inches. He caught a glimpse of gray hair.

Morgan grabbed the carton of eggs that had fallen to the ground when Lance tackled her. Golden yolks dripped from the cardboard. She waved the eggs over the top of the bench. "Elijah Jackson sent us with eggs for you."

The shed door opened, and a small, gray-haired woman stepped out. She wore khaki slacks and rubber boots. Leather gloves, a wide-brimmed hat, and a neat bun finished off her outfit. She could have been headed for a garden club meeting, except for the shotgun in her hands.

"Why didn't you say so?" She tucked the shotgun into the crook of her arm and walked toward them.

"Please set the gun down, Ms. Wright." Lance got to his feet.

"This is my property, so you put your gun away first, young man." She chuckled. "I won't shoot you. You can calm down."

Lance debated. She didn't look like a threat. But his pulse was hammering like the bass drum at an Iron Maiden concert. His body remembered what it felt like to be shot, and it wanted no part of a repeat.

Still holding the egg carton, Morgan raised her hands, palms out in the traditional surrender gesture. A glob of egg yolk dripped to the ground.

"Call me Abigail," Ms. Wright said.

Lance tensed as she walked closer.

She shot him an exasperated look. "Put the gun away."

Though his instincts screamed otherwise, Lance slid his handgun into his holster.

Abigail approved with a nod. "Now, who are you and what do you want?"

Morgan slowly slid a business card from the side pocket of her tote bag and introduced them. "Mr. Jackson said you could tell us more about Crystal Fox."

The muzzle of the shotgun tipped to the ground as Abigail reached for the card and inspected it. "I heard Crystal hanged herself."

In rural areas, gossip spread like fire through straw.

"We're not sure what happened," Morgan said. "Did you know her well?"

Abigail turned and headed for the rear porch of the house. "Let's go inside."

They followed her into the cottage. The back door opened into a mudroom. She stood her shotgun in the corner and hung her jacket on a hook by the door, then removed her gloves. Abigail led them into what Lance was sure she called the *parlor*. Flowers covered every surface. They filled vases, dotted the wallpaper, patterned the throw rugs. Flowers were even carved into the wood of the ornate furniture. The room was crowded with knickknacks and fancy, uncomfortable-looking furniture. Lance leaned on the wall, eyeing the fussy camelback sofa as if it would attack. The cluttered decor was claustrophobic.

"Your home is lovely." Morgan perched on the edge of a blue velvet chair.

"I love flowers." Abigail sat on the sofa. Her

body was nearly hidden by an enormous orange arrangement on the coffee table. "Sorry about the shotgun. I'm a little paranoid since that good-for-nothing grandson of Elijah's broke in here last month. Caught him halfway out the window with my silver candlesticks in his hand. I sent that little creep running. He was a dozen feet away from a load of birdshot in his butt."

"That's awful." Morgan unbuttoned her coat, set her bag at her feet, and took out her notebook.

"It's a damned shame. He used to be a cute little kid. You can't trust anybody once heroin gets its claws into them." Abigail shook her head and clucked in disgust. "Now what do you want to know about Crystal?"

"How long did she work for you?" Lance stifled a sneeze. The clashing scents of different flowers clogged his throat.

"She cleaned motel rooms for me on and off for more than twenty years." Abigail folded her hands in her lap. "She'd get better jobs, but she couldn't hold on to them. She always came back. It's a dirty job. I have no illusions about my business or my clients."

What kind of motel does Abigail own?

"Was Crystal a good worker?" Morgan plucked a leaf from her hair and discreetly tucked it into the side pocket of her bag.

Abigail laughed. "Not in the least. But she showed up more often than not. I used to pay her at the end of every day. If I gave her a full week's pay, she'd spend the next three days in a bar."

Warm, Lance opened his jacket. "Do you remember her daughter, Mary?"

"I do." Abigail nodded. "Crystal tried to get her to work at the motel, but Mary wanted no part of it. She was a lazy girl, and she turned up her nose at the idea of cleaning up after other people. She preferred to work on her back."

"I thought she was a waitress." Morgan crossed her ankles.

"She worked part time at PJ's," Abigail said. "But she used the waitressing job to troll for clients in her more lucrative enterprise."

"How do you know she was a prostitute?" Lance pulled at the neck of his shirt. With adrenaline still sliding through his veins, the heat in the cottage was suffocating him.

"She brought clients to my motel on a regular basis. I was never sure if she did it because I had the cheapest rooms in the area or to spite her mother." Abigail pointed a slim, dainty finger at him. "Mary was a nasty girl."

"Would you recognize one of these clients after all these years?" Lance's chest went tight.

Will Abigail verify that my father was sleeping with Mary?

"Maybe." She narrowed her eyes.

"Could we come back with some pictures?"

194

Lance asked. *Why didn't I think to bring a photo of my dad?*

Deep down, he didn't want to own the possibility that the sheriff was right.

Abigail thought about his question for a few seconds. "Did Crystal really kill herself?"

"That will be for the medical examiner to determine," Lance said.

"I heard her daughter's body was found." Abigail picked up a small pair of shears from the coffee table. She clipped the dead head of a flower from the arrangement in front of her. "A reporter on the news speculated that's why she did it."

"You sound like you don't believe it," Morgan said.

"Crystal wasn't a very good mother," Abigail said. "She never put Mary's needs before hers. Most of the time, her child seemed like an afterthought. Mary had been gone for weeks before Crystal reported her missing. It's not like she's been pining away for her lost child for the last two decades."

"Mary was murdered," Lance said. "It's *her* death we're investigating."

Abigail paused, pruners hovering in midair. "We all thought Mary left for greener pastures. She hated it here. All she ever talked about was getting out of town."

"Do you know of anyone in Mary's or Crystal's

lives back then who could have been a threat?" Lance asked.

"Crystal's husband, Warren, comes to mind." Abigail ferreted out another limp bloom and cut it off. "Crystal married him when Mary was about ten. I always thought he had the wrong sort of interest in that little girl, if you know what I mean."

Lance's gut twisted. "You think Warren Fox abused Mary?"

Warren Fox shot to the top of Lance's mental list.

"Yes. And that's what I told Crystal." Abigail shook her shears at Morgan. "But that woman was too wrapped up in herself. I don't know whether she didn't want to believe it or if she just didn't care all that much. Back then, Warren was a truck driver. He brought home cash, and cash made Crystal happy."

Morgan looked up from her notes. "What makes you think Warren molested Mary?"

"The way he looked at that child made my skin crawl." Frowning, Abigail shifted some greenery. "Mary would do anything to stay out of his reach. She started acting out shortly after the marriage, and she made sexual jokes she was entirely too young to understand. I put two and two together. It wasn't rocket science. Besides, owning and operating a low-end motel has given me a fairly good creep detector."

I'll bet.

The idea turned Lance's stomach. If it were true, maybe Mary had threatened to rat out Warren.

"What happened to Warren?" He didn't remember seeing a man's clothes or other personal belongings in Crystal's house.

"A few years ago, he got fired for drinking on the job. So naturally, he started drinking more, which led to him beating Crystal. She kicked him out. At one point, she had a restraining order against him, but it expired. He works at the county recycling center now." Abigail deadheaded another flower stalk. The wilted head fell to the table.

"Did Mary ever say anything to you to confirm Warren was molesting her?" Morgan's pen waited poised over her notebook.

"No." Abigail shook her head. "But it wouldn't surprise me if Mary had tried to blackmail him. She was the scheming sort."

Morgan made more notes. "In the weeks before she died, did Mary bring anyone in particular to the motel?"

"She had regulars." Abigail nodded. "I worked the registration desk back then too. I might be old, but my memory is still intact."

Lance wondered if scheming Mary could have blackmailed any other clients. "Did any of Mary's clients seem violent? Did you ever see her with bruises afterward?"

"There was this one man. Mary said he liked it rough, and she always looked shaken when he was through with her. What was his name?" Abigail tapped her shears in her palm. "Most of Mary's clients would use fake names. You have no idea how many men register in my hotel as Mr. Smith."

"You don't check driver's licenses?" Morgan asked.

"Honey"—Abigail's tone shifted to aren't-you-sweet—"most people who rent rooms by the hour generally prefer anonymous cash transactions."

"What do you remember about this man?" Lance asked.

"He used a ridiculous fake name. It stood out." She pressed her forefinger to her pursed lips; then her face brightened. "Mr. Joshua." Her eyes rolled in a what-an-idiot expression. "Those *Lethal Weapon* movies were really big back then, with all their martial arts fighting. But this guy didn't look like he could fight traffic. He was too clean cut."

Morgan leaned forward. "Would you recognize a picture of him?"

"I might," Abigail said.

"Mary was reported missing in August 1994. We'd like to know about the clients she entertained that month. Do you keep old registration information?" Lance asked.

"Yes." Abigail nodded. "Back then I still used a

paper system, but I kept everything in the storage room. I keep meaning to clean it out. There's no reason to keep records that old, but I never seem to get around to it even though I'm there most evenings."

Lance's surprise must have shown on his face.

"Yes. I am too old to put in that many hours, but like I said, you can't trust anybody anymore." Abigail let a deep breath out through her nose. "I have been thinking about selling the place. The world is going to hell in a handbasket. Even the quality of my low-life clients has deteriorated. Used to be I only had to worry about vomiting drunks and married cheaters. Last year, I had two people overdose in my rooms. I don't need that kind of stress in my life."

"Could we stop by the motel and look at the old registries?" Lance asked.

"I'm usually there between six p.m. and midnight," Abigail said. "That's our busiest time of the day."

"Thank you." Morgan stood.

"You're welcome. Mary didn't have much of a chance with Crystal for a mother, and she certainly didn't deserve to be murdered." Abigail showed them out.

Back in the Jeep, Lance started the engine and stared through the windshield. "The sheriff thinks my dad was one of Mary's clients. He was right about Mary not being a nice person. Maybe he's right about my father too. I don't know how I would ever tell my mother that."

Had Lance been *that* wrong about his father?

His phone buzzed, and MOM displayed on the screen.

"Mom?" he answered. But her words were too fast and jumbled to understand. "Hold on. Calm down. What's wrong?"

His mother took a huge, audible gulp of air. "The sheriff is on TV. He says Vic is a person of interest in Mary Fox's death."

"I'll be right there." Lance lowered the phone, put the Jeep into gear, and relayed the call to Morgan.

"Oh, no." Morgan fastened her seat belt. "Let's go."

"Don't you have to pick up Sophie and Gianna?" Lance backed out of the driveway.

Morgan shook her head. "It's OK. I'll call Mac. He'll get them."

Lance pulled onto the road and stepped on the gas. "But then he'll have to leave your grandfather alone."

Morgan turned and took his hand. "It's all right. Grandpa can behave himself for thirty minutes. My family will always pitch in. That's what we do. We help each other, even if our responsibilities sometimes seem like the same deck of cards that gets shuffled and dealt out to new people each morning."

"But I want to be there for you and your girls"—frustration filled Lance—"not take you away from your family."

"Life isn't neat and clean. Family responsibilities aren't divvied up in perfectly equal slices all the time. Look at my family. I live with Grandpa and Stella is nearby. So we handle his needs. Mac isn't family at all, but he does more for Grandpa than my brother, Ian, or my sister, Peyton, because Mac is local."

Lance couldn't articulate his feelings, how much he wanted to be a part of her family, because in the end, it just might not be possible.

Chapter Twenty-One

Thirty minutes later, Lance stood in his mother's office, watching the computer monitor over her shoulder. On the screen, the sheriff stood behind a podium. The image changed to a mocked-up picture of what Vic Kruger might have looked like if he had aged to the present day.

"Mr. Kruger has been missing since August 10, 1994. He is now a person of interest in the murder of Mary Fox." The sheriff leaned closer to the microphone. "If anyone has information as to his whereabouts, please call the sheriff's department."

A phone number scrolled across the bottom of the screen. The sheriff ended the press conference and stepped away from the podium. The video froze.

"I'm sorry, Mom. I can't believe he made that announcement without warning us."

But he could. Lance had let a few instances of decent manners soften his opinion of the sheriff. King did what suited King.

"You have nothing to apologize for." She patted his hand. Her nails were bitten below the quick, so far down that several of them had scabs. "The sheriff is just doing his job, though he's headed down the wrong path. Your father would never have hurt that girl."

But Lance couldn't be so sure. He'd already learned that many of his childhood perceptions had been dead wrong.

"I mean it, Lance. Your father was a good man." His mother's body stiffened. She looked more angry than upset. "The sheriff is way off base. He's wasting all of our time."

Morgan leaned in the doorway. "Lunch is ready."

"You're a dear." His mom got up from her chair and followed Morgan into the kitchen. "I don't know that I can eat."

"You should try." Morgan wrapped an arm around his mom's shoulders. She'd heated tomato soup and made grilled cheese sandwiches for three, one of his mother's favorite wintertime meals. Morgan always paid attention to the little things.

His mother sighed and sat at the table. "All right."

"Did I tell you what Sophie did this morning?" Morgan launched into a story of Ava tattling on Sophie for coloring on the wall, and Sophie cutting all the hair off Ava's dolls in retribution.

Distracted, his mom ate half her sandwich.

"I'm almost surprised she didn't slide a toy horse head into Ava's bed." Morgan chuckled.

"That Sophie must be a handful." His mom dipped her spoon into her soup.

"She is." Lance finished his grilled cheese without tasting it.

"I'd love to meet your children," Jenny said to Morgan.

Lance tossed his napkin onto his empty plate. His mother depended on routine. Morgan's oldest two girls were predictable, but Sophie was a freight train full of chaos. Could his mother handle it?

He studied the lift of her chin and stubborn set to her jaw. Maybe. Just maybe she could. She seemed determined to improve her life.

But it was too soon to speculate about the future. First, they had to get through the current crisis.

"About those e-mail and phone records the sheriff wanted." His mom got up and fetched a slip of paper and a pen from a kitchen drawer. "As you know, my phone and e-mail are both with my Internet provider. Here's the log-in and password to my account." She handed him the paper. "The sheriff can sift through my personal e-mails until his eyeballs cross from boredom. I did not give him access to my professional accounts. He'll have to get a subpoena for those. I will not compromise my clients' privacy."

Sometimes his mom's intelligence got lost in all the craziness of her life. A trip to the grocery store was beyond her capabilities, but she could design and maintain websites, detect cyber security issues, and teach computer science.

Lance took the paper, hoping the information satisfied the sheriff.

"Don't worry. He won't find anything in my e-mails," his mother said.

Lance hoped she was right.

He turned to Morgan. "Let's take this information to the sheriff and get back to work."

They'd uncovered their first big break in the case. It was time to find Warren Fox.

Chapter Twenty-Two

Morgan sat in the passenger seat of the Jeep, talking to Sharp on the speakerphone. She kept one eye on Lance in the driver's seat. He gripped the steering wheel like he was going to rip it out of the dashboard.

Morgan leaned closer to the speaker. "We dropped Jenny's e-mail and phone account information with the sheriff."

Which was one of the reasons Lance looked ready to snap off a head.

"We have two possible suspects." Morgan summed up the information Abigail Wright had given them on Crystal's husband, Warren Fox, and Mary's mysterious client, Mr. Joshua. "We plan on visiting Abigail at the Roadside Motel at seven. Until then, there's Warren Fox to check out."

"You two go talk to Warren," Sharp said. "I'm on my way to PJ's now. Come to the office when you're done with Warren, and we'll compare notes."

Morgan ended the call and Lance drove to the Randolph County recycling center. An eight-foot-tall chain-link fence surrounded the property. Lance turned in at the gate. A sign posted the hours as Monday through Friday, seven a.m. to three p.m. Lance pulled up in front of a small building labeled OFFICE. Behind it was a row of dumpsters. Several other outbuildings were scattered around the property. The only vehicle in sight, a black Chevy pickup truck, sat alongside the office. Morgan made a note of the license plate.

They got out of the car. Morgan's heel sank into the rutted gravel, and she instantly regretted not taking the time to change from her suit to more durable clothing.

Lance peered in the shed. "He's not in there. I'm going to look around."

He turned and walked around the building.

"I'll be right there. I need to change my shoes before I break an ankle." She leaned into the vehicle and brought out the pair of black flats she always carried in her tote. With one hand on the open vehicle door, she changed her shoes. Straightening, she was struck with the sense of being watched. Unease spread through her as she slowly turned in a circle.

A man stood in the doorway to one of the nearby buildings. He wore olive-green coveralls and a leer that disgusted Morgan from ten feet away. She closed the Jeep door and faced him. "I'm looking for Warren Fox."

He stepped into the sunlight and crossed the gravel to stand in front of her. "I'm Warren."

The sour smell of alcohol emanated from his

every pore, as if he'd been pickling in gin for weeks.

"Morgan Dane." She offered him her card.

He inspected it, his face transforming from leer to rage.

"Another fucking lawyer." With one motion, he grabbed her by the bicep and dragged her closer. "You can tell my fucking bitch of a wife that she ain't getting anything from me."

His finger dug in to her arm. Nerves—and anger—surged through Morgan's veins.

That answers my question about whether Warren would hurt a woman.

"Take your hand off me. Now." Morgan slid her hand inside her coat to find the handgun just behind her right hip. She'd had enough of being threatened this week. Warren would never try to manhandle Lance, but because Morgan was a woman he assumed he could intimidate her, the same way Esposito had.

Warren's eyes narrowed. "I ain't paying that bitch a cent."

Either Warren didn't know Crystal was dead or he was one hell of an actor.

"So you said, but I'm not here about money. Let go of me before you are very sorry." She slid the Glock from its holster.

"Why? Are you gonna sue me? I ain't got squat. *Fucking* Crystal kicked me out of my own *fucking* house, then she has the nerve to ask for *fucking* money." His grip on her arm tightened, his finger digging in to her flesh. "I'm not signing any *fucking* divorce papers, and I'm not giving her a *fucking* nickel." He leaned closer, getting right into her face, his breath smelling flammable. A lit match would send him up in flames like too much lighter fluid on a charcoal grill. "You bitches all stick together."

Morgan turned her face away.

"I'll wring your pretty neck." He released her arm and wrapped his hands around her throat. He didn't squeeze hard enough to choke her, but the pressure of his thumbs on her windpipe made her gag. Fear leaped in her chest, and her heart jumped.

Enough!

Morgan drew her handgun and pressed the muzzle into the soft flesh of his groin.

He froze. His grip loosened, and Morgan swallowed.

"I said let me go." And now she needed to wash her neck. With bleach.

The idiot appeared to consider trying to take the gun.

"Don't do it. My father was a cop. My grandfather was a cop. My sister is a cop. My brother is NYPD SWAT. If you move one millimeter toward my weapon, I *will* shoot your man bits off."

His fingers opened, and he raised his hands.

Before he could step backward, his body went airborne. In one swift movement, Lance spun Warren away from Morgan, kicked Warren's feet out from under him, and introduced his face to the gravel.

"Didn't anyone ever tell you to ask permission before you touch a lady?" Lance twisted both of Warren's hands behind his back. He glanced up at Morgan. "Are you all right?"

"I'm fine." She returned her weapon to its holster and rubbed her neck. "Other than I feel like I need to shower."

Nerves and adrenaline tumbled through her belly, the combination making her queasy, as usual.

"Get off me." Warren twisted his face around, his eyes snapping and the muscles in his jaw twitching.

"Shut up." Lance put a knee into Warren's lower back.

"Crystal is dead," Morgan said.

"What?" Warren wheezed.

Lance eased his weight off his back.

"Didn't the police notify you?" she asked. "You're still her husband."

"Yes." A flicker of something crossed Warren's face. "There was a cop on my doorstep last night, but I don't answer my door to cops."

Can't imagine why.

"I'm sorry for your loss," Morgan said out of habit. "I thought you knew."

"You're serious." Surprise finally dawned on Warren's face. "She's dead?"

"Yes." Morgan nodded.

"Holy shit." He squirmed. "Am I under arrest?"

"No." Regret filled Lance's answer.

"Then let me up," Warren whined. "You're hurting my back."

Morgan rubbed her bicep.

"Can you behave?" Lance asked.

Warren nodded, and Lance hauled him to his feet.

Lance jabbed a finger in his face. "If you so much as look at her with anything short of respect, I'm putting you right back down."

"Fucking police brutality," Warren complained. "I should sue."

"Guess what, Warren?" Lance's lip curled in a snarl. "I'm not a cop."

Warren swallowed. "Who are you?"

"I work for her," Lance said. "She's a lawyer."

Confusion wrinkled Warren's thick Neanderthal forehead. "How did Crystal die?"

Morgan clicked her pen. "She was found hanging in her home."

Warren's face went slack. "She killed herself?"

Morgan didn't answer. "Does that surprise you?"

Warren snorted. "Crystal is—was—way too selfish to kill herself."

"Is there anyone who might want to murder her? Besides you?"

Warren's face paled, and he took two steps backward. "I didn't touch her! I haven't even seen Crystal in months."

Since Warren was already off balance, Morgan tossed him a curveball. "When was the last time you saw Mary?"

"Mary?" Confusion puckered Warren's face. "She left town more than twenty years ago."

"Tell us about your relationship with Mary," Morgan said.

Warren's gaze flickered to the ground. "Not much to tell. She never liked me."

"How old was Mary when you married Crystal?" Morgan asked.

"Ten." Warren's tone shifted to wary.

Morgan made a note. "When was the last time you saw her?"

"I don't know." Warren avoided eye contact.

Liar.

"Mary is dead too." Morgan watched his eyes. "Did you know that?"

"No." Warren's gaze snapped back to hers. "I thought she'd left town."

Maybe the truth. Some people lied so often, they had trouble keeping their facts straight. Warren struck Morgan as one of those people. Accomplished liars knew to keep their answers short and not to embellish.

"Mary was murdered," Morgan said.

Warren backed up another step. "Well, I didn't do it."

But the news that his stepdaughter was dead didn't bother him.

Lance stepped sideways behind Warren as if he were afraid Warren would run. "Why would we think you killed your stepdaughter?"

"Because you're here." Warren's lips mashed flat. His arms folded over his chest in stubborn defiance. "I'm not answering any more questions."

Morgan and Lance couldn't make him, but they could tell the sheriff what they knew about Warren.

Warren walked away. Back in the car, Morgan watched him disappear into the shed.

"To quote Sheriff King"—Lance dropped his voice two octaves and drawled a decent impersonation of the sheriff's voice—"he's guilty of something."

Chapter Twenty-Three

As they drove back to the office, Morgan added to her notes on the interview. She liked to get the details down while they were fresh in her mind.

Sharp was in the building when they arrived. Before Morgan could get to her coffee maker, he handed her a cup of green tea. "This won't give you a headache."

She sipped it on her way into her office. "All right, but no complaining if I'm slower than usual."

He followed her in, chuckling. "There is nothing slow about you."

Morgan hung up her coat and set her tote on her desk.

Lance came in, a mug in his hand, and stared at the whiteboard. "So, where are we?"

"We have suspects!" Sharp rubbed his hands together. "Finally."

"Beats the hell out of not having any," Lance agreed.

"Let's have it." Sharp curled his fingers in a bring-it-on gesture.

Morgan consulted her notes. "Number one: Warren Fox."

"Who is he, and why do we think he might have killed Mary?" Sharp reached for a marker.

"Warren is Mary's stepfather. Abigail Wright, who owns the Roadside Motel where Crystal sometimes worked, suspected he molested Mary." Morgan's tone turned to disgust. "She was ten when Warren married her mother."

Sharp wrote *child molester* with a question mark under Warren's name.

"When we told him she was dead, he didn't ask a single question." Lance leaned against the wall, folded his arms across his chest, and studied the board.

"He didn't ask how Mary died or if her body had been found." Morgan flipped the page in her notebook. "He wasn't at all curious about his stepdaughter's murder."

"Either he doesn't care or he already knows," Sharp said. "Possible motive?"

Lance sighed. "Maybe Mary tried to blackmail him, and he killed her to keep her quiet."

"How did your father get involved?" Sharp asked.

"PJ's is the common link between my father and Mary. Maybe he saw Mary and Warren argue there?" Lance frowned. "That seems weak. Could there be some way my father saw Warren kill her or force her into his car?"

Sharp wrote the question on the board, then turned to face them again. "Suspect number two?"

Morgan read from her notes. "One of Mary's customers, the mysterious Mr. Joshua."

"Reason?" Sharp's marker hovered in front of the board.

"He liked it rough," Lance said. "Possibly too rough. Mary was strangled. That's an intimate death. Could he have gotten carried away or perhaps Mary made him angry and he choked her?"

Sharp nodded. "She wouldn't be the first prostitute strangled by a client."

"Blackmail could work here as motivation as well," Morgan added. "We don't know Mr. Joshua's real identity. He could have been married or there was some other reason that consorting with a prostitute would be devastating to his life or livelihood."

Sharp capped his marker. "I went to PJ's this afternoon. P. J. Hoolihan still owns the place. His son tends the bar now. P. J. had a stroke and retired a couple of years ago. He bought a house and chunk of land in Grey's Hollow. I'm driving out to talk to him tonight."

"Later tonight, Morgan and I are headed to the Roadside Motel to look at Abigail's old hotel records."

Sharp glanced at his cell phone. "Since we have an hour or two of downtime, we should break for dinner. We can't go full tilt 24/7. It isn't healthy, and we have no idea how long this case will drag on."

"You're right," Morgan said. "I'm going to run home for dinner and see my girls."

Lance nodded. "I should stop at the ice rink and give Coach Zach a hand with the team. I've been neglecting the kids lately."

Morgan's phone vibrated. She checked the screen. "It's Mac. Excuse me. I have to take this."

She went into the hallway and accepted the call. "Mac, is everything all right?"

"It's nothing major," Mac said. "Ava stayed after school to try out for the school play." He cleared his throat. "She got into a fight. She's in the principal's office."

Shock paralyzed Morgan for a heartbeat. "*Ava* got into a fight?"

"That's what the principal said." Mac sighed. "Do you want me to go get her or do you want to handle it?"

"I'll get her. Thanks, Mac." Worried, Morgan ended the call, returned to her office, and explained the situation to Lance and Sharp. "I'm sorry. I have to pick her up, and I don't even have my car here."

"I'll take you, but this makes no sense." Lance frowned. "Ava is the biggest Goody Two-shoes around."

"I know! She is the Queen of Rules." Morgan tossed some paperwork into her tote and followed Lance out to his Jeep.

He drove to the school. By the time he parked in the lot, Morgan's stomach was tied in guilty knots. She'd been working long hours. Was Ava feeling neglected?

They crossed the pavement, and Lance opened the entry door for her. In the waiting area of the main office, a secretary faced a few plastic chairs. Ava sat in the corner. Her eyes were red-rimmed, and tears streaked her face. One empty chair separated her from a boy who looked to be at least eight and a woman Morgan assumed to be his mother. Mother and son had the same red hair, and there was a clear family resemblance.

Ava's knees were drawn up to her chest, and she cringed into the corner as if she couldn't get far enough away from the boy and his mother. No wonder. The mother was glaring at her, while the boy eyed Ava with a small, smug smile.

As soon as she spotted Morgan, Ava launched herself across the room. Morgan stooped and caught her, wrapping her arms around her daughter's shaking body. "*Shh.* It's OK."

"It most certainly is *not* OK." The red-headed woman stood and scowled at them. Her forehead wrinkled as she scanned Lance from head to boots. She turned back to Morgan with a frown. "Your daughter kicked my son in his, um, private parts."

The principal walked out of her office. "Ms. Dane, you're *finally* here. Now we can discuss the incident." One eyebrow lifted over her stern dark eyes as she glanced at Lance.

Morgan introduced him. "Principal Small, this is Lance Kruger."

She gestured toward a small conference room next to her office. "Mrs. Sloan is waiting."

Mrs. Sloan was the music teacher.

"Wait here," the mother said to her son as she walked toward the open door.

"I'll be in after I've spoken with my daughter." Morgan straightened, keeping one hand on Ava's shoulder.

"We've already been waiting." The principal crossed her arms over her chest.

"I appreciate that. I'll be right in." Morgan steered Ava out the door and into the hallway and squatted to her level. Lance leaned on the wall. She brushed Ava's hair off her face. Her skin was hot and sweaty. "Take a deep breath and tell me what happened."

Ava's breath hitched. "Bret kept pulling my hair." She sniffed and dragged her hand under her nose. "I kept asking him to stop, but . . ." *Sniff.* "He kept doing it. It hurt."

"Did you tell the teacher?" Morgan asked.

Ava nodded. "Mrs. Sloan said he probably likes me. If he likes me, why did he keep hurting me?"

"Your teacher is wrong." Morgan bit back her irritation. "Boys don't hurt girls they like."

They do it because they enjoy it, and if no one teaches them manners, they grow up to be men with no respect for others, like Warren Fox or ADA Esposito.

"So the teacher didn't make him stop?" Morgan asked.

Ava shook her head. "He did it harder after I told." She rubbed a spot behind her ear. Fresh tears welled in her eyes. "He said I'd be sorry if I told on him again."

Morgan fished a tissue from her tote and gave it to Ava. Then she gently turned her around and checked the spot she was rubbing on her scalp. Anger did a slow burn up her windpipe. Ava had a swollen, scabbed bald spot the size of a dime.

That bully had ripped out a chunk of Ava's hair.

Lance leaned over her. His face went taut.

Morgan breathed through a spike of rage. "So you kicked Bret?"

Ava's head did a slow, exaggerated bob. "Grandpa showed me how to make a boy stop touching me."

Grandpa . . .

A smile tugged at Morgan's mouth. She and her sisters had received the same lesson from Grandpa, and it had served them just as well.

"Mrs. Sloan said I was in big trouble." Ava wiped her nose with the tissue. "Am I?"

"No." Morgan hugged her. "You did the right thing. You asked for help first and defended yourself as a last resort. I will handle Mrs. Sloan."

She stood, took her daughter's hand, and the three of them went back into the principal's office.

"Would you mind staying out here with Ava?" she asked Lance.

"I'd be happy to." Lance held out his hand and Ava took it. She moved closer to him, plastering her little body to his leg. When he sat in one of the plastic chairs, she crawled onto his lap. He wrapped his thick arms around the little girl. She leaned against his chest and finally relaxed, no doubt feeling safe for the first time all afternoon.

Morgan was almost ashamed at the small surge of pleasure she felt when the bully shifted to the last seat in the row to put one more chair between him and Lance.

Almost.

The teacher, the principal, and the boy's mother were all sitting at a round table in a small conference room.

The principal gestured toward the teacher. "Mrs. Sloan is in charge of the school play tryouts."

Mrs. Sloan narrowed her eyes. "During today's session, your daughter kicked Bret. She could have seriously injured him."

Morgan sat. "Did my daughter come to you for help?"

"Well, yes." Mrs. Sloan pursed her lips. "But it was such a trivial thing. Children are so touchy these days. They really need to toughen up."

"Exactly what did Ava ask you to do?" Morgan asked.

Mrs. Sloan lifted her chin. "She wanted me to make Bret stop tugging her hair."

"Did she use the word *tug?*" Morgan settled into cross-examination mode.

"I don't recall her exact words." Mrs. Sloan sniffed.

"How did you address the issue?" Morgan leveled her with a steady gaze.

Mrs. Sloan shifted in her chair. "I told him to stop. Kids will be kids. Your daughter needs to develop a thicker skin."

"Keeping one's hands to oneself is a simple concept all children can master," Morgan clarified. She was having none of those boys-will-be-boys excuses.

Bret's mother humphed. "I'm sure Bret was just being friendly."

Morgan ignored her. The woman obviously had no clue what her son was up to.

"Did you follow through?" Morgan asked Mrs. Sloan. She pictured a distracted teacher, irritated by what she considered to be a trivial interruption.

"I don't know what you're getting at, Ms. Dane," the principal chimed in. "Your daughter admitted to kicking Bret. End of story."

"Oh, no it isn't. That isn't even close to the end," Morgan said. "You have a responsibility to protect my daughter while she is in your care. You didn't do that. You forced a six-year-old to defend herself against a much larger child. Bret ripped out a chunk of Ava's hair violently enough that her scalp bled."

"I . . ." Mrs. Sloan leaned back from the table.

When the woman appeared to be at a loss for words, Morgan continued. "This boy is older than Ava. He's twice her size, and he was clearly bullying my daughter. You didn't make him stop. *He* should be in trouble, not my daughter."

The self-satisfied smile fell away from the mother's face.

Were some kids born mean or did they learn it from their parents?

It didn't matter.

Not all children were nice. Not all people were nice. It was a fact of life, which was the reason Grandpa had made sure all the children in his family could look out for themselves.

"We always punish all participants in a physical fight," the principal said in an end-of-discussion tone. "Our school has a zero-tolerance policy. I have no discretion. Both children will receive a two-day suspension. Today is Wednesday. Ava can return to school on Monday."

"You're suspending my daughter from school? She's *six!*" Disbelief flooded Morgan. "Bullying is a permissible activity?"

"I have no choice," the principal said. "Bret will be punished as well. Those are the rules."

"Bret threatened and physically attacked Ava," Morgan said. "If an adult committed these acts against another adult, they could be charged with assault and battery."

The color drained from the principal's face. "They're just children."

Morgan leaned forward a few inches, her gaze locking on the principal's. "If I reached over and yanked out a handful of your hair, what would you do? Would you consider that trivial? Would you brush it off? I'm taller and stronger than you. I could do it easily."

Morgan let three heartbeats of silence pass. "So you wouldn't tolerate that behavior for yourself, but you expect my daughter to *toughen up?* Seems to me she is plenty tough."

"I didn't know he had actually hurt her." Mrs. Sloan's voice weakened.

You didn't bother to find out.

"If children are afraid to stand up for themselves, then your policy protects and enables bullies." Morgan turned to the principal. "Did you know I used to be an assistant district attorney, and now I'm a criminal defense lawyer?"

"No." The principal looked as if that information made her physically ill.

Morgan addressed the boy's mother. "Did you know that parents of bullies can be sued?"

Bret's mother's mouth hung open a full inch. Sadly, the only thing that appeared to get the woman's attention was the thought of the incident costing her money, not the fact that her son had hurt another child.

"Now you do." Morgan stood. "You can all expect an e-mail summing up today's discussion. Since this is a district policy issue, I'll copy the school board and superintendent. But as far as I'm concerned, my daughter handled the situation admirably."

No one responded, but then Morgan hadn't really expected them to. She also didn't expect that Bret would bother Ava again. Not that she had any faith in his mother's ability to discipline her son. It was Ava's well-placed kick that had earned Bret's attention. Most bullies didn't pick on kids who fought back.

"Goodbye." Frustrated, Morgan left the room.

Ava sat up. "Am I in trouble?"

"No, honey. But you're going to have a couple of days off from school. Maybe you and Gianna can do something fun."

"But I want to go to school." Ava's eyes filled with tears, and she sagged back against Lance.

"I know, honey. I'm sorry." Morgan touched her daughter's head. "But you did the right thing. You can always defend yourself."

Lance shot Morgan a tight-lipped look. He stood with Ava still wrapped in his arms. "Let's get you home."

He set her down, and she slid her tiny hand into

his giant one as if it was the most natural thing in the world.

"Can we get some ice cream?" Ava asked with a thin smile.

Morgan looked at her daughter's teary, swollen face. "Absolutely. Let's get some for everyone."

" 'Specially Grandpa." Ava's step lightened as soon as they left the building.

"Yes. Especially Grandpa," Morgan agreed.

They climbed into the vehicle.

"Why don't you stay with your kids tonight," Lance said as he started the engine. "I'll take Sharp with me."

"Are you sure?" Morgan glanced in the back seat. The sight of a sad-faced Ava resting her head on the side of her booster seat tugged at Morgan's heart. Balancing her career and motherhood felt like she was juggling a raw egg, a live grenade, and a chainsaw. At any moment, something could break, blow up, or slice her to pieces.

"Sharp and I can handle one interview. Ava needs you tonight."

"You're right, and thank you."

Lance inclined his head toward the rear seat. "*She* is the most important thing today."

They bought several containers of ice cream, and Lance dropped Morgan and Ava at home. Morgan was greeted with the usual chaos of kids and dogs.

Mac was standing behind the crew. "If you

don't need anything else tonight, I'm going to head home and see Stella before she goes back to work. She has some kind of meeting tonight."

"We're fine." She gave Mac a hug. "Thank you for everything."

He left. Morgan locked the front door and tossed her coat and bag over a chair. She took the ice cream into the kitchen and put the containers into the freezer.

Gianna peeked in the oven. "Mac and cheese is almost ready. Girls, let's go wash up."

"Gianna made garlic bread," Mia yelled as the girls followed Gianna from the room.

"What happened at school?" Grandpa asked.

Morgan filled him in.

"I'm not exactly making friends at the school." Morgan couldn't shut off the instant replay of the scene in the principal's office. How many times could she second-guess herself? "Do you think I overreacted?"

She thought of Warren Fox grabbing her, the stench of him, the bruises he'd left on her arm. The incident with Esposito hadn't been violent, but he'd also tried to intimidate her. She touched her throat, where Tyler Green's hands had left a ring of bruises two months ago. And now she had to consider the possibility that Tyler was stalking her.

Had today's incident with Ava hit a personal chord and had she let her emotions get the best of her?

Grandpa snorted. "Should you have let it go to *make nice* with the teacher and principal?"

"No." Morgan reached for a pile of mail on the counter. "I won't kowtow to school administrators who would rather look the other way than address a difficult issue. I guarantee Bret's days as a bully aren't over."

"But he probably won't target Ava again." Grandpa sounded pleased. "At least not unless he's wearing a cup."

"I'm going to have kids at that school for the next nine years," Morgan said. "They probably have me marked as a troublemaker."

"Or maybe your response will change the way the school handles this kind of behavior."

"Maybe." Morgan hadn't thought of it that way. "But I was angry. Really angry, and I don't lose my temper often. I'm an adult. But this—this really threw me."

"Someone hurt your baby, and you went mama bear on their asses." Grandpa crossed his arms. "Now they know not to mess with you *or* Ava. Nothing wrong with that."

Morgan flipped through the mail. Mostly junk. She set it down. On the counter next to the envelopes was a squat brown box. Morgan's name and address were printed on the top, but there was no return address. "What's this?"

Grandpa craned his neck to look at the package. "Gianna said the neighbor from two doors down dropped it off. She said someone left it on her porch this afternoon. The delivery service must have gotten the houses mixed up."

"There's no postmark or bar code." Morgan's instincts went on alert.

Obviously, so had Grandpa's. "I should have noticed. Don't touch it. We should call Stella."

"Let's not get ahead of ourselves. This could be anything." Morgan went to the chair at the front door and took a pair of vinyl gloves from her tote. Back in the kitchen, she used a pair of scissors to slit the tape at the end of the box. When she opened it, she found photographs nestled in crumpled brown packing paper.

Morgan lifted the stack. The first picture was her leaving the courthouse. The photographer had clearly followed her. The stack of images followed her from the courthouse across the parking lot to her minivan. There were photos of her arriving home as well, getting out of her minivan, walking into the front door, and greeting her kids.

My kids!

A chill swept through her, settling in her chest. Her hands trembled. Seeing her little girls in the sights of a stalker made Morgan ill with terror.

But the children clearly weren't the focus of the sender's rage. Each picture had a bloodred *X* drawn across Morgan's face. Some of the lines were scratched into the photographs, as if the hand that held the marker had pressed hard enough to break the felt tip.

The last photograph was an eight-by-ten shot of Morgan's face. Instead of red Xs, bullet holes riddled the picture, as if it had been used for target practice. On the bottom of the page was a message written in blocky print.

PAYBACK IS A BITCH.

Chapter Twenty-Four

The little house stood alone on a quiet section of country road. There were no other houses, no other vehicles in sight.

No one close enough to hear a scream.

He doubled-checked the address. 212 County Line Road, residence of the next person on his list.

He parked his car down the street and watched the house. Except for one room at the front of the house, the rest of the windows were dark. What would two old people do on a weekday evening? They'd sit in the living room and watch TV.

When nothing moved for ten minutes, he moved his car farther away and parked it behind a stand of trees. Then he stepped out of the vehicle and tugged on a ski mask and a pair of gloves. His black sweatpants and hoodie would blend into the dark. Slinging a black pillowcase over one shoulder, he walked through the side yard, past a vegetable garden tilled for the winter.

Cloud cover kept the yard dark. He couldn't risk being seen until the last moment. With two of them inside, this needed to be a surprise. A light shone in the first window. He ducked under it and moved to the next. Rising onto his toes, he cupped his hand over his eyes and peered through the dark glass at the empty kitchen. Light spilled from a doorway that led into the living room.

Then he waited, listening.

The sound of a television blared through the house. P. J. and his wife must be stone-deaf. He circled around the back and opposite side of the house, giving each window a cautious look and getting a general layout of the interior. In addition to the main living area in the front of the house, he noted a kitchen and three bedrooms. The second bedroom had been converted into an office. Children's furniture and toys decorated the third. Grandchildren?

The rear door had nine panes of glass in the top half. He could see straight through into the living room. Two gray heads were visible over the back of a sofa. An old man would not be able to put up much of a fight. An elderly woman didn't pose much of a threat either.

He eyed the flashlight in his hand. It would be just as easy to bash them both over the head. But impulsive behavior is what got him into this mess. He couldn't take the chance that one of them would have time to call for help. With two targets, he had to be quick. Besides, there was no one around to hear a gunshot.

He put a gloved hand on the doorknob. It turned. Clearly, P. J. and his wife didn't think there was a need to keep their doors locked in the middle of the country. Normally, they'd be right. Just not tonight.

Pushing the door open, he stepped over the threshold and crept down the short hallway, past a laundry room and half bath. In the next doorway, he peered around the molding. Neither gray head had moved, and the television would cover any sound of his footsteps. He walked closer, pulling his gun from his pocket, easing each foot forward, his steps silent on the carpet. The woman was bent over a crossword puzzle. P. J. aimed the remote at the screen and surfed channels until he came to a news station.

The old man's hand shook. Could he even stand up? His pale-blue shirt and jeans bagged on his skinny frame. His flesh sunk into his cheeks, as if he was already halfway to being a corpse. The old woman was equally frail. She couldn't weigh a hundred pounds. P. J.'s wife suddenly froze and turned her head. He hadn't made any noise. She must have sensed him. She jumped to her feet, opened her mouth, and screamed.

P. J. stumbled to his feet and pointed one arthritic, shaky finger at him. "Stop right there!"

The old man squinted at him. "I know you."

Most people hesitated before killing another human being. But not him. He didn't hesitate for a millisecond.

He aimed at the old man and pulled the trigger.

A red spot bloomed across the pale-blue shirt. The old man dropped to his knees.

"No!" the old woman shrieked. She lunged to her husband's side. Sobbing, she pressed her hands over the bullet wound. Disbelief wiped her face clean of expression as she looked up at him, blinking, crying, not comprehending what had happened.

She wasn't on his list, but he could hardly let her go.

Before she could get over her initial shock, he pulled the trigger again and shot her in the face. Blood and brains sprayed across the carpet. She slumped sideways over the body of her husband.

He walked closer, checking the man's pulse first, then the woman's. Both were good and dead. He crossed more names off his mental list.

Now to finish setting the scene.

The diamond on the woman's engagement ring was a decent size. He pried it off her finger and dropped it in the pillowcase. Then he stepped over the bodies and went into the bedroom. On the dresser, he lifted a jewelry box and dumped it into his bag. Moving faster now, he went to the nightstand and emptied the old man's wallet, leaving the leather billfold empty and open.

He returned to the living room, turned out the contents of a desk, and found a small stack of cash. Leaving the drawer upside down on the carpet, he shoved the money into the pillowcase.

He passed on an iPad and laptop. He wanted no part of anything that was GPS-equipped. He opened more drawers, leaving them hanging open with their contents draping over the edges. Then he moved on to the kitchen.

The sound of a car door slamming stopped him cold.

Someone was outside.

He set down the pillowcase by the back door and crept to the living room window, peering around the frame.

A shadow walked up the front path.

Chapter Twenty-Five

Sharp parked in front of P. J. Hoolihan's little house in Grey's Hollow. After his stroke three years before, P. J. Hoolihan and his wife had moved to this compact rancher. According to his son, P. J. needed one floor, but the Hoolihans were country people. A senior community just would not do. They needed the calm and quiet of having their own land around them.

He disconnected his phone from the car charger. The battery had barely charged. He stuffed it in his pocket. Maybe the connection had been loose.

Sharp went up the walk and knocked on the front door. No one answered. Sharp turned and scanned the front yard. A small sedan sat in the driveway. The hairs on the back of Sharp's neck quivered.

Cupping his hand over his eyes, he peered through the narrow window next to the door.

In between the sofa and TV, two bodies were sprawled. Dark spots arced away from the bodies on the carpet.

No!

Pulling out his phone, he called 911. Cognizant of the crime scene, Sharp pulled gloves out of his pocket and tugged them onto his hands. He tried the doorknob and nearly fell inside when the door opened.

He'd been a cop for twenty-five years, but he flinched when he got an up-close-and-personal look at the living room.

P. J. stared up at the ceiling. He'd been shot dead center in the chest. But his wife . . .

She was lying across her husband's belly. Half her face was gone. Bits of bone and blood had been sprayed across the pale carpet. Bloody matter spattered across the television screen. Sharp crouched next to the bodies. Pulling off a glove, he pressed his fingertips to P. J.'s neck, then checked his wife for a pulse. Both were dead, but just barely. Their hearts weren't pumping blood from their wounds, but gravity was still at work. Blood oozed from Mrs. Hoolihan's face. P. J. must have died quickly. His chest wound hadn't bled much.

Was the shooter still close by?

Sharp's mind spun. Whoever had shot these poor people didn't want P. J. to talk about Mary. Why? Probably because the shooter had killed Mary. Had he killed Vic too?

Sharp scanned the room, taking in the upended drawers and general ransacked appearance. This was no burglary. Sharp wasn't buying the cover-up for a second.

A shadow moved outside the window.

The shooter had gone out the back door and circled around.

Sharp crept to the door. The man outside could be the key to the twenty-three-year-old mystery that had ruined two lives and consumed Sharp's career.

He eased the door open a few inches and peered through the gap.

The figure had reached a line of decorative trees planted on what Sharp assumed was the property line. He must have a vehicle stashed somewhere.

And if he had a vehicle, maybe it could be used to identify him.

Sharp slipped out the door, pushing it almost closed behind him. Straining his eyes in the dark, he searched for the figure in the shadows but saw nothing. Crouching low, he jogged across the grass toward the trees. If he could just get a look at the guy or his car or his license plate.

Anything.

If Sharp stopped to call the sheriff, the shooter would be long gone before help came.

Sharp reached the trees. Hiding behind a mature pine, he peered around the trunk but still saw no one. Had the shooter gotten away? Sharp listened for the sound of an engine but all he heard was the wind rustling in the treetops—and the hammering of his own heart.

Somewhere out there was a killer with a gun he wasn't afraid to use. A killer who needed to be stopped.

Sharp stole across ten feet of open space to the next tree. This one wasn't quite wide enough to provide adequate cover. He didn't waste time behind it, but jogged toward the next one.

Thirty feet away, a figure stepped out from behind a tree. A gun fired with a small burst of orange light. A flash of searing pain hit Sharp's arm. He dove to the ground, rolling behind a tree. Panting, he glanced around the trunk and saw the black-clad figure disappear into the deeper woods. A few seconds later, an engine started, and he heard a vehicle driving away.

Rolling to his back, Sharp pressed a hand over his bicep. Blood welled between his fingers.

Shit!

He climbed to his feet and walked back to his car to wait. After digging out his first aid kit from the trunk of his car, he removed his ruined jacket and cut the sleeve from his shirt. The bullet had grazed his bicep. He needed stitches, but he wouldn't bleed to death any time soon. He doused the bloody furrow with antiseptic, which felt like he'd soaked his arm with gasoline and lit it with a match. He opened his car door, sat sideways on the seat, and put his head between his knees. When the ground stopped tilting, he sat up and covered the wound with a bandage.

Deputies arrived one by one. Thirty minutes later, the sheriff still hadn't made an appearance. Maybe he'd get lucky. Maybe Sheriff King wasn't available. The sheriff was spread thinly this week. He couldn't be everywhere. Sharp was feeling good about the possibility as the responding deputy took his statement.

Another fifteen minutes later, the sound of a vehicle approaching caught his attention. The sheriff's car parked in the road.

Sharp gritted his teeth. His arm throbbed. He was not in the mood to deal with Sheriff King.

King stomped across the road, put his hand on his hips, and leaned in at Sharp. "What are you doing here, Sharp?"

Sharp shrugged. "I came to ask P. J. some questions about Mary." He glanced at the medical examiner's van parking at the curb. "Seems like someone didn't want P. J. to talk."

Sheriff King jabbed a finger at Sharp's nose. "Don't go anywhere."

Sharp leaned on his car, folded his arms across his chest, and waited. His bicep burned like someone was holding it over a bonfire.

Twenty minutes later, the sheriff walked out of the house, tugging off his gloves. "I was supposed to interview P. J. in the morning." The sheriff glared. "Tell me everything that happened."

Sharp gave his statement again.

"Let me get this straight. You are not armed, yet you followed the shooter." The sheriff shook his head.

"Yeah." In hindsight, that hadn't been a shining

moment for Sharp's common sense. "Adrenaline got the better of me."

And anger and desperation. He'd been after this man for more than two decades. Tonight, he'd been obsessed with getting him, the man who'd killed Mary and Crystal—and maybe Vic too.

"What did the shooter look like?" King asked.

"I don't know. It was dark. He was dressed in loose black clothes and a hat. His face was covered with a ski mask. He was too far away for me to get an accurate height or size. He was average to tall. Thin to normal weight."

"The best you can do is average to tall, in dark clothes, not fat."

"Yes." Sharp ran the chase through his mind again. "Have you discovered anything about Mary that P. J. could have known? Something important enough to have gotten her killed?"

Sheriff King glared. "I'm not going to share information about an active homicide investigation. This is my case. Stay out of it."

"Mary Fox's death is tied to Vic Kruger's disappearance," Sharp said. His arm throbbed with its own heartbeat, and if he didn't lie down soon, he might throw up.

The sheriff spun around and took two steps in the opposite direction. He propped his hands on his hips and bowed his head, his posture all give-me-strength. His entire torso inflated and deflated with a huge breath. He turned to face

Sharp again. "If you get in my way, you and Kruger will both end up in a cell on impeding-an-investigation charges."

"We haven't impeded your investigation at all." The pain in Sharp's arm took the heat out of his argument, and he was starting to feel light-headed. "Don't you want to know why P. J. Hoolihan and his wife were murdered before you had a chance to talk to him about Mary Fox?"

The sheriff's answer was an angry huff and glare. "You look like you're going to pass out. Do you need an ambulance?"

"No." Which was a stupid thing to say. Of course he did.

King rolled his eyes. "Well, you can't drive yourself to the hospital. Give me five minutes. I'll get a deputy to drive your ass to the ER."

"Thanks," Sharp said, grudgingly.

"Leave your keys in your vehicle in case we need to move it." The sheriff stomped away.

Sharp wanted to protest, but he didn't. He was in enough trouble with the sheriff. No one was going to steal his vehicle from an active crime scene.

While he waited, Sharp called Lance.

"Where are you?" Sharp asked.

"Just left hockey practice. I'm on my way to the Roadside Motel," Lance answered.

"Somebody shot P. J. and his wife." Sharp

summed up the last hour. "A bullet grazed my arm. I'm getting a ride to the hospital."

"You were shot?" Lance shouted.

Sharp lifted the phone away from his ear. "It's just a scratch."

"Scratches don't need to be treated at the hospital."

"I need a couple of stitches," Sharp admitted. "And a clean shirt."

"I'm on my way." Under Lance's voice was the sound of tires grating on a road. An engine accelerated. Wherever he was, Lance was turning around. "I'll meet you at the ER."

Sharp ended the call. A deputy waved him over to a patrol vehicle. Sharp got into the passenger seat. He stared out the side window all the way to the hospital.

What had P. J. known?

Chapter Twenty-Six

Lance pulled the ER curtain aside. Once he saw Sharp sitting up on the gurney, Lance breathed easier. A nurse was wrapping a bandage around Sharp's bicep.

"What's the damage?" Lance set the clean shirt he'd brought on the gurney.

"Fifteen stitches." The nurse taped the gauze down and stepped away to strip off her blue gloves. "I'll be back with your discharge paperwork."

Wincing, Sharp reached for his shirt. Lance reached over and pulled the shirt over his arm and shoulder. Then he helped him into his black fleece jacket.

"Thanks." Sharp picked at the hole in his jacket sleeve.

"That could have been your head," Lance said.

"I know. I'm sorry."

"Now what happened?" Lance asked.

Sharp told him about finding P. J. and his wife dead, chasing the killer, and getting shot. By the time he'd finished the story, the nurse had returned.

"The stitches should come out in seven to ten days." She handed Sharp a pile of papers. "There's a prescription for pain medication in there."

Tucking the folded paper into his pocket, Sharp slid off the gurney. His movements were slow and stiff, not at all like his usual bouncy, energetic gait. He obviously hurt more than he would admit.

He could have been killed. If the bullet had struck him a few inches to the side, he'd have a sucking chest wound instead of a minor graze. Lance rubbed a knot just below his breastbone. Sharp had never been shot. He was freakishly healthy. He'd never even been in a fender bender. To Lance, he'd always seemed invincible. But even Sharp's impressive physical condition couldn't hide the fact that he wasn't Superman. Bullets were everyone's Kryptonite.

They walked out to the Jeep.

"I need to go get my car," Sharp said.

Lance shook his head. "Tomorrow. You shouldn't drive tonight."

He felt rather than saw Sharp roll his eyes. "I'm OK, Lance."

"I know." Lance drove toward the office.

Sharp shook his head. "Let's drive out to the Roadside Motel." Sharp leaned on the headrest and closed his eyes.

Lance kept the car on course. "We're stopping at the office so you can pick up your gun. I know you don't like guns, but if someone shoots at you, you should be able to shoot back."

"You're right." Sharp sighed.

Lance pulled up in front of the office. Sharp's Prius was parked in the driveway.

"How did my car get here?" Sharp asked.

"The sheriff must have had someone drop it off."

"Damn it." Sharp smacked the armrest. "Just when I want to foster a deep hatred for that man, he does something decent."

Lance pulled up to the curb. Sharp got out of the vehicle, stopped at the Prius to collect the key, and went up the exterior staircase to his apartment. He came back a few minutes later wearing his sidearm and a jacket without a bullet hole.

"Are you sure you want to come along to the Roadside Motel?" Lance asked as Sharp climbed into the passenger seat. "You're not moving with your usual grace."

"I'm fine." Sharp grunted and checked his watch. "Let's get to it."

Before Lance could pull away from the curb, his phone vibrated. He didn't recognize the number of the caller. He pressed "Answer." "Kruger."

"Lance?" a male voice asked.

"Yes." Lance put the Jeep into drive.

"This is Kevin Munro, your mom's . . . friend."

Kevin?

Alarmed, Lance shifted back to park. "What's going on?"

"I'm worried about Jenny." Kevin's voice rose in pitch. "We talk every evening. I've messaged her three times and called her twice. She hasn't answered. She always returns my messages within twenty minutes or so."

"Maybe she's working." But even as Lance said it, he knew the argument didn't hold water. His mom spent most of her day online. She worked online. If she received three messages from Kevin, she would have messaged him back.

"I don't know," Kevin said. He sounded anxious.

"I'll go check on her right now." Lance turned the Jeep around.

"You'll let me know?" Kevin asked.

"Of course." Lance stepped on the accelerator. He ended the call.

Sharp was already on his phone. He shook his head. "She isn't answering."

Lance pressed his foot down harder. His mother always answered Sharp's calls.

"She could be meditating or doing yoga." Sharp grabbed the armrest as Lance made a quick turn.

"Maybe."

But neither one of them believed it. His mom was too predictable. Too routine oriented.

He cut three minutes off the drive, his heart racing faster than the Jeep's engine. Sharp dialed her number twice more, but no one picked up either call.

Lance roared into the driveway. He had the vehicle door open before the Jeep was in park. They raced to the front door. Lance turned his key in the lock and shoved open the door. From the foyer, he could see into the empty, dark living room. His mother's home was quiet. Not unusual. She spent most of her waking hours in her office at the back of the house. But beneath the absence of sound lay a disturbing *stillness* that stirred the hairs on the back of his neck.

Something was wrong. Very wrong.

He started down the hallway, dread balling up in his gut. "Mom?"

Silence ticked by, punctuated by the hum of the refrigerator and the echo of his heartbeat in his ears.

Sharp was right behind him, calling for his mom, his steps quickening as if he felt it too. "Jenny?"

With panic tightening his lungs, Lance entered the kitchen. The tidy room was empty, but one chair was pushed away from the table.

"Mom?" Lance's voice rose with his apprehension as he continued into the short corridor that led to the bedrooms. His mother's office had once been the third bedroom. The desk light was on, but the computer monitors were dark.

Lance emerged from the office and turned toward his mother's bedroom. The door was closed, a thin strip of light showing at its base. He knocked. Maybe she'd been in the shower.

But even as the thought passed through his mind, he rejected it. His mother showered in the morning. Jennifer Kruger didn't just decide to alter her personal routine on a whim.

He knocked on the door. "Mom, it's Lance. Open the door."

He curled his knuckles and banged again, harder. Nothing.

"I'm coming in!" he shouted. Sweat dampened the back of his shirt.

The door was locked. He ran his hand along the top of the doorframe, where the simple, cylindrical interior door keys had been kept since he was a boy. He found the key and used it to pop the push-button lock. The door opened.

The bedroom was empty.

With Sharp close on his heels, Lance moved quickly across the carpet to the closed door of the master bathroom. He banged just once, then tried the door. The knob didn't give. He unlocked the door and pushed. The door cracked a few inches and stopped, something was blocking it.

"Mom!" Lance pushed against the door enough to get his head inside.

Not some*thing*. His mother.

She lay on the floor, curled in a fetal position, her legs on the bathmat, her torso and face on the tile. Her face was turned away from him, but her body was still and her skin matched the bone-colored tiles.

He froze for half of a second, his heart stuttering, his gaze on her ribcage watching for respirations, but he saw none.

She couldn't be dead. She couldn't.

Sharp called 911 while Lance muscled the door open enough to squeeze through sideways. Dropping to one knee, he rested two shaking fingers on his mother's neck. Her pulse beat in a weak rhythm against his fingertips, and he caught the faint movement of her ribs as she took a shallow breath.

Relief rushed through him like a fighter jet. "She's alive."

Sharp gave the dispatcher the address and requested paramedics and an ambulance, then he climbed over her and crouched on the other side of her body in the small bathroom. Lance took her pulse and counted her respirations before moving her legs and opening the door all the way. Grabbing the blanket from her bed, he draped it over her.

"Maybe she fell and hit her head." Sharp ran a gentle hand over her scalp. "I don't feel any bumps or blood, but that doesn't mean much."

Lance stood and scanned the bathroom. When he'd first rushed in, he'd only seen her body. Now his gaze locked on to the sink and the two orange prescription bottles in the white bowl.

Both open. Both empty.

No!

She wouldn't.

His gaze tracked back to his mother's face.

Sharp had followed Lance's gaze. He was tough, but his face paled as he took in the empty bottles.

Lance dropped to his knees. "Oh, Mom." He bowed his head and put a hand on her forehead, then brushed a lock of hair away from her face. She didn't react. Her eyelids didn't even flutter. "I didn't see this coming."

Sharp grabbed his arm. "This is not. Your. Fault."

"I know." Lance took her hand in one of his. Her fingers were cold. He tugged the blanket over her shoulders, then checked her pulse and respirations again. "She seemed all right when I left her earlier. How could I have completely missed the signs? I was just here a few hours ago."

"She's breathing," Sharp said. "Don't count her out."

Her heart rate was the same, but her respirations had slowed. He counted her breaths and kept his fingers on her pulse point, ready to start CPR the instant her breathing ceased or her heart stopped beating.

Time seemed to tick by in slow motion.

Even with his mother's long and troubled

history, he still couldn't believe she'd try to kill herself.

Ten minutes later, sirens approached. Lance went to the door and let the paramedics in. They rushed the gurney into the bedroom and left it just outside the bathroom while they assessed his mother. Lance stood outside the door, hands curled into frustrated fists at his sides.

Sharp put his hand on Lance's shoulder, pulling him backward. "Give them some room."

The medics took her vital signs and started an IV, their rapid efficiency projecting the severity of the situation. One injected something into the IV line.

Sharp scrubbed a hand across the top of his head. Disbelief creased his face. "This doesn't seem like your mom. Even when she's been self-destructive, she's never been suicidal. In fact, when her anxiety takes over, she isn't thinking clearly enough to do anything except crawl into a dark place."

"I don't know what to think," Lance said.

"Exactly what did she take?" one of the paramedics asked.

"The bottles are in the sink," Lance said. "One's for depression. She takes the other for anxiety and panic attacks. I had just refilled them last week so the bottles were nearly full. The anxiety medication is relatively new."

Once, she took several more medications, but

the new drug seemed to take the place of several of her old ones. Lance dropped his head and hooked a hand around the back of his neck.

Sharp frowned. "Are you OK?"

"Yeah." But Lance didn't know how he felt. His body was numb. But there was also pain. Pain buried so deep in his heart, it was going to take a scalpel to carve it out.

"Respiratory depression," a paramedic called out. "We're going to intubate her."

Lance closed his eyes, his mother's words replaying in his head.

I don't want to be a burden on you.

Had she been afraid another breakdown would be hard on *him?*

The paramedics loaded his mother onto the gurney and wheeled her out.

Anger, at himself, at the situation, at the fucking world, overcame him for a minute. He turned to the wall and let it out. His fist went through the sheetrock. Pain shot through his knuckles, dissipating his rage.

Sharp grabbed his hand and examined it. "Good thing you didn't hit a stud."

His knuckles were scraped, but the damage was minor.

Sharp lifted Lance's keys from his hand. "I'm driving."

Lance didn't argue. They went outside. He climbed into the passenger seat and stared at the swirling red ambulance lights all the way to the hospital.

The ambulance pulled into the ER bay.

"You should call Morgan." Sharp parked the car in the emergency lot.

Lance shook his head. "Not yet. May as well wait until we find out how she is."

"Morgan would want to know. She'd want to be here."

Lance checked the time. Seven o'clock. He pictured Morgan sitting on the closed lid of the toilet, supervising bath time, then curling up with her kids to read bedtime stories. "There's nothing she can do right now. I'll call her as soon as I know something."

The only thing to do was wait.

Chapter Twenty-Seven

Morgan paced the living room. Picturing the nasty photos and message, she didn't know whether to be terrified or furious. Both worked, she decided.

"Stella took the photographs to the fingerprint examiner," Grandpa said. "She'll call when she has some information."

"There won't be fingerprints." Morgan's stalker was far too clever. Her blood iced over when she thought of him parked on her street, using a telephoto lens to take pictures of her hugging her kids.

"We're safe here." Grandpa tapped the blanket on his lap. He'd stashed his own handgun under it. "We're both armed. We have an excellent security system, and Rocket will let us know if anyone's outside."

She took a deep breath. Grandpa was right. Her sister had also arranged for patrol units to drive past the house during the night.

"On another note, I finished reviewing Sharp's file on Vic Kruger's disappearance," Grandpa said. "He crossed every *t* and dotted every *i*." Grandpa frowned. "I can't think of any other leads he could have chased at the time."

"Thanks for trying."

"I'm happy to be useful. I wish I could have helped more." Grandpa rolled himself away from the table. "I'll be in my room."

"I'm going to bed too. Goodnight." Morgan set her gun on top of her armoire, out of reach of the children. Then she put on her pajama bottoms and an old T-shirt and got into bed. She was still staring at the ceiling when her phone buzzed. She grabbed it from the table, hoping it was an update from Lance. Snoozer and Rocket stirred, then went back to sleep.

But Sharp's number displayed on the screen.

She answered. "Yes?"

"Did he call you?" Sharp asked.

"No." Morgan sat up, her heart tight. "What did Abigail say?"

"We didn't make it to the motel." Sharp's voice lifted goose bumps on Morgan's skin.

"What happened?"

"Jenny tried to kill herself." Sharp's voice broke. "She took a whole bunch of pills."

"No." Disbelief rolled through her for a few seconds. Then Morgan jumped out of bed, stripped off her pajamas, and stepped into a pair of jeans. "Is Lance at the hospital?" She shoved her feet into the old sneakers she kept by the bed for middle-of-the-night dog walks.

"No. He went home to get some sleep. Jenny's on a ventilator and it'll likely take several days for the drugs to clear her system. The nurses told him to save his strength for when she wakes up. They don't know about permanent organ or brain damage yet."

Oh, no.

"Is he all right?" Morgan asked.

"He said he wanted to be alone, but I think he's in shock." Sharp sighed hard. "He needs you."

Under her concern, disappointment raced through her.

He didn't call me.

"I'm on my way." Morgan ended the call, then phoned her sister. Stella agreed to come right over. She was at the door in ten minutes. Mac waited in the car and followed her to Lance's house.

It was just past midnight when Morgan arrived.

She heard the piano from the front stoop, the despondent melody wrenching her heart. Lance's version of "Hurt" was more Johnny Cash than Nine Inch Nails. Tonight, emotion lent gravel to his voice that sent a chill up Morgan's arms.

She let herself in with her key. Sadness filled the house as fully as the music. Morgan went to the dining room, where his grand piano stood in place of a table. He played, a glass of whiskey perched above the keyboard.

"Sharp called me." She slid onto the piano bench next to him. "I wish you had."

He stopped playing. His hands hovered over the keys, his fingers quivering as if he couldn't find the right notes. "I know, and I'm sorry. I'm not thinking straight."

She wrapped an arm around his broad shoulders, her heart breaking for him. "That's OK."

With his gaze fixed on the keyboard, Lance shook his head. "I can't even process what happened tonight." Grief emanated from him, as poignant as the song he'd just played. A sigh rolled through his frame. He breathed again, his chest expanding with painful effort. "I'm used to handling my disasters alone. You have so much on your plate already."

"Is our relationship that one-sided? If that's true, then I'm the one who should be apologizing to you."

He glanced at her, his brows dropping in confusion. "I don't understand. You and your girls deserve someone who can make you a priority in his life."

"I know you don't get it, and that's the problem." Morgan searched for the right words. "I don't need to be ranked in your life. There's no need to queue loved ones in order of importance. People all have different needs at different times. I know that you're used to going it mostly alone, but that's not the best way."

He took a small sip of his whiskey.

"*You* help *me* all the time," she said. "You protect me and my family. You welcomed me and my girls and my *nanny* into your home when we needed a place to stay. You helped my grandfather shower last week!" Her voice rose, frustration undoing her, and she took two breaths to get it under control. "But you resist letting us help you. Why?"

"You've already been through so much. You deserve happiness."

How could she get through to him? "You must not think very much of me."

He lifted his head. Confusion cut through the grief in his eyes. "What?"

"Do you think I could just walk away from you because you're having a personal crisis? That I'm the kind of person who could turn her back on you because, for a change, *you* need *me?*"

He looked away. His hands curled into fists and landed on the keyboard with a soft cacophony of notes.

"And if you're thinking of being all manly and saying you don't need help, don't bother," she said. "The question was rhetorical."

How could she make him understand? He seemed beyond words, almost in shock. But if there was one thing she understood, it was grief, that dark place that had sucked her in for two years. The numbness, the hollow, empty pressure that had eaten her alive from the inside out. She couldn't let it drown him the way that it had held her under. There had been times she hadn't been able to take a deep breath.

But how? He wouldn't even hold eye contact with her.

Morgan turned on the piano bench to face him. Sliding one leg over his, she straddled his lap. "I'm not going anywhere."

His hands settled lightly on her hips, and he leaned back, almost warily, putting as much space between them as their positions would allow.

She settled on his thighs, looped her hands around his neck, and looked down at him. The agony that sharpened his face tore at her.

"Morgan . . ." His voice was harsh, as if he had a hard time speaking.

"Shh." She kissed him lightly on the temple. When she straightened, his eyes were closed, his jaw tight with restraint.

His lids opened, revealing blue eyes filled with pain and doubt. "I don't know what you want from me."

"Absolutely nothing," she said. "Because it's my turn."

"You don't have to do this." He shook his head.

"Since you seem to be a little confused about the mechanics of a relationship, I'm going to lay it out for you. Straight. No bullshit." She caught and held his gaze. "A successful adult relationship requires support and sharing on *both* sides. It's not a one-way street where one person does all the giving and the other does all the taking."

He blinked, his gaze dropping.

She took his face in her hands and lifted his chin, but still he wouldn't look at her. "I love you."

Her eyes filled with tears. She'd wanted the first time she'd said the words to be a romantic moment, but he needed to hear them now.

His gaze snapped back to hers.

She slid her thumbs along his square jaw, her hands cupping it, the stubble rough in her palms. The strength in him amazed her. How had he coped all these years with only one close personal relationship? Sharp was the only person Lance had allowed into his pain, probably because Sharp had been a part of it from the beginning, when Lance had been too young to push him away. And knowing Sharp, he would have bulldozed his way past any walls Lance would have put up.

Her words didn't seem to sink in, so she said them again, her heart warming. She meant it when she'd said she wasn't letting him go. "I love you. And not to be conceited or anything, I'm fairly sure you feel the same way. A few months ago, I didn't think I'd ever be happy again. I didn't think it was possible to find love a second time. But I did. With you."

His eyes misted. His grip on her waist tightened.

But she wasn't finished. This incredible man had accepted the chaos of her family. He'd banished the darkness from her soul and shown her the light of a brand-new day.

"You listen to me, mister. There is no way in hell I'm letting you go. You're stuck with me. Whatever problems either of us face, we'll deal with them together. Have I made myself clear?"

Lance swallowed, the muscles of his neck working hard. He cleared his throat. "I don't know what to say."

"You don't have to say anything." She pressed her mouth to his, pouring her heart into this kiss. Despite her position, she didn't intend the kiss to be sexual. She'd just wanted to command his attention, to make contact, to warm what was a soul-deep and bitter cold. She lifted her head, her hands sliding down to rest on his shoulders.

Had she gotten through to him?

Chapter Twenty-Eight

Lance's breath trembled in his chest.

She broke him. Every word, every kiss, every caress, battered him down, until the barrier he'd spent decades building around his heart shattered into a thousand pieces like a block of ice dropped from a ten-story building.

She pressed her lips to his jaw, sliding them along his cheek, finding his mouth again.

And once his defenses were gone, there was no containing the flood of emotions that had been safely walled behind them.

Staring into her determined eyes, he was struck dumb by her sheer perfection. Her intelligence and strength and generosity.

The way she loved with full force and didn't accept his bullshit excuses.

And the fact that she'd chosen *him* blew him away.

He tucked a lock of her hair behind her ear. "What did I do to deserve you?"

A small smile curved one side of her mouth. "You were you."

He kissed her. She leaned back in his arms, her softness yielding to the hardness of his body. But he didn't mistake her soft body or kind heart for weakness. She was the strongest woman—strongest person—he'd ever met.

Behind the determination in her blue eyes were purple smudges of exhaustion.

He scooped her into his arms and carried her to his bedroom. He lay her gently on the bed and stretched out alongside her. "Are you sure you want to deal with the chaos of my life?"

"I thought I'd made myself clear."

"Crystal. Just making sure." Despite the horror of the last few days, a smile pulled at his mouth. His hand skimmed the feminine curve of her hip.

He'd been waiting to tell her he loved her. His excuses included not wanting to overwhelm her or scare her off. Now he realized he'd been protecting his own heart in fear that she didn't return his love, waiting for her to say it first. He'd rather face bullets than lose her.

But no more being an emotional coward for him. She deserved better.

He brought her hand to his lips. "I love you. Heart and soul. Body and spirit and any other stupid you-complete-me cliché you can think of."

She took his hand and interlaced their fingers. "Then we'll get through this together."

"I don't know how I ever thought I could do it alone." He'd been an idiot.

She'd given him some of her strength. He felt like a starved man who'd accidentally stumbled into a buffet.

"Do you want to talk about it?" She brushed her fingertips along his temple.

"Not now." He rolled to his back.

Morgan leaned on his chest, again forcing contact with him when his instinct was to pull away.

He was going to have to break that habit.

"Now I have something to tell you," Morgan said. "When I got home tonight, there was a package waiting for me."

The story she told him wiped away the numbness and replaced it with raging fire.

"I want to find Tyler Green and beat him senseless." He stuffed a pillow behind his shoulders and looked her in the eyes.

"We can't do that." She lay her head on his chest and spread her fingers over his heart. "We're not even positive that it's him."

But Lance disagreed. "Tyler is a scumbag. He's already assaulted you. He deserves a good beating."

"Now you sound like Sheriff King, going rogue and dispensing your own brand of justice."

"That's not a flattering comparison."

"But it's a fair one," Morgan said. "Our legal system might not be perfect, but we need to work within its framework. You cannot punish a man if you have no real evidence he's guilty."

Lance snorted. She was right, but he didn't like feeling helpless. He wanted to slay all the dragons for Morgan.

"Everyone is protected for now, and Stella is working on identifying my stalker. The best thing we can do tonight is put it out of our minds and try to get a few hours of sleep."

But Lance stared at the ceiling, unable to think of anything else. He was certain of only one thing. He would not let her out of his sight until he'd dealt with Tyler.

Chapter Twenty-Nine

Sharp stepped into Jenny's house. A dark-blue sedan pulled up to the curb. Stella and her partner, Detective Brody McNamara, climbed out and hurried up the walk. Sharp held the door open for them.

Brody crossed the threshold. "Heard you were shot tonight. You all right?"

"It was minor," Sharp lied. His arm was killing him, the stitches on fire and pulling with every movement. But urgency kept him going. "Thanks for coming."

He went through to the bedroom. Stella and Brody followed him.

"What can we do?" Stella asked.

Medical paraphernalia littered the carpet. His mind's eye replayed the horror of the evening. The paramedics working on Jenny. Lance standing just behind them, his hands linked and pressed to the top of his head, his eyes lost.

His heart broken.

Sharp pushed away the pity.

"Something is wrong here," he said.

Stella and her partner exchanged a look.

Sharp raised his hands. "I know I'm too close to the case to be objective, which is why I asked you to come. But I know Jenny."

He could feel it, a puzzle piece that didn't quite fit. His instincts were waving a frigging red flag at him.

What did I miss?

"Two people involved in this case have died this week," Sharp said. "One appeared to be a robbery. The other looked like a suicide. Jenny would be number three. Coincidences give me hives."

"That's why we're here." Stella reached into the pocket of her black jacket for a pair of purple nitrile gloves. "Someone sent my sister threatening photos yesterday afternoon."

"What?" Sharp asked.

Stella told him about Morgan's package. "It seems whoever left the box knew about the security cameras at the house. They left it on the neighbor's porch in the afternoon when no one was home."

"That's smart," Sharp said. "Do you think it's Tyler Green?"

"We're going to talk to him in the morning," Stella said. "I just thought you should know."

"Thanks." Sharp sighed. "Keep me updated?"

"Will do." Stella pivoted, taking the room in. "Now, let's find out what happened to Jenny."

There was nothing to suggest this was anything other than a suicide attempt, but they'd come at his request.

Brody gloved up too. "Tell us about her."

They knew her basic stats. Sharp needed to fill in the personal information.

Sharp rambled on about Jenny's issues as he scanned the room, trying to see the evidence with fresh eyes. "Jenny keeps a strict routine to her days. She used to be a hoarder, but now she overcompensates with OCD neatness."

Her bed was made. Two cats slept in the center of the comforter. The nightstand and dresser were tidy as always. No clutter in sight. It was as if having one item out of place would put her at risk for free-falling back into chaos.

Sharp wandered to the bathroom doorway. "There were two prescription bottles in the sink, both empty. The paramedics took them to the hospital with her."

Why the sink?

Sharp pulled on a pair of gloves. With the edge of a finger, he opened the medicine cabinet. Personal products stood in neat rows. Brody walked up behind him.

"They're in alphabetical order," Brody said over Sharp's shoulder.

"I told you she has OCD tendencies," Sharp said. "Why would she drop her empty bottles in the sink? The trashcan is right there." He pointed to the wastepaper basket tucked between the vanity and toilet. "And I don't see a cup in here. If she took the pills in the bathroom, she would have needed water."

"Maybe she took the glass to the kitchen," Stella suggested.

"But we found her on the bathroom floor, and if she had time to go to the kitchen and back, why didn't she throw away the pill bottles? For that matter, why didn't she go lie down in bed?"

"She could have returned to the bathroom because she felt sick." Stella opened the three vanity drawers and checked the cabinet under the sink. She crouched and looked through the trash in the can. Frowning, she straightened. "I'm not sure what I'm looking for."

"Me either." Sharp left the bathroom. "But every time I've seen Jenny lose it, she wasn't cognizant enough to plan a suicide. She was incoherent, wild. Her eyes were dazed and glazed. Utterly terrified beyond comprehension. She'd literally crawl into her closet."

"But you don't know what she was like before she hid?" Stella asked. "Or how long the attack lasted before she took action? Or if this time was completely different."

Good point.

"No," he admitted. "But in the early days of her illness, there was a great deal of trial and error with medications. Lately, things have been better."

"What were her triggers?" Brody opened the closet.

Jenny's clothes were sorted by type and color.

They hung in their usual, evenly spaced order. There was no sign that she'd moved anything aside to make a hiding place.

"Once it was the loss of electricity during a winter storm," Sharp said. "The schools closed. Lance came home early and found her in the closet in an almost catatonic state. He was twelve."

Lance had stayed with Sharp until Jenny got out of the hospital a week later. Then Sharp had installed a generator in their house so that would never happen again.

"About a year later, she had another episode when Lance was two hours late coming home from hockey practice. Another parent was giving him a ride. The car broke down, and they had to wait for a tow truck. Jenny had convinced herself that he was dead." She'd called Sharp, and he'd found Lance and brought him home, but by then she'd been too far gone. "She hasn't had an episode like that for a long time. The doctors said that fluctuating hormones had made her medications hard to balance. The last ten years she's been more stable. Not normal, but stable."

"But she was upset by the discovery of her husband's car this week," Brody said.

"Yes." Sharp followed Stella and Brody into the kitchen. "But she was taking the news better than I had expected."

Sharp scanned the kitchen. "That chair pulled

away from the table is very unlike Jenny. She likes everything in its place."

He went to the sink. Empty. Sharp opened the dishwasher, his focus zooming in on two dessert plates standing on the upper rack. "This is wrong."

Stella came to stand next to him. "What?"

Sharp pointed. "Jenny would never put a dish on the top rack, only glasses and mugs."

"Do you think someone else was here?" Brody asked.

"Yes," Sharp said. "That's exactly how it feels."

There were too many little things out of place.

Excitement hummed through Sharp's veins. No matter how upset Jenny was, she would never, ever change the way she loaded the dishwasher.

"Would Jenny let a stranger into her house?" Stella asked.

"I don't think so," Sharp said. "But I can't be sure."

"Does she run her dishwasher every day?" Stella asked.

"Yes," Sharp said. "Without fail."

Stella pointed to the interior. "I see two coffee cups on the top rack."

She lifted a cup and turned it over. Dried coffee residue was stuck to the bottom of the cup.

Sharp peered over her shoulder. "Jenny thoroughly washes her dishes before they go into the machine. Someone else put those cups in here."

"Let's bag these cups as evidence," Stella said.

"Since there are two dessert dishes here as well," Sharp said, "it's possible she had company."

"We'll take the plates as well," Brody said from across the room.

Sharp went to the refrigerator and opened it. There was nothing unusual inside.

Brody went to the garbage can and stepped on the foot pedal. "There are pie scrapings in the trash. Looks like a whole slice."

"Pie is Jenny's favorite food. Why would she cut herself a slice and then throw it away?" Sharp asked. "And for that matter, where is the pie? I don't remember if Lance brought her one this week, but if he did, the box should be on the counter or in the trash."

"No box in the trash," Brody said.

"I'll go check the garbage can outside." Stella took a small flashlight from her jacket pocket and walked out of the kitchen. She returned a few minutes later. "No pie box."

"So where did it go?" Sharp asked.

Brody scanned the kitchen. "Maybe her guest brought it and took it away."

"This whole thing just doesn't feel right." Sharp's wound ached. He stuck his hand in his jacket pocket to give his arm a rest. "Jenny doesn't get visitors."

"Staging a suicide is very unlikely. But then,

so is having two back-to-back suicides related to the same case." Brody's gaze roamed the room before returning to Sharp's face. "But if you're right . . ."

"Then she's in danger," Sharp finished. He knew he was right. He knew Jenny better than anyone else, maybe even better than Lance did. She clung to her routine like a rock climber dug in to handholds, as if letting go of any small part of her routine would send her plummeting into another downward spiral. The more anxious she was, the more she would insist on following her rituals.

"Let's get a forensic team in here," Brody said. "I want the house printed. We'll get the cups, plates, and pie scrapings tested."

"We should also get the doctors to run a full drug panel," Stella said, "in case she was given something other than her own prescriptions."

"I need to get someone into her room to protect her." Sharp froze. "Can you spare an officer?"

Brody shook his head. "There's no way the chief would approve putting a guard on Jenny. We don't have any real evidence this was a crime, and the hospital will be watching her closely in the ICU."

"Not closely enough." Sharp paced across the small room and back. "I wish I could be in two places at once."

"Give me a minute. Let me see what I can

do." Brody took out his phone and stepped into the next room. He came back in two minutes. "Hannah will go right over to the hospital and stay with Jenny."

"Hannah?" Sharp asked. "Is she a cop?"

Brody shook his head. "No. Hannah Barrett is my girlfriend. She's a lawyer, but she had a unique upbringing. I promise you; no one will get past Hannah. She will keep Jenny safe."

"Why would someone try to kill Jenny?" Stella asked.

"There's only one reason I can think of," Sharp said. "It must be related to Victor's disappearance. She must know something."

Chapter Thirty

She wasn't dead.

How could he have miscalculated?

He'd estimated her body weight. He'd counted the pills and crushed them into powder, then mixed some into her coffee and some into her pie. He'd even added a shot of heroin to her pie for good measure. He'd been worried she'd taste the drugs, but she'd eaten every bit. He'd rinsed the damned plate and put it in the dishwasher himself.

She should not have survived.

How was she still alive?

Tugging his baseball cap lower on his forehead, he slipped into the secure ICU wing with another visitor, falling into step beside him. He lowered his chin, hunched his shoulders, and averted his face from the ceiling-mounted cameras.

The ICU hallway bustled with bodies. Gathered around a doorway marked with the number three, nurses and doctors suited up as if they were going to Mars. Full body gowns, face shields, double gloves. An alarm clanged, the light above the door flashed. Doctors shouted orders. More than a dozen medical personnel crowded the fishbowl room.

He kept walking, kept his distance.

Blended in.

The hospital staff was busy trying to stop someone from dying. They paid him no attention. Even the staff not involved with the critical patient were distracted, watching the life-and-death drama unfold.

He continued to room eight, walking right past, barely slowing to look inside, and stopped in front of the next room. He stood in the doorway, pretending to watch a shrunken old man sleep, all alone. The curtains over the glass walls of Jenny Kruger's room were open. He could see inside.

Jenny lay still. Wires and tubes snaked around her. Liquid dripped into an IV line in her arm. A ventilator at the bedside puffed in a steady rhythm, and a bank of monitors kept track of every heartbeat and every breath. Sometimes, medical personnel grew too dependent on those monitors and didn't come into rooms often enough. He'd been hoping to sneak in during a lull in the nurse's attention. He nearly flinched as he spotted a woman sitting beside Jenny's bed, a book open in her lap.

The woman stood, glancing around, as if sensing his scrutiny. She did a quick scan of Jenny's equipment, then sat back down. Her interest in her book seemed to wane. Her gaze strayed to the door, watchful. In jeans and boots, she was tall, with short blonde hair and a sharp face. A slight bulge under her sweater suggested she might be armed. The suburban hospital didn't have metal detectors.

Who was she?

She didn't look exactly like a cop, but she didn't look like she'd take any crap from anybody either.

Shoving his hands into his pockets, he considered his options.

A janitor in green coveralls pushed a large, wheeled trash receptacle down the hallway. The janitor stopped at each doorway, ducked into the room, and emptied the nonmedical waste into his cart. Coughing into his fist to cover his face, he stepped aside as the janitor emptied the old man's trashcan.

His fingers closed around the syringe in his pocket. Heroin. Injected into the muscle, it would take some time to work. He would be long gone before Jenny Kruger began to react to the drug in her system. Her body was already compromised. She'd be dead in a few hours. No one would suspect she'd been given an overdose of heroin while lying in a hospital bed.

His plan had been to wait until no one was watching, then slip in and give her the injection. It would take a minute or two, at best. There were always codes and other emergencies that distracted the ICU staff, like the one up the hall. But the blonde woman's presence screwed up everything.

He could wait until she left the room. She'd have to step out at some point. She must eat.

But that would take time he didn't have.

He had things to do. People to see. Not that any of them were as important as Jenny.

The minute she opened her eyes—and her mouth—his game was over.

He'd kept his secret for twenty-three years. He sure as hell wasn't giving up now.

She appeared to be in some sort of coma. There was a chance she could still die without his interference. He couldn't kill Jenny and the blonde at the same time, not without attracting attention. Especially if the blonde was armed.

An ICU death had to be silent, swift, and stealthy. It needed to look like an unfortunate complication of Jenny's overdose.

Adjusting his baseball cap, he dropped his chin and walked down the hall. He'd have to come back later.

He left the ICU wing the same way he'd come in. In room three, a nurse pulled a sheet over the patient's face. The sense of letdown and failure was palpable in the people slowly trickling from the room. A few had tears in their eyes and on their faces. They consoled each other with hugs and shoulder pats.

They'd cared. They'd tried. The patient had still died.

Maybe he'd get lucky and the same would happen to Jenny.

He pressed the silver square on the wall. The automatic double doors opened with a dramatic swoosh. He'd be back. He had no choice. He had to think of some way to make sure that Jenny Kruger never woke up.

Chapter Thirty-One

Morgan borrowed a pair of sweatpants and a T-shirt and wandered into the kitchen. Lance stood at the counter, cracking eggs into a bowl. He picked up a whisk and began to beat the eggs.

She walked up behind him and wrapped her arms around his waist. "I can't believe you let Sharp throw away your coffee machine."

"He says coffee strains your adrenal glands. Green tea is healthier."

"I'm sure he's right, but green tea does not give my brain the swift kick in the pants that it needs."

Lance had embraced Sharp's crunchy, organic lifestyle. Morgan had not.

He nodded toward the cabinet. "I bought you a surprise."

She opened the cabinet. A single-serve Keurig machine sat on the shelf. Craving caffeine, she imagined a beam of sunlight and a chorus of angels.

"In case I didn't say it enough last night, I love you." She lifted the machine from the shelf.

He leaned over and kissed her. "I love you too. You have no idea how much."

"You showed me with coffee." She put the machine on the counter, set it up, and pressed start. "Way better than diamonds."

"I'll remember that." Lance poured the eggs into the pan.

The doorbell rang.

"I'll get it." Morgan went to the foyer and peeked through the narrow window next to the door. She called over her shoulder as she opened the door, "It's Sharp."

Sharp breezed in the door. "How is he?"

"Hanging in." Morgan led the way back to the kitchen. "How are you feeling?"

"I'm all right." But Sharp moved stiffly and held his arm close to his body.

"Hungry?" Lance asked Sharp. "The eggs are organic."

"No, thanks." Sharp shook his head. "I have good news for you."

Frowning, Lance stirred the eggs. "About what?"

"I asked Stella and Brody to look over your mother's house last night," Sharp said.

"Why?" Lance transferred the eggs to two plates. He handed one to Morgan and picked up a fork.

Sharp leaned on the counter. Dark circles underscored his eyes. He'd clearly been up all night. "Because I don't think she tried to kill herself."

Lance paused, a forkful of eggs halfway to his mouth. "I'm almost afraid to ask why you think that."

Sharp explained what he and Stella and Brody had found the night before. "Someone was in your mother's house yesterday."

Morgan didn't know whether she should be relieved. Was it better if someone had tried to kill Jenny or if she'd done it herself?

"She would never let a stranger in." Lance set down his fork, his food untouched.

"I know," Sharp said. "Brody said he'd try to have the tests expedited. He'll also ask the doctors to run a full drug panel on your mom. How soon did they say until you can talk to her?"

"The critical care doctor estimates about forty-eight hours," Lance said. "I spoke to the nurse earlier this morning. There's been no change in her condition."

"I'm glad she's in ICU," Sharp said. "The regular floors are too accessible."

A chill zipped across Morgan's skin. "She shouldn't be alone."

"I have to stay with her." Lance dumped his plate on the counter and moved toward the kitchen doorway. "If someone tried to kill her, there must be a reason, which means they'll try again when they learn they weren't successful."

Sharp raised a stop hand and stepped in front of Lance, blocking his path. "I've already got your mom covered. Brody's girl, Hannah, is already in the ICU, sitting by your mom's bed."

"Hannah Barrett?" Lance tried to get around him.

"That's Mac's sister," Morgan said. "I would trust her."

"Yes. Brody says Hannah can handle it." Sharp put a hand on Lance's shoulder. "We need to find out who did this. That's the only way your mom is ever going to be safe."

"You're right, but where do we go from here?" Lance rubbed his eyes. "Nothing makes sense."

"But we're clearly making someone nervous," Sharp pointed out. "Let's see if we can poke a few more badgers. I'd like to look at your mother's recent e-mail and phone activity. I can't imagine her just opening the door to a stranger."

"Unless they called her first," Lance finished the thought. "I just gave that information to the sheriff. I'll write her account log-ins down for you."

"I have to get dressed." Morgan turned toward the bedroom. "I wish we could confirm Crystal's death wasn't a suicide. I'd like more evidence than our gut feelings."

"This is when not being a cop makes the job tough." Sharp pushed off the counter and paced in a circle. "The official autopsy results might not be issued for months."

"We need to go through the pictures again and see if anything jumps out at us," Morgan said.

"We've already looked at them." Sharp shook

his head. "What we really need is someone who has seen more homicide scenes than the three of us. My experience is more all-purpose detective. I've only seen a few hangings. But who can we trust with pictures we shouldn't have? Do you think your grandfather would be willing to help?"

"I'm sure he would," Morgan said. "He has much more experience working homicides than all of us put together. I'll call him."

"Call him from the Jeep," Lance said.

"Give me two minutes." Morgan hurried to the bedroom and dressed in the old jeans and T-shirt she'd been wearing the night before. She used the second minute to brush her teeth.

She walked out of the bedroom, and Lance grabbed his keys from the counter. "Let's go."

"I'll meet you at the office," Sharp said. "Your grandfather and I can review the photos."

"I'll call Abigail and see if we can get into the Roadside Motel this morning," Morgan said. "I don't want to wait until tonight."

They drove back to Morgan's house. Grandpa agreed, just as Morgan expected. She changed her clothes while Lance got him ready. Muscling her grandfather in and out of the Jeep was a production, but an hour later, Sharp and Lance maneuvered his wheelchair over the threshold of Sharp Investigations.

"You called Abigail Wright?" Sharp asked.

"Yes," Morgan said. "She said to go ahead to the motel. She called the manager and told him to let us into the storage room. She'll meet us there as soon as she's done with her garden club meeting."

Leaving Grandpa and Sharp at the office, Lance and Morgan headed to the Roadside Motel.

"I expected the place to be sleazy," he said. "But this just doesn't fit the image of a motel owned by a little old lady who plays the organ for her church and runs the local garden club."

The motel was a dirty-looking strip of rooms on a rural stretch of highway. There were no other buildings in sight. No doubt the location afforded privacy for guests who didn't want their patronage made public. The sign at the edge of the parking lot read VACANCY. The office was located on the left end.

"They rent rooms by the hour. We're going to need a shower after this," Morgan said. "At least I'm dressed down."

"I wish we had PPEs to zip into," Lance agreed. "I don't even want to think about what a spray of luminol and a black light would show in any of these rooms."

They went into the office. A young man with a puffy neck beard sat on a high stool behind a counter watching a small TV. He slid off his stool as they walked in. "You need a room?"

"No." Morgan shook her head. "Abigail said

we could look in the storage room. She was going to call ahead."

"Cool." He led them through the office into a back room and unlocked a door into a small windowless chamber. He flipped a wall switch. Overhead lights illuminated a dusty space that smelled of mold. Filing cabinets lined one entire wall. A desk was pushed up against the other.

Morgan pressed a finger under her nose and stifled a sneeze.

"The old records are in the filing cabinets. They aren't organized very well, so good luck." The clerk left them to it.

"I'll start on the left." Morgan tossed her coat over the desk and rolled up the sleeves of her sweater.

Lance pulled on gloves and handed her a pair. Then he started with the cabinet on the right. He slid a file out and opened it, then checked another. He moved through two cabinets, randomly reading dates.

For the next half hour, Morgan worked her way through several drawers. "I found 1994."

She dug through the row of files and came up with a yellowed book. "Here is August."

Lance went to her side and peered over her shoulder as she flipped through the book, only touching the edges of the paper. Depending on conditions, fingerprints could be developed on porous surfaces like paper many years after the prints were deposited. She stopped on August tenth. The entries were written in blue pen.

She hovered her finger over the page. "Here it is."

Lance read the entry. "Mr. Joshua."

"He checked in at seven p.m. Paid for an hour." Morgan slid the registry into a large envelope. She labeled the envelope with her name, the date, and location found, then turned back to the filing cabinet. "Let's see if we can find his registration form."

Thirty minutes later, Lance pulled it from another filing cabinet. "Got it."

They looked at it together. "There's no personal information. No car license plate. He listed his home address as 123 Main Street, Anytown, NY. The phone number is 123-4567."

"But we know he was here."

Morgan went to the window and scanned the parking lot. A red sedan was parked in front of the office. "Abigail is here."

"Then let's go talk to her." Lance closed the file cabinet drawer. "You have the photo of my father to show Abigail?"

"I do. Are you all right?" Morgan asked. He was about to find out if his father had been a prostitute's client.

"Yes." Lance opened the door for her. "Look. I've spent a lifetime putting my dad on a pedestal. He was just a man. What if he wasn't perfect? He did his best to take care of me and my mother. I have to open my eyes if I want to learn the truth."

She gave his hand a squeeze before they went into the main office.

Abigail was on the computer behind the desk. "Did you find what you were looking for?"

"I think so." Morgan pulled the photo of Vic she'd taken from the whiteboard out of her tote.

Next to her, Lance tensed and stepped away to look out the window at the parking lot.

Morgan pointed to Vic. "Do you recognize this man as one of Mary's clients?"

Abigail squinted at the photo. She lifted her reading glasses from the chain around her neck and set them on her nose. "He doesn't look familiar at all."

Morgan could sense Lance's relief from six feet away.

"But I know this man. He was one of Mary's regulars." Abigail leaned closer and tapped the photograph. "This is Mr. Joshua."

Her fingertip landed on Brian Leed's face.

Stunned, Morgan stared at the photo.

Lance crossed the room in two long strides. "Are you sure?"

"Positive," Abigail said. "He drove a black Pontiac Trans Am. He'd try to hide it behind the building, but the engine was loud. When he'd leave the parking lot, gravel would shoot all over."

Morgan caught Lance's eye. He looked as shocked as she felt.

Brian Leed was Mr. Joshua.

"Thank you." Morgan lifted the envelope that held the register. "Is it all right if we take the register with us? We'll bring it back."

Given that the killer was snapping at their heels on this investigation, Morgan didn't want to leave the register behind. She'd rather personally deliver it to the sheriff.

Abigail nodded. "Sure."

Morgan pivoted toward the door, then turned back. The revelation about Brian had almost made her forget about Crystal's ex. "When was the last time you saw Warren Fox?"

Abigail took off her glasses. "He was slinking around here about two weeks ago, bugging Crystal. He wanted to move back in with her."

So much for his statement that he hadn't seen Crystal in months. Was anyone in this case telling the truth?

"Please be careful, Abigail," Morgan said. "Having information regarding this case has proven to be unhealthy for others."

Abigail reached under the counter and brought up a shotgun. "Thank you for your concern, dear. I'll be sure to take extra care."

Morgan followed Lance outside, and they climbed into the Jeep.

Lance tapped a finger on the steering wheel.

"Seems like everyone is lying. Didn't Brian Leed have some kind of sports car under a tarp in his garage?"

"He did," Morgan said. "Brian Leed is Mr. Joshua. He was a regular client of Mary's. He was with her the night your dad disappeared."

Lance put the Jeep into gear. "Which was also the night Mary was probably killed. Time to pay Brian another visit."

Chapter Thirty-Two

Trying to keep his temper in check, Lance parked in front of Brian Leed's house. The garage door was up. In the driveway, Brian was rubbing a chamois over the shining fender of a sleek black Porsche 911.

Lance and Morgan walked up the sidewalk to stand next to the car.

"Hey, Brian." Lance scanned the car. "What year is that?"

"She's a 2007." Brian inspected his work.

"Low miles?" Lance asked.

"Eighty thousand." Brian shook his head. "Cars like this are made to be driven. It's a sin to let them sit in a garage."

Brian knows all about sin . . .

Anger simmered low in Lance's chest. He lifted his gaze to the sky for a few seconds to get himself back under control.

"What brings you back here?" Brian buffed a spot on the side mirror.

"A few follow-up questions," Lance said. "You've always had a black sports car, haven't you?"

"I've had a few, sure." Brian wiped a bead of water from the hood.

"What did you drive back in the day?" Lance

asked. "All I can remember is that it was loud."

"That would have been the Trans Am." Brian whistled. "That was a sweet car. I couldn't afford a Porsche back then, not with kids to raise. And you're right." He grinned. "That engine didn't purr. It roared."

Lance bent over and looked inside the car. "Money was tight?"

"Kids are expensive." Brian turned away from his car, his grin fading and his eyes narrowing as if he just realized Lance's tone wasn't casual. His eyes darted back and forth between Morgan and Lance. Suspicion lit his gaze. "You know what? I have an appointment. Is there a specific reason you're here?"

Your alibi is circling the drain.

"There is." Lance moved forward, resentment curling his hand into a fist. All these years, Brian had been lying.

Morgan put a hand on Lance's arm, as if she could restrain him. "You might not want your neighbors to overhear the questions we're going to ask you."

Brian rocked back on his heels, assessing them. "You're not the police." His tone turned smug. "I don't have to talk to you at all."

"If you'd rather talk to the sheriff, that can be arranged." Lance took his phone from his pocket. "I'll call him right now."

Brian's throat undulated. Muscles on the sides of his jaw shifted, as if he was clenching his jaw. He glanced up the street, then shifted back to his toes and turned toward the open garage. "All right, but I don't have much time."

They followed him into the house. He didn't offer them coffee or a chair. He spun around. "What's this about?"

Lance stopped in the middle of the kitchen. "How much did Mary charge you for sex?"

Brian's face went whiter than the quartz countertop. He backed up a step. "I don't know what you're talking about."

"Does the name Mr. Joshua ring a bell?" Morgan asked.

"No." Brian took another step, stopping when his back hit the wall.

"You were my father's friend." The words scratched Lance's throat on the way out. "And you lied to the police about the night he went missing. What else did you lie about?"

Did Brian kill Mary? What about Crystal? Lance couldn't even process the thought that Brian had tried to kill Jenny.

Brian glared back, and his chest puffed out. "You need to leave."

"It must have been hard to squeeze money for a prostitute into the family budget." Rage crawled around inside Lance's chest, making itself comfortable, as if it was in for the long haul.

"You paid Mary Fox for sex on a regular basis." Morgan stepped closer, her shoulder edging in front of Lance's, clearly concerned he was going to throttle Brian. "The owner of the Roadside Motel identified you as one of Mary's clients. You used the alias Mr. Joshua, and you were with her at the motel the night Vic went missing. I think we can reasonably hypothesize that was the same night Mary was killed."

"Get out." Brian's face reddened.

Lance pressed closer, edging Morgan aside. He wanted to grab Brian by the neck and shake the information out of him. "What else do you know about the night my father disappeared?"

"Nothing." Brian's eyes shuttered.

"What happened that night, Brian?" Morgan's hands wrapped around Lance's bicep.

But her slim fingers had no hope of holding him back. Lance leaned in, until he was right in Brian's face. "Where is my father?"

"I don't know," Brian yelled.

Lance shook off Morgan's hand and grabbed Brian by the front of his polo shirt. "Did you kill Mary?"

"God. No." Brian tried to lean away, but the wall behind him limited his movement. "And that's the truth. I didn't see your father that night. I dropped Mary back at PJ's afterward." Brian didn't try to look away. "That's the last time I saw her. I didn't know she was dead until you told me."

Was that the truth? Brian had already proven himself to be a gifted liar.

Lance eased back, putting some space between them. Brian's sliminess felt contagious. He was supposed to have been Vic's buddy, someone his dad confided in about his troubled marriage, his wife's fragility, his son's vulnerability. Brian had betrayed one of his best friends.

"Twenty-three years ago, someone murdered Mary Fox." Lance barely recognized his own voice. "But since her bones were found, two possible witnesses have died, and someone tried to kill my mother. Where were you last night?"

"I had a meeting and then dinner with a client," Brian said. "I was tied up from five o'clock until ten."

"Would this client back you up?"

"Yes." Brian nodded. "It was a business dinner. There's no reason why he wouldn't. We were at a restaurant. I have a credit card receipt."

He took out his wallet and pulled out a receipt. Lance glanced at it. The time stamp was nine thirty-six. The date was correct, and the dinner was expensive enough to have lasted several hours. If Brian's alibi was legitimate, it would clear him of P. J.'s death and the attempt on Jenny's life.

"I'd be very, very careful," Lance said.

"Someone is making sure anyone who had information about Mary's death can't talk."

Brian looked over Lance's shoulder. "Shit."

Lance spun around. Natalie was standing in the doorway. Had she been there long enough to hear Brian confess to adultery?

"You bastard!" she shouted.

Seems like she had. While Brian's face was dead white, Natalie's cheeks had flushed an angry red.

"Nat . . ." Brian's throat worked as he swallowed hard.

"I always knew you cheated on me, but a hooker?" Natalie took two steps, moving through the doorway into the kitchen. "Who knows what kind of diseases you're carrying."

"It was just her," Brian stammered. "There haven't been—"

"Oh, shut up. Do you think I'm stupid? You've always been a cheater. But you couldn't be discreet about it?" she yelled. "You're even lazy about cheating. How many whores have there been, Brian?"

"No more. I swear. Mary wasn't really a hooker. She was . . ." Brian seemed unable to fill in that blank.

"A fucking hooker!" Natalie screamed. "You paid her for sex. This is simple stuff."

"You never liked sex." Brian's eyes went mean. "Men have needs."

"It wasn't *sex* I didn't like. It was sex with *you*." Natalie gritted her teeth. Her furious gaze darted to Lance and Morgan. Humiliation hovered under her rage and helplessness for a few seconds. Then her attention snapped back to her husband with the force of a mousetrap. "Brian can't get it up unless there's some violence involved. He's into inflicting pain. I'm not into receiving it. Did Mary let you yank her around by the hair? Did she like to be tied up and have you hurt and humiliate her? You realize that none of that dominant shit really compensates for a small penis, right?"

Brian looked like he was going to have a stroke at any second. His mouth opened and closed, gaping as if he couldn't suck in any oxygen.

"You're pathetic," she spat.

Lance eased sideways, distancing himself from Brian and the stream of wrath his wife was pouring on him.

"Natalie." Morgan's voice was soft and soothing. "Where were you the night Lance's father disappeared?"

Lance froze.

Did Natalie kill Mary?

"I was here. *Someone* had to be home with the children." Natalie's focus never left Brian's face.

No one would be able to give her an alibi.

"Did you kill Mary?" Morgan asked in a gentle voice, her tone suggesting an admission

298

would be totally understandable under the circumstances.

Natalie blinked. Her attention flickered to Morgan. "Why would I kill her? It wasn't her fault that my husband is disgusting." A tear rolled down her cheek. She didn't seem to notice. Her attention returned to Brian, fresh fury flickering in her eyes. "I didn't even know it was Mary until just now."

Brian hadn't just betrayed Vic. He'd betrayed his wife too. Everything about him was a lie.

Who was he sleeping with now?

"Natalie, is there anyone who can verify that you were here that night?" Morgan asked.

"No. The kids were all in bed." More angry tears spilled from Natalie's eyes. "But you can believe me when I say that the only person I have ever wanted to kill is Brian." She reached into her purse and pulled out a huge handgun.

Lance took three steps sideways, stepping in front of Morgan, one arm sweeping out to tuck her behind him, the other drawing his sidearm. But the only reason he'd shoot Natalie was if she turned the gun on him and Morgan. Brian was on his own. Life lesson: If you lie down with dogs, you might not get up again.

"Where did you get that?" Brian screeched.

"I bought it, dumbass," she shot back. "It's not hard. You go out late at night. I'm here by myself. You don't like dogs. I wanted it for protection."

"Put it down! You're not going to shoot me." Brian took a step forward, his face smug.

Lance thought she might.

"Dude, I wouldn't do that," Lance said.

Natalie's gun went off. The rooster cookie jar exploded a few feet to Brian's right, sending ceramic shards and cookie bits in all directions.

Brian turned toward an open doorway to his left, but Natalie fired another shot, cutting off his path. Trapped, Brian searched the room for a way out. "You're going to kill me."

"Oh, please. I've been taking lessons for months, not that you would notice. Do you think I'd buy a gun if I didn't know how to shoot it? If I had wanted to hit you, you'd be bleeding." She lowered the gun, pointing it at the floor. "Get out of my house."

"It's not—"

The gun muzzle lifted an inch.

"Brian . . ." Lance warned in a what-are-you-thinking tone.

"You have three seconds." Natalie tapped the toe of her sensible shoe on the kitchen tile. "One."

Brian complained, "But this is my—"

"Two," Natalie said.

Brian slid along the wall. Natalie moved out of his way, keeping several feet of space between them, but she didn't turn her back on him. She spun in a slow circle as he passed her.

The front door slammed. A few seconds later, a powerful engine started up, and they heard the Porsche roar away.

"He'll be back." Natalie stuffed her gun into her purse. "Best purchase I've made in years. I was just never the sort of person who could stand up for myself."

"What changed?" Morgan asked.

"A few months ago, a friend of mine finally talked me into going to a support group. Hearing other women talk about getting out of bad marriages made me think I could do it too. I've been secretly planning to leave him for months. Kicking him out feels even better."

"We should go." Lance nudged Morgan's arm. Someone probably called the police. Gunshots were not normal in this neighborhood.

Natalie walked across the kitchen, pieces of ceramic crunching under her shoes. She pulled a dust pan from the pantry and began to sweep up.

"Are you all right?" Morgan asked.

Natalie paused for a few seconds. "I feel better than I have in years. It makes me angry that I wasted so much of my life. I could have been happy. Why did I put up with that asshole all this time?"

The question sounded rhetorical. Lance kept his mouth shut.

Natalie swept up a pile of red-and-yellow crockery pieces. "I always hated that cookie jar. Brian bought it for me." She nudged the decapitated rooster head with a toe and then ground it under her shoe. "Stupid cock."

Lance didn't wait for the police to show. He took Morgan's elbow and steered her toward the front door. "The last thing I need right now is another run-in with the sheriff's department."

"True," she agreed as they went outside. "You won't be able to solve the case from a cell."

"You asked Natalie about her activity the night my dad disappeared. Do you really think she could have done it?" Lance got behind the wheel. He glanced up and down the street but didn't see any curious neighbors or police.

Morgan slid into the passenger seat. "Now that I think about it, no. I would lean toward a male killer. Strangling a young woman and putting her into the trunk of a car would take physical strength. I doubt I could lift a dead body. Hanging Crystal took some muscle too."

"We'll have to tell Sheriff King about Brian." Lance drove away. "Brian lied in his police statements."

"He lied to Sharp twenty-three years ago," Morgan said. "The statute of limitations would have run out on making a false statement many years ago."

"But admitting he falsified his statement means he has no alibi for Mary's murder."

"And he also admitted that he was with her that

night," Morgan said. "He said he dropped her at PJ's, but who can believe a chronic liar?"

"But if Brian had an alibi for P. J. Hoolihan's death and the attempt on my mother's life, then he probably didn't kill Mary."

Chapter Thirty-Three

Morgan stepped into her office. Her grandfather was studying the whiteboard from his wheelchair. He held one of Sharp's green protein shakes in his hand. Next to him, Sharp pointed at the board with a dry erase marker.

"What have you two been up to?" She touched her grandfather's shoulder on the way to her desk.

"Sharp made me this drink." Her grandfather examined his glass. "It looks disgusting, but the taste isn't bad."

"We've found a couple of new leads, thanks to your grandfather," Sharp said. "Art hasn't forgotten anything about investigating."

Lance came in. Four adults crowded the small room.

Sharp set down his marker. "Tell us what happened with Brian Leed."

By the time Lance finished the story, Sharp and Grandpa were shaking their heads.

Sharp snorted. "Nice to see Karma getting payback. I can't believe he lied all these years."

"I'd keep Brian at the top of the suspect list for Mary's murder." Grandpa drained his glass. "We suspect the current murderer is the same person who killed Mary, but we don't know that for certain. And forgive me if I don't take his word for it that he dropped Mary back off at PJ's that night. Or about anything else. Once a liar, always a liar."

"His word is worthless." Sharp drew a big fat star next to Brian's name.

"Warren Fox is a liar too. He told us he hadn't seen Crystal in months, but Abigail said he'd been hanging around the motel harassing her recently." Lance pointed to the board. "We need to follow up with him."

"Stan needs a follow-up interview too," Morgan said. "If Brian lied about their whereabouts, then so did Stan. Was he covering for a friend, or was there another reason he lied?"

"We have more lies than truth at this point." Lance shook his head.

"Now, what did you two discover today?" Morgan asked Sharp.

"First, your grandfather found indications that Crystal could have been murdered." Sharp opened a laptop on Morgan's desk.

The four gathered around the computer. Sharp pulled up a photo of Crystal. The gruesome image made Morgan flinch, even though she'd seen it before.

Grandpa pointed to the screen, where he'd zoomed in on Crystal's hands. "Look at her fingertips."

"Her fingernail is broken," Morgan said. "And

I see a yellow thread and a little blood under the nail."

"Good eye." Grandpa zoomed in even more. "She pulled at the rope. She has some scratches on her neck too, which *could* indicate that she was struggling against an attacker. *Or* once her brain figured out she was dying, her survival instincts kicked in and she tried to get the rope off her neck. Without a drop long enough to break the neck, it can take a few minutes to die by hanging."

Morgan had a mental image of the woman's body flailing, her feet kicking, knocking over the chair, her fingers tearing at the noose around her neck. "But at that point, she couldn't free herself."

"Right." Grandpa went to another image, a close-up of the rope around her neck. "Do you see the way the rope has shifted on her throat?"

Morgan leaned in and pointed to the screen. "This abrasion?"

Next to her, Lance said, "I would expect the rope to move a little when she stepped off the chair."

"Yes," Grandpa said. "But to me, this looks like it could be two distinct ligature marks, a horizontal line *and* an angled line, with the abrasion connecting them."

And here's where Grandpa's experience with the dead made all the difference.

Morgan sat back. "As if someone stood behind

her and choked her with the rope and *then* strung her up."

"And the noose shifted position when her body weight hit the rope." Lance straightened. "Maybe she didn't commit suicide. Maybe she *was* murdered."

"We can't prove it," Sharp said.

"How do we tell the ME?" Morgan asked. "We aren't supposed to have these photos."

"We don't," Lance said. "Frank won't miss it. He'll have the actual body. The marks will be even clearer to him. Is this enough for the medical examiner to find the death suspicious?"

"Depends what else the autopsy turned up." Grandpa studied the screen for a few seconds.

Without his insight, *they* wouldn't have had this information until the official autopsy was released, which could take months, since the medical examiner would wait for lab results and the tox screen before he would issue an official cause of death. Sheriff King would never share preliminary autopsy results.

"What now?" Lance asked.

Morgan studied the board. "What did Crystal and P. J. and Jenny all know?"

"Crystal and P. J. have a tighter connection: a relationship with Mary. But I can't see how Jenny fits into this." Sharp tapped his closed marker on his chin. "She was home when Vic went missing."

He started a new column for Crystal's death. "Art has some other ideas as well."

"Feels good to be useful." Grandpa closed the laptop and stared at the board. "The more I looked at the file, the more I thought this was never about your dad, Lance. Vic had a wife sinking into mental illness, financial problems, and a ten-year-old he was trying to shield from all of that. He didn't have time to misbehave. He could barely squeeze out an hour or so a week to have a beer with his pals. He couldn't even play baseball anymore. He'd quit his baseball team because he didn't have time for it."

Sharp cradled his injured arm. "Until Mary's bones turned up, we had no other crime to link to Vic's disappearance."

Grandpa nodded. "And since her bones were discovered, you've been looking for a connection between Vic and Mary. It's possible Brian was that link, but what if there is no connection?"

"You think my father was collateral damage?" Lance asked.

Morgan watched Lance. What was he feeling? How could he discuss his father's fate objectively? His face was strained, his mouth grim.

"It's possible that Vic was accidentally swept up in something relating to Mary." Sharp set his marker on the bottom edge of the board. "But Art and I have been researching other events around the time of Vic's disappearance, thinking he and Mary might both have been caught in something entirely unrelated."

"Have you found anything?" Morgan asked.

Sharp paced. "During the week of August 10, 1994, the biggest events were a fatal car accident on the interstate, two burglaries, and three drunks arrested for assault."

"At first, we found nothing unusual about any of these events," Grandpa said. "Until we dug deeper and learned that Lou Ford, one of the drunks, died from a traumatic head injury."

"I don't see how that could possibly be related," Lance said.

"He was arrested during a bar fight on August 10." Sharp paused. "At PJ's."

"Oh." Lance dropped into a chair and rubbed his temples. "Brian said he dropped Mary at PJ's around eight p.m."

Grandpa shuffled some papers. "Lou Ford was arrested at eight thirty."

Morgan tapped a pen on her desk. "If Brian *was* telling the truth, Mary might have seen the fight."

"Then what? How does Mary end up dead?"

"She saw something?" Lance suggested. "Maybe there was more to the bar fight than the cops were told. Who was the arresting officer?"

Sharp consulted his notes. "Deputy Owen Walsh. Owen retired and moved to Florida a few years ago. Ford's family sued the sheriff's department."

"What were the grounds for the lawsuit?" Morgan perked up.

Sharp continued. "The other two men were taken directly to the ER for stitches. Ford appeared to be uninjured, just intoxicated. He was brought to the sheriff's station and put in the holding cell, where he died. The ME found a head injury during the autopsy. The family won a small civil settlement. Ford had a long history of drunk and disorderly conduct. This wasn't his first bar fight. Multiple witnesses stated he was the aggressor. The jury was unsympathetic. They found for the plaintiff, but the settlement was too small to matter. No charges were ever filed on Deputy Walsh, though the department changed several policies as a result of the case."

"We need to talk to Owen Walsh." Lance said.

Sharp nodded. "I already left a message on his cell phone. Ford was fifty-five years old and unmarried when he died. His sister brought the lawsuit against the sheriff's department. I'm trying to track her down. She moved out of the area. I'll keep following up with Owen Walsh and Ford's sister."

"This case keeps getting more complicated," Morgan said.

"But wait. There's more," Sharp added. "I also found out that the ADA plea bargained Ricky

Jackson's case. He has to complete a drug rehab program."

"That the kid who was robbing Crystal's house while her body hung dead in her bedroom?" Grandpa asked.

"That's the one." Lance cracked his shoulder. "We should talk to Mr. Jackson again. When we interviewed him, we didn't know Warren might have molested Mary when she was a child."

Grandpa slumped in his chair. Despite the brighter look in his eyes, his shoulders sagged.

She put her hand on his shoulder. "Are you all right?"

"I'm fine." He patted her hand.

"Lance and I will take you home," she said, worried.

Grandpa didn't argue, which meant he was truly exhausted.

"Morgan and I will pay Warren another visit." Lance stood and rolled his neck.

"I didn't get to review these." Grandpa held up a stack of papers. "Can I take them home with me?"

"I'll make you copies." Sharp took the pages and carried them out of the room. He brought them back a few minutes later and put them in a folder for Grandpa. "Thanks again for your help, Art."

Sharp didn't look healthy either. His face was drawn and pale, and he moved with the stiff gait of an old man. Morgan was running on coffee, and Lance had to be feeling the effects of too little sleep and too much stress.

But they had no time for a break. The killer was ahead of them at every step of the investigation.

Chapter Thirty-Four

Lance carried the bag of groceries he and Morgan had picked up for Elijah Jackson to the old man's doorstep. The afternoon had turned gray and cold. Shivering next to him, Morgan knocked.

The old man opened the door and motioned them in. "Come in."

Mr. Jackson's eyes misted as Lance brought the groceries inside. "I don't know how to thank you."

"You don't have to." Lance followed him down the hall into the kitchen and set the bag on the counter. A small fire smoldered in the next room.

Morgan unbuttoned her coat, started to take it off, then slipped it back onto her shoulders.

Lance took off his leather jacket and hung it on the back of a chair. The inside of the house wasn't much warmer than outside. Did the old man have heat except for the fireplace? Lance walked to the window. A small pile of wood was stacked beside the rear porch. A very small pile.

Mr. Jackson smiled as he lifted a sack of coffee from the bag, then unloaded the rest of the food. "Pie! I haven't had pie in ages. Sit down. I'll make a pot of coffee."

Lance had voted to stick to staples. Morgan had insisted coffee and pie *were* staples.

"Thank you, but we can't stay," Morgan said. "We just wanted to ask you a few quick questions."

"Ask me anything you want. I'm going to make coffee. I've been out for a month." The old man's mood seemed lighter and his posture straighter as he filled the coffee machine. He opened an upper cabinet.

"We heard Ricky was offered an alternative sentence of drug rehabilitation," Morgan said. "That's good, right?"

Mr. Jackson paused, leaning both hands on the counter. "It would be, if they helped get him into a program. And if I could afford to pay. Ricky doesn't have insurance, and every center I called today is booked for months. He has to stay in jail until he gets into a program. I know he can't be trusted out on his own, but someone at church told me he can get heroin in jail. I never imagined such a thing. I'd love to get him help. I lost my son to drugs. I'd do anything to get my grandson back."

"There are centers that charge on a sliding scale based on how much you can afford," Morgan said. "You should be able to do an online search. That should speed things up, though he'll probably have to wait his turn. Space is limited."

"I don't have a computer." Mr. Jackson took a mug from the cabinet. "I suppose I could go down to the library and use the one there."

"I can help you with that," Morgan volunteered. As always.

He smiled at her. "You would do that?"

She nodded. "I could look up the information faster than you could drive to the library."

"You're a doll," Mr. Jackson said.

Lance moved the conversation along. He had no doubt Morgan would be semiadopting Mr. Jackson, like she did everyone else. "We wanted to ask you about Crystal's husband."

"Warren?" Mr. Jackson's face pinched. "He's useless."

"Have you seen him around Crystal's house lately?" Lance asked.

Mr. Jackson poured a mug of coffee and inhaled over the cup. "Warren is always hanging around. I assumed they were getting back together."

"Did you see him the day Crystal died?" Lance asked.

"No, but he was there last Sunday. I saw his truck at her house on my way home from church." Mr. Jackson sipped, his eyes closing in satisfaction.

"Did you ever see Warren threaten Crystal?" Morgan asked.

Mr. Jackson set down his mug. "No, I didn't spend any time with either one of them. I'm sorry. I really can't tell you anything else. Are you sure you don't want pie?"

"No, we need to leave, but thank you for your help." Lance put on his jacket. "We'll see ourselves out."

Morgan followed Lance, then turned back. "One more question. Did you ever suspect Warren molested Mary when she was a child?"

Mr. Jackson frowned. "No, but I wouldn't put it past him."

"Thank you again," Morgan said.

They left Mr. Jackson cutting a slice of pie, almost giddy.

"I told you coffee and pie were important," Morgan said, sliding into the passenger seat of the Jeep. "That poor man has very few pleasures in life."

Lance drove toward the recycling center. He glanced at the clock. Two p.m. "We can still catch Warren at work. Once he gets home, he'll never open his door to us."

Lance drove to the recycling center and parked the Jeep. He climbed out of the vehicle.

Morgan walked around the rear of the SUV and fell into step beside him. "Let's stick together this time."

"I don't think Warren will mess with you again." But Lance would stay close, just in case. There was too much going on, too many people lying, too many possible motives and victims.

They entered the small recycling office building. Instead of Warren Fox, a black-haired man sat at a beat-up desk watching something on his smart phone.

Lance stopped in front of the desk. "We were looking for Warren."

"He called in sick," the black-haired man said without taking his eyes off his screen.

"Thanks." Morgan led the way out of the building and climbed into the Jeep.

Lance slid behind the wheel. "Do we have Warren's home address?"

"Yes."

While Morgan dug out the address and plugged it into her phone maps app, Lance called the hospital and checked on his mother's condition. Nothing had changed.

As he started the engine, his phone rang. "It's Sharp."

He answered the call.

Sharp didn't wait for a greeting. "Sheriff King wants to see us at the sheriff's station. He actually threatened to arrest us if we're not there in thirty minutes."

"I'm on my way," Lance said. "I'll bring the lawyer."

"Please do. I believe we're going to need her."

Chapter Thirty-Five

In the conference room at the sheriff's station, Morgan kept a hand on Lance's arm. On her other side, Sharp held his injured arm close and shifted in his chair as if he couldn't get comfortable.

"I'm trying to solve a murder. Why are you competing with me?" The sheriff paced the narrow space between the table and the wall. "Especially you." He pointed at Lance. "Don't you want to know what happened to your father?"

"Of course we do," Morgan answered, afraid of what Lance might say.

"I went to see Abigail Wright at the Roadside Motel. I asked her for the motel registry for August 10, 1994. Guess what she told me? That you already took it!" The sheriff turned and flattened both hands on the conference table. "This is an active murder case. I should arrest all three of you for impeding an investigation."

Morgan met his gaze without blinking. "But we might all be more successful if we worked together rather than running parallel investigations."

"You took evidence from the motel." The sheriff's words were measured, as if he was working to keep his voice level.

"And we fully intended to turn it over to

you," Morgan said, producing the large paper envelope from her tote. "Inside you'll find both the hotel registry and the registration form for *Mr. Joshua*."

"Why did you take it?" King asked.

"At the rate potential witnesses are dying, we thought the registry might not be safe at the motel," Morgan said.

The sheriff snorted. He didn't believe her.

"We think Crystal Fox was murdered," Sharp said.

"The preliminary autopsy results are inconclusive." The sheriff lowered his bulk into his chair and dragged a yellow legal pad in front of him.

Sharp folded his hands. "The Scarlet Falls PD is investigating Jenny Kruger's supposed suicide attempt as a potential attempted murder."

"I heard about her overdose." Sheriff King's gaze shifted to Lance. "How is your mother?"

Lance lifted a shoulder. "Her condition is still critical."

"I'm sorry to hear that." The sheriff frowned, picked up a pencil, and made a note on his legal pad. "She seems like a nice lady."

Sharp outlined the inconsistencies at Jenny's house. "Don't you think it's a little coincidental to have two suicides in the same number of days, both associated with Mary Fox's case? And what about P. J. Hoolihan and his wife? P. J. knew

Mary. Was P. J. tending the bar on the night of August 10? Do you really think they died in a bungled burglary?"

"I never said I did." The sheriff leaned closer to the table, slid the register out of the envelope, and opened it. "Save me some time. What am I looking for?"

"Brian Leed was Mary's client and he went by the name Mr. Joshua," Morgan said. "Mr. Joshua was with Mary on August 10 at the motel."

The sheriff snapped his pencil in half.

"Brian Leed lied about his whereabouts the night Vic disappeared," Morgan said. "He wasn't with Stan. He was with Mary. Brian told us that he dropped Mary off at PJ's around eight p.m."

"Hell." The sheriff scribbled on his note pad with the broken pencil stub. "Is anyone telling the truth?"

"We also learned there was a bar fight on that night." Sharp jerked a thumb toward the door. "And that a man died in the holding cell."

The sheriff held up a hand. "Wait. Now you think a bar fight is related to Mary's murder?"

"We're exploring all options," Morgan said. "We don't have any evidence to link the bar fight to Mary, other than it happened at PJ's the night Vic went missing, and she was likely there at the time."

"I'll look into it." The sheriff wrote a note and circled it. Then laid his pencil down.

"We'd like a copy of those three arrest reports from the bar fight," Sharp said.

"No!" The sheriff slammed a hand down on the table. The pencil halves jumped. "Stay away from this case. Do you remember what happened the last time you stuck your noses in a dangerous situation?" King paused for two heartbeats. "I had to come in and save your butts."

The sheriff *had* come to Morgan and Lance's rescue the previous month.

King stood and swept a hand toward the door. "Get out of my station before I find some reason to arrest all three of you."

Lance opened his mouth. Morgan shushed him with a hand on his shoulder.

"One more thing." Morgan extended an olive branch. She didn't think the sheriff would really arrest them. He was just frustrated. They had beat him to several important clues. "Warren Fox's truck was at Crystal's house the Sunday before she died."

"I know that. I talked to her neighbor. Do you think I'm sitting on my hands all day? I'm investigating the case." The sheriff's eyes were dark, and Morgan sensed his patience was depleted.

Time to go.

If they weren't under arrest, technically the sheriff couldn't hold them or make them answer questions, but they did have to respect his authority. This was all a balancing act.

"Please call us if you have any other questions," Morgan said. "We want to cooperate fully with your investigation. Like I said before, we could accomplish much more as a team."

He glared.

"We gave you Brian," she reminded him.

Sheriff King looked only slightly less furious as they filed out of the conference room. Morgan wasted no time herding Lance and Sharp out the door before either one of them said anything to set the sheriff off again.

They walked across the parking lot toward their vehicles. The temperature was dropping as the sun set.

Sharp paused next to his Prius. "If the sheriff is not going to give us those arrest records, we need access to the police blotter. Nowadays, many police departments post their arrests online. But years ago, the *Randolph County Times* used to publish police activity on a weekly basis. They used to call it 'The Weekly Round Up.' "

"I don't suppose those archives are online?" Morgan shivered and stuck her hands in her pockets.

"No." Sharp shook his head. "I suspect I'll have to dig through the old microfiche files in the library basement."

Morgan stamped her feet. "I didn't even know microfiche still existed."

"It does here. The basement of the library is

circa 1979. Randolph County doesn't have the funds to tackle old records." Sharp stretched his arm, as if it was stiff. "They're busy trying to stay afloat. I'll let you know what I find." He glanced at his phone. "My battery is dead again. I need to pick up a new phone."

"Any luck with the deputy who arrested Ford . . . Owen Walsh?" Morgan asked.

"No. I left another message," Sharp said. "He hasn't returned my calls. I'm going to call an associate in Florida and ask him to interview Walsh. It's harder to ignore someone who is standing on your doorstep. I'll let you know if I hear from him. I'm meeting the boys at The Pub for an early dinner. Maybe one of them remembers the case."

The boys were all over fifty. Sharp met regularly with his retired or almost-retired local law enforcement buddies.

"Do you still want to look for Warren Fox?" Lance asked Morgan.

"Yes." Morgan hugged her coat tighter around her body, then pulled up her map app. Her phone calculated new directions from their current location. "I don't like not knowing where Warren is."

"Or what he's doing."

Morgan's phone rang in her hand. "It's Stella." She answered the call.

Stella sounded rushed. "I just got off the phone

with the Redhaven police." Redhaven was a small town about fifteen miles from Scarlet Falls. "They arrested Tyler Green yesterday around noon for violating a restraining order against his ex."

Morgan froze. "Did you say noon?"

"Yes." Stella's voice darkened. "Tyler Green didn't send you that package yesterday."

A nasty wind nipped at Morgan's exposed face. "Shit."

"You be careful," Stella said.

"I will." Morgan ended the call. A chill slid through her bones, and she fastened the top button of her coat. "Did you hear Stella?"

Lance's face was set. "Yes."

Morgan shoved her hands into her coat pockets. "If Tyler isn't my stalker, then who is it?"

"I can think of one other person who is both angry and petty." Lance crossed his arms.

A scene in the courthouse popped into her mind. Morgan hunched against the wind. "Esposito?"

"He tried to bully you," Sharp said.

He had.

"But he's the ADA . . ." Morgan had a hard time believing the new prosecutor would be *that* angry she'd outmaneuvered him.

"He looks like the type who doesn't like to lose," Lance pointed out.

Sharp added, "He didn't care about guilt or innocence, only about winning his case."

"He's a good candidate," Morgan agreed.

"One more thing. Esposito was handling Tyler's case," Lance said. "Do you think it's possible he reduced the assault charges against Tyler out of spite? Maybe that was part of a grand plan to harass and intimidate you."

"Ninety percent of cases are plea bargained. We can't prove Esposito had any motive in letting Tyler out beyond getting the case cleared." But it made perfect sense. Unfortunately, there wasn't anything she could do about it. Criminal charges were at the discretion of the prosecutor's office. "Look, we have to put my stalker on the back burner for now. We need to focus on figuring out who's killing people."

Chapter Thirty-Six

If at first you don't succeed, try and try again.

But also, try harder.

And try smarter.

He pulled the green cap lower on his forehead. His gloved fingers gripped the rolling trashcan as he pushed it from room to room. He kept his chin down and made sure the security badge hanging from his belt loop faced backward. He looked nothing like the Hispanic janitor whose ID he'd stolen. With his attention on his task, his face was turned away from the surveillance cameras overhead.

The hallways were quiet. No one even glanced at him. Cleaning staff was practically invisible. The nurse covering Jenny Kruger's room and the one next to it was behind the counter talking on the landline.

He walked past Jenny Kruger's room. The blonde was still there. Didn't she need to sleep at some point? He wasn't getting into Jenny's room. He needed another plan. He spied a supply cart parked just outside her door. A label on the front of the cart was marked with Jenny's room number. And on top rested two large IV bags. Saline, he guessed from the size and the fact that they were out in the open. Medication was kept under lock and key.

If he could just get to the front of Jenny's room without anyone noticing him, he could slip the heroin into her saline. The extra time it would take for the drug to enter her system would give him the opportunity to slip away before any alarms were raised.

The old man still occupied the next room. He went to the bedside. Slipping syringe number one from his pocket, he slid it into the IV port and pushed the plunger. He was no medical professional, but an air bubble was the least of this old man's problems. A few seconds later, he dumped the old man's trash in his rolling can and left the room with unhurried strides.

Mindful of the security cameras, he adjusted his posture accordingly to keep his face averted. He'd worn some padding under the baggy coveralls to disguise his body shape. No one gave him a second glance as he moved from room to room.

He was three rooms down the hall when alarms sounded. A minute later, a Code Blue blared over the speaker. Footsteps rushed. He poked his head into the hallway to find that everyone else was doing the same. Scrub-clad bodies crowded the old man's room, including the shared nurse. Staff hustled in and out of the room.

Even the staff not involved with the code gravitated to the drama. He moved closer, stopping just before Jenny Kruger's doorway to stand behind two short nurses. From here, he could see over their heads into the old man's room. Someone climbed onto the bed to deliver chest compressions. Another readied a defibrillator. Injections were given. A man in blue scrubs watched the monitors and shouted orders. Well-organized chaos ensued.

The crowd's mood shifted as efforts to revive the old man failed.

He glanced at the supply cart by Jenny's door. The bags of IV saline still sat on the top shelf. Keeping his hands low, he eased sideways, pulled a second syringe from his pocket, and injected it into the self-healing orange port on the bag. Because the heroin would be diluted, he added another shot. That should do it. On top of everything else in Jennifer Kruger's body, that should stop her heart.

People began to drift away from the old man's room, disappointment emanating from their postures and gestures. He backed away from the cart and retreated down the hall before the rest of the crowd dissipated. He pushed his trash can to the end of the hall and abandoned it in a utility room before hitting the silver square on the wall and exiting the ICU.

The timing was a bit tricky. He didn't know when the saline would be administered or how long it would take to drip into Jenny Kruger's veins, but it didn't matter. Before the night was over, Jenny would be dead.

Chapter Thirty-Seven

Morgan warmed her hands in front of the dashboard heat vents. The temperature was dropping as the light waned.

Lance followed directions to a small brick apartment building not far from the Grey's Hollow train station. The building was divided into eight apartments. Four up and four down. Warren lived in a downstairs end unit. Morgan and Lance got out of the Jeep, crossed the sidewalk, and walked up the concrete path. Lance knocked on his front door. No one answered. Morgan wasn't surprised.

Turning, she scanned the parking area in front of the building. "I don't see his truck."

Even if Warren were home, would he answer the door to them?

Stepping into the grass, Morgan cupped her hand over her eyes and tried to peer through the front window.

"See anything?" Lance asked.

"No, the curtains are drawn." She stepped back onto the path.

Lance walked around the unit, but blinds covered the windows. At the front window, he angled off and tried to look through the half-inch gap between the curtains. "Can't see anything."

A middle-aged man wearing blue coveralls came out of the apartment next door. Frowning, he raised a suspicious eyebrow at Lance.

"Hello." Morgan walked toward him, smiling while trying to look innocent.

The man didn't look convinced. "Can I help you?"

Morgan turned up the wattage of her smile and reached into her pocket for a business card. "We're looking for Warren Fox—"

"We're private investigators." Lance put a hand on her arm, keeping it in her pocket. "Warren might have inherited some money. Have you seen him?"

"Sorry." The neighbor relaxed and shook his head. "I wish I could help, but I haven't seen Warren today. You should try the county recycling center. I don't know what time he gets off, but that's where he works."

"Do you know Warren well?" Morgan asked.

"No." His curt tone implied that was by choice.

"Do you have any idea where else he might be?" Lance asked. "He's going to want to talk to us."

The neighbor adjusted the zipper of his coveralls. "You could try the Black Tavern. That's his watering hole. You'll have to excuse me. I have to get to work." He turned and walked toward a sedan parked in front of the building.

"Thank you," Morgan called after him.

They went back to the Jeep.

"You lied to him." Morgan closed her door with more force than necessary. "What if he tells the sheriff?"

"I said *might,*" Lance clarified. "And that's why we didn't give him a business card or our names."

Morgan sighed. "The sheriff will know it was us. This is the kind of behavior that puts you on Sheriff King's bad side."

"He's impossible."

Morgan was sure the sheriff felt the same way about Lance.

"I know you're frustrated, but we have to pick our battles," she said. "Like it or not, he is the law. There are some fights we just can't win. It's better to willingly give on some issues, makes you look cooperative."

"I know. You're right, but people are dying." Frustration sharpened Lance's words. "My mother almost died, and we still have no idea what happened to my father."

"Why don't we go see your mother now?" Morgan suggested.

He consulted the map on his smart phone. "We'll stop at the Black Tavern first. It's just up the road, and the hospital is in the other direction."

He backed away from the curb. The tavern was only a half mile from the apartment. Warren could stumble home blind drunk. Remembering his breath on her face, Morgan thought the location was probably convenient for him.

Lance parked, and they went inside. Clearly a neighborhood dive, the tavern was small, holding barely a dozen booths and the same number of stools at a worn bar. The air smelled like sour beer and lifelong disappointment. A chalkboard on the wall announced beer on tap was one dollar during happy hour. At five thirty, a handful of patrons took advantage of the special. They stared at a hockey game playing on a wall-mounted flat screen. Several slumped, already appearing intoxicated though happy hour had just begun.

Two men on the end of the bar eyeballed Morgan. Lance changed sides, putting his body between her and the men. The gesture was unnecessary but appreciated.

They went up to the bar. Grit on the floor crunched under Morgan's feet.

Below the short sleeves of his black T-shirt, the bartender sported two full sleeves of tattoos. "What can I get you?" he asked.

Morgan leaned across the bar. "We're looking for Warren Fox."

The bartender barely glanced at her.

Lance rested his forearms on the bar. In a low voice, he said, "Warren might have inherited some money."

The bartender scratched a red bump on a tattoo of a robot on his wrist. There were more marks on the insides of his arms. *Addict.* A friendly smile wasn't going to influence him. Addicts only cared about one thing, money to buy their next hit.

Lance slipped a folded twenty-dollar bill from his pocket and set it on the bar. He held a second between his forefingers. *That* got the bartender's attention. He pocketed the money and gave Lance his full attention. "I'd like to help, but I haven't seen Warren today."

"How often does he usually come in?" Lance asked.

"Almost every night." The bartender pointed to the other end of the bar. "He's usually on that stool by four thirty."

Warren hadn't been at work, and he wasn't at his usual hangout. Was he guilty, in danger, or simply drunk somewhere other than the bar?

"When was the last time you saw him?" Lance asked.

"Come to think of it, Warren wasn't here last night either." The bartender scratched his belly.

His itchiness felt contagious. Morgan eased back a few inches.

"Maybe he decided to drink at home." The bartender shrugged. "Or he could be broke. That slut he was married to was after his paycheck. Maybe she got some of it."

Lance passed the second bill over the bar. "Do you know anywhere else Warren might hang out?"

"Sorry." The bartender took the cash. "As far as I know, he's at work, here, or home."

"Thanks." Lance steered Morgan toward the other patrons, keeping her tucked just slightly behind his left arm. He took another twenty from his pocket. "Does anyone here know where Warren Fox might be?"

Morgan had little doubt that the other patrons had overheard Lance's conversation with the bartender.

"You could try his wife's place." An old drunk swayed on the closest stool. "He was trying to get back with her. Hated the bitch, but loved her too, if you know what I mean."

Not really.

"Anyone have any better information?" Lance waved the folded bill.

The other men sighed and turned back to their beers.

Lance handed the old man the twenty, then steered Morgan out of the bar. The fresh air was cold but welcome.

"Warren hasn't been in the bar in two nights." Morgan reached into her tote and pulled out a small bottle of hand sanitizer. She offered it to him.

He shook his head. "You didn't touch any-thing."

"I still feel dirty." She rubbed a spot of gel between her hands. He was right, but the sting of Purell in her nose made her feel cleaner. "Nasty place. The bartender is an addict."

Lance nodded. "Which is why he gave us info on Warren for forty bucks without a hint of guilt."

They got into the Jeep.

"We should call the sheriff." Morgan smoothed her coat and fastened her seat belt. "Given the history of this investigation, Warren could be dead inside his apartment."

"As much as it pains me to admit it, I agree," Lance said. "You call him."

Morgan sighed and made the call. She covered the speaker with her fingers. "No answer." She left a message for him to call her about the case.

"That works perfectly. We did our duty and didn't have to deal with the sheriff."

"I still feel guilty." Morgan lowered her phone to her thigh. "Should we call 911?"

Lance steered the Jeep onto the on-ramp. "I suppose we can't let ourselves in?"

"No. Definitely not." Morgan made the call, giving the dispatcher her name and asking for a welfare check at Warren Fox's address. "They won't rush a welfare check."

"If he's dead, an hour or two won't make any difference."

The hospital was a thirty-minute drive from the Black Tavern. It was nearly seven o'clock by the time Lance parked in the lot. "I'm sorry. We should have stopped for food."

"I'm fine." Morgan pulled two candy bars from her tote and offered him one.

He shook his head. "I'm not hungry."

She stashed one back in her bag and ate the other as they walked across the parking lot. They went through the automatic doors, collected visitor badges at the front desk, and took the elevator to the third floor. They walked down the hall toward the ICU. A lab tech was exiting, and they slipped in while the doors were still open.

Morgan picked up on a somber energy the minute they walked into the ward. Staff talked in hushed, subdued voices. Lance's steps quickened. He felt it too. Morgan took his hand in a strong grip.

Someone had died.

Chapter Thirty-Eight

Lance could feel the sorrow, as palpable as a drop in room temperature.

They hadn't called him.

It can't be Mom.

He paused just before he reached his mother's doorway, dread weighing his steps like his boots were filled with concrete. He and his mother had fought her mental illness for decades. Her demons had taken up permanent residence. But every time they'd advanced, she'd rallied and driven them back. Her whole life had been one battle after another. She won some and lost others. But overall, she'd been winning the war. Inch by inch, she'd chipped away at their advantage. She'd finally made real gains, only to fall victim to someone's sick game.

As he pushed forward for the last two strides, Morgan's grip on his hand tightened.

But everything in the room looked the same. His mother slept. The ventilator hissed. The heart monitor beeped in a steady rhythm.

It's not her.

When he exhaled, he was light-headed for a few seconds.

In the chair near the bed, Hannah Barrett looked up from her book. Her face was grim, her eyes sad. Lance glanced into the next room. The sheet had been pulled up over the patient's head. Two women in scrubs were unplugging equipment and tubes, coiling the untethered ends onto the bed.

The old man was dead.

Equal amounts of relief and guilt flooded Lance. The old man was someone's father or grandfather. Someone would be brokenhearted at the news.

Hand in hand with Morgan, he went into his mother's room. The nurse bustled in and hung a new IV bag. Her eyes and nose were red from crying.

"How is she?" Lance asked.

"She's hanging in there." She sniffed, then gave him an update on her vital signs. "Her kidney function showed some improvement today." She flushed the IV port, attached the new bag of fluids, and pressed buttons on the infusion pump.

The bed and medical equipment filled one half of the large room. A supply and computer station was built into the other. The wall that edged the hallway was made of glass, with a curtain that could be drawn across if needed.

The nurse scanned the monitors and then went to the computer and typed. "Let me know if you need anything." She left the room.

Hannah stood and greeted them.

"I can't thank you enough for being here," Lance said.

"I don't mind." Hannah brushed a lock of short, spiky blonde hair off her face. "Do you have any idea who might have done this to her?"

"We have a few solid suspects." *But not solid enough,* thought Lance. "You've been here all day?"

Hannah nodded. "Brody will be here soon to relieve me for the evening, and Stella said she'd take the night shift. One of us will be with her all the time."

"I'm grateful," he said.

"No one can be in two places at once." Hannah moved toward the door. "Since you're here, I'm going to stretch my legs and grab a cup of tea."

Morgan squeezed his hand. "Do you want a few minutes alone with her?"

Lance nodded. Morgan and Hannah left the room.

He went to the bedside and took his mother's hand. Her fingers were freezing. He wrapped his hand around hers to warm it. The doctors thought she would survive, but would she? And if she did, what kind of permanent damage had her body sustained?

The nurse seemed satisfied with her progress, but Lance didn't see any improvement. His mother's face was lifeless, her skin colorless, almost blue tinted. Her lips had no color at all. In fact, she seemed to be fading as he watched.

One of the machines beside the bed began to

beep. The nurse appeared in the doorway, her mouth turned down as she watched the monitors. An alarm sounded.

Lance startled. Sweat broke between his shoulder blades, and his stomach flipped over. "What's wrong?"

"Her heart rate is decreasing," the nurse said. She pressed a button and the blood pressure cuff inflated.

A doctor rushed into the room.

"Heart rate and blood pressure are down." The nurse rattled off numbers and readings. "Her vitals were all normal ten minutes ago."

More nurses hurried into the room. Someone nudged Lance out of the way. He stepped sideways, toward the doorway.

"Fingernails are blue." The doctor lifted his mother's eyelids with his thumb. "Her pupils are constricted." He went to the computer and scrolled. "If she wasn't in the ICU, I'd say she is presenting as a new opioid overdose. Her original drug panel came back positive for opioids."

They'd been right.

"Someone poisoned her," Lance said. "This wasn't a suicide attempt."

Could someone have sneaked into the ICU and given his mother a drug?

"Was anyone else in this room?" Lance scanned the room, then the doorway. People rushed past. Medical personnel wore IDs. Visitors checked in at the desk in the lobby and received ID badges. But how hard would it be to sneak into the hospital? This was not the city. The community hospital gave excellent care, but they didn't even have metal detectors. But even if someone did manage to get into the ward, Hannah said she'd been with his mother the entire day. That's the whole reason she was here. Had she gone out for coffee or to use the restroom?

The doctor shot a look at him. "Are you suggesting . . ."

"Someone tried to kill her once," Lance said. "I don't know how they could have gained access to her here, but this is a busy place."

More medical personnel crowded around the bed.

"Could a medication have been swapped?" Lance moved farther out of the way, until his shoulder hit the glass wall next to the door.

"We have strict dispensing protocols." The doctor watched the monitors while he talked to Lance. "Medications are checked and double-checked."

"Her heart rate is still falling," someone called out.

"We'll try naloxone." The doctor called out.

Lance glanced over his shoulder. On the other side of the glass, two bags of saline lay on a cart, along with other supplies. In the open. Unattended.

He stepped forward. "The nurse changed her IV fluid bag five minutes before this happened."

The doctor unplugged the IV. "Get a fresh bag of saline."

"Not one that was sitting in the hallway," Lance shouted as the nurse bolted for the door. He watched, helpless, as the ICU staff worked. Bodies blocked the view of his mother.

"Keep that bag," Lance called to the nurse moving the bag off the hook. "It could be evidence."

She set it aside.

A nurse administered an injection through the IV line. Naloxone, also known as Narcan, blocked the effects of opioids and reversed an overdose. When he'd been a patrol officer, Lance had carried a dose in his vehicle. Heroin addiction and overdoses had drastically increased over the past decade. Narcan acted fast, sending a true addict into almost immediate withdrawal. If his mother had been given opioids, the antidote would work within minutes.

If Lance was wrong, then Narcan would have no impact on her condition. But she would continue to deteriorate, and they would have lost valuable time.

Come on.

Lance's heartbeat echoed in his ears. Sweat dripped down his back, and the fists at his sides went clammy. Everything inside him curled up into a tight ball, waiting. Cold slid over him like a blanket, as if his emotions were preparing for the worst.

Please.

He was so numb, so focused, he didn't see Morgan and Hannah in the hallway.

"What happened?" Morgan grabbed his arm.

But he couldn't take his eyes off the heart monitor.

Tick tock.

"Her heart rate is up," the doctor said. "And climbing."

The ICU staff drew a collective breath. In ten minutes, her pulse and blood pressure had returned to normal levels.

Lance let out the air he'd been holding in his lungs.

Morgan slipped her arm around his waist. "Are you all right?"

"Yes." He rubbed his face. It was wet. He dried it with the heels of his hands.

"Come into the hall." Morgan steered him out of the room. "What happened?"

He explained.

"I didn't even step out of the room for coffee," Hannah said. "The nurses brought me food. No one was in her room except the nurse and doctors, and only the nurse administered medication." Her eyes narrowed. "I watched."

"It had to be the saline." Lance dragged in air,

his lungs shaky. He felt like he'd lived three days in the last fifteen minutes. "Tampered with out in the hall. I need to call Stella or Brody. They can pull the hospital surveillance tapes." He glanced through the glass wall. Nurses and doctors still surrounded his mother.

"I'll call Brody," Hannah said. Phone in hand, she walked down the hallway.

The doctor emerged from the room. "She seems to be stable."

"How much of a setback will this be for my mother?" Lance asked. She'd already been at risk for organ damage.

"We can't say just yet." The doctor yanked his gloves off. "I don't know how this could have happened."

A woman walked by, her hand over her face. Sobbing, she entered the room next to his mother's.

The old man.

"Did you have a code earlier?" Lance asked.

The doctor followed his gaze. "Yes. Not long ago. But he'd been sick for a long time. He'd been here for weeks. His death was not a shock."

"But codes are chaotic," Lance said.

"They are," the doctor said turning back toward Jenny. "Excuse me." He went back into her room and checked her vital signs on the monitors again.

Morgan's face went grim. "A code would provide a convenient distraction."

"They should check the old man for opioids," Lance said. "In case he was murdered."

Hannah returned. "Stella is coming with Brody. They're going to request a police guard for your mother."

But the saline had been tampered with before it even entered his mother's room. This killer had murdered by strangulation, hanging, shooting, and poison. He was using whatever method would get the job done.

"I'm going to call Sharp and tell him what happened." Morgan moved down the hall.

Who knew how long it would be before his mother woke up? And if she would be able to identify her poisoner . . . Lance pushed that thought away. He couldn't deal with the possibility of her sustaining brain damage. Not now. Tonight, he had to keep her alive.

Brody and Stella arrived and took charge of the investigation. Lance gave them a summary. As he described the events of the night, the numbness retreated like a shadow at noon, leaving anger as bright and clean as winter sunlight in its place.

He would find the man who did this.

Maybe he was the same man who'd killed Lance's father. Maybe not. But Lance knew that whoever had hurt his mother would have those answers.

"A patrol officer is bringing up a drug field test kit," Stella said. "We'll be able to tell you in a few minutes if the saline was contaminated."

Lance paced while the officer arrived and opened his notebook-size case in the corner of Jenny's room. While the ICU staff attended to Lance's mother, the officer selected a pouch from his kit. He took a small sample of the saline solution. Police officers often needed to test substances for the presence of narcotics. Lance had performed enough field tests in his career. It was far better to identify a random white powder in the field than to arrest someone for possession of crack cocaine when the powder was actually baking soda.

In five minutes, the officer looked up from his mini chemistry kit. "Positive for opioids."

Jenny had been poisoned. Twice.

Chapter Thirty-Nine

Morgan watched the scene unfold as Sharp's cell switched over to voice mail. She left a quick message, her attention on Lance, pacing the hallway near his mother's doorway. Confirmation of the poisoning triggered a quick response both from the investigators and Lance.

The cops switched into high gear.

Tension radiated from Lance like heat from a furnace. His body remained in perpetual motion, as if his emotions were too turbulent for him to keep still.

As if he were barely keeping himself in check.

He was a man of action. His natural inclination was to funnel fear and sadness into a battle plan.

Brody and Stella questioned hospital staff, retrieved the surveillance videos, and called for a forensic team.

Morgan's phone buzzed. She pulled it from her purse. Her grandfather's cell number displayed on the screen. A quick burst of nerves scattered her pulse. Grandpa didn't call her without a good reason. Were the girls OK? She stopped at the end of the corridor and answered the call. "Is everything all right?"

"Everything is fine." He paused.

Her spine straightened. Something was wrong. "But?"

"I was reviewing Jenny's e-mails and phone records today. She doesn't get many calls that aren't from Lance, you, or Sharp, but yesterday, she received a call from a strange number. I thought it might be a telemarketer, but I thought I'd dig. Took me a while to get the caller's identity. Things have changed a bit since I ran investigations. You'll never guess who called Jenny."

"Who?" Morgan asked.

"Stan Adams."

Morgan's mind connected dots.

"I thought you'd want to know right away," Grandpa said.

"I do." Morgan told him what had happened to Jenny.

"No." Grandpa swore, a rare event. "I wish I could be more helpful."

"You've been very helpful."

"Keep me updated," Grandpa said. "Love you."

"Love you back." Morgan ended the call.

She caught Lance's gaze.

He strode down the hall. "What is it?"

"That was my grandfather." Morgan swallowed. "He reviewed your mother's e-mail and phone records. Someone called her yesterday."

Lance's attention sharpened to a knifepoint. "Who?"

"Stan Adams."

They knew Stan had lied about his whereabouts the night Vic disappeared, but they hadn't had a chance to question him again.

Lance turned and headed for the door.

Morgan hurried after him. "Where are you going?"

Whatever else happened tonight, she would not let him go off on his own. He was wired.

"To talk to Stan," he said over his shoulder.

"Stop," she called.

Lance turned.

"We need to tell Stella and Brody."

Lance shook his head. "They'll have to pull their own copy of the phone records, but that will take time, and they're going to be tied up at this scene all night. It'll be morning before they're free to interview Stan."

"You can't cut them out of this."

"No. We'll message them the information from the Jeep." Lance pivoted and strode away.

"Don't you think we should call the sheriff too?" Morgan asked, falling into step with him.

Lance pushed out of the ICU. "No. He'll just tell us to stay away from Stan."

Morgan hurried to keep up. "He is going to blow a vein if we don't share this with him."

And won't that make working with him in the future fun.

"Let him stroke out." Lance stalked to the

elevator and stabbed the button. "We've played by the rules, and where did that get us?"

"None of that is King's fault." Morgan faced him, putting her hands on his shoulders. "This is not a good idea. I know Sheriff King is a pain in the ass, but he's smart, and he's been right behind us every step of this investigation."

"If we involve him, he'll put us off the case. Considering King doesn't follow the rule of law, it's totally hypocritical on his part."

"Remember last time we kept the sheriff out of our plans? We almost died." Morgan shivered, thinking about that night in the woods.

"Maybe it would be best if you didn't come with me."

His words stung, but she could see the rage pacing through him, as frustrated and pent up as a big cat in a cage.

"I'm coming with you," Morgan said, afraid he'd leave her behind. God only knew what he'd do without her to temper him. "We are a team."

Lance met her gaze, his eyes softening for just a second. "OK."

He jabbed at the elevator button again.

"What about your mother?" she asked.

Lance glanced back at the closed doors of the ICU. "Brody and Stella are here. More cops are coming. She's as safe as she can be for now. But here's the thing. Brody and Stella and the forensic team will be at the hospital most of tonight. The hospital environment will create challenges for the investigation and the collection of forensic evidence. The ICU staff won't allow patient care to be compromised. But as soon as the investigation team leaves, how will anyone protect her? We can't post a lab outside her door and test every drug she needs right before it's administered. Whoever is trying to kill her is smart and flexible. He has no MO. He's killing for self-preservation, and he doesn't care how he gets the job done or how many people become collateral damage along the way. That old man in the next room did nothing, but I am going to bet that he was murdered just to create a diversion so the killer could get to my mother."

The elevator doors opened, and Lance stalked inside. Morgan followed him. She briefly considered messaging the sheriff in secret, but loyalty warred with caution. Lance would take it as a betrayal. It would *be* a betrayal. He was already hurting beyond comprehension. His mother was his only family. How could she ask him to let someone else handle this threat to her life?

Lance was right. The sheriff would order them away from Stan, and Sheriff King *was* hampered by the law. Which was the same reason Morgan and Lance had ended up in trouble last time. The entire situation felt too much like déjà vu for Morgan's comfort.

But this time, she would make sure they exercised proper caution. They were both armed, and they weren't alone in the woods in the dark.

The elevator descended, and the doors opened.

"We're only going to talk to Stan," she said as they stepped out.

"Right."

The cold air hit them halfway across the tiled lobby as the door slid open to admit visitors. They passed a young couple. A colorful bunch of *Get Well Soon* balloons floated behind them. Outside, the night smelled like snow. Morgan buttoned her coat in a rush. They hustled across the parking lot to the Jeep. Morgan plucked the keys from Lance's hand. She didn't trust him behind the wheel, and she wanted some control over their movements. He let her have the keys.

Morgan opened the vehicle door and spoke over the roof. "We have to let Sharp know where we're going. Someone needs to keep tabs on us."

"Fair enough."

"And we will take every other reasonable precaution. One step at a time tonight, OK?" She would ask him to proceed carefully, but she wouldn't demand he walk away. If it was her family at risk, she would be unstoppable too.

A defeated sigh hissed from him. "OK."

"We're not going to do anything dangerous."

But she recognized the words as ridiculous even as they tumbled from her cold lips. "I love you."

They were on their way to question a potential killer.

Chapter Forty

Lance sent messages to Brody and Sharp.

"Are you all right?" Morgan reached across the console and offered her hand.

He took it. In a world of uncertainty, filled with lies and betrayal, what she offered him was pure. He'd been a crazy man to even think about turning away her love.

She loves me.

When this was all over, he was going to process that. For now, he had to keep swimming forward so he didn't sink.

"No. Yes. I don't know," he said honestly.

"You look angry."

"I am angry." His jaw was so tight, he could crack walnuts in his molars. "My father went missing, and everyone was so concerned for themselves, they lied to the police and possibly hindered the investigation."

"I know," Morgan said. "But you won't get any information out of Stan if you're too confrontational."

"How about I hold him out a window by his ankles? That might convince him to cooperate."

Morgan squeezed his fingers. "Let's make that Plan B. Plan A is to get him to talk without violence."

But if Stan had anything to do with his father's disappearance or the attempt to kill his mother . . .

"I won't drag you into anything dangerous," he said. "I love your girls too much to risk their mother's life. Call Stan and get him to meet us somewhere public."

A public location would also keep Lance from beating the man into a pulp on the spot.

Morgan called Stan's cell. She put him on speakerphone. "Hello, Mr. Adams. Lance Kruger and I have a few follow-up questions for you. Do you have some time this evening?"

"Not really," Stan said, his words clipped. Other voices and background activity came over the line. "The firm is dealing with an issue tonight. Can it wait until morning?"

"I'm sorry," Morgan said. "It's important."

"Fine," Stan said. "But you'll have to come to my office." He disconnected without saying goodbye.

Morgan drove out of the hospital parking lot. Her phone went off. She handed it to Lance. "It's a message from Stella. Can you read it?"

He entered her passcode and read the message. "Stella says, WHERE ARE YOU? Do you want to answer her?"

"No." Morgan sighed. "You told Brody what my grandfather found. She'll figure out where we're going."

A few minutes later, the phone beeped with an incoming call.

Lance read the display on Morgan's phone. "It's your sister."

"Don't answer it," Morgan said. "With her and Brody working your mother's case, she has the power to order us away from Stan."

He lowered her phone. "I'm sorry if this will cause tension between you and your sister."

"It won't be the first time." Morgan turned left onto the main road. "You told Sharp where we were going?"

"Sent him a detailed message."

"As long as someone knows."

The accounting firm was located in a five-story office building, practically a high-rise in this rural community. Lance and Morgan went into the lobby and took the elevator to the fourth floor. The firm was small, two senior accountants, two juniors, and a handful of administrative staff, but their offices took up the entire fourth floor. Large silver letters spelled out ADAMS & BOOKER on the wall opposite the elevator bank.

In the boring black-and-gray reception area, Morgan handed her business card to the middle-aged brunette behind the desk. "We're here to see Mr. Adams."

Behind the receptionist, harried people bustled.

"Is he expecting you?" the brunette asked.

"Yes." Morgan smiled.

Lance didn't try to copy her. He was not capable of putting on a friendly expression. He hung back and did his best to appear nonthreatening.

Based on the receptionist's worried side-eye, he wasn't successful.

She pointed to a hallway. "Second door on the left."

Morgan stepped in front of Lance. Her glance back at him was worried, like he was going to do something violent. Lance wouldn't, even though he might like to. He wanted answers.

He wanted the man who hurt his mother locked up.

He wanted to know what happened to his father.

He wanted justice.

Stan's office door was open. Lance closed it after he and Morgan were inside. In khaki trousers and a blue button-down, Stan looked like he was headed for the golf course. He glanced up from his computer screen as they walked in. Standing, he extended his hand across the desk. Morgan and Lance shook his hand and sat in the two chairs facing his desk.

"Thank you for seeing us on such short notice," Morgan began.

"You said you had some follow-up questions." Stan rocked back in his chair. "I don't have much time."

"I hope it's nothing serious," Morgan said.

"No." He waved off her concern. "Just a last-minute request from a client."

"Nice of you all to scramble to accommodate him."

"He's one of our biggest clients," Stan explained. "These things happen."

The small talk was giving Lance heartburn. He leaned forward, his forearms on his knees, 100 percent of his attention on Stan's face. "My mother overdosed last night."

"Oh, no." Stan's head shifted back. "I'm so sorry. Is she . . . ?"

"It's still touch and go," Lance said. "Did you talk to her this week?"

Stan's hand dropped to his blotter. He toyed with a paper clip, rolling it around on his fingertips. "I called her yesterday."

"You didn't stop and see her?" Lance asked.

Stan shook his head. "No. I offered, but she said she didn't accept visitors."

That, at least, was true. But how could Lance believe a single word Stan said? He'd already caught him in a lie.

"Why did you call her?" Morgan asked.

"After we'd talked, I felt guilty." Stan watched the paper clip spin. "I was your dad's friend, and I let him down. I didn't look after his family. I didn't check on you. I didn't make sure your mother was all right."

"Where were you again that night?" Lance forced the question out of a tight throat.

"I already told you. I was with Brian at the ball field." Stan licked his lips. He spun the paper clip in nervous circles.

His khakis should have self-combusted.

Tension built in Lance's chest, and he quelled the urge to reach across the desk and choke Stan with his own collar.

"That's interesting"—Morgan shifted into her cross-examination tone—"because we know that Brian was lying about that night. He wasn't with you."

Stan dropped the paper clip, but he remained silent.

"Why did you lie to the police?" Morgan asked.

Stan contemplated her question for a few seconds, his fingers finding the paper clip on the blotter. Was he deciding whether to tell the truth or another carefully phrased lie?

How would they ever know? Lance straightened, planting his hands on the armrest, occupying them in case he was overcome with the desire to wring Stan's neck.

Thankfully, Morgan was here. She grounded him.

"Because Brian asked me to," Stan admitted, his tone shifted to disgust. "I assume you know where he was?"

"With Mary Fox." Morgan nodded.

"He didn't want Natalie to find out about Mary." Stan dropped his paper clip, clasped his hands, and rested them on the blotter. "You have to understand. At the time, no crime had been committed. Brian didn't see why he should destroy his marriage for nothing."

"My father was *nothing?*" Lance asked.

Stan winced. "I didn't mean your father was nothing. But we didn't think anything bad had happened to him. He'd been under a great deal of pressure. We thought your dad just lost it and went somewhere to decompress for a couple of days. Vic was my good friend."

"Not good enough for you and Brian to give the police accurate information," Lance said.

"You covered for Brian so he could cheat on his wife," Morgan pointed out.

Stan bowed his head over his clasped hands. "I can't argue with that, but Brian's marriage was his business, not mine. I didn't think it had anything to do with your dad."

"And afterward?" Lance's mouth tasted bitter. "When my father never came back?"

Stan's shoulders sagged. "Once we'd told the police detective one story, we could hardly change it. I had no idea where Vic was. I only knew where Brian was and who he was with that night. At the time, there were no connections between your dad and Mary." He lifted his chin and met Lance's eyes. "I'm sorry."

Too little, too late.

"Where were you this afternoon?" Morgan asked.

"I was here, all day." Stan gestured toward his closed door. "The receptionist can vouch for me."

"So where were you the night my father went missing?" Lance asked.

"Home. Alone." Stan glanced away for a fraction of a second. Sweat beaded on his upper lip.

Liar.

"That's the best you can do?" Lance's fingers curled around the armrests.

"We know why Brian lied," Morgan said. "But I seriously doubt you would falsify a statement to the police just so your friend's wife wouldn't find out he was with a hooker. We've already established you're not the most loyal friend. If you lied to the police, you were also up to something that night."

Stan's lips mashed flat, as if he wouldn't speak another word.

"Did you see Brian and Mary that night?" Lance asked.

No answer.

"Were you at PJ's?" Lance pressed.

"I have nothing else to say." Stan gestured toward the door. "Please leave. Don't come back."

"We won't." Lance stood. "The next person you'll be talking to is the sheriff."

Lance couldn't wait to sic Sheriff King on Stan.

Morgan held him by the arm all the way out the

door. Lance didn't remember taking the elevator or walking across the lobby. The next thing he knew, the cold air was slapping him in the face.

"He was lying." Lance headed for his Jeep. "He wasn't home alone."

"Probably not," Morgan agreed. "What was Stan doing that was worth lying to the police about? And how do we find out where he was twenty-three years later?"

"He wasn't married, so he wasn't hiding a woman." Lance put a hand on the door handle and talked over the roof of the Jeep. "Maybe he was with a *married* woman."

"Maybe, but after all these years, would he still lie about that?" Morgan asked. "In my mind, he was doing something illegal, something that might still affect his life if the truth came out."

Chapter Forty-One

Morgan settled in the driver's seat, the steering wheel freezing under her hands. "If Stan has an alibi for today, he couldn't have been at the hospital."

"Maybe. Maybe not." Lance's breath fogged in front of his face like a personal storm cloud. "He's lying about the night my dad disappeared. I've no reason to believe anything else he says."

"But he has witnesses for today," Morgan pointed out.

"He has employees who will say what he wants them to say. The hospital is a fifteen-minute drive from here. He could have slipped out and done the deed. With driving time, it would have taken less than an hour. The receptionist must take a lunch break."

"I still feel like we're missing something." Morgan drummed her fingers on the wheel. "Our only suspects are Brian and Stan, yet both had alibis for at least some of the recent murders."

"What if they were working together?" Lance asked. "Their original false alibi was joint."

"It's possible. But what was their motivation? If Brian killed Mary because she was going to tell his wife, how did Stan get involved?"

"Brian called him for help disposing of the body," Lance suggested.

"It's possible, but I feel like we're still missing a key piece of information." The theory wasn't ringing true to Morgan. "It's one thing to cover for your pal, but quite another to help him commit murder."

"And it doesn't explain what happened to my father." Lance closed his eyes and rubbed the bridge of his nose with both hands.

"Unless Vic saw Brian kill Mary."

"And my father wouldn't help them cover it up." Lance dropped his hands into his lap. "Even though I know Brian and Stan both lied, I still have a hard time believing they would have killed my father."

"What do we do?" Morgan asked.

"We get comfortable." Lance cracked his neck. "I have no ideas other than good old-fashioned surveillance. Stan is our best lead at this point. I want to stick with him and see where he goes after work." He glanced at Morgan. "He might be late. Do you want me to take you home?"

"No." Morgan glanced sideways.

Lance seemed to have gotten his temper under control, but she didn't trust him to go off on his own.

She reached behind the seat for her tote and pulled it onto her lap. Unzipping it, she dug for the case file and handed it to Lance. "Stan drives a black Mercedes. Let's find it in case he goes out the back door."

Lance read off the license plate number. Morgan started the engine and turned on the heat. She drove the Jeep up and down the rows until they spotted Stan's car. She parked in the darkest spot she could find several rows away.

Turning off the engine, she fished her leftover candy bar from her bag. She tore the wrapper and waved it at him. "Want half?"

He shook his head. "Don't eat that."

Too late.

She chewed and swallowed. "It has peanuts in it. Nuts are healthy."

Lance was always prepared for an impromptu stakeout. He kept his Jeep stocked with emergency supplies. He opened the console and took out two protein bars. From a bag behind his seat, he removed two water bottles and offered her one.

She took it but didn't open it. Who knew how long they'd have to wait? After three pregnancies, it was safest to minimize fluid intake on stakeouts of indeterminate length.

She fished gloves from her pockets and turned up her collar. He handed her a protein bar, but she put it aside as well. The chocolate would keep her going for a while. It could be a long night. They'd have to ration their supplies. She settled lower in her seat. Lance did the same.

Time passed with a creeping slowness that reminded her of Salvador Dali's melting clocks.

Just after eleven p.m., Stan exited the building.

Morgan perked up. "There he is."

Hunching his shoulders against the wind, Stan hustled across the parking lot and slid into his Mercedes. The headlights turned on. A minute later, he drove out of the lot.

Morgan followed him. With the roads nearly deserted, she eased off the accelerator and stayed well back. When Stan turned into his development, she drove past, then turned around to double back.

"Kill the headlights before you make the turn," Lance said.

Exterior lights blazed in the new development, eliminating the need for headlights.

Two blocks away, she slid the Jeep to the curb, choosing the darkest place between street lamps. They watched Stan park in his driveway. Lights shone in the front windows of the big house. Stan got out of his car. Closing the door, he stopped and scanned the street. Did he feel them watching him?

Stan went into the house. The first-floor windows went dark a minute later.

"Maybe he's going straight to bed," Morgan said. That's what she would do.

"It's late," Lance agreed.

"Do we continue to watch him? If he was going

anywhere else, he wouldn't have driven straight home."

"Unless he saw us."

"If he saw us, we might as well leave. He won't lead us anywhere if he knows we're watching."

Lance shifted in his seat. "Drive around the next block."

Morgan cruised past Stan's house and turned left three times.

"Pull over here," Lance said. "Under that tree."

Morgan parked at the curb around the corner from Stan's house. "It's so bright here. I feel exposed."

Not only were the lots covered in landscaping lights, but the houses were close together. There were no dark places to hide.

"It's the best we can do in this neighborhood," Lance said. "From a home security perspective, I applaud the lack of dark shadows for burglars to lurk. But for our purposes tonight, it's damned inconvenient."

They climbed out of the Jeep. They locked the vehicle's doors manually and closed their doors as softly as possible.

"Hold my hand." Lance reached toward her.

She slid her hand into his.

Lance tugged her onto the sidewalk. "We're just a nice couple taking a stroll."

For a minute, that's exactly what she wished they were. The crisp night air chilled her face, but her coat blocked the worst of the cold, and the heat of his body penetrated her thin leather glove. A snow flurry drifted down, slow as a feather, and landed on her arm.

If they weren't on a stakeout, their walk would be romantic.

Tires crunched on asphalt.

"Look casual." Lance pulled Morgan closer, wrapping his arm around her shoulders.

Morgan glanced over her shoulder. "Uh-oh."

A black-and-white sheriff's vehicle pulled up to the curb a few feet ahead of them. Sheriff King climbed out of his car, crossed the strip of grass next to the curb, and stepped onto the sidewalk, blocking their way. "What are you doing here?"

"Taking a walk," Lance said.

"Don't smart-ass me." The glare of the streetlamp overhead cast the sheriff's face in harsh, angry shadows.

Waves of animosity—and testosterone—shimmered between the two men.

"Stan Adams called me to say you have been harassing and stalking him," the sheriff said.

Morgan squeezed Lance's hand. "Don't say anything."

The sheriff propped his hands on his hips. "Didn't I tell you both to stay away from this case?"

Lance said, "My mother is lying in a hospital bed—"

"Stop. Talking," Morgan said in a louder voice.

The sheriff pointed at Lance. "You should listen to the lawyer."

But Lance's temper had obviously kicked his sense out of the way. "I have every right to protect my family."

"You don't have squat." The sheriff paused after each word for effect.

Morgan nudged an elbow in between the men and tried to defuse the situation. "We just found out that Stan Adams called Jenny Kruger yesterday, but you knew that, right? You have access to her phone records."

The sheriff's lips mashed flat. She couldn't tell if he knew or not.

Lance leaned forward, as if he was going to speak. Morgan tugged him back.

"Jenny was poisoned with opioids," she said. "Tonight at the hospital, someone tried to do it again."

"Do you have proof of that?" Sheriff King asked.

"It just happened," Morgan said. "Her saline solution was spiked. The Scarlet Falls PD has just begun their investigation."

"So you just thought you'd take matters into your own hands?" King asked.

Lance shook his head. "And this is why we didn't want to call you."

"I've had it with you." The sheriff's finger

stabbed in the air toward Lance. "The only way I'm going to keep you both out of my way is to put you in a cell. You're both under arrest."

"You can't be serious." Lance took a step forward.

So did the sheriff. "I don't make jokes."

It was true. The sheriff had no sense of humor.

"Just do what he says." Morgan gripped Lance's bicep. The muscles were hard and tense under her fingers.

"Both of you, hand over your weapons." King held out an empty hand.

They slid their guns from their holsters and offered them butts first.

The sheriff took both. "Put your hands on top of your heads. Lace your fingers."

Lance tensed, but he followed instructions.

"Now you first, Kruger." The sheriff crooked a forefinger at Lance. "Give me your coat."

Lance slid out of his leather jacket and handed it over. "You can't arrest us."

"I most certainly can. Remember the last time you went off half-cocked?" The sheriff tossed Lance's jacket over the hood of his car. "You almost got yourself and Ms. Dane killed. Now turn around."

Lance complied.

Pulling Lance's hands down one at a time, Sheriff King snapped handcuffs onto his wrists. He gave Lance a thorough pat-down, emptying the many pockets of Lance's cargos and piling the contents on top of Lance's jacket. Pocketknife, a fully loaded magazine for his Glock, and a handful of plastic zip-ties. The sheriff guided him into the back of the police vehicle.

"Now you, counselor." The sheriff pointed to her. "Let's have your coat."

Morgan took off her coat and handed it over. The cold air swept through her, and she shivered as she turned around.

"Turn out your jeans pockets," he said. "Use two fingers."

She turned her jeans pockets inside out and handed him the keys to the Jeep. The rest of her belongings were in her tote bag, which she'd left in the Jeep. The sheriff handcuffed her and gave her a cursory pat-down, skipping the more intimate areas of her body, something she was positive he would not do when arresting a female stranger. He was being a gentleman while he arrested her, a fact that was ridiculous all on its own.

"What are the charges?" Morgan asked.

"I'm starting with loitering, harassment, stalking, and impeding an investigation," he said. "I'm sure I'll think of some more during the drive."

With a solid hand on her arm, he guided her to the back door of the vehicle. Then he put a gentle hand on the top of her head as she slid into the vehicle.

Scooting across the bench seat in handcuffs was harder than Morgan anticipated. The door closed. The physical restraint of the handcuffs and the cage separating the back and front seats felt claustrophobic. She glanced over her shoulder and watched the sheriff going through their coat pockets. Lance's jacket held his cell phone, a miniature screwdriver, and a small flashlight. From Morgan's coat, the sheriff pulled her phone, a wad of tissues, a lip balm, and two lollipops. The second lollipop was sticky and covered in lint, having been licked and rewrapped when Sophie had discovered she didn't like green apple. With a disgusted sneer, the sheriff wiped his hand on the thigh of his uniform, then bagged their personal possessions.

"I can't believe he's arresting us." Lance glared out the side window.

"We'll call Sharp from the station," Morgan said. "He'll get us out."

Lance shook his head. "Knowing the sheriff, he'll stick us in a holding cell overnight just to prove he can."

"I messaged Sharp earlier. He knows where we are. He'll look for us."

"He won't think to call the sheriff."

"Probably not," Morgan agreed. "We'll survive a night in a holding cell."

"You know what cells are like." Lance frowned at her. "*You* don't belong in one."

In her former life as a prosecutor, Morgan had interviewed plenty of criminals. Holding cells, like other jail and prison facilities, were disgusting, filthy places with open toilets and the lingering scent of vomit. From the outside, the sights and smells could gag someone with a strong stomach. The thought of being locked in one wasn't pleasant.

"I'm aware of that, but there's nothing we can do about it now." Morgan was less surprised at their arrest than Lance. He and the sheriff had butted heads one too many times. They were equally hardheaded, but the sheriff had the law on his side. Sheriff King had warned them, and Lance was right: King was just arrogant enough to want to prove he had the upper hand.

The sheriff collected their belongings and put them in his trunk.

Morgan turned to Lance. "You need to remain silent. I mean it. Don't say a single word to the sheriff or anyone else at the station."

Male and female prisoners were not held together. She suspected Lance would be put in the holding cell, and the sheriff would handcuff her to a bench somewhere. She sensed they had finally pushed King over the line.

"Cooperate, but exercise your right to be silent. Anything you say *will* be used against you. *Anything.*"

"I know." Lance's shoulders fell. "I'm sorry.

I should have listened to you tonight. You were right. We should have called the sheriff and told him about Stan. Now we've lost a whole night."

"It'll be all right." Morgan shivered.

Lance shifted closer, pressing his shoulder against hers. "I can't help protect my mother from a jail cell, and now that we're getting locked up, Stan is free to do what he wants."

"Stella and Brody are with your mother tonight," Morgan said.

The sheriff climbed into the driver's seat, ending their conversation. As the vehicle pulled away from the curb, Morgan turned and glanced back at Stan's bright-as-day neighborhood. Stan had seen them following his car, and he'd gone on the offensive, smartly turning the tables on them.

No one was watching him now.

Chapter Forty-Two

Through the window of the sheriff's vehicle, Lance watched the dark landscape roll by. Flurries whizzed past. They stopped at an intersection, and the sheriff turned left when he should have made a right. Where was he taking them?

"Hey," Lance called through the wire mesh that divided the front and rear seats. "The sheriff's station is the other direction."

"We're not going to the station," the sheriff said. "You need to be taught a lesson."

Lance glanced at Morgan.

The sheriff was angry enough to inflict some payback on Lance, but surely King wouldn't hurt *her*. Would he?

"Whatever you have in mind for me, drop Morgan somewhere," Lance said to King's reflection in the rearview mirror.

King ignored him.

Morgan nudged Lance with her elbow, her eyes wide and worried. But what could Lance do? They were handcuffed in the back of a police car, a place designed specifically to keep people contained.

The landscape became more and more rural. The sheriff turned onto a long country road.

Lance snapped to attention. He knew where they were going.

Grey Lake.

A few minutes later, the trees opened. The lake shimmered in the darkness. But the car continued past the area where his father's Buick had been dragged from the water. Two miles later, the sheriff turned onto a dirt lane in a thick patch of forest. Discomfort shifted to paranoia as the trees closed around the car. The car rolled to a stop. A small clearing opened to their left.

The sheriff stepped out of the vehicle and opened the rear door. "Get out."

Was he going to leave them out here? He'd taken their coats, and the temperature was hovering around freezing. As far as Lance knew, the closest houses were on the other side of the lake. The hike was *at least* five miles.

"No." Lance shook his head. Next to him, Morgan shivered.

The sheriff reached into the car, grabbed her by the arm, and pulled her out of the vehicle.

"Hey," Lance yelled, anger and terror churning inside him. "Don't hurt her!"

"Then get your ass out here," King called, dragging Morgan into the beam of the headlights. Still holding her bicep, King crooked a finger at Lance. Morgan's face was as pale as the snowflakes swirling around her dark hair.

Lance scrambled out of the car. Whatever the

sheriff had planned, Lance couldn't let Morgan face it alone. He walked across the clearing and stopped in front of the sheriff. King released Morgan's arm and stepped away from her, toward the car.

"You can't leave us out here." Facing the sheriff, Lance put his body between King and Morgan. They were in the middle of nowhere. With the falling temperatures, Morgan wouldn't make it. Surely, the sheriff knew that.

But King didn't respond.

"Dispatch will have a record of Stan's call," Lance argued. "They'll know we were with you."

"Stan didn't call. Do you really think that dumbass spotted you?" The sheriff snorted. "I was looking for you. You weren't that hard to find. You're predictable, and I'm a very good hunter. It's all about knowing your prey and being able to predict its movements."

"Sharp will figure it out." Lance tried to think of an argument, even though it would be futile. The sheriff had already gone beyond the law.

Beyond reason.

"I'm not worried about Sharp," King said.

Morgan seemed to shake off her shock. "What do you mean, leave us out here? You can't do that." The chatter of her teeth punctuated her words.

"I can do whatever I want," King said in a

voice as cold as the falling snow. "But I have no intention of leaving you out here to freeze."

Lance took a deep breath. What a prick! The frigid air felt like needles in his lungs. Was this all an attempt to intimidate them? To scare them out of ever crossing him again?

Morgan's whole body was shaking now, and her shoulders hunched against the cold. The misery on her face stoked rage inside Lance's chest. If the sheriff thought he could get away with a stunt like this with a PI and a lawyer . . .

Wait.

Even the sheriff's ego wasn't that big. A PI didn't have much clout, but a respected lawyer, a former prosecutor, did. Plus, Morgan had connections. Nearly every member of her family was or had been in law enforcement.

"This is kidnapping," Morgan said in a quivering voice. "You'll never get away with it."

No, the sheriff wouldn't get away with leaving them to hike out of the woods in the cold. He had no intention of letting them hike anywhere. Lance could see it in King's eyes. A veil of detachment slid down like a curtain. Anger and frustration faded. The cool that replaced emotion in his eyes was stone cold.

He was going to kill them.

But why?

Lance's belly chilled, as if he'd swallowed snow. He had no time to analyze the sheriff's motive. Whatever the reasons, Lance could not let Morgan die.

Instead of drawing his service weapon, King reached into his pocket. Lance shifted onto the balls of his feet. The sheriff had a spare gun. Before he cleared it from his pocket, Lance charged him. His shoulder hit the sheriff in the ribs, knocking him off balance. King stumbled backward. Without his arms for balance, Lance went down too. But he was younger and more athletic than the sheriff. He landed on his opposite shoulder and rolled. Momentum carried him back to his feet.

"Morgan, run!" he shouted.

She turned and fled into the woods. The sheriff turned onto his stomach, got one foot under his body, and reached for his weapon again. Lance rushed him again, body slamming him a second time. Prepared, the sheriff stayed on his feet. Lance jumped back and drilled a front kick into his solar plexus, but the sheriff was wearing his body armor, and the kick had little impact, except to throw him off balance one more time.

King recovered quickly and reached for his weapon again, his face a mask of determination.

If he killed Lance, Morgan would be easy to hunt down.

Jumping forward, Lance brought his forehead down onto the sheriff's nose. Blood squirted, and the sheriff went down on his ass. But King had his gun out of its holster. Before he could aim, Lance kicked his arm and sprinted for the trees.

A gunshot echoed through the woods. The bullet hit a tree a few feet to Lance's right. A piece of debris struck Lance in the face, but the sting barely lasted a second. He turned around a large pine and zigzagged.

He had two objectives: stay alive and find Morgan.

Chapter Forty-Three

A gunshot rang through the thin air. Startled, Morgan stumbled. With her hands behind her back, she had no hands to catch her fall. She went down on one knee. Pain shot through her kneecap, but it was fleeting and adrenaline blotted it out.

Lance!

Had King shot him?

Branches crashed. Lance?

Or King . . .

Continue to run or circle back?

Morgan's lungs burned. Her thighs burned. Everything burned.

The most running she'd done in the last six years was teaching Ava how to ride a bike. Trying to find any sort of stride on the uneven forest floor with her hands bound behind her back felt impossible. She didn't want to leave Lance behind if he was wounded. But if he wasn't wounded, he would catch up easily. *She* would be the one to slow *him* down.

She put her feet together and squatted until her chest pressed against her thighs. She slid her bound hands under her butt until they were behind her knees. Then she rocked onto her back and wiggled her feet through one at a time.

When she stood, her hands were in front of her body.

A rock the size of a fist on the ground caught her eye. She grabbed it, pushed to her feet, and broke into a jog. Out of breath, she sucked the freezing air in through her mouth. If it was King on her trail, he'd hear her gasping for air from a half mile away. Lungs on fire, she ducked behind a tree.

The crashing came closer.

Once she stopped moving, Morgan shivered. She pressed against the tree trunk, using it as a shield and wind-block.

Please, let it be Lance.

Steeling herself, she peered around the tree and raised the rock over her head. A body flew toward her. Black pants. Black shirt. Legs churning. Strides sure and swift despite the hands bound behind him.

Lance.

Relief weakened her for a second. Then she pushed away from the tree and staggered toward him.

"Keep going." He barely broke stride, his voice just a whisper.

She stumbled after him. She had no idea how far her initial sprint had taken her, except that it wasn't far enough.

He slowed his pace and lined his shoulder up with hers. For him, the pace was a light jog.

"Where is he?" she whispered in three pants.

"I don't know," Lance said, his words barely audible over the sound of her footsteps. He frowned at her. "Let's walk for a minute."

She slowed to a walk. A stitch in her side doubled her over. She pressed her hands against it.

He glanced over his shoulder. "Fairly sure I broke his nose, but I doubt that will slow him down for long. We need to keep moving. You got through your handcuffs?"

"I fell." She huffed and puffed, her lungs working like fireplace bellows to catch up on airflow. But the incoming air was so cold, she felt like she was inhaling needles. "Seemed like a good time."

He nodded and veered to the left.

Morgan jerked her hands to the right. "But the road is that way."

"It's unlikely that a car will come by this late at night. The road is too open. He'll catch us. There are houses on the other side of the lake." He scanned the darkness. "Our best chance is to keep the lake on one side."

Morgan's gasps and heart rate slowed, but with the reduced activity, the cold hit her hard.

"Can you move faster now?" he asked.

She nodded and broke into a heavy, toe-dragging jog. She tripped. A thin branch cracked under her foot, the sound carrying through the quiet woods. She regained her balance, but the temperature and exhaustion were taking their toll. Her movements were clumsy.

She was running as fast as she could. He wasn't even breathing hard. He could move a lot faster without her. She would slow him down. He was going to get killed because of her.

"You should run ahead and get help," she said. "I won't make it. It's too cold, and I'm too out of shape."

"I will not leave you. We are stronger together, remember?"

But tonight, she was the weak link in their partnership. Physically, she could not match Lance's strength and conditioning.

She hadn't even begun to process what the sheriff had done. Did this mean King had killed Crystal and the Hoolihans? What about Mary? Had the sheriff tried to kill Lance's mother? *Why?*

Whatever it was must be related to Mary's death and Vic's disappearance. King had been the chief deputy in 1994. Only one thing linked the sheriff's department to August 10, 1994: Lou Ford's death.

A mental image of Eric's bruised face appeared in her mind. *My face hit the floor when the sheriff handcuffed me.*

The sheriff had used excessive force when he'd arrested Eric. Had he been involved in Ford's death? How? King hadn't been the arresting officer. As chief deputy, had he initiated a cover-up?

Morgan tripped over a rock and stumbled to her knees. The pain brought her back to the present.

Lance took her fall as an opportunity to roll to his back and work his cuffed hands in front of his body the same way she had.

She got her foot under her body and stood, swaying from lack of oxygen.

They paused for a moment. Morgan caught her breath. Lance listened.

He put his lips to her ear. "I don't hear him."

"He's out there." Morgan felt the sheriff behind them, a shadowy presence, a threat that her body recognized even if her eyes and ears couldn't discern his location.

"Stop thinking," he whispered. "Just put one foot in front of the other."

But they both knew that King wouldn't let them go. He was out there. And he was coming after them.

Chapter Forty-Four

He should have known Kruger wouldn't go down without a fight.

Face aching, he climbed to his feet and holstered his pistol. Kruger was too far away to hit with a handgun. He watched the handcuffed man disappear into the trees. Kruger moved with impressive speed and agility.

But he wasn't worried.

He walked to the rear of his vehicle and opened the trunk. Opening his first aid kit, he mopped the blood from his face. He punched an instant ice pack and held it over his throbbing nose. Kruger had likely broken it. A few minutes with an ice pack now might stave off some swelling. Clogged nasal passages would slow him down.

Besides, he was in no rush. They were miles away from help, and even Kruger couldn't run at top speed through the woods in the dark. The PI would have to slow down or risk breaking an ankle. But even if Kruger could make good time, he didn't have to catch Kruger. He only had to catch Ms. Dane. The counselor was smart, loyal, and determined, but she was not athletic.

And Kruger would never leave her.

The key to a successful hunt is knowing your prey and being able to predict its behavior.

They were both handcuffed and unarmed. No one knew where they were.

He moved aside the evidence bag containing Kruger's and Dane's personal possessions. When he'd stashed their phones in the trunk, he'd removed the batteries. No one would be able to track them. Their last known location was outside Stan Adams's house. If Dane's sister on the SFPD went looking for her, that was where she'd start.

Maybe he could plant some evidence at Stan's house . . .

He'd sort it out later. Tonight, his focus had to be on stopping Kruger and Dane. Those two were relentless. They'd discovered Lou Ford's death. It was only a matter of time until they tied Ford's death to Mary's.

He removed the battery from his own phone. He wanted no GPS record of *his* upcoming trek through the woods either.

After laying the ice pack aside, he took four ibuprofen tablets from his kit and swallowed them with water. He stripped off his coat and uniform shirt and tossed his Kevlar vest into the trunk. Kruger and Dane weren't armed, and the vest would slow him down. Instead, he layered a long-sleeve thermal shirt and a fleece pullover, then put his coat back on. He exchanged his campaign hat for a wool cap.

Then he began loading his many pockets:

water, protein bars, spare fully loaded magazines, a flashlight he wouldn't use unless necessary, a compass, fire starter sticks, and matches. He didn't plan to be out all night, but a good hunter was always prepared. Reaching back into the trunk, he added a silver emergency blanket.

His hunting cabin was at the end of this lane. He knew every game trail in the woods around the lake well. He would not let Kruger and Dane get away. His future depended on catching them.

He returned the first aid kit to his trunk and removed his AR-15 from the rack mounted under his trunk lid, wishing he'd thought to bring his personal hunting rifle. For deer hunting, he preferred the 30-06. His personal rifle fired a larger, heavier bullet with more stopping power at a greater distance. He'd seen too many deer shot with the light AR-15 rounds get up and run, needing to be finished off with another shot. But he'd have to be close to hit his target in the dark anyway. And if possible, he wouldn't use his official weapon.

He stooped and picked up the handgun he'd dropped when Kruger kicked him. He'd taken it off a stupid kid a few months before and kept it, just in case he would need a gun to toss next to a suspect. He slid it into his pocket. He'd planned to use the throwaway weapon to kill Kruger and Dane before they'd gotten away.

He hadn't expected to have to hunt them down.

Kruger's rush had thrown a wrench into his plans. He should have expected it. The PI was more dangerous than he'd thought. He wouldn't underestimate him again.

The rifle felt balanced and comfortable in his hands. It would do. He closed the trunk and turned to the woods.

Time to go hunting.

Chapter Forty-Five

Sharp left the store with a new phone in his hand, his account data freshly downloaded from his cloud account to the device. A series of messages from Lance popped onto the screen. Sharp read them, stunned by the news that someone had tried to kill Jenny in the ICU, and that Stan was now the top suspect. He dialed Lance's number, but the call went directly to voice mail.

He left a message. "Call me after you and Morgan question Stan. One of the boys set up a meeting for me with someone who was at the sheriff's station on August 10, 1994. I'll let you know if I learn anything interesting."

Sharp pressed "End," slid his phone into his pocket, and drove to the meeting location, Bridge Park. He stopped his Prius in front of the Revolutionary War monument and parked next to an old Chevy Chevette at the base of the old stone bridge that spanned the Scarlet River. A figure hunched on one of the three wooden benches facing the water.

Sharp zipped his jacket, making sure his sidearm was accessible. He might not like to carry a weapon, but considering the rate people were dropping in this case, he'd make an exception.

He got out of the car. Snow fell in lazy eddies of wind and gathered on the grass as he walked across it.

The figure on the bench stood. "Are you Sharp?"

"Ned?"

"Yes." Ned eased back onto the bench. He was in his seventies. The black wool coat and fedora he wore were old and threadbare.

"We could have met somewhere warmer." Sharp turned his face away from the wind.

Ned shook his head. "This meeting is not public. I'm only talking to you because I owe Bill. He pulled my kid out of a car wreck years ago." He craned his neck to give the area a nervous scan.

"What are you afraid of?" Sharp asked.

"Have you seen all the dead people lately?" Ned's tone hinted that his fear was justified and obvious. "Bill says you're investigating the skeleton they pulled out of the lake a few days ago."

"Yes," Sharp said. "The skeleton was identified as Mary Fox. She disappeared August 10, 1994. Bill tells me you were working that night."

Ned nodded. "But no one knows I saw anything, and that's exactly how I want it to stay." He took a deep, audible breath. "I was a janitor in those days. I took care of the sheriff's station and a couple of other small county buildings. Sheriff's station got cleaned twice a week." He toyed with a hole in the thumb of his black leather glove. "I was in the maintenance closet, getting ready to mop floors. There was a commotion in the hallway. The door was open a couple of inches. I looked out. The sheriff, he was Chief Deputy King back then, he was bringing a young woman in through the back door."

A chill settled low in Sharp's gut. *Mary?*

Ned continued. "There wasn't a camera covering every single inch of the station in those days. The back corridor was a blind spot. Deputy Walsh was struggling with a drunk. King cuffed the woman to a ring next to the payphone that used to be there. He handed her a quarter, told her to make her call, and went to help Walsh. The drunk was raising a ruckus, shouting and cursing and thrashing around. Neither King nor Walsh had any patience left. They beat on him, then it got real quiet."

Lou Ford.

Ned paused to catch his breath. He raised his eyes and stared out over the river. "I backed into the dark part of that closet. I didn't want either of them to know I saw. I didn't come out until they were both gone."

"What happened to the woman?" Sharp asked.

"I heard King offer her a deal. He'd drop the charges against her if she promised to keep her mouth shut about what she saw." Ned paused.

"He took her right out the back door. Never brought her inside the station."

King might have offered Mary a deal, but he didn't live up to his end of the bargain.

Ned set his hands on his thighs and pushed to his feet. "I don't know anything else. That's all I saw." He raised a hand, palm toward Sharp. "Before you ask, I will not testify. Nor will I admit this conversation ever took place. Not unless King is six feet underground or in a prison cell. He isn't the kind of man who lets things go."

"You think Sheriff King is killing people?" Sharp asked.

"There ain't anybody else left. Walsh moved to Florida. I heard he was dying." Ned shivered. "Walsh, he was shook up when he realized the prisoner was dead, but King just shrugged it off, like it was no big deal. The sheriff is one cold-blooded SOB."

"Thanks, Ned."

"Nothing to thank me for. We never talked." Ned walked toward the beat-up Chevy.

Sharp went back to his car and started the engine. Holding his hands to the heat vents, he chewed Ned's revelation down to the bone.

King must have killed Mary.

Once Sharp's brain made that connection, everything started to make sense. Events slid into place, clicking like the tumblers in a lock when the right key was inserted. They'd thought King was running a parallel investigation. In reality, he had known all the players ahead of time and had used his *investigation* time to kill off any potential witnesses.

If Brian had dropped Mary back at PJ's that night, Mary must have been arrested at the same time as Lou Ford. The other two men had been taken directly to the ER. It made sense that every deputy on duty had been called to the bar fight. At least one would have accompanied the additional two men to the ER. If King saw Mary proposition someone, he might have arrested her too. If P. J. saw King arrest Mary, then once Mary's body turned up and they connected Mary's death to the bar fight . . .

They'd put those pieces together right in the sheriff's conference room, which put Sharp, Lance, and Morgan all at risk.

Sharp picked up his phone, a sick feeling rolling around in his belly. He dialed Lance. Still no answer. Sharp's unease grew as he tried Morgan's line. She didn't pick up either. He sent them each a text. Morgan, always worried about family emergencies, paid close attention to her phone.

Sharp lowered his phone to his leg, his brain still churning out possibilities.

What happened to Vic? And why kill Crystal and try to kill Jenny?

What if Mary made that phone call? She would

have called Crystal. So Crystal would have known that Mary had been in the station. Was King eliminating anyone who knew that he'd arrested Mary that night?

P. J. and Crystal would have been able to link King and Mary on August 10, a connection that didn't matter until Mary's body turned up. But Sharp had no theories about how Vic or Jenny played into the scenario.

His phone buzzed a few seconds later. Hoping it was Lance, Sharp snapped it up. Disappointment filled him as he read the name of his Florida PI contact on the screen.

He answered, "Sharp here."

The Florida PI got right to business. "Owen Walsh is in a hospice facility, dying of cancer. He's medicated and sleeping right now. He doesn't have any family to object, so I'm hanging here with him, hoping he wakes up and wants to talk. I'll let you know if I learn anything."

"Thanks," Sharp said. "Pressure him about Lou Ford's death. Convince him he wants to go to his maker with a clean conscience."

"You had a break in the case?"

"I did. Now I need a deathbed confession." Ending the call, Sharp lowered the phone and stared at it.

Morgan should have returned his message by now.

He accessed the app that would let him track

Lance's phone. The *wait* symbol rotated and rotated and rotated.

Phone not found.

Ned's statement played in Sharp's head on repeat.

The sheriff is one cold-blooded SOB.

Sharp needed to find Lance and Morgan, fast, and he needed help.

He dialed Brody.

Chapter Forty-Six

A half inch of snow dusted the ground. Spotting a game trail, Lance pulled Morgan onto it. The cleared ground would be easier for her to navigate with fewer large obstacles to trip her up.

On the downside, they would also be easier to track if they followed the path. But at this point, he didn't know how far the sheriff was behind them. King wasn't a runner, but he was an experienced hunter and outdoorsman. They were going to be easy to follow no matter where they ran.

Lance hoped the trail led to the lake. If they kept the water to their right, that would eliminate one side of possible attack. The sheriff would have to come up behind them or on their left flank.

Lance had no doubt King would catch up with them eventually. Morgan was freezing and exhausted and running on pure willpower. But he couldn't let her stop. Once she was still, hypothermia would take over, though he could carry her at that point. They had no coats, no food, no water, and no method of communication. Their only option was to keep moving and pray they found help before King found them.

Wishing he could get out of the handcuffs,

Lance eyed Morgan's hair. As gorgeous as it was tumbling around her shoulders, today would have been a good day for one of her courtroom buns and the dozen hairpins that secured them. He was a decent lock pick. "No chance you have a hairpin on you?"

"No, sorry." Her teeth chattered and her words quivered.

Helplessness flooded Lance. There was nothing he could do to protect her. He squinted through the woods. Had they even traveled a mile yet?

How close was King? The sheriff would be warm and dry and armed. He'd be in no rush. He'd hunt them with steady, dogged determination.

The snow picked up, just hard enough for them to leave footprints, not hard enough to fill in those prints as they walked. Their dark clothes, which had been excellent camouflage earlier in the evening, now silhouetted them against a white backdrop.

The cold blew through the thin sleeves of his shirt, and a shiver swept through his bones. If this night dragged on long enough, the cold would kill them as surely as a bullet.

Morgan stumbled again. Lance caught her arm in his hands. Could he hide her somewhere, then lead the sheriff away? He rejected the option. If the sheriff shot him, she was done. A fire would lead the sheriff right to her, and without one, hypothermia would kill her before morning.

The sound of water moving in the darkness caught his attention. The lake?

Evergreen boughs closed in on the trail, smacking him in the face and blotting out the scant light from the overcast sky. He released Morgan's arm to separate the branches. As they neared the sound, he realized it wasn't the lake he'd heard but a stream, which likely fed into Grey Lake.

The trail opened suddenly, the ground dropped off, and Lance teetered on the edge of an embankment. If it hadn't been for the white of the snow at his feet, he wouldn't have noticed the steep drop-off.

He stepped into Morgan's path.

Morgan bumped into his back, then froze.

Leaning over his shoulder, she pressed her lips to his ear. "What is it?"

He leaned to the side so she could see. With her body touching his, he felt the intense shivering racking her body. She was shaking so hard she could barely stay upright.

Ahead, the stream cut through a deep gully twenty feet below the game trail. During the spring, it likely ran much higher on its banks. There had to be a path leading down to the water.

Turning his head, he whispered, "Keep moving," and nudged her gently along a two-foot-wide path that ran along the side of the gully. Morgan's lack of balance worried him.

"Put your hand on my shoulder," he said.

Her grip was weak and trembling. He was freezing. Morgan had less body fat and lower overall body mass than he did. Her long limbs and thin body gave her more surface area from which to lose heat.

But there wasn't a damned thing he could do to help her. With King on their trail, they couldn't stop to build a fire or shelter.

They had to find a place to cross the stream. The snow helped illuminate the ground at their feet, but the topography forced them to slow down. They shuffled along, careful with each footstep. The quiet of the snowy woods was broken only by the gurgle of the stream.

Lance looked as far ahead as the darkness would allow. He had roughly twenty feet of decent visibility. Beyond that, the woods were a dark nothing.

Ahead, the path widened, the embankment becoming gradual enough that they should be able to scramble down without killing themselves.

He pointed with both hands and looked over his shoulder at Morgan at his left flank. She nodded and kept walking.

The snowfall picked up. A glance at the trail behind them showed the flakes settling into their tracks. Maybe King wouldn't find them. Maybe they had a chance after all.

Morgan stumbled. Lance spun and lunged for

her, but her feet slid over the edge. She clawed at nearby branches for a handhold. Lance caught her arm, his feet skidding a few inches in the snow. He fought for traction, his boots sliding closer and closer to the edge. Her eyes were wide open and shining with fear.

If she fell . . .

Lance's boot hit a rock. Bracing against it, he hauled her back up onto the path, pivoted, and pushed her away from the edge, his heart hammering. She fell to her knees, but she was safe.

Rocks shifted. The ground dropped out from under Lance's feet. He plunged downward, his body banging into tree trunks, broken branches tearing at his limbs. A hot bolt of pain licked at his leg. He slammed into a rock. A bone cracked, and pain rocketed through his side.

Then everything went black.

Chapter Forty-Seven

Morgan knelt on the edge of the embankment. A rush of panic lent her body renewed strength. Holding on to a tree, she leaned over the edge. "Lance?"

She shifted her weight, trying to get a better view through the foliage. Beneath her knees, the ground crumbled. Another fat section broke away and tumbled down the slope. Morgan scrambled for solid footing.

Where is he?

Feet first, she stepped down and planted her boot on a tree root. Her fingers slipped from their grip on the tree. When she found a new handhold on a rock, she left a smear of blood behind. She used snow to wipe the blood away, then pulled the sleeve of her sweater over the cut. She didn't want to leave *that* obvious a trail, but she was too cold, too numb to feel the cut on her palm. She moved carefully, making sure each new hand- and foothold was secure before releasing the previous grip. She wouldn't be able to help Lance if she fell too, and having her hands cuffed together made the descent awkward.

It seemed to take forever to work her way into the gully.

She was near the bottom when she spotted his

black-clad form and bright-blond hair on the snow. He lay still at the base of the slope, a few inches from the meandering stream.

If he'd tumbled farther, he would have drowned.

He has to be all right.

As if answering her thoughts, he stirred. His head lifted and turned as he scanned the stream bed.

She slid down the remaining few feet of bank and dropped to her knees beside him. She tried to run her hands over his body to assess his injuries, but she couldn't feel anything. Her hands and feet felt like heavy blocks of ice. She slid her hands over his legs. Her fingers came away from his calf wet with fresh blood. She parted a slash in his pants. A deep gash ran through his calf. Blood ran from the wound. But she doubted the cut was the reason he hadn't risen. "Where else are you hurt?"

"Ribs, leg," he said through blue-white lips. "Help me up."

"Are you sure?"

He hoisted his body into a sitting position, his face went gray, and the skin of his face stretched tight as a drum. Despite the cold, his injuries clearly weren't numb. "We have to keep moving."

"We need to stop that bleeding." She got her shoulder under his arm. The handcuffs got in the way. With his feet under him, he walked two steps and doubled over, his hands pressing against his ribs.

"Broken?" she asked.

"I don't know. Maybe not."

"Hold on. We're leaving a blood trail in the snow." But what could she use to stop the bleeding? They had no supplies. Nothing. Her belt or his bootlace weren't any good without a bandage of some sort. She must have something she could tie around his leg . . . There was only one thing she could think of.

She snaked her freezing hands into the neck of her sweater and slipped her bra straps down her shoulders. Unhooking the straps with frozen fingers was harder, but she fumbled through it. She gave Lance her back. "Unhook my bra."

Lance made a choking sound. "What?"

"It's the only thing I can think of to use as a bandage."

"Smart." His fingers slid up the back of her sweater. With the shoulder straps already unhooked, her bra fell to her waist, and she tugged it out from under her sweater.

"This is going to hurt. You might want to sit down." She folded it in half.

"Getting up was too hard." He grabbed a tree limb and held tight.

She pressed the folded bra against the wound, then used the straps to tie it in place. Not secure enough. She took off her belt and wrapped it around his calf. It held, and the light padding of her bra absorbed the blood.

"That's the best I can do," she said.

"I'm impressed." Lance took a step forward. His face creased with pain, but he was no longer dripping blood. "We need to assess our options."

"We have options?" Walking next to him, Morgan brought her arms close to her body, her hands under her chin. Snowflakes dotted the sleeves of her wool sweater. Her brain was frozen. She could barely think.

"We can continue to follow the water. Once we reach the lake, at least we'll have a clear direction and distance to travel. But thanks to my fall, we're moving very slowly now."

Morgan glanced behind her at the clear lines of footprints in the snow. "And he's going to catch us."

She picked up a tree limb and dragged it behind them, trying to obscure their tracks. In real life, it didn't work as well as it did in the movies.

Lance squinted over his shoulder. "We know he's a hunter. He's experienced in the woods. He'll have provisions, and he has time on his side."

"We can move faster if you lean on me," she offered.

"I'm too heavy, and you're already exhausted. One of us needs to be able to break away and run if necessary." Holding his ribs, he frowned at his leg. "That's not going to be me now."

"You would never leave me, and I would never leave you, so I rule that one out."

He sighed. "You're going to have to have an open mind. When I said we had options, I never said any of them were good options."

"What's option number two?" she asked.

His sideways glance told her she was going to like this choice even less than the last.

"You leave me and run for help," he said.

The choking sound that came out of her mouth was part exhaustion, part horror. The thought of their lives being dependent on her being able to run far or fast under good conditions was terrifying. She'd been raised in the city. Her family hadn't moved to Scarlet Falls until after her father had been killed in the line of duty. She'd been in high school. The woods were not her natural habitat, and in this cold, she felt like a baby giraffe taking its first steps. Every inch of her shook. She was barely putting one foot in front of the other. At any second she could face-plant in the snow.

"How far would I get?" she asked. "Even injured, you'd probably get farther than I would."

He shook his head. How badly *was* he hurt?

"We're back to me not leaving you out here."

"I'm not helpless," he said.

"What kind of long gun does the sheriff's

department carry?" She side-eyed him. "This is no insult to your masculinity, but you don't stand a chance against an AR-15."

"Look, if only one of us is going to get out of this, it has to be you. I don't have three kids at home. Your girls have already lost their father. I will not allow them to lose their mother too."

And there it was. Lance's very nature. He was so different from her late husband in almost every way. John had been tall and thin, with a lighthearted and easygoing personality. Lance was athletic, heavily muscled, and intense to his core. But the two men she had fallen in love with had one essential quality in common. Deep in their hearts, they were both heroes. John had given his life for his country, and Lance was prepared to die for her and her girls right here and now.

But she couldn't accept the thought of letting him sacrifice himself for her. "We have to think of something else."

But what?

"We need to outthink the sheriff. We need a plan." She grasped for an idea.

What had King said?

It's all about knowing your prey and being able to predict its movements.

More numb than cold, she tripped over her own boot. As she righted herself, her knees buckled. She grabbed a tree to stay upright.

If you get out of this alive, you will start exercising. But future promises weren't going to help her now.

"We need to do something he doesn't expect," she said. "We need to use his own behavioral patterns to predict his movements. What is his end goal?"

Lance turned back to the path. His leg was bleeding again. "The only thing that King wants is us to be dead."

A twig cracked. Lance shoved Morgan into the bushes. "Hide."

She fell on her hands and knees, crawling under the branches of a blue spruce.

Chapter Forty-Eight

Crouching, King scanned the ground. Their footprints were ridiculously easy to follow in the snow. This wasn't even going to be a challenge. They couldn't be too far ahead, or the snow would have obliterated their tracks.

They were following a game trail toward Grey Lake. Once they reached it, Kruger would take them around to the populated side of the lake. It was a solid plan.

But Ms. Dane was not in top condition. She was smart and tough, but physically, she was soft. It was no insult. She was a hell of a woman, though maybe a bit too intelligent. In his opinion, women shouldn't try to compete with men. But even with that one flaw, Ms. Dane was the first woman he'd ever admired. Not that he desired her. He had no interest in a relationship with anyone. He liked being alone. But for the first time, he might have a real regret after he killed someone.

Not that it would stop him.

If he had to choose between Ms. Dane and himself, the choice was damned simple. Besides, women made men weak. Ms. Dane would be the end of Kruger. Like a wolf targeting the weakest, trailing member of the herd, King only had to catch up with her. Kruger would be at her side.

He'd kill the pair of them and dispose of their bodies. No one would find them. Either he'd borrow a boat and sink them in the middle of the lake. Or he'd bury them where he'd left Vic in '94.

Wouldn't it be ironic to put Kruger next to the father he'd been looking for all these years?

He straightened and followed the trail of footprints. The snow had brightened the landscape enough that he didn't need his flashlight. He followed their trail. They were headed toward the stream that fed the lake. The woods opened at the edge of a gully. If he hadn't known it was there, he might have slid into it.

The footprints turned toward the lake, following the flow of the water. He kept as far away from the drop-off as possible, stopping when the ground in front of him fell away. He crouched again. Digging the flashlight from his pocket, he risked a quick look at the trail. He did not want to end up in the gully. But beneath the fresh landslide, he saw a clear path through broken foliage. Something large had gone over the edge.

One of them had fallen.

Anticipation surged through his veins as he illuminated the slope, searching for a way down. He picked his way carefully down to the bottom of the embankment and examined the ground. They'd spent some time here, and the tracks leading away were different. He spotted something red in the snow. Blood. One of them was injured. That's why the footprints were closer together—more shuffling and less striding. The stream ran though the bottom of a deep gully. The embankments were steep, hard enough for a fit man to climb, let alone an injured person. They'd be stuck in the gully until it reached the lake. This would almost be too easy.

He followed their trail, breaking into a light jog. Excitement invigorated him. The hunt was almost over.

After he'd eliminated Kruger and Dane, he'd take care of Sharp. Then he was home free. Every thread between him and Mary would be severed.

Almost all, he corrected. But Owen Walsh would be dead soon enough. Paranoid Owen, who had been riddled with guilt and fear for more than two decades. Owen had called him the second Lincoln Sharp had attempted to make contact. Now Owen had only weeks to live. Cancer was eating him with the same efficiency as his conscience had over the years. Soon, Owen would be gone, and he would be the only one who knew what had happened that night.

In the parking lot of PJ's, he assessed the fallout. Three drunken fools had beaten the crap out of each other over a woman.

411

If the three men had been less drunk and more intelligent, at least one of them would have realized that Mary was a hooker. She would have done all of them in turn for the right amount of money. What a bunch of assholes.

As chief deputy, it was his responsibility to sort the mess out.

He pointed to one of the deputies on duty. "Bill, you follow these two idiots to the ER. When they've been cleared, bring them into the station for processing." He turned to another deputy. "Owen, you drive this asshole to the station." He handed off Lou Ford, still cursing and arguing and being a drunken pain in the ass. Lou was a frequent flyer in the drunk and disorderly department.

Mary tried to slink off through the parking lot, but he spotted her.

"You're under arrest too," he said once he'd caught up with her.

She propped a fist on her hip. "You're kidding?"

"We both know I have no sense of humor." He cuffed her and put her in his patrol car. Like Lou Ford, it wasn't her first ride in his back seat. "P. J. is tired of you soliciting customers. He says you're fired, by the way."

He followed Owen back to the station. Mary was compliant. But not even a quart of Wild Turkey would make Lou Ford cooperate. He cursed and thrashed and dragged his feet. They entered the back door of the station, and he brought Mary into the corridor.

"Don't I get a phone call?" She sulked. "I need to call my mama."

"Little help here," Owen called out from the doorway. Lou had planted his feet like a mule, leaning back and refusing to budge.

Son of a . . . He unlocked one of Mary's handcuffs and fastened it to the ring next to the payphone. Digging in his pocket, he came up with a quarter. "Here. Make your call."

He walked to the doorway. Taking Lou's opposite arm, he pulled. But Lou leaned over and retched. Disgust and anger reared up inside him.

"Do not puke in my station!" he yelled.

Owen had clearly had enough of this shit too. He raised a fist. At the same time that Owen punched Lou in the head, King kicked out. One sweep of his big, black cop shoe knocked Lou's feet out from under him. Already leaning over and unbalanced, the drunk went down hard, his posture sending him over to the right. His head hit the wall with the sickening clunk of bone on cinderblock.

Lou sprawled on the floor and didn't move.

"What did you do?" Owen yelled.

He poked Lou with a toe. Still no movement.

Owen bent over the body. One hand went to the drunk's neck. He looked up and mouthed, "He's dead."

King lifted a shoulder. "He was a waste of oxygen, and his liver wouldn't have lasted too much longer anyway."

The man's death didn't bother him, but he'd have to think fast to avoid a legal fallout. The only worry on his mind was his future.

"Now what do we do?" Owen stood. Removing his campaign hat, he rubbed the top of his skull as if he was trying to stimulate his brain.

Good luck.

Owen was a decent cop, but he was no Einstein.

And this situation was going to need a solid plan. Finesse would be required.

Owen dropped his hand and shoved his hat back on his head. "We have to call the sheriff."

"No." King would do whatever was necessary to fix this. "My career is not going down for this piece of shit."

"What do we do?" Owen gestured to the body at their feet. "We can't just pretend it didn't happen."

"Why not?" He reached for one of Lou's arms. "We'll put him in the cell to sleep it off, like we've done before. Nothing unusual about that. When he doesn't wake up, we'll be surprised."

Owen hesitated.

"He just got into a bar fight," he argued. "Who's to say he didn't get hit in the head at PJ's?"

The best lies were the simple ones.

"OK." Owen's arm shook as they picked up the body and dragged it into the holding cell.

The station was empty. The only other staff member on duty was the dispatcher, and he had a room to himself. They positioned Owen on his side on the cot, his body curled up as if asleep. Then they left him there.

King closed the cell door and smiled. "Done."

"You're forgetting something." Owen's gaze indicated the doorway that led into the rear corridor.

Mary.

He had forgotten about her. Unfortunately for Mary, she was a witness.

"Come on." He moved toward the doorway.

"What are you going to do?" Owen asked.

"Just follow me."

Mary was still cuffed to the ring in the wall. Her eyes widened as he approached her, the whites glowing in the dim corridor. She pressed her back against the wall. She knew what she'd seen and what it meant.

"How about we make a deal, Mary?" King walked closer.

She swallowed, the column of her throat undulating. "Wh-at?" Her voice trembled.

"I'll drop the charges. You forget you were here tonight."

Mary's quick nod was tense and desperate.

He took off her handcuffs. "I'll even drive you back to PJ's."

With one hand on her bicep, he guided her out the rear door and into the back seat of his car. He glanced over his shoulder at Owen. "Do your paperwork on Ford as if he passed out—then go back out like normal. We'll find him dead later."

Owen nodded.

Then King drove out into the country-side, away from Grey's Hollow and into neighboring Scarlet Falls. If a client killed Mary, he'd want to put some distance between her body and the crime scene.

Mary pressed her hands to the side window. "This ain't the way to PJ's."

At a rest stop, he pulled off the road and parked. There were no other cars in sight. Insects hummed in the warm August night. He got out of the car and opened the rear door.

"Get out," he said.

She obeyed. Between the hem of her miniskirt and her fuck-me heels, she wobbled as she climbed from the back seat. She sidled along the car fender. He closed the rear door.

As he turned to reach for her arm, she kicked out. His hips jerked sideways. Her foot struck him high on the thigh and grazed his groin. His knees buckled, and she bolted, stepping right out of her shoes.

Shit!

Cupping his balls, he limped after her.

He recovered his stride after a couple of minutes, but she'd put a hundred feet between them. Barefoot, she hit the side of the road, turned, and ran straight up the yellow line. Ahead, her bare legs churned, but he was gaining on her.

Until he saw the one thing that could ruin his plan.

Headlights.

Screaming, Mary stayed in the center of the road and waved her arms. The vehicle slowed, then stopped. A man got out of a sedan and stepped into the beams of his headlights.

"Help me!" Mary yelled, glancing over her shoulder. "He's going to kill me."

He closed the gap just as Mary reached her Good Samaritan.

The man was tall and athletic-looking. "Is everything all right, Deputy?"

"Just fine. I'm arresting this woman," he said, cuffing Mary's arms behind her back.

"No." Mary struggled. "He's going to kill me! Please. Help."

The man shifted his weight. Hell, even if the man left now, he was a risk. A witness. Thanks to Mary's outbursts, the man would remember her.

"She's been drinking." He took Mary by the arm and tugged her back. "You can get back in your car now, sir. I have everything under control."

The man pivoted, slowly, uncertainly.

When the man's back was turned, he pulled his baton off his duty belt and hit him over the head. The man's legs crumbled. He went down hard.

Mary screamed again.

He had to get her off this road.

"Shut up." Anger roared inside him as he knocked her to the ground and straddled her. With her hands cuffed behind her back, she couldn't resist. His fingers were around her throat. He squeezed until she was still and lifeless and fucking quiet.

He stopped, panting.

She was dead.

Fuck! That hadn't been part of the plan.

Her death should have looked like an accident. No chance of that with his finger marks around her neck.

Now what?

Now he had two more deaths to cover up, that's what.

He'd have to improvise. He ran to the vehicle and opened the trunk. Hauling Mary off the pavement, he put her inside. Then he dragged the man to the back of the car and muscled him in too. Sliding behind the wheel, he opened the glove compartment and found the registration. Victor Kruger lived in Scarlet Falls.

Correction: *Had* lived in Scarlet Falls.

He needed a plan to get rid of both bodies and the car. The car he could sink in Grey Lake. If he put Victor at the wheel of his car, the deaths could look like a combination murder and suicide. But they would have no connection to one another. Murder-suicides were typically crimes of passion, born of the desperation that came from twisted love.

If these bodies were ever discovered, what he needed was a way to make it appear as if Victor killed Mary and then left town. The car could go in the lake with Mary in the trunk. He'd bury Vic in the woods. He knew just the spot. When it was done, he'd call Owen for a pickup. Owen was an accessory. He'd keep his mouth shut.

A twig cracked ahead, pulling his attention back to his task. Kruger and Dane must be just ahead. He slowed his pace, easing along the trail. The footprints muddied in the snow, as if they'd stopped to rest. His gaze fell to the spot of blood in the snow ahead. He walked closer. They couldn't be far, not with one of them still bleeding.

The footprints disappeared into the thick foliage of an evergreen tree. Could they be trying to hide? With slow and silent steps, he eased forward and separated the branches of the evergreen. She huddled on the ground, wet, cold, and scraggly as a lost kitten.

"Ms. Dane. Nice to see you." He gestured with the barrel of the rifle. Her hand was bloody.

Ms. Dane lifted her hands. Her skin and lips were blue, and she staggered as she tried to get to her feet. Even if he hadn't found her, she wouldn't have lasted much longer. She was running on pure determination, which he admitted, she had in spades.

It was a shame she had to die.

"Where's Kruger?" he asked.

"He went ahead for help." She swayed on her feet. "I can't walk anymore."

Kruger would never leave her.

"Liar." King whipped the rifle around and smacked her in the face with the butt of the stock. She crumpled to the ground and lay in the snow, unmoving. He hadn't delivered a full-force blow, hadn't meant to knock her out, only to stun her. But she was a more delicate creature than he was accustomed to handling. Whatever. At this point, he needed to be flexible and keep his eyes on the prize. Now he would use her as bait.

He aimed the rifle at her face. "Come on out, Kruger. I know you can hear me. You have three seconds to show yourself before I pull the trigger."

Chapter Forty-Nine

Heart hammering, Lance stared at the sheriff's back. Wavering, he hesitated for a fraction of a second. If he jumped the sheriff, King could shoot Morgan. But if he didn't, King would definitely shoot them both. He could not, under any circumstances, allow either of them to be taken prisoner by King. That would be the end.

Surprise—and the sheriff's own confidence—would be Lance's best weapons.

He took as deep a breath as his ribs would allow. Pushing off his good leg, he launched himself at the sheriff's back. He looped his cuffed hands over the sheriff's head. Pulling hard, he yanked the chain joining the cuffs into the sheriff's windpipe. The sheriff dropped the rifle. His hands went to his throat. He grabbed Lance's arms and tried to relieve the pressure. But Lance had the upper hand, and he wasn't letting go. If this didn't work, he and Morgan were both dead.

There would be no more running. No more game of cat and mouse. The mice didn't have any more chase left in them.

The sheriff gagged, a sick choking sound emanating from his throat as he fought to breathe. He thrashed, clawing at Lance's hands and using his size and weight to attempt to pull Lance off balance.

King was large, strong, and trained in defense and arrest tactics. He dropped one hand to his belt and freed a knife from its sheath. Reaching over his shoulder, King jabbed the point at Lance's head. Lance ducked his head out of the knife's path, but the effort cost him leverage.

The sheriff grabbed Lance's wrist with his other hand, eased the pressure on his own throat, and heaved Lance forward with brute strength. King pinned Lance's wrist just below his own collarbone. Lance dropped his weight and fought to hold his position.

The knife came at Lance's eye next. He shifted his head. His arms trembled. Agony seared through his ribcage. Exhausted, hypothermic, and injured, he was nearing his limit. It would be now or never.

"Last chance!" he yelled in the sheriff's ear. "Drop the knife."

King's answer was another sweeping arc of the blade toward Lance's face.

Lance shifted away, fighting to maintain the hold on King's neck. If he had two good legs, he'd put a knee into the sheriff's back for leverage. But with his injuries, he was lucky to be standing.

The knife swept toward his head again. He caught a flash of metal as the blade whispered past his eye, missing his eyeball by millimeters. His eyebrow stung where the sharp point nicked him.

The sheriff grunted and pulled hard on Lance's wrist, attempting to give himself more breathing room. Lance planted his forearms on the sheriff's upper back and rolled his arms inward. If he could press on the side of the sheriff's neck, he could cut off the blood supply to his brain.

But King wouldn't give up the leverage. With a grunt, the sheriff lowered the knife and stabbed under his own armpit, aiming at Lance's midsection. The blade kissed his belly with a flicker of heat.

Lance opened his mouth to tell Morgan to run. He couldn't hold King much longer. He couldn't maneuver or gain leverage. But he didn't have any air to shout either. Every ounce of remaining strength in his body pulled against the sheriff's neck.

The pine trees around him spun. He couldn't breathe. Tiny stars rushed at his eyes, and his vision began to tunnel.

They weren't going to make it. The sheriff was a bull. Lance could hold on, but he couldn't finish him.

A thud sounded next to Lance's ear, and the sheriff went limp. His body sagged, and Lance saw Morgan standing behind him, the sheriff's

AR-15 raised butt-down over her shoulder. She'd knocked the sheriff out.

It was over.

Relief drained his adrenaline high, leaving him weak and shaky.

Lance released his hold on the sheriff's neck. The weight of the falling body dragged him off balance and onto the ground. Lance fell sideways. His shoulder hit the snowy grass. He rolled over to his back. Snow fell on his face as he stared up at the dark sky and snowy treetops.

At Morgan.

She stood over the sheriff's prone body, the AR-15 in her hands pointed straight at King's head. Dark hair waved around her face, and snow whirled around her. In a moment of almost giddy light-headedness, Lance imagined her as Wonder Woman.

He blamed oxygen deprivation.

"Now what?" Morgan shook. She looked like she could barely hold on to the rifle.

"Cover me. Shoot him if he moves a muscle." Lance staggered to his feet. After testing the sheriff's consciousness with a solid kick, he took his weapon and searched his belt for a handcuff key. Finding it, Lance unlocked the cuffs on his wrists. Setting them aside, he worked the sheriff's coat off. Then he peeled off King's next two layers before rolling the sheriff to the base of a tree and cuffing his hands around the trunk. He collected the knife from where it had fallen and searched the rest of the sheriff's pockets.

Lance brought Morgan the coat. After removing her handcuffs, he wrapped the heavy coat around her.

She slipped her arms into the sleeves. Lance zipped it to her chin. Then he dressed in the sheriff's extra shirts, a thin base layer and a fleece zip-up. They were still warm from King's body, but Lance didn't care.

Heat was heat.

Setting the rifle aside, Morgan dug in the pockets of the sheriff's coat and started pulling out all the supplies a good woodsman packs when going into the forest: protein bars, flashlight, compass, a reflective emergency blanket. "Matches and fire starter sticks. We can build a fire."

She also found a handgun that was not a police issue. She returned it to the pocket.

"We'll fill this with snow and let it melt." She shook an empty water bottle.

"I don't want to spend the night out here," Lance said. He wanted to get the hell out of the woods, but his ribs felt like he'd been run over by a car.

"How far are we from the nearest building?" Morgan asked.

Lance scanned the area. "I'm honestly not sure.

It seems like we covered some ground, but I'm betting we didn't get that far. Could be a few miles."

"We're both hypothermic and likely risking frostbite," Morgan said. "Getting warm has to be our first priority. I vote for a makeshift shelter and a fire. Then we reassess our physical condition. Right at this moment, I wouldn't make it another mile."

Lance nodded. She was right. Breathing was becoming more painful.

She glanced at the sheriff's prone body. "He'll freeze to death if we leave him there."

"Probably." Lance didn't care. "After everything he's done, he deserves to freeze to death."

"That's exactly what King would say."

Damn.

She was always right, but the moral high ground felt as attainable as Mount Everest.

"*Fine.* But *you* get warm first." Lance began looking for dry wood, not an easy task in the snow, when it felt like a truck was parked on his chest. But he scoured the underside of a fallen log for enough to get a flame going. Morgan, dwarfed in King's coat and gloves, brought some dryish sticks and pine needles to the spot under the fir tree, where they were sheltered from the worst of the snowfall. If Lance could get the fire going and eat a protein bar, maybe he'd find a way to pull a few branches over them for better protection from the elements.

But Morgan was already on it. "I'm stealing your bootlaces."

She arced two branches over them, forming a fir tree lean-to that blocked the wind. She tied them in place with his laces.

In twenty minutes, they had enough flames to warm their hands over. Lance added some twigs and coaxed the flames higher. Then he grudgingly spread the emergency blanket over the sheriff.

Huddled around their tiny fire, they ate the sheriff's power bars and drank melted snow. Lance leaned back against the tree, pain and exhaustion finally besting him now that the acute danger had been neutralized. He balanced the AR-15 across his thighs, the muzzle aimed in the sheriff's direction. Morgan had King's service revolver in her hand and the extra handgun in her pocket. She leaned on his shoulder. Twenty feet outside their small shelter, the sheriff didn't move.

The sound of a snapping twig startled Lance. Pain sliced through his ribs, stealing his breath. He must have fallen asleep.

Something rustled the foliage, farther away this time.

Lance lifted the rifle in his lap, scanning the clearing, looking for the sheriff. But another rustle in the distance told him King was running away.

Next to him, Morgan came awake in an instant. She mouthed, "What is it?"

He whispered, "King is gone."

A little while later, voices floated through the trees from the direction opposite where King had run.

Ten minutes passed before Mac and Sharp walked into the clearing in backpacks and hiking gear.

Relief swept through Lance, warming him as much as the fire had.

Morgan stumbled to her feet, and Mac caught her in a hug.

Sharp dropped to one knee next to Lance. "Are you alive?"

"Yes." Lance struggled to sit up. The sky was lighter. Was it close to dawn? "How did you find us?"

"Hold on, let me give the rescue party our coordinates." Sharp spoke into his radio. After he lowered it, he jerked a thumb toward Mac. "That guy is freaky good in the woods. He tracks like one of the K-9s."

"We didn't wait for the official rescue party to get it together," Mac said. "The two of us could move faster anyway."

Sharp set his backpack on the ground and opened it. "But they aren't far behind us. We'll have you both out of here in no time. Since you're not dying, we won't call for a helicopter. Mac is trying to figure out the closest spot we can rendezvous with a four-wheeler."

Lance straightened. Pain in his side nearly split him in half. "King got away. It must have been just before you arrived. He was handcuffed around that tree. I must have dozed off." Lance wanted to kick himself.

"*Passed out* is probably a more accurate description," Sharp said. "You're in rough shape."

Mac was crouching where King's prone body should have been. Mac stood and scanned the ground. "He went north. We can catch him if we move now."

"I'm surprised you didn't kill him." Sharp handed Lance a bag of trail mix.

Lance ate a handful of raisins and nuts. "I wanted to."

And if he had, he wouldn't be worried about the sheriff getting away right now.

"I'll bet you did." Sharp handed him a bottle of water and patted his shoulder. "You did good. Everything is going to be all right. We'll find him."

"You'll wait for the police to catch him, right?" On the other side of the fire, Morgan sat on a rock. She smiled at him through the smoke.

"Right," Sharp grumbled.

Lance leaned back against the tree. He knew who had killed his father, and the sheriff couldn't possibly get far. He and Morgan were alive and together. Everything *would* be all right, as long as he had her.

Chapter Fifty

An hour later, Sharp hiked through the forest behind four state troopers. He could see why Mac Barrett was an asset to his search and rescue team. He loped along the trail in an effortless gait, tracking the sheriff like a frigging golden retriever.

The trail led into a clearing. A cabin sat in the center of the open space. Fresh tracks in the snow led to the front door. King was inside. They all knew it. Tension connected the team members like an invisible current.

The troopers fanned out, motioning for Sharp and Mac to fall behind them.

Grudgingly, they did.

But not far.

One trooper scouted ahead. Crouching beneath a window, he took a selfie stick and his cell phone from his pocket. Raising the phone just above the windowsill, he used his camera to spy inside. He lowered the phone and crept back to the group. "He's standing in the middle of the room. He's armed and injured."

"Think we have any chance of talking him into laying down his weapon and coming outside?" the leader asked.

All the men shared a *there's no way in hell that would ever happen* look.

"Then let's go get him." The leader motioned toward the cabin.

The troopers flanked the entrance. With no warning knock, they breached the door, sweeping through the doorway. Boots thudded on wood as they shouted commands.

"Police!"

"Let me see your hands!"

"Drop the weapon!"

Sharp angled himself so he could see through the doorway.

The sheriff stood in the center of the main room. His face was blotched, his nose was twice its normal size, and his eyes were bloodshot. In one hand, he pointed a handgun toward the floor. He cradled his other, swollen hand against his body.

King had dislocated his thumb to escape the handcuffs.

Crazy bastard.

"Put the weapon down, Sheriff," the lead trooper ordered.

They all knew King. They'd worked together. But they would still put a bullet in him to stop him if they had to.

King looked beyond the cops, to Sharp. Their eyes met. King's mouth curled into a snarl.

"Put the weapon down or I *will* shoot you!" the trooper yelled.

Sharp knew in that moment of eye contact that

King would not let the troopers arrest him. Nor would he take the chance of a nonlethal bullet wound. He would never go to jail.

In one swift movement, the sheriff brought the gun to his mouth and pulled the trigger, blowing off the back of his head. Blood and bits of brain splattered across the worn wood behind him.

King went out on his own terms.

Sharp didn't give a rat's ass how he went out, as long as he ended up six feet underground.

Chapter Fifty-One

Late the next morning, Morgan sat in Lance's kitchen and drained her second cup of coffee. Lance was still asleep. He'd refused to stay at the hospital the night before. They'd returned to his house in the gray hours just before dawn, crawled into his bed, and slept like corpses.

The doorbell rang. Not wanting the noise to wake Lance, she hurried to the door and opened it. Mac and Stella stood on the front step, with all three of Morgan's girls in tow.

"Where's Wance?" Sophie tried to zoom past Morgan's legs.

Morgan made a grab for her daughter. "He's sleeping."

Sophie folded her arms and sulked. "I want to see him."

"I know," Morgan said. "I'll go in and see if he's awake yet. Sharp is in the kitchen."

"We'll take the kids into the kitchen." Stella held up a box of donuts. "Who wants a donut?"

"Save me one," Morgan said over her shoulder.

"Do you really deserve a donut?" Stella asked. "If it were Christmas, I'd fill your stocking with coal for the stunt you pulled last night."

Morgan and Lance had given their statements at the hospital the previous night.

"I apologized twenty times already." Guilt poked Morgan. "I should have answered your call. I should have told you where we were going. I'm sorry."

Stella humphed. "Maybe *one* donut." She shook a finger at Morgan. "But you have to drink one of Sharp's nasty concoctions."

"I promise." Morgan held up three fingers like a Girl Scout.

Shaking her head, Stella retreated down the hall. Her sister loved her. No matter what.

Morgan opened Lance's bedroom door.

"You don't have to be quiet," he said. "I'm awake."

His eyes were open. Shirtless, he pushed the sheet down to his waist. Purple bruises mottled his ribcage. A small bandage on his side and another on his eyebrow covered the shallow knife wounds he'd sustained in his fight with Sheriff King. Just looking at him bare-chested made Morgan shiver. She'd layered her silk long underwear under a wool sweater. After their night in the woods, she might never be warm enough again.

Morgan eased onto the side of the bed, taking care not to jostle him. "The kids are here. They were worried about you, so Stella and Mac brought them to visit. I hope that's all right."

"Of course it's OK." Lance took her hand and traced the small bandage on her palm. "I'm fine."

She shook her head. "You have three fractured ribs and twenty stitches in your leg. You should have stayed in the hospital last night."

"*Observation* is hospital code for waking you up every thirty minutes. I needed actual sleep, and it could have been worse." He touched a tender spot on her temple, where the butt end of King's rifle had left a bruise.

"Unfortunately, I can't argue with that."

They'd been very, very lucky.

Lance put his palms on the bed and pushed his body toward the headboard. His face went tight with pain.

"You need a pill." Morgan reached for a pillow and tucked it behind him. When he made a face, she said, "Remember what the doctor said. If you don't take the medication, you won't breathe deeply enough, and you'll be at risk for pneumonia."

"Yes, ma'am." He eased onto the pillow, relaxing again once he was still.

Morgan's own bruises were numerous, but just being alive and with Lance was enough to ease her stiffness. Every time she thought about what *could* have happened, her throat clogged and her heart clenched.

She opened the prescription bottle and put two tablets in his hand, then handed him a glass of water on the nightstand. Morgan moved the medication to the top of his medicine cabinet, out of the reach of her kids. She moved the sheet and blanket aside to check the bandage on his calf. He wore just his boxers. More bruises had darkened on his body overnight. Angry, dark patches covered his torso and limbs like a purple camouflage print. The sheer number and expanse of them spoke volumes of how hard he'd fought to save them.

The bedroom door opened, and Sharp swept in, carrying a green shake. "How are you?"

"How about a little privacy, Sharp?" Lance pulled the sheet over his legs and tugged it to his waist.

Sharp rolled his eyes, walked to the bedside, and set the shake on the nightstand. "You need nutrients."

"I just woke up," Lance grumbled.

"I made breakfast for you too." Sharp speared Morgan with a direct gaze. "Don't you dare dig in to those donuts I saw in the kitchen. You're not in as serious condition as Lance, but your body has some repairs to make too."

She sighed. She'd really been looking forward to one of those donuts and a vat of coffee.

"How's your arm?" she asked Sharp.

"Starting to heal, thank you." He handed Lance the shake with a short speech about vitamins, amino acids, protein, and anti-inflammatory compounds.

"I believe you. I'm drinking." Lance accepted

the shake and took a long swallow. "What happened to your hand?"

Sharp poked at a bandage on his finger. "I went to pick up that little dog at the vet this morning. She bit me. The vet said it seems the dog hates men."

"Oh, no," Morgan said. "I'll bet Warren Fox had something to do with that."

"Speaking of Warren," Sharp said, "he's fine. He was passed out drunk when you knocked on his door. He'd run his vehicle into a ditch a half mile from his house and stumbled home."

"At least he isn't dead," Morgan said. "What are we going to do with the dog? I can't have a dog that bites. I have three kids." But she'd never take the dog to the shelter.

"No worries. I already found her a home. I took her to Natalie Leed's house. When I told Natalie the dog was homeless and hated men, she said that was perfect. So did she, at the moment. It was love at first sight." Sharp grinned. "Oh, and guess what Stan Adams has been hiding? A gambling problem."

"How do you know?" Lance raised the glass.

"He was arrested this morning," Sharp said. "That problem at his firm wasn't a request from a client. It was missing money. Stan has been *borrowing* from the firm to pay his debts. Apparently, his partner has had him under investigation for a while."

"I wonder how long that's been going on, or whether it has anything to do with Stan's refusal to say where he really was the night my dad went missing." Lance drank.

Sharp shrugged. "I doubt he'll say now that he's lawyered up."

Watching Sharp fuss over Lance, Morgan turned toward the door. "I'll get you an ice pack."

Sophie bolted past. Morgan tried to grab her, but the child was wiry and quick. She launched herself onto the bed. She made no attempt to touch him, but the mattress rocked. Lance's face turned pale.

Morgan hurried back to the bed, reaching for Sophie, but Lance shook his head. "I've got her."

He set the shake down and put both hands around Sophie's waist to stop her movements.

Sophie's eyes widened as she stared at his bruised chest.

"It looks worse than it is," he said.

"It wooks wike it hurts." She leaned forward and kissed the darkest, largest bruise across his ribs.

His face went whiter, and his eyes looked like they were going to roll back in his head as her lips touched the skin over his fractured bones. Sophie leaned back and folded her legs under her body with a little bounce.

"Oh, honey." Morgan winced. "Lance needs to rest. Don't—"

Lance held up a hand. Despite the paleness of his face, his eyes were misty. "She's fine. I need to get up anyway."

"But you don't need to be catapulted to your feet," Morgan said. "Sophie, did you get a donut?"

The little girl turned and frowned at Morgan. "I want to stay wif Wance."

"How about I come into the kitchen?" Lance suggested.

Sophie eyed his injuries with a dubious expression, as if she didn't believe he could or should be getting up, but she agreed. "OK."

Sharp lifted her off the bed, clearly trying to stave off another trampoline session. He set her on the floor, and she darted out of the room.

"I'll go make some vegetable omelets," Sharp said. "When you're up to it, Stella has business to discuss with you both."

Sharp had phoned to tell them about King's suicide while they were in the ER. Morgan had not been surprised. The only rules King had followed were his own.

When they'd been discharged from the hospital, Morgan had stayed with Lance to keep an eye on him. He'd insisted he was all right, but she hadn't wanted him to be alone. They'd fallen asleep as soon as they'd gotten back to his house. Morgan had kept one hand on his body all night long, as if she needed to be continuously reassured that he was safe and whole.

"Did the state police find anything at King's cabin?" By anything, Lance clearly meant *remains*.

Sharp said, "The forensics team was still searching the cabin. In light of Vic's body still being missing, I suggested they bring in a cadaver dog. I'll bet your dad isn't far from the lake."

But they still didn't know *why* Vic had died. Would they ever? After all they'd been through, Lance and his mother deserved closure.

"I want to go out there," Lance said, obviously feeling the same way. "And I need to visit my mother."

They'd checked on her after he'd been discharged. She'd still been holding her own.

"See how you feel standing up first, all right?" Sharp followed Sophie out of the room, pulling the door closed behind him.

"I'll get you some clothes." Morgan opened his dresser drawer and took out a pair of sweatpants and a T-shirt. She brought them to the bed. Lance was sitting up with his legs over the side. She knelt in front of him, sparing him the agony of bending in half to get his pants on.

"I can dress myself," Lance protested.

"I'm sorry about Sophie. I hope she didn't hurt you."

Lance swallowed. "She didn't."

"Liar," Morgan said.

"Don't make me laugh." He laughed, then

put a hand over his ribs. "I'm flattered. In the beginning I didn't think I'd be able to win her over."

Morgan pictured Sophie bouncing on the mattress. "Be careful what you wish for."

Chapter Fifty-Two

The next day, Lance stood on the grass behind Sheriff King's small hunting cabin. Next to him, Morgan held his hand. The day was bright and clear. The sun shone on the water and warmed the top of his head.

Having done her job and alerted within thirty minutes of being brought to the site, the cadaver dog sat on the sidelines while a state police forensic team dug careful shovelfuls of earth out from under the turf. The hole was three feet deep, and they were still digging.

Morgan had detoured to see the inside of the cabin. She hadn't seen the sheriff's body, but the bloodstain on the wall had been enough to convince her that the sheriff was dead.

That it was all over.

Well, almost.

They still didn't know where Vic was or why he'd been killed.

Morgan shivered and zipped her parka to her chin.

Stella and Brody walked across the grass to join them.

Brody stared out over the lake. "How typical of King to off himself and leave us totally in the dark. No note, no explanation, no nothing."

"I never would have guessed King was behind everything," Lance said. "But when I think about it now, it makes complete sense. He had access to all the witnesses. He only killed those who could connect him with Mary. I have to assume Crystal was the person Mary called from the police station that night. So she knew Mary had been arrested."

"And P. J. knew King had arrested Mary too," Stella said. "We arranged for a local detective in Florida to interview Owen Walsh. When he arrived, a PI was in the room." Sharp's associate. "The PI had already convinced Owen to talk."

Lance stiffened. His ribs ached. The last missing piece of his puzzle was about to fall into place.

"Owen is dying of stomach cancer. He seemed relieved to confess." Stella turned to Lance. "Owen confirmed the story the janitor told Sharp about Owen and King beating Lou Ford. Ford died in the back of the sheriff's station." She took a breath, giving Lance a second to brace himself. "This part of the story is secondhand. King told Owen what happened when he called from Grey Lake asking Owen to pick him up. King drove Mary out to a rest stop in Scarlet Falls to kill her, but she got away from him. Your dad was driving along the road, saw the girl running, and stopped to help. King killed him, buried him here, then sank the car in the lake with Mary in the trunk.

He called Owen to pick him up on the road near Grey Lake, and Owen drove him back to his car at the rest stop."

So simple. Just a few sentences summed up his father's death. It didn't seem right. But all of the pieces fell into place perfectly.

Disbelief and anger did a slow tumble through Lance's belly. They'd interacted with the sheriff on several cases over the past few months. King had faced Lance over and over with no sign of guilt. What kind of man could do that? A psychopath. No empathy. No remorse. King hadn't shown any guilt because he hadn't felt any.

Lance glanced out over the glittering surface of the lake. He was finally getting the closure he'd wanted for decades, but now that he had it, he couldn't seem to process it.

He pressed his arm against Morgan's. He had time, and he had her. The rest would work itself out.

Stella turned to Morgan. "You know Tyler Green was never your stalker, right?"

"Yes," Morgan said. "He was in jail when the photos were left on our neighbor's porch."

"You'll never guess what we found in King's cabin. A canister of hornet foam spray and an empty gallon container of beef blood. The sheriff made his own blood bait for catfishing. He had a freezer full of it." Stella shook her head.

"Why would the sheriff slit your tires and pour blood in your car?" Lance asked. "Other than the general knowledge that he was a cold-blooded killer. Everything else that he did had a specific reason, but those acts seem just plain nasty . . . almost vengeful."

Morgan's face went grim. "I can only think of one reason. He was angry that I told the DA he coerced a false confession out of Eric."

"His ego couldn't take having a woman rat him out," Lance said.

Morgan shook her head. "Yet he always seemed to almost like me."

Lance sighed. "King was clearly a psychopath. They mimic the emotions of others. They are very manipulative, charming even." He thought of the sheriff's polite act with his mother. "He was displaying the behavior he thought would make him blend in better."

"That's exactly how Ted Bundy convinced young women to trust him," Morgan agreed.

"There's more," Stella said. "The hospital security tape shows a big man in jeans and a baseball cap outside your mother's room, Lance. He kept his face shadowed or turned away from the camera, but it could have been him. And the night she was poisoned in the ICU, we have a video of someone we believe is him disguised as a janitor. He went into the room next to your mom's and waited for the old man to code.

Then during the commotion, it appears that he injected something into the bag of saline outside your mom's room. He'd been researching your mother's medication on his home computer. He had access to confiscated heroin and guns."

The police and forensics units had been busy, but then the SFPD, the state police, and the county resources had all been on the job.

"He planned everything." Lance felt numb. How could someone kill so many people just to cover up one mistake?

Psychopaths only think of their own needs and how to manipulate others to attain them.

"We found something," one of the forensic techs yelled.

Lance moved toward the hole, but Morgan held him back with a hand on his elbow.

"Let Stella and Brody go first," she said. "You might not want to see."

He smiled at her. "I need to see this the same way you needed to see the inside of King's cabin."

Her grip on his arm tightened.

"It's a skull," someone shouted.

Lance took one look in the gravesite. The skull stared back at him from the dirt. Grief flooded him. That was his dad in the bottom of that hole. Even from outside the grave, Lance could see the fissure over the brow ridge. Blunt force trauma. King's baton?

Lance swallowed hard, stood back, and let the team work. He'd waited twenty-three years. What was another couple of hours?

"Let's sit down." Morgan tugged him toward a carved-out log bench facing the water.

He let her guide him to the seat.

But he didn't have to wait that long.

An hour later, Stella walked over with a clear plastic evidence bag. Inside was a man's silver wedding ring. Stella pointed to the inside of the band.

JENNY & VIC FOREVER.

"Thanks," Lance said, his voice hoarse.

Stella returned the ring to the forensic team, then walked back toward Morgan and Lance.

The official identification would take time, but Lance knew this was it. He'd found his father. Vic Kruger hadn't abandoned his family. He'd stopped to help a woman in distress, and he'd been killed for it.

His mother had been right all along. His father had been a good man.

Emotions crowded Lance's chest. Too many to sort through all at once. His next breath dragged in and out of his lungs, making his ribs ache through the pain medicine.

"How are you?" Morgan took his hand. She was wearing thick gloves, but the grasp of her hand grounded him.

"OK. I knew as soon as we got here that this

would be the place." He turned away from the rippling water.

Morgan's big blue eyes were filled with concern. "Are you all right?"

"I am." Under the sadness lurching through his heart, there was a new stillness, as if he was on a turbulent flight that suddenly smoothed out.

Morgan tightened her grip on his hand.

"I have to go see my mother now," he said.

Jenny had woken that morning, groggy, out-of-sorts, and terrified at being in the hospital. But Lance had gone to the ICU, and she'd calmed down. She was going to be all right, at least physically. Who knew what kind of mental scars the incident would leave? But if there was one thing Lance was learning, it was to handle one disaster at a time. She was going to live. They'd deal with the fallout later.

"I'll go with you." Morgan stood. "I know you're worried about bringing her home, but I want you to accept that I'm here to help. I love your mom."

"Thank you."

"It's what family does."

He didn't argue. He wanted her with him. Why he'd ever thought differently was a mystery to him now.

"Brody and I would like to tag along," Stella said. "We need your mother to answer some questions if she's up to it."

"I don't know how coherent or cooperative she'll be," Lance warned, heading toward the Jeep.

"Understood. You tell us what she can tolerate." Stella waved for Brody, and he strode across the grass toward them. "This scene belongs to the state police. They don't need us here."

"I want to stop at my mom's house and pick up her computer," Lance said to Morgan. "She'll feel better if she has something to do."

They left the crime scene, stopped at Jenny's, and then drove to the hospital.

To Lance's surprise, his mother was out of the ICU and in a regular room. Lance walked in first, with Morgan right behind him.

She sat up and reached her hand out for his. Taking it, he sat on the edge of the bed. Morgan stood beside him.

His mom squinted at him. Her eyes were a little bit fuzzy. "What happened to your face?"

She obviously didn't remember him stopping by that morning. Her voice slurred, as if she were mildly sedated. Probably for the best. She'd experienced enough stress to freak out the most stable person.

"It's just a few scratches. But I have some news for you." He told her the basics of what happened with the sheriff, leaving out the details of King's attempt to kill him and Morgan. She didn't need to know *everything*.

"They found Dad." Lance told her what they'd found at the sheriff's cabin.

When he'd finished his story, she seemed . . . relieved. "I knew it. I knew he didn't leave us."

"You were right."

His mom sniffed. "Now we can put him to rest properly."

And carry his memory untainted. Until this moment, Lance hadn't realized how important it was that his father's name be cleared.

"How are you doing here?" Lance asked.

His mother's eyes filled with tears. "I want to go home. The doctor thinks I can go home tomorrow or the next day." She licked her lips. "I don't like being here. I want to go home today."

"I know." Lance patted her forearm. "Are you up to answering a few questions from the police?"

"I don't know." His mom pulled her hand away and picked at a cuticle.

Lance took her hand back, holding it firmly between his own palms. "It's all right if you're not ready. The man responsible is dead. Cleaning up the loose ends of the investigation can wait."

"I can try." She struggled to sit up. "Would you hand me my water?"

"Sure." Lance raised the head of the bed and lifted the water cup to his mother's lips. Then he nodded to Morgan, who went out into the hall, returning a minute later with Stella. Brody hung by the doorway, within earshot, but not crowding Lance's mother.

Morgan introduced her sister.

"Who visited you the day you got sick?" Stella asked.

"Sheriff King came to ask me more questions about Vic's disappearance," Jenny said. "He brought pie, but it wasn't very good. When he went to the bathroom, I scraped most of it into the trash. I didn't want to insult him, so I left a few bites to finish when he came out."

The fact that she'd only eaten a few bites had saved her life.

"He used the bathroom twice in thirty minutes. I thought maybe he was having prostate problems. I had no idea . . ." His mother shivered.

He must have gone into the bathroom to steal her medication. Then again to leave the pill vials in the sink and set the stage for her fake suicide attempt.

"None of us did." Lance still couldn't wrap his head around the truth.

"Do you have any idea why Sheriff King might have tried to poison you?" Stella asked.

"No." His mother shook her head. "But I do remember where I'd seen him before. It wasn't just on TV. Of course, he looked different. He was much younger back then, which is why I didn't remember him right away when he came into my house the first time. He was on duty the night Vic went missing. I remember driving past a rest stop when I was out looking for Vic. There were two sheriffs' cars in the lot. I stopped to ask them if they'd seen a Buick Century."

Lance and Morgan shared a glance.

And the very last piece of the puzzle fell into place.

"Mom, did you mention this to Sheriff King when he came alone to question you?" Lance asked.

She nodded. "I did. He said something about it being a small world."

And he'd tried to kill her before she could give him away.

Stella asked a few more questions, then bowed out. "Is it OK if I contact you again, Mrs. Kruger? You answered our big question, but I'm sure we'll have details to iron out as we wrap up the investigation."

His mom nodded. "I suppose that would be all right."

"Thank you for your help today." Stella said goodbye and she and Brody left.

His mom released their hands. "You both look terrible. You should go home and get some rest."

"Would you like to have a video call with Kevin?" Lance asked.

His mother lifted her chin. Her eyes brightened. "I would love that."

Lance connected her laptop to the hospital's

Wi-Fi network. Morgan rolled the bedside table over to the bed. A few minutes later, Kevin's face appeared on the screen.

Jenny smiled.

"We'll leave you two to talk." Lance kissed her on the cheek. "I love you, Mom."

"Love you too." She smiled at Morgan. "Take care of each other."

"We will." Lance followed Morgan out of the room.

That's exactly what they did best.

Lance stood on the sidelines of the ice arena and watched Eric send a hockey puck into the goal. The buzzer rang and the small crowd cheered.

Next to him, Morgan clapped her hands around Sophie, who sat on her mother's hip. Ava and Mia stood on the bench so they could see over the wall.

"Did we win?" Sophie kicked Morgan's sides as if she was riding a pony.

"Yes, we won." Morgan pointed to the score board. "The blinking number four is Lance's team."

"Yay!" Sophie squealed.

The team skated by Lance, pulling off their gloves and high-fiving him as they zoomed past. By the time the last member had slapped his hand, Lance was holding his ribs.

"Lance pwomised to take us on the ice after the game." Sophie squirmed.

"Oh, honey." Morgan hugged her daughter. "Lance isn't quite up to that yet."

"I can manage," Lance said, looking mildly offended.

Morgan gave him a look. "The doctor said your ribs would take six weeks to heal. It's been two days. You shouldn't even be here."

"I wasn't missing this game." Lance had neglected the kids on his hockey team enough.

After finally learning the truth about his dad, Lance was ready to live. Really live.

One selfish man had changed the course of his life. Lance had lost an entire future with his dad. He'd spent twenty-three years mired in the fallout. Two decades of pain, of doubt, of just being happy to get through the day.

But now that it was over, he realized that life was too precious to waste a minute of it. He had a second chance at happiness with Morgan and her girls. He was grabbing it with both hands and holding on. No more being satisfied with the bare minimum life had to offer.

He had a whole future out there, and it was bright and shiny and new.

"I'll take her." Eric handed his gloves and helmet over the wall to Lance and held his hands up.

"Pweeeeeese," Sophie begged.

"All right." Morgan carried Sophie to the opening that led onto the ice. Ava and Mia hovered close behind her. The rest of the team crowded around the girls. Eric took Sophie's hands and let her shuffle across the ice in front of him. The only girl on Lance's team, Jamie, offered Ava and Mia her hands.

"Not too fast," Morgan called out.

"They'll be fine." Lance leaned on the wall next to her. "They're barely moving."

"I know." But she would still worry. "How do you feel?"

"Very happy to be alive." He kissed her temple. "And very happy to have you."

"Are you sure you'll be all right by yourself tonight?" she asked. She'd stayed at his house the night before.

"Yes," he said. "Though I'm tempted to say no, just so you'll spend the night with me."

She turned. "The girls would be all right with me staying over to take care of you. They were all worried. You're lucky Sophie isn't here playing doctor."

Lance laughed. Pain encircled his ribs. He put a hand on his side. "Her bedside manner needs work."

Morgan checked her phone. "We should go soon. The girls will be hungry. Come for dinner?"

"I'd like that."

"My girls love you."

"I know." He turned. "I was worried about that for a while."

"Worried?"

"A relationship with your kids is a whole different kind of responsibility. I didn't want to disappoint them if my taking care of my mother got in the way. Your girls deserve better."

"You would never do that." Morgan took his face in her hands. She kissed his cheek. "And I would never be with a man who wasn't good for my girls, but I love that you were worried about them. You are a good man, Lance Kruger. I love you, and my kids love you. I'm afraid there's nothing you can do about it. You're stuck with all of us, the whole crazy, chaotic bunch."

He pulled her mouth to his. "I was an idiot to resist."

"Resistance is futile," she said against his mouth.

He kissed her. "In that case, I surrender."

And he did, heart and soul.

Acknowledgments

As always, credit goes to my agent, Jill Marsal, and to the entire team at Montlake Romance, especially my managing editor, Anh Schluep, my developmental editor, Charlotte Herscher, and author herder/tech goddess Jessica Poore.

Special thanks to writer friends Leanne Sparks, Rayna Vause, Kendra Elliot, Toni Anderson, Selena Laurence, Amy Gamet, and Jill Sanders for much-needed motivation in finishing this book.

About the Author

Wall Street Journal bestselling author Melinda Leigh is a fully recovered banker. A lifelong lover of books, she started writing as a way to preserve her sanity when her youngest child entered first grade. During the next few years, she joined Romance Writers of America, learned a few things about writing a novel, and decided the process was way more fun than analyzing financial statements. Melinda's debut novel, *She Can Run*, was nominated for Best First Novel by the International Thriller Writers. She's also garnered Golden Leaf and Silver Falchion Awards, along with nominations for a RITA and three Daphne du Maurier Awards. Her other novels include *She Can Tell*, *She Can Scream*, *She Can Hide*, *She Can Kill*, *Midnight Exposure*, *Midnight Sacrifice*, *Midnight Betrayal*, *Midnight Obsession*, *Hour of Need*, *Minutes to Kill*, *Seconds to Live*, *Say You're Sorry*, and *Her Last Goodbye*. She holds a second-degree black belt in Kenpo karate; teaches women's self-defense; and lives in a messy house with her husband, two teenagers, a couple of dogs, and two rescue cats.